TO THE GRAVE

Steve Robinson

Published in 2012 by FeedARead Publishing
1st Edition

A CIP catalogue record for this title is available from the British Library.

www.steve-robinson.me

For the Nans

Prologue

Jefferson Tayte was sitting at the table in his hotel room, wondering how his latest assignment had come to this. It should have been easy. All he had to do was reconnect an adopted woman with her birth parents. She'd even been able to give him a name and address, albeit as it was in 1944. Now he was thousands of miles from home, staring into the barrel of a Walther P99 semi-automatic handgun.

"Head or heart?" the man sitting opposite him said.

"What?"

Tayte had heard the question but he had to ask to make sure he'd heard it right. The man didn't say it again. He just moved the muzzle of the gun slowly from Tayte's chest to his head and back again. He was a younger man, Tayte thought: early thirties, dressed in a navy pinstripe suit, shirt open at the neck. And he was leaner, too, much leaner, and he would be all the more agile for it.

"I guess I can't talk you out of this, can I?"

"No," the man said.

"And if I go for the door, you'll shoot me in the back, right?"

"No."

"No?"

The man shook his head only slightly. "You wouldn't make it out of your seat," he said through thin lips that sat dead straight on his face.

Tayte tried to swallow but he couldn't. He knew he was going to die. A part of him had known it the minute he'd walked into the room and saw this man sitting there. They were both very calm about it and somehow Tayte wasn't surprised by how he felt. He knew it was going to happen. They were resolved between them to kill and be killed. *Head or heart?* What kind of a choice was that?

"Does it matter?"

"Not to me," the man said. He shifted as he adjusted the round, frameless glasses that were pinched to the bridge of his nose. "But if you choose heart, there's a small chance the first bullet will miss. Your head on the other hand..."

Tayte tried to imagine what a head shot would be like. Quicker perhaps, but what if the bullet went in through his eye? He winced. It didn't bear thinking about. He really did not want to be having these thoughts.

"Will it hurt?"

"I'm not going to tell you that you won't feel a thing, Mr Tayte. But this is not personal. I'm not here to hurt you. Either way, the pain won't last long."

Tayte turned away and looked out through the window, thinking that this man was as cool as the January night that had settled an early frost on the cars below. He breathed deeply and wondered where the time had gone. His time. He thought how ironic it was that he should die a lonely man in some nondescript hotel room trying to connect another client with her birth parents while he still had no idea about his own. How could he die without knowing who he was? He scoffed, thinking that death would certainly spare him that pain.

How had it come to this?

"Head or heart?" the man opposite him repeated.

Chapter One

Five days ago.

It was a Friday afternoon and Jefferson Tayte was with his client at her home in Washington DC, a few miles east of the capital and not many miles from his own home on the other side of the Potomac river. They were sitting opposite each other by an open fireplace that had served to chase the January chill from Tayte's fingers and toes since the heating in his much loved Ford Thunderbird had decided to pack up on him during one of the coldest spells he'd known in years. The thin white shirt and loose-fit, tan linen suit he was wearing felt entirely inadequate.

He'd first met Eliza Gray two weeks earlier when she'd called his number from the advertisement he ran in the classifieds section of the Washington City Paper. Assignments had been plentiful of late, if bordering on mundane at times, so when she'd told him that a suitcase had been sent to her with an anonymous note saying that the contents belonged to her real mother and that the sender thought she should have them, he called to see her right away. The note said nothing more than that and it had come as something of a shock to Eliza because in all her sixty-six years she had no idea that she'd been adopted. Her late, adoptive parents never told her.

That was one of the reasons Tayte had taken the assignment. It was a little outside his usual routine, but he understood how Eliza felt and he wanted to help her fill the void he knew was growing inside her if he could. The first thing he'd done was to prove the note's claim that Eliza had been adopted. He'd called his friend, Marcus Brown, an eminent genealogist who worked at the National Archives in London, and asked him to see if his client had an entry in the Adopted Children Register. The index to the register was only available publicly on microfiche at six locations in England and Marcus had been happy to go along to the City of Westminster Archives Centre to check.

When Marcus had called back to say that he'd found Eliza's index reference, Tayte downloaded the forms she had to fill in and they sent them off the same day. A week later she attended a mandatory interview with a local adoption advisor and a few days after that she received two certificates. The first was her amended birth certificate, which looked like a regular birth certificate but gave her adopted name, Elizabeth, and the names and address of her adoptive parents. The second was a copy of her original, confidential birth certificate to which the amended record was linked. It showed her original name of Virginia and no father was listed, which was as Tayte had expected.

The other reason he'd taken the assignment was the red suitcase that was beside him on the sofa, and if he was honest with himself his own intrigue around how and why it came to be there had got the better of him. Eliza hadn't kept the packaging, which was a shame because he knew it would have offered some clue as to who had sent it.

Tayte picked the suitcase up and set it down on his knees. It was a small suitcase, like a child's suitcase, and it put him in mind of the kind of thing he'd seen in the small hands of countless British evacuees in photographs taken during World War II. It looked pristine apart from the dust that had settled a tacky grime into the locks and hinges, which over the years had tarnished the metal. He thought it had to be at least seventy years old and it had that familiar, musty odour he knew could never be removed - although judging by its condition it had travelled very little.

"I wanted to take another look before I set off, Mrs Gray," Tayte said. "I hope I haven't inconvenienced you."

"Of course you haven't." Eliza threw him a smile. "And I thought we were on first name terms now."

"Yes, of course. Eliza," Tayte said, smiling back.

He thought she looked much younger than her years. She had shoulder length, red-brown hair, a slim frame and youthful dress sense. And he liked the energy she exuded as she spoke, despite everything that had happened to her in recent years. He imagined she must have been a very active woman before the car accident that had taken her husband's life and left her in need of walking sticks for the remainder of hers. He found it easy to admire people like that, who kept smiling through no matter what.

"I'd like to take the book with me if that's okay," he continued, opening the suitcase. "I thought it might help open a few doors. You know, prove my authenticity should the need arise."

"Go right ahead," Eliza said. "Take the whole suitcase if you like."

Tayte laughed through his nose. "That's okay. The book will do just fine."

It was a pale pink hardback library copy of *Madame Bovary* by

Gustave Flaubert. It had been amongst the few layers of clothing that were in the suitcase with several personal items such as a hairbrush, a half used lipstick and other items of makeup, and a toothbrush wrapped in an off-white facecloth. There was also a teddy bear with a button in its ear that read, 'Made in England by Merrythought Ltd'. The case seemed full of things that a young girl might not want to be separated from given the choice and it was the reason they had been separated that intrigued Tayte the most.

Eliza poured coffee from the percolator Tayte had helped bring in from the kitchen when he'd first arrived.

"You don't take sugar, do you?" Eliza said.

Tayte looked up from the book. "No thanks." He patted his stomach. "At least, I'm trying not to."

Eliza's smile broadened as she sat back again. "So, tell me what you've managed to find out," she said as she tried to get comfortable again. "You wouldn't believe how restless I've been since your last visit."

Tayte thought he would, but he didn't want to get into his own ancestry issues just now. He opened the book and eyed the library card that was still inside the jacket.

"Philomena Lasseter," he read aloud, and Eliza's eyes grew wider at hearing what she now knew to be her birth mother's name.

The name and address of the girl whose belongings had been sent with the note were written in the book, and with that information Tayte had thought it would be a breeze to find Philomena, especially after he'd written to the address and confirmed that the Lasseter family still lived there to this day. He'd received a phone call from a man named Jonathan Lasseter who was keen to speak to him.

And that's when it had all gone wrong.

Tayte had expected to learn something about the girl whose suitcase had found its way to Washington after all these years, but any hope he had of an easy assignment was dashed when Jonathan told him he knew very little about Philomena. By the time the conversation had ended he was of the impression that her life was little more than a rumour. Tayte had seen the warning signs, but they had only served to further pique his interest; like when he'd seen Eliza's original birth certificate and noted that her mother's name was recorded as Mena Fitch, not Philomena Lasseter, although the address given was the same as the address found inside the copy of *Madame Bovary*.

"The news isn't as good as I'd hoped for," Tayte admitted, closing the suitcase. "When I spoke to Jonathan, he told me that Philomena was something of a family mystery. He said he'd heard of her and that he'd seen a few old photographs, but he also said that he hadn't seen any beyond the war years, when Philomena would have been in her late teens."

"So she could have died during the war?" Eliza said.

"That's a possibility, but I don't think so. You see, while I was waiting for a response to my letter, I started looking for Philomena's vital records online - in the UK birth, marriage and death indexes. It's an uncommon name, which helps a great deal. From the address I had, I was able to identify the parish where she was born and I found the record of her birth in Leicester, England in August 1927, making her seventeen years old when this library card was stamped in September 1944."

"But there's no record of her death?" Eliza said, second-guessing him.

Tayte shook his head. "No record of any marriage either. From the information on her birth certificate I could identify her parents, Margaret Lasseter, nee Fitch - which is where the name on your original birth certificate comes from - and George Lasseter, who was a general medical practitioner at the time. I searched for Philomena under both Lasseter and Fitch, but I couldn't find anything relevant."

"Any clue as to who my father might be?" Eliza asked.

Tayte opened the book to the page where a piece of material had been placed inside it like a bookmark. "Even less to go on there," he said, removing what he recognised as a military nametape. It was a piece of olive-drab cloth with the name, 'Danielson' sewn into it. "All we have so far is this, but it could be anything or nothing."

"Or it could be a clue," Eliza said.

"Yes, it could, but by itself it doesn't mean a thing." He slid it back into the book. "It could have been picked up just about anywhere in 1944."

Eliza shifted in her seat and Tayte could see that even sitting too long in one position was uncomfortable for her.

"Didn't you find anything else?" she asked.

Tayte pushed his hair back off his brow. He had a thick crop of black hair that never looked tidy for long no matter what he did with it. "I made some general checks online," he said. "I went through all the newspaper archives I could and I looked at several other resources for any mention of anyone called Philomena Lasseter or Mena Fitch. I checked the British electoral registers, too, and the online London Gazette where enrolled changes of name by deed poll are printed." He shook his head. "My results aren't conclusive, but so far I can see why her life became a family mystery."

"But you do think she could still be alive?" Eliza said, as though holding on to that hope.

"If she is she'd be eighty-four years old, so there's every chance, yes. But I can't do any more to confirm that from here." Tayte bit his lip as he added, "I'm booked on an overnight flight to London."

"I thought you said you weren't going for a few days yet, or was it next week?"

"I know, but I was just putting it off because I don't like to fly and sitting around worrying about it just makes it worse. I'm all packed."

"Well now that's the spirit, Mr Tayte." Eliza said. "What doesn't kill you, eh?" she added, and Tayte wished she hadn't.

"I need to go and talk to the family," he said. "I figure I'll have all weekend to find out what I can from them and when the local record office opens on Monday I'll go and see what they can tell me. I've arranged to meet Jonathan Lasseter and his wife at their home tomorrow afternoon."

Eliza was on the edge of her seat now, clearly excited by this sudden sense of urgency. "Is there someone who can go with you?"

Tayte had to think about that. A moment later he shook his head and said, "No. There's no one."

"Well Madame Bovary will have to keep you company. She'll help take your mind off things."

Tayte just smiled and glanced down at the book he was still holding. *If only it was that simple*, he thought.

"I want to know everything about her," Eliza said. "What kind of life she led, and -" She paused. "And I'd like to understand why she gave me away."

"Of course," Tayte said. "I'll do my best."

"And you'll keep me updated? I won't be able to sleep otherwise."

"Just as soon as I have anything to update you with."

"Good. Well have a safe trip and if you need anything just let me know."

Eliza reached for her walking sticks like she was about to get up and Tayte could see that she was eager for him to get started, despite the fact that he couldn't make his plane take off any sooner.

"There's no need to see me out," he said, getting up himself. He leant in and gently shook her hand, which seemed tiny in his. "I'll call you tomorrow once I've touched down," he added, forcing positive thoughts into his head as he imagined himself at the baggage reclaim at Heathrow, stressed as he knew he would be by then, but alive and kicking and whistling an up-beat show tune to calm his nerves.

Eliza kept hold of his hand. "I'd like to keep this just between ourselves until we know more. You understand?"

"Of course," Tayte said, knowing that she had an extensive family around her: three sons and a daughter living in DC with children of their own. The arrival of the suitcase had affected their perceived ancestry and it was entirely his client's call as to if and when she wanted to tell them.

She let go of Tayte's hand and as he turned away he eyed the little red suitcase again and wondered, as he had wondered all week, who had sent it and how they came by it. And he wondered why it had been sent now, some seventy years later. Something had happened to prompt it, but what? Tayte had no idea just now but he intended to find out. As he left the house, heading for his car, he gazed up into the clear sky and snapped his collar higher to keep the late afternoon chill off his neck. He thought about the girl again. *Philomena Lasseter.* He'd been thinking about her a lot. Who was she? Why was her name recorded on his client's original birth certificate under her mother's maiden name of Fitch? And why had she been separated from her suitcase all those years ago?

Chapter Two

December 1943.

It was Christmas morning and Mena Lasseter awoke early, harbouring the sensation that she had been disturbed by something that now, in waking, left no obvious clue as to its source. The blackout curtains at the window held her bedroom in total darkness and it was so quiet that she fancied she could hear the air around her, hissing in her ears. She sat up and pulled at the heavy curtains behind her until they revealed a misty, moonlit landscape of leafless trees and frosted fields and just the hint of a salmon daybreak to the east. When she opened them more fully the moonlight washed in from the Leicestershire countryside, casting diagonal crosses onto the oak-beamed walls from the blast tape that had been in place between the leaded lights since the bombings began. The moon painted everything with its silver brush, stealing all the colours.

But not quite all.

As Mena turned away from the window and looked into the room across a cheerless bedspread, past the foot of an ironwork bedstead and the chaise beyond, she saw something beside her washbasin that she hadn't seen in such a long time that the sight of it brought a lump to her throat. It was an orange - a beautiful plump orange that was as vivid amidst the early morning grey as if it were in full sunlight. She threw aside her bedcovers and ran to it, unable to resist piercing its peel as she clutched it to her nose, drawing in the sweet memory of its scent. She laughed quietly to herself, choking back a tear and just smiling at it because she understood its significance: Eddie was home for Christmas, and what a gift.

Mena - whose devout Catholic mother had named her Philomena after Saint Philomena the wonder worker - was sixteen years old and several months younger than she wanted to be. She was tall for her age and knew she could easily pass for seventeen, which was the age she needed to be before she could join the Women's Land Army, but her mother - staunch upholder of the Decalogue that she was - would not permit Mena to lie about her age, even if most of the other girls of her acquaintance were doing it.

But August wasn't so far away, she kept telling herself. She could make do with being a fire-watcher until then and she also worked part-time as a volunteer, wheeling books through the wards at the Leicester Royal Infirmary and the general hospital in Evington, often reading to the patients. She was still doing her bit, like her sister, Mary-Grace, who had enlisted with the Auxiliary Territorial Service two years ago and was no doubt having a glorious war, driving around in her motorcar, delivering important documents to important people.

And there were her three brothers. No one could ask more of them. In the thick of it since 1940, Mena hadn't seen Michael, James or Peter in far too long. She envied them their freedom, despite the mortal danger and the hardship that was all too evident from their letters. Edward Buckley - dear, sweet Eddie, who had always been like a fourth brother to her - was already a commissioned regular when the war began. His childhood belonged to Oadby and it owed much of its happiness to the Lasseter family, before the Buckleys moved away to Hampshire.

Mena pulled the orange to her nightdress and sighed. *Mary will be so thrilled to see him,* she thought, genuinely happy for her. And yet a part of her envied her sister his return. She set the orange down, thinking to steal back to her room with a knife after breakfast, to eat it in secret, knowing that it would taste all the sweeter after whatever powdered egg creation was in store for them again this festive morning. Her hand had barely left the orange when the distinct sound of a creaking floorboard beyond her bedroom door drew her attention. Her smile grew when she realised that this must have been the sound that had stirred her from sleep. Was Eddie still there, delivering his oranges in the night like Santa Claus?

She opened the door with a flourish, expecting to catch Father Christmas in the act. But as she leapt through the doorway and the cool moonlight followed her, she found her own father instead, glowing in a pool of candlelight. He was dressed, not in a red tunic and trousers, but in slippers and a new striped dressing gown that was not unlike the curtains that used to hang in one of the spare bedrooms. He had one foot on the stairs at the top of the landing and a startled expression creased his already worry-lined face.

"Pop!" Mena said, still smiling.

Everyone called him, Pop. Although Eddie, who was more than welcome to, was such a stickler for correctness that out of respect he still called him Mr Lasseter or sir - despite Mr Lasseter's numerous protestations over the years that he should at least call him George.

Pop was a tall man: lean and lanky, with a balding pate and a wiry grey moustache that he kept meticulously trimmed. He clutched a bony hand to his chest and staggered forward like a bad actor in the throes of a poorly written death scene and Mena thought he was about to fall down the stairs. She rushed to him, her smile faltering, but as she arrived he wheeled on her, balancing on the top step with all the nimbleness of a man half his fifty-four years. His free hand grabbed her.

"Gotcha!" he said, laughing disproportionately to the joke until Mena slapped his arm playfully and reminded him of the hour.

"Shh!" she said. "You'll wake everyone."

Pop nodded and quickly buttoned his smile, though his steely eyes were still laughing.

Mena hugged him. "Merry Christmas, Pop."

"Merry Christmas, my lovely Mena," Her father replied. "Now back to bed with you until I've lit the fires and this old house has had a chance to warm up."

Mena reached her bedroom door and turned back. "Will there be an extra setting for Christmas dinner?" she whispered, sure of the answer.

Her father's smile renewed. "Just you wait and see, my girl. Wait and see."

The Lasseters lived just outside the village of Oadby, which was a few miles east of Leicester, between Evington to the north and Wigston to the south. The war for them had so far been kind, if *kind* is a word that can sit alongside *war* so comfortably. But it had been kind in as much as they were still receiving regular letters from Michael, James and Peter, who were all serving in the European Theatre of Operations and living on the outskirts of Oadby in a crooked old farmhouse that seemed too big without the boys - despite the two refugee children who had been assigned to them - meant that they had not suffered the bombs that had fallen on Leicester. Neither had they fallen victim to those bombs that had been dumped on the villages when the bombers returned from their numerous raids on Coventry. And the war had been kind to them perhaps because they were financially better off than most families in Oadby, which meant that when the war began they had a better stock of things with which to *make do and mend.*

When Mena returned to her bed, she found that she was incapable of sleep. She tried a book from the pile of classics on the floor beside her, but neither Dumas nor Stevenson could hold her attention. Instead, she wrapped herself in her bedcovers and sat in her favourite chair by the window where she watched the sunrise. It was a perfect morning: no snow, but the frost was thick enough to give the illusion and if it wasn't going to snow then a clear and crisp sunny day was just what she liked. The mist had all but gone now and the world outside her window was no longer silver but orange like her gift, which was back in her hands, slowly turning in her lap.

She was deep in thought, her gaze fixed on the horizon while she wondered how her brothers were today. She said good morning to each of their remembered faces, which she did every morning, silently praying for their safe return. She knew that their Christmas fare would be better than hers again this year. They would have real roast turkey and roast potatoes, with cranberry sauce and pickles, peas and corn, spread with real butter, too, no doubt. At least, she liked to think they would. She thought about the 'mock turkey' she'd helped her mother prepare: sausage-meat with chopped apple and onion and two parsnips for the legs. It tasted nothing like turkey, but as with so many things now, it was all about appearance.

Appearance. Mena hadn't given much thought to what she would wear today, but with the arrival of her orange, she knew that she had to come up with something special. She felt it her duty to look her best - all part of the war effort and doing one's bit, which brought her to the makeup issue. That was another matter altogether and one on which her mother avidly disapproved. But it was Christmas Day and she was every bit sixteen and a half years old. The only thing that concerned her was how to improvise with what remained of the few items she'd managed to scrounge off Mary on her last visit a few months ago - she didn't want to arrive at breakfast looking like a rag doll.

There was a *Boots* in Leicester and she was dying to try their *No.7* range. She hadn't been there in a while, but the last time she looked they had foundation cream and complexion milk, which cost three shillings each, rouge cream and nine different shades of face powder. The lipstick came in so many colours, it was like being in a sweet shop, but Pop wouldn't waste the money even if her mother had approved. 'We've no knowing how long this war will last,' he'd say, and that would be the end of it. She hoped Mary would come up trumps with a few leftover essentials for her Christmas present this year, so she could make a better job of things for the evening.

Mena unwrapped herself from the bedspread and sat at her dressing table. She set the orange down in the sunlight from the window and frowned at herself. Her hair was too straight for what she had in mind. She wanted long golden waves for the daytime, straight at the sides to frame her face before gently curling onto her shoulders like that Hollywood actress she'd seen in a movie last summer: Veronica Lake. For the evening it had to be an up-do. Nothing looked classier.

She opened a drawer and found a few large rollers and her makeup kit - such as it was. The only item of real makeup she had was a stub of lipstick that she had to get at with a cotton bud because what little remained was recessed far into the tube. She had rouge for her cheeks but that wasn't really makeup. She'd crushed a square of watercolour paint into as fine a powder as she could manage using the mortar and pestle from the kitchen once when her mother was out, and she had to use it sparingly on moist cheeks so as not to overdo it or out came the rag doll. She had nothing at all for her eyes, but then her father had always told her how pretty they were - much like her grandmother's, only paler, more slate-blue, so she considered herself lucky there.

Some of her friends were washing their legs with black tea or smearing gravy browning on them because no one was manufacturing silk stockings any more; they needed the silk and the production looms to make parachutes. She'd tried gravy browning once, but Xavier - or Manfred, she couldn't remember which of the Great Danes it was - had spoilt the already poor effect by licking her legs under the table. And besides, she had no eyeliner pencil to draw the seams with anyway. Ankle socks would have to do.

Chapter Three

By the time Mena was ready to make her appearance to the rest of the household, she could already hear the hubbub of what promised to be a very special Christmas morning. For at least half an hour she'd been listening to the clatter of pans and the tramping of ten-year-old feet as the twins from London chased one another about the place; their incessant energy bolstered by the occasion and their own expectations of what new things Christmas would bring. She could hear her mother shouting at them to settle down or there would be no presents this year. Then it would go quiet for no more than two minutes before the pandemonium started up again. Occasionally, beneath all this, she heard Pop's voice. She could only hear the soothing tone of it - words without distinction - but longer periods of calm always followed and it was during one such calm period that she heard another voice, conjoined with the hum of her father's. It was another man - a much younger man.

Mena smiled at the Hollywood star in the mirror and thought that the woman who winked back at her would do very well.

"Philomena!"

Her mother's voice was shrill. It rose to such a high pitch that Mena jolted as if being startled from a daydream, knowing that that was the sound of her mother's final call. She slipped her socked feet into a pair of white-and-black saddle shoes and hurriedly tied the laces. Then she ran to the door and only paused to straighten her dress when she reached the bottom of the stairs. She took a moment to compose herself in the hall mirror and thought the coat-stand to the right of the front door looked a little heavier than usual and those were definitely not her father's boots beneath the parlour palm at the base of the jardinière. Pop's voice drew her across the parquet floor to the sitting room door where she waited and listened. She could make out his words perfectly now.

"Oh, I'm kept busy," Pop said in response to a question Mena had been too late to hear. "I make most of my house calls in the villages now. There was a nasty bout of flu doing the rounds not so long ago, but the extra petrol coupons keep the old Morris running so I get about well enough. Now what about you? 1st Airborne treating you well, are they?"

"As well as any man might expect under the circumstances," the other man said.

"Yes, well perhaps it will all be over by next Christmas, eh? Did you hear Churchill's announcement on the wireless last night?"

"No, sir. I'm sorry to say I missed it. We arrived quite late."

"Of course. Still, it's not like we weren't expecting it, there's been enough speculation these past months. I'm sure it will come as no surprise to you to hear that Eisenhower's been appointed Supreme Commander of the Allied Expeditionary Force."

"I'd sooner see one of our boys in the role."

"Quite," Pop said. "But I believe the decision was largely based on the nationality of the country with the highest commitment of troops."

"And the usual politics, no doubt."

"Oh, no doubt at all. Although politically the decision carries with it certain guarantees. If the coming operations in the ETO are to be led by the Yanks, then any failure will ultimately be seen by the world as their failure. From a political standpoint their full support and their unwavering attention are secured now for the duration."

Mena was distracted by the arrival of the twins. First one then the other came sliding past her like a déja-vu episode in grey socks and identical yellow candlewick dressing gowns. They slid all the way to the foot of the stairs without registering she was there and they raced up them like stampeding elephants, slowly followed by Xavier and Manfred who both nuzzled her hand as they nonchalantly passed.

Another clatter of pans from the kitchen forced Mena to call out, "I'll just be a minute, Mother." Then she tapped on the door, turned the doorknob and stepped through into the sitting room, which was bright with dusty sunlight and suddenly full of smiles.

Both men were standing beside a fire that by now was spitting vigorously at the brass fireguard. A pair of knitted Christmas-stockings hung from a blackened beam and towards the window to her right, over an arrangement of floral-print furniture, a small Christmas tree looked proud despite the lack of any new ornament again this year. The twins had been kept busy one afternoon on the lead-up to Christmas, making animals from Pop's pipe-cleaners, but they ended up looking more like hairy caterpillars to everyone except the twins.

Mena's smile met Pop's first. He was wearing a jacket and tie: the same old comfortable tweed jacket with the sagging pockets that he wore when he made his rounds. His smile was pinched at one corner to keep his pipe from falling out and he had a hand in one of his jacket pockets as usual, which was why they had sagged over the years. Mena's attention was quickly drawn to the man beside him who was beaming back at her.

"Eddie!" she said. She saluted him. "Or should I call you Captain Buckley now? Pop told us all about it."

Edward Buckley pulled a straight face. He saluted back and stamped his heel. He laughed. "Merry Christmas, Mena. And Eddie will do just fine as always."

She threw herself at him. "I knew it was you," she said, hugging him so tightly she thought she would crease his uniform.

"What? Even with the tash?"

"It's barely there," Mena said. "But very becoming an officer." She studied his face like he was on inspection: the tidy brown hair, which she thought a little too shiny, and the hazel eyes that co-ordinated well with the drab colour of his uniform. "Thanks for the orange," she added as she withdrew.

"You're welcome, I'm sure," Edward said. "Now let me get a good look at you." A moment later he added, "Wow! Don't you look pretty in that dress? Blue always was my favourite colour and those polka dots set it off a treat. Are they yellow or cream?"

Mena frowned. "They used to be white."

"Well, whatever colour they are, they're my favourite, too."

She slapped his arm and laughed. "You're just saying that."

"I never say anything I don't mean," Edward said. "I told your father I'd make it here in time for Christmas and here I am."

Pop leant in towards the fireplace and blew his pipe-smoke at the flue. "And we're glad to have you. I only wish you could stay longer."

"When must you go?" Mena asked, alarmed by the suggestion that their fruit-bearing guest had to leave again so soon.

"I might just fit in a little tea before I head back, but only if it's early. A car should be here for me around six."

"We'll make sure of it," Pop said.

There was a tap at the door and Mena turned towards it as it opened, expecting to see her mother. It was Mary; another smile to replace the one she had suddenly lost. She looked amazing, Mena thought. She was out of uniform, in heels, which helped, and real stockings too, she supposed. She wore a light-grey jacket, belted at the waist and a matching skirt that was fitted all the way to her knees so that she waddled like a duck when she came into the room. At least that's how Mena saw things, but the smile on Edward's face as he rushed to meet her suggested to Mena that he liked the effect. What really set the look off was the fact that she was already wearing her strawberry-blonde hair in the same kind of up-do Mena had planned for herself that evening. Mary must have known that Eddie would be gone again by then.

There followed a kiss that lasted all of five seconds but which felt to Mena more like five minutes. Her father looked away into the fireplace and continued to puff on his pipe as Mena watched her sister's ankle slide the length of her slender calf and back again. She wished her calves were that slender. She thought how unfair it was that she should still carry the softness of her childhood just as she was beginning to feel like a woman, but she figured the Land Army would soon sort that out. It would be a 'healthy, happy job' according to the poster she had in her room and there was certainly nothing soft about the pitchfork-wielding girl in the green pullover and khaki corduroy breeches depicted in the advertisement. Mena saw Edward whisper into Mary's ear and Mary whispered something back. She couldn't hear what it was, but it set the young lovers giggling. A year ago, perhaps two, Mena would have charged in and insisted they tell her what they were giggling about, but she was all grown-up now and knew better.

When at last Mary and Edward managed to peel themselves apart they came hand in hand to the fireplace, smiling broadly and already glowing long before they reached it. Mary seemed to see Mena then for the first time.

"Is that our Mena?" she said. "No, it can't be."

Mena knew her sister was teasing, but it was the first time she'd made herself up at home and she was enjoying the compliments. She couldn't suppress her smile, however hard she tried to. She gave a little curtsey and lowered her head to hide her blush.

"You look beautiful," Mary said. She leant in and they touched cheeks. "Merry Christmas, sis," she added. Then she kissed her father and said, "You too, Pop. Merry Christmas."

There was no preceding knock at the sitting-room door the next time it opened and the sight of her mother standing in the glow of the frame reminded Mena that she had been by the fire too long. Margaret Lasseter looked flushed as she continued to wipe her hands on the stained apron that covered her cornflower-blue day-dress. She was a slim woman, almost as tall as Pop, with short mousy hair, sharp-set features and eyes that missed nothing. There was the hint of a smile there somewhere, probably for the benefit of their guest, but Mena knew she was in trouble.

"Sorry, Mother, I was just coming."

"Well hurry along, girl!" Margaret said. She smiled more fully, yet unconvincingly, at Edward. "Edward's brought Christmas with him this year," she added. "Enough to last the week, I should think. Real turkey, too, and there's bacon for breakfast and a dozen real eggs." She was talking to the room now. Then directly to Mena, she added, "It all has to be prepared, you know. Quickly girl. Unless you want us all eating dinner at tea-time."

Mena quickened her pace, but as she approached the doorway, she faltered. Her mother's feigned smile had all but collapsed, replaced by disbelief as she clutched at the wooden crucifix she always wore on a rough length of string around her neck. Another step and Mena could hear the air drawing in through her nose and she knew she was really in for it when she saw her mother's lips begin to tremble and shift as if in utterance of some silent prayer.

It came without further warning.

Mena reached the door and that dirty apron was suddenly in her face, rubbing and scratching and tearing at her mouth. She felt her mother's firm hand on the back of her head suddenly and she was led out of the room, bent almost double.

"You little Jezebel!" her mother said, loud in Mena's ear.

Then through the opening sniffle of her tears, Mena heard her father call out, "Now Margaret, there's no harm in -"

The door closed.

"Wash it off!" her mother said. She shoved Mena towards the stairs. "And don't you come down again until you've prayed for His forgiveness."

Mena felt the back of her mother's hand slap and sting across the back of her legs, causing her to skip the next three steps at once.

"And be quick about it!"

Chapter Four

Mena sat in front of her dressing table mirror and cried into her hands for a full ten minutes. When she stopped crying she spent several minutes more just staring at the rag doll before her, thinking about her favourite book and wishing that, like Alice, she could disappear into her own reflection and find that other world. She barely noticed the door open behind her; barely saw Mary enter the room and squeeze a flannel into the washbasin. But she felt the cool, damp cloth on her skin and she saw the rag doll in the mirror begin to fade as Mary drew the flannel soothingly across her face, back and forth, caressing not scratching, until the rag doll was gone.

"It's never fair," Mary said. "And believe me, I've had my share. And don't blame Pop," she added. "He's had his share, too."

A comb reached through Mena's hair. It felt nice, like lying on damp sand on a warm day at the beach as the sea combs foaming bubbles along your entire body. She drew a relaxed breath and slowly let it go.

"Do you remember when Mother first caught me kissing Edward?" Mary said. "Of course you don't. That all happened off stage, but you must have wondered where I'd been for so long? 'Mary-Grace!' she'd yelled at me."

Mena saw a little girl in the mirror now. Not the woman who had sat there earlier, full of wanton smiles and sultry expressions; Veronica Lake was long gone.

"No?" Mary continued. "Well I was in my room the rest of that day and all the next day, too. Locked in my clothes-cupboard to be exact, with nothing to eat or drink. I was fourteen then. You would only have been about eight."

Mena missed the combing when it stopped. She felt an Alice band slide into place and she saw Mary's face in the mirror beside her own.

"There," Mary said. "I think Mother will approve now, don't you?"

Mena nodded. Then beneath her gaze she saw a white handkerchief parcel slide onto the dressing table.

"Don't I always look after you?" Mary said. "I thought this might cheer you up. I was going to give it to you tonight, but I think you'd better have it now."

Mena looked at her sister and then back to the parcel. She picked it up and pulled at a loose end of the material where Pop's initials were embroidered. The handkerchief draped open and her eyes immediately fell upon the words, *Boots No.7*. She looked at Mary again, this time flicking straight back to the gift. She couldn't believe it. There were several items and they looked brand new. She turned and hugged Mary.

"Just don't let Mother catch you wearing it this time," Mary said. "When she makes you hand over your makeup, give her the old stuff. She'll be happy enough."

"Thank-you, thank-you, thank-you," Mena said.

"Don't mention it. Now come on, it's Christmas. Put all this behind you and come and have some breakfast."

It had seemed to Mena that the Christmas of 1943 would go down in her memory as the worst Christmas ever, but the day quickly regained its rhythm. At seeing Mena again her mother had simply smiled at her like any proud mother might, kissed her forehead and said, "Look at you. That's much better, isn't it? Now pass me down that skillet, there's a dear." And that was the end of it.

Mena was last to sit down to breakfast, which they ate in the conservatory at the back of the house, looking out over leaf-strewn grounds and skeletal trees towards Evington. Pop was quick to pacify any lingering discomfort over the make-up incident with a few jokes that had everyone laughing more out of sympathy than good humour. And with Edward there, winking at her as soon as she sat down as if to ask if she was okay, Mena could only think of her new make-up and smile back to the affirmative.

Ordinarily it was the custom - or duty as far as Margaret Lasseter was concerned - to attend morning Mass at St Mary's in Wigston on Christmas Day. But soon after petrol rationing began, despite the extra coupons Pop received for his rounds, the journey to the church in the Morris could no longer be justified. At any other time, Mena knew that her mother would think nothing of taking them all on the near eight mile return bicycle ride, but today, with Edward there, there was just too much to do. Accordingly, prayers were said often and in such times were never more heartfelt.

After breakfast it had been Mary's suggestion that they should visit with a few of their close neighbours to share some of the treats Edward had brought with him. This delighted her mother who was quick to agree, saying that it was as saintly a thought as any she'd heard.

"That's our Mary," Margaret said with a smile. "Our Mary full of grace."

This occupied the rest of the morning and their own Christmas dinner was all the more rushed for it, but no one seemed to mind except the twins, who were always hungry. Presents traditionally came after dinner at the Lasseter house, which again no one except the twins seemed to mind. The pair had rushed away from the dining table as soon as the last *Amen* had fallen; off into the sitting room to the decorated tree and the gifts beneath it. These were typically homemade or practical things like Pop's 'new' dressing gown or a bar of soap. The twins were soon pulled away again though to help with the washing up and it was late afternoon by the time a few drinks had been poured and the presents had been unwrapped.

The sun was low and paling at the windows. Outside, the frost had already begun its return to Oadby, but the fire kept the cold distant. Mary and Edward were on the settee, as inseparable as they had been all day. Margaret was in her usual chair by the fireplace and Pop stood by the grate because it was the only place in the house where he was allowed to smoke his pipe. Mena was sitting on the floor, cross-legged as she watched the twins, who were quiet for what seemed like the first time all day as they tried to work out how to play their new board game, *Touring England*. Mena knew it was one of her brothers' old games, but it was new to the twins and they seemed content enough with it, pushing their cardboard cars around the countryside with no understanding or concern for the rules. Behind them on their own settee, which over time had come to need the throw that covered it, Xavier and Manfred were sleeping, or looked to be.

The Lasseters had a Pye radiogram that always sat on top of the sideboard. The case was brown Bakelite and it had a fan shaped window for the frequency numbers. Pop would sit there for hours some evenings, turning the dial, listening for German spies broadcasting cryptic messages - a sure sign that *Jerry* had reached England's shores. The whistling and the static hiss annoyed the rest of the family, especially the dogs, so Pop was often left alone to his twiddling. They never missed *In Town Tonight* though and at nine o'clock the dial would turn without fail to the BBC Home Service for the news programme.

They were listening to Sandy MacPherson now, playing his organ music as he often did, throwing in something festive every now and then. Mena had no idea what the tune they were listening to was called; there were so many. "Too many," Pop always said. She liked the Vera Lynn programme, *Sincerely Yours*, which her mother liked too, so she heard that show a lot. And she loved listening to anything by Glenn Miller and his band, whose music seemed to set her free, if only for three minutes at a time. The band had become very popular since the war began, but not with her mother so she had to be clever about it, often interrupting Pop, who never seemed to mind. He would give her a conspiratorial nod as she crept in at certain times and she always thought he liked the element of danger that followed after her if Mother ever found out.

Margaret Lasseter took a sip of sherry and set her glass down on the table beside her chair. "Must you really leave us so soon, Edward," she said. "I don't know how we shall ever repay your kindness."

Mena watched her sister's arm knot tighter through Edwards. Their hands touched and their fingers fidgeted. She thought she saw Mary nudge Edward's thigh. Then Mary quickly hid her smile in her Vermouth.

"Well, there is something," Edward began. He glanced at Mary then looked back into the room.

He was blushing, Mena thought. She saw that nudge again from Mary and noticed that her sister's smile had broadened behind her glass.

"What is it, Edward?" Margaret said.

This time Mary nudged Edward so hard he moved. He turned to Pop, coughed into his hand and said, "May I speak with you, sir?"

Despite the blush and the warmth of the fire, Mena saw the colour drain from Edward's cheeks as he stood.

Pop set his glass of Mackeson's down on the mantle. "Of course, lad. You know you can speak freely here. There's no need to ask."

Edward cleared his throat again. "I believe on this occasion there is, sir." His posture became authoritative, straightening like he was standing to attention. "Alone, if you please."

Pop's brows arched. He puffed on his pipe, blew the smoke into the fire then set it down on the mantle. He put a hand on Edward's shoulder. "We can go into the study," he said as he led a worried looking Edward Buckley out of the room.

They were not gone long.

Mena heard their laughter first, followed by their loud, smiling voices on the other side of the door before it opened. Mary was already on her feet and Mena thought she looked like she was about to explode. She hopped on the spot and silently clapped her hands together several times.

"Bring out the champagne glasses, Mother," Pop said. He had the neck of a bottle in one hand; the other was hastily twisting at the wire. "I've been keeping this by for you two," he added.

There was a tinkle of glass from the drinks cabinet and Margaret's eyes sparkled in their reflection as she brought them out. "Oh, this is the best news," she said, distributing the glasses.

Mary had an arm through Edward's and her eyes were locked with his until the *pop* of the champagne cork broke the spell. It bounced off the ceiling and into the Christmas tree and Mary shot after it as Xavier and Manfred began to bark and circle between everyone.

"Edward has asked for consent to marry our daughter," Pop announced. "And I have given it my full blessing!" He finished pouring the champagne, half filling a glass for Mena. The twins were still sucking *Coca-Cola* through striped paper straws.

"You must marry Mary at St Mary's," Margaret said and she laughed, adding, "I'll not be able to say that after this glass of champagne!"

Edward nodded. "There was never any question, Mrs Lasseter." He smiled at Mary as she returned with a grin and held the recovered cork up for him to see.

"And will you call me Margaret after the wedding?"

Edward laughed through his nose. "I promise to try."

Pop raised his glass. "Congratulations to the pair of you."

"Yes, congratulations," Margaret added as the glasses met and tinkled. "And when is the big day to be? A spring wedding perhaps? If you can wait that long."

Edward and Mary exchanged glances and both began to speak at once. "We were -"

Edward continued. "We rather thought it best to wait until this wretched war was over," he said. "I want to do what's right for Mary and what with the rationing and our families scattered to the four winds..."

"Quite," Pop said, though his expression seemed to question Edward's judgment.

Margaret voiced their concern. "Do you think that's wise, Edward dear? I mean, with everything that's going on... Well you have to live each day, don't you?"

"Mother!" Mary said.

"Well you do, dear. There's no knowing if Edward will -"

Edward cut in. "We're completely decided on the matter." He looked into Mary's eyes again and held them as he spoke. His voice softened. "I have no idea if I'll make it through this war, Mrs Lasseter, but I do believe I'll stand a better chance if I have your daughter's hand waiting for me at the end of it."

Margaret put a hand to her mouth. "Oh, Edward," she said, and she hugged him like all three of her own boys were there in her embrace.

Much later, after Edward had left and the cold moon was high over Oadby, Mena sat in her chair by the window and looked out over the crystalline landscape. Pop had not long retired for the night - always last to bed and first to rise - and the house was still again, but she couldn't sleep. She pulled her blanket up beneath her chin and continued to wonder why everything about her life was so unfair.

Why couldn't I have been born before Mary?

Things would have been different then, she supposed. Perhaps then she would be allowed to wear make-up and she would have been allowed to *join-up* and get away from home as Mary had. Perhaps then she would have been the one her mother had matched with Edward Buckley so long ago and now she would be getting married and setting up her own home, somewhere far from Oadby and everything else about her life that was wrong.

A creaking floorboard interrupted her thoughts. She imagined Pop had had one too many glasses of stout too close to bedtime, but a moment later her bedroom door opened. It was Mary, dressed in a pale-yellow nightdress that matched her own.

"I couldn't sleep," Mary said as she came into the room.

"Oh?"

"I was worried about you."

"Worried about me?" Mena laughed to herself. "Whatever for?"

Mary approached the window and sat opposite Mena on the edge of the bed. "You've hardly said a word all evening. Now I find you sitting up in your chair. You can't sleep either?"

"I'm not tired."

"Is it because Edward and I are getting married?"

Mena looked out the window and the moon seemed to reflect her melancholy.

"It is, isn't it?" Mary said. She squatted beside the chair, between

Mena and the moon. "It won't change anything, Mena."

Without looking at Mary, Mena got up and jumped onto her bed. "It will. It will," she said. "It will change everything and I'll be left here alone with Mother!" She was under the covers before Mary had the chance to stand up again and from beneath them she heard her sister laugh in that gentle way that always told her what a silly little girl she was being.

"You can come and stay with us whenever you like," Mary said. "You know that."

Mena felt the bedcovers slide back over her face. She did nothing to stop them.

"It won't be half as bad as you think," Mary added.

Mena was back in the moonlit room, staring into her sister's eyes. She felt a soft hand brush a tear from her cheek.

"How long have you known?" Mena said.

"About a month. Edward had been in Italy until the end of summer. They lost Major-General Hopkinson in the fight and I think Edward and his unit must have had it pretty rough. In November most of the division were sent home. He wrote and said he needed to see me, but he couldn't get away so I pulled a few strings and went to him. He came here today so he could ask Pop."

"Why didn't you tell me, or write to Mother?"

"Some things are private," Mary said. "Even between us. And I wanted it to be a surprise." She laughed. "I'm sure Mother's been waiting for Edward to propose to me longer than I have. I wanted to see her face. Can you understand that? Can you forgive me?"

Mena sat up and threw her arms around Mary. "It's me who needs forgiveness. I've been selfish and I'm sorry. I didn't even offer my congratulations. I wish you both every happiness, of course I do."

"Friends again then?"

Mena nodded.

"Anyway," Mary said. "The way things are it's not likely to happen any time soon. You'll feel different by the time the war's over, I'm sure."

Mena smiled at last. "Maybe I'll have my own husband by then," she said. "Someone to carry *me* away."

"Maybe you will. But you're too young to worry about all that, aren't you?"

Mena didn't think so.

Chapter Five

Jefferson Tayte was in England on a train heading north out of London's St Pancras station. He hadn't expected to be back again so soon, but he was glad to be there without really knowing why. Perhaps it was that he felt some connection through what little he knew about his mother, or maybe it was just because it meant that he'd survived the flight. He'd called his client to let her know he'd arrived safely and now he had his phone pressed to his ear again, trying hard to follow his own conversation over the noise around him. It was Saturday afternoon and he was sharing the carriage with a host of jubilant football fans returning from what was evidently a win for the away team.

"Toulouse?" he said. He wasn't sure he'd heard right. "What's Marcus doing in France?"

He listened to the answer with one finger pressed to his other ear to block out the chant that had just started up further along the carriage. He thought that must be why he couldn't reach his friend on his cellphone - Marcus didn't want to pay extra for international calls.

"What was that, Emmy?" he said. "Research?"

He listened as Marcus's wife told him that her husband had been so wrapped up in his latest project that she'd hardly seen him lately. Tayte understood that lifestyle only too well.

"Okay, he said. "Well, I'll try and call again. I just wanted to thank him for helping me out the other week. I know he must have called in a few favours at the GRO to speed things up with the documents. I thought it would be great to see you both before I head home." He paused, listening. "Yeah, I know. It has been far too long."

He said goodbye and put his phone back in his jacket, wondering whose family history his good friend Marcus Brown was working on in France. He was curious, but as Marcus was incommunicado there wasn't much he could do about it.

"American?"

The man sitting too snuggly in the aisle seat next to Tayte pulled him from his thoughts and Tayte smiled and nodded back. The man's wife and daughter were sitting opposite them: wife reading a book, daughter buried in a handheld video game with the earphones thankfully plugged in. Judging from the *Harrod's* bag on the table and the other assorted bags at their feet they were returning from a shopping trip.

The man put his newspaper down. "Don't mind this rabble," he said, indicating the red and black football shirts that lined the carriage. "We've had a win, that's all. Sheffield FC that is. So are you on holiday? Vacation?"

Tayte was still a little wired from the flight and he wasn't really in the mood to open his life up to a stranger on a train, but he didn't want to be rude. "I'm kind of here on family business," he said, being deliberately vague about his profession as a family historian then realising that the man must have thought he meant he was going to a funeral.

"Oh," the man said. "I see. Well, I'm sorry to hear that."

The man went back to his newspaper then and Tayte turned away and looked out the window. Beyond the dim reflection of his dark, unshaved face the view was bleak. It had been raining when they set out from London and now that they had cleared the city, wet snow was falling and sticking to the glass. He watched the snowflakes spatter and race across the window and he thought about the girl again. He'd been thinking about her since he'd left DC, often rolling her name around in his head: *Philomena Lasseter*. He liked the way it sounded. He'd gone over his limited research several times on the plane until the details on her birth certificate were fixed in his memory. It had helped take his mind off the flight, even if he'd been unable to learn anything more from it. Now he was in England though, he hoped that was soon going to change.

He turned his thoughts back to the phone call he'd just made, thinking about Marcus and the old days. Although they kept in touch, Tayte hadn't seen him in years and he regretted not seeing him on his last visit. The assignment in Cornwall had kept him so busy though that he hadn't had time to give Marcus much thought, let alone do anything about it. He planned to rectify that this time around and he hoped Marcus would be back from France before he had to return home.

They had first met soon after Tayte left high school and became interested in genealogy - not long after he'd found out that he'd been adopted, which had brought about a sudden, unrelenting need to learn the tools of the trade he'd been in ever since. Marcus Brown was the teacher and Tayte was the hungry pupil, and no one had helped him more; although he often thought that if someone like Marcus couldn't find out who he was, what chance did he have? No one was better qualified than the estimable Marcus Brown and yet neither of them, their skills combined, had even come close. It served to remind Tayte how hopeless it was to keep trying, but every time he voiced such thoughts his friend would remind him of one simple truth. He could hear Marcus telling him it for the first time - could picture him pulling at his goatee as he often did when he had anything thought provoking to say.

"They say there's only one certainty in life, Jefferson. Know what it is?"

Tayte had been twenty-three years old and he knew well enough. "Death," he'd said.

"That's right, but it's not the only certainty, is it?"

"It's not?"

"No," Marcus said. "The other certainty is that wherever you want to go, whatever you want to be or do, or find in your case, you will certainly never get there if you give up. Now pick your chin up off the floor and stop feeling sorry for yourself. You've got work to do."

Sometimes Tayte wished Marcus hadn't told him that. Sometimes he'd wanted to give up, or thought he had. But in the end he knew Marcus was right and he wanted to pick up the pieces again. It just seemed that they had exhausted every angle over the years and right now he had no new angle to explore.

He pictured the photograph of his mother that he'd been given at the reading of his adoptive parents' will. He recalled the address in South America that was written on the back: the Catholic mission in San Rafael, Sinaloa where she'd left him, and how it had led him to Mexico and Sister Manriquez. He'd been fortunate that she was still there after the seventeen years that had passed since she'd taken him in from a mother who had refused to impart any information about herself.

"For the child's own protection," his mother had said with an English accent - or so the Sister had told him.

She recalled little else from that fleeting visit, her focus drawn as it was to the crying bundle in her arms as she took it and watched his mother leave. She'd been alone - just her and an open top jeep that Sister Manriquez had told him she'd sped off in just as quickly as she'd arrived, leaving her with the baby - with him - in her arms. He supposed his mother was running from something or someone, but from what or whom he had no idea. He'd spent weeks in that area, looking around and asking questions, knowing how futile it was.

Tayte shook his head and scoffed. He checked his watch and the glowing red LED digits told him he'd be in Leicester in around forty-five minutes; too much time to spend in a past he'd rather not revisit just now. He reached between his knees into his briefcase and his hand fell onto a bag of Hershey's chocolate miniatures. He'd bought two bags at the airport on the way out for courage and one of them was already long gone despite the promise he'd made to himself to cut back. He wasn't going to open this bag, though. He planned to save it for the return flight and only if he really needed it, unless some other emergency came along.

He found the book he was looking for - the copy of *Madame Bovary* he'd brought with him - thinking he had time for some light reading before the train arrived in Leicester. He'd started it on the plane and he wanted to read it because he knew the girl had. He was using the nametape as a bookmark, too. He slipped it out from the pages and read the name again, smoothing his thumb over the stitching as he did so, wondering again as he slouched in his seat who Danielson was and what part, if any, he had played in Philomena's story and the arrival of her suitcase at Eliza Gray's home all these years later.

Chapter Six

May 1944.

Mena Lasseter had a red bicycle with a silver bell and a basket over the front wheel. It had been Mary's once, back when it was yellow and Mena was too small to reach the pedals; when she would sit with her feet on the bar and her hands locked around her sister for support. She was on her way back through the village at last, just passing St Peter's church by the low brick wall that retained all the old headstones. She wore a cream cardigan over a sage-green, button-through dress that kept riding up on the breeze, but she didn't care. It was a glorious Friday afternoon and although the air was cool, the late spring sun felt warm on her face and the gardens and fields in and around Oadby were bursting with colour.

She glanced up at the clock that was set high into the church's prominent spire and instantly sped up. *Joan Cartwright is such a gossip,* she thought, grinning in spite of the fact that she knew she was going to be late for tea and more importantly that her mother would not be happy. She turned the corner too fast and had to *tring* her bell at an elderly woman in a raincoat who had just stepped out to cross the road.

"Sorry, Mrs Andrews!" Mena called, not waiting for a response, pedalling faster now that the road had straightened again and she could see the allotments that marked the edge of the village.

Mena had been with her best friend Joan Cartwright all afternoon and Joan's particular brand of gossip had a way of making Mena forget all purpose, especially as the subject matter today concerned the American soldiers who were currently pouring into Leicester. Some of their town friends, of Joan's acquaintance more than Mena's, had even been on dates already. One of them, Alice, whom Mena did know, had been locked in her bedroom to keep her from fraternising with the GIs, who were generally thought to be dangerous. Mena was surprised that her own mother hadn't done the same thing, but she supposed there was little point given that, unless she was fire-watching, she wasn't allowed out after tea anyway, which was all the more reason for her present haste.

Her brakes made a rubbery squeal that shook the bicycle as she pulled up and turned off the road onto a shortcut she knew. A track led through the allotments to a bridle path, which cut along the edge of the fields that the Lasseter house backed onto. She would be very late by the time she arrived home and she knew it, but there was something about the day that made her worry less and smile more. Perhaps it was the myriad wild flowers and the blossom that hung like candyfloss in the trees, or the recently mown gardens whose borders were crowded with brightly coloured tulips and hyacinths. She sucked in the giddy scent of it all, enriched as it was by evening's onset, and felt as carefree as spring itself. She thought to pick some bluebells by way of a peace offering for her mother, but that would have made her later still so she pushed on.

She was out of breath by the time she reached the gate at the bottom of the garden. She nudged through and pedalled hard down the brick pathway that wound through the lawns, past the Anderson shelter to her right and the old well to her left that was now no more than a garden ornament. When she arrived in the yard beside the house, she jumped off her bicycle before it had stopped and left the pedals spinning by the coal-shed as she burst in through the back door.

"Sorry, I'm late!" she called, still panting. There was the smell of old chip-fat on the air, which made her stomach groan, and there were dirty pans in the sink. She removed her shoes and hurried into the dining room where the Lasseters always had their tea. She opened the door and began her excuses. "I was just -"

Her words trailed off when she saw that the room was empty. Then laughter drew her away and she crossed the hall to the sitting room, aware now that she was so late she'd missed the meal altogether. Her mother looked unhappy to see her, but Pop's smile made up for it. Edward Buckley was there so that would save her, she thought. The 1st Airborne had been billeted all over Leicestershire, awaiting orders. Edward had a few days furlough and was staying with the family in the hope that Mary would soon be home. There was someone else with him: a young man, also in military garb. He rose with Edward as she entered and then both men sat down again as she closed the door.

Mena cast a smile into the room, avoiding eye contact with her mother. Pop spoke first.

"Couldn't you find Mr Gibbons?"

Mena faltered in her reply. She'd been sent out early that afternoon with a prescription for old Fred Gibbons in Wigston. She often ran such errands for her father - doing her bit.

"I was -" she began.

Then she saw the dubious squint in her mother's eyes and turned to Pop again who winked at her and she caught on.

"He wasn't home," she said, and in her mind she crossed her chest for the lie. "I had to ride all over the place. It was such a nice day and I suppose he must have -"

"Enough, enough," Margaret said. "Did you find him or not?"

"Yes, Mother."

"Then sit down. You can have supper later. We have a guest." Margaret's smile returned. "This is Mr Danielson," she added. "He's from America."

"Folks just call me Danny on account of my surname," their guest said with an accent that seemed to flatten the vowels and draw them out as he spoke, or so Mena thought.

He was perched on the edge of the settee, like he was uncomfortable with the idea of getting too relaxed. His rank insignia was that of Staff Sergeant and he wore his Class A uniform: gleaming russet-brown shoes and a sharp edged, olive-drab, four button tunic and trousers with a khaki tie in the neck. The jacket carried a number of badges and brass buttons, the most notable of which was an *'Airborne'* insignia on the left arm with the letters *AA* sitting boldly beneath it.

Between his hands was a flat-folded forage cap that had a parachute emblem on the side. He was pressing it between his fingers, turning it over every now and then. He looked at least twenty, Mena thought, and she liked his close-trimmed hairstyle, which was so blonde it was almost white. He had a pronounced jaw-line that looked unbreakable, she thought, and his blue eyes were the kind that held your attention. At least, they held Mena's.

Margaret's smile broadened. "Danny's a friend of Edward's," she said. "He thought it would be nice to bring him home for tea to meet an English family. Apparently everyone's doing it."

"Brought fresh eggs with him too," Pop said, smiling through his pipe.

Margaret cleared her throat and to Mena she said, "Yes, well I'm afraid the twins have eaten yours, dear."

Mena was starving. Real eggs and home cooked chips. She sighed through her nose and smiled awkwardly. Then she sat in the chair opposite her mother and turned to face Edward.

"Hello Eddie," she said. "Anything from Mary yet?"

“She’ll be home first thing,” Edward replied, beaming. “I don’t know how I shall sleep tonight.”

Mena tilted her head towards their guest and began to stare. “Mena Lasseter,” she announced, suddenly finding that her mouth was dry. “I’m pleased to meet you.”

“Likewise ma’am,” Danny said. He squatted forward, stretched a long, substantial looking arm across the gap and shook Mena’s hand.

Edward gave a chirpy laugh. “Danny here almost got himself into trouble this afternoon,” he said. “That’s how we met.”

“Oh?”

“No fault of his own, mind,” Edward added. “I was having a drink with a couple of chums down at the *Dog*. It was pretty quiet in there except for a bunch of flyboys who’d had one or two sherbets too many. We couldn’t see them where we were sitting, but we could hear them all right. Having a dig at you over the pay difference weren’t they, Danny?”

Danny grinned. “Hell, they’d have started up over just about anything, I reckon.” He shot a glance at Margaret. “Pardon my language, ma’am.”

Margaret returned a forgiving half-smile and Danny continued.

“Well, I didn’t much like the odds,” he said, “but there was no way I was getting outta there without a fight. I stood to meet them as they came over - ready to give it my best. Then Eddie here stepped out.”

Edward laughed. “We couldn’t just sit there and let you take a pasting, could we? It was Dougie Peters who pointed your insignia out. We’d been fighting alongside you 82nd boys in Italy. You might be *All American* but we’re all airborne together so up we got.” Edward laughed again. “I can still see their faces when I said to Peters, ‘Now it’s a fair fight!’”

“They didn’t even finish their beers,” Danny said, laughing along with him.

He had a perfect mouth, Mena thought. She liked the way his smile lifted slightly in one corner and how the intensity in his eyes seemed to lift with it.

“Good for you, Edward,” Pop said. “Those RAF sorts think they own the place. We’re surrounded by airfields, Danny. It’ll be nice to see some different uniforms about the place.”

“The 504th are camped at Shady Lane,” Edward said to Mena.

“Camp Stoughton, we call it,” Danny added.

Mena continued to smile at Danny, nodding her head. She wished she wasn't in such a state. Her hair felt wretched and her face was no doubt ruddy and glistening from the ride home.

"They kept us in for two weeks quarantine when we arrived," Danny said.

"Came into Liverpool, I hear," Pop said.

"We sure did, and it was a welcome sight after Italy. We sailed up through the Med on a tub called the Capetown Castle. I think it used to be a cruise ship." He paused and for a long moment he stared at the cap in his hands. "We lost too many friends back there," he added. "I guess that's why we're here now."

"Regrouping?" Pop said.

Danny nodded. I don't know how long it'll take to get back to operational status, but no one's in any hurry. Green fields and friendly faces, and a comfy cot to sleep on. It sure ain't Italy."

Mena found herself fishing for eye contact, but Danny was looking at his cap again, slowly wringing it back and forth in his hands like his mind was elsewhere. There was an element of vulnerability about him that Mena liked. It made her want to know him better, perhaps to understand why.

Danny drew a breath through his teeth and pressed his hands onto his thighs. "Well I should be getting along." He stood up. "Thank you kindly for your hospitality ma'am," he said to Margaret. "It was real swell of you."

The rest of the room rose with him.

"You must come back again," Margaret said.

"Mmm," Pop agreed, still hanging onto his pipe. "And bring a *buddy* next time."

"Careful," Edward said. "You'll have the whole of the 504th knocking at your door before you know it and it will all be my fault!"

Danny laughed. "Don't worry, ma'am. They don't let us all out at once."

"Well come back soon," Margaret said, shaking his hand.

"I'd sure like that," Danny said, and as he made for the door Mena caught his eyes at last and she held them, thinking how much she would like that too.

Chapter Seven

The next day was not so bright: no rain yet, but there was a scurrying breeze and the sky over Leicestershire was filled with the kind of gathering grey clouds that told Mena rain was soon to follow. Gone was the sun-washed vibrancy of yesterday, muted now in shade. Yet today, Mena saw Oadby just as she had seen it then, as if everything reminded her of the day she first met Danny.

Mary had arrived home early that morning, as Edward had said she would. It was early afternoon now. The Saturday chores were done and the errands run. Pop had been called out on a house visit and Margaret Lasseter had gone to queue with her ration book - and the twins. Sightings of Mary and Edward had been scarce since breakfast and since Edward was with them it meant that they had sausages, which although not on the ration were hard to get and made a pleasant change to the monotony of wheat flakes or porridge.

Mena was by the French doors in the conservatory when Mary and Edward reappeared. She was sitting on the floor between Xavier and Manfred, gazing towards Evington, deep in thought as she toyed affectionately with their floppy ears.

"Are you sure you won't come to the pictures?" Mary said. "We'd love you to join us, wouldn't we, Edward?"

"Yes, of course," Edward said. "Just like old times."

"Don't pretend you haven't been looking forward to it," Mary added.

They were taking the bus into Leicester and it had been arranged that the next time Mary was home they would see a movie. Rita Hayworth was starring in *Cover Girl* and Mary was right, she had been looking forward to it. Until yesterday. Until Danny Danielson.

"I can't, really," Mena said.

Mary came closer and knelt beside her. "Why-ever not?"

"I told Mother I'd look after this soppy pair until she gets back."

Mary ran a hand down Xavier's spine. "That doesn't sound like you, Mena Lasseter. What are you up to?"

Mena felt a smile rise inside her. "Nothing, really." She looked away and tried to hide her face by nuzzling into the back of Manfred's huge head, brushing her nose back and forth on his coat until he rolled over and licked her chin.

Mary stood up. "Well, be good."

"See you later," Edward added as they left. "We'll save you some popcorn if they have any."

Fifteen minutes after Mary and Edward had gone, Mena was cycling away from Oadby on the Stoughton Road wearing her best day-dress beneath a beige raincoat, with a scarf in her hair and contraband cherry-red lipstick on her lips. There were fields to either side of her and she saw few people, although she turned away whenever she did in case someone recognised her. As she neared the end of the road, a US-military jeep passed her in the opposite direction and a covered truck followed it with plenty of whistling from the back. At the junction she turned left onto Gartree Road then right into Shady Lane by the golf course.

Shady Lane looked its best in full sun, she thought, when the contrast between the leafy canopy above her and the swatches of sunlight on the lane below was at its most intense. The bluebells that lined the lane's deep verges looked happier then; although today, for Mena at least, they were still smiling even though the lane, which stretched away beyond sight, was so grey it was almost dark.

She had cycled about halfway down when she heard what sounded like a party going on somewhere ahead. A little further and she could see a number of bicycles scattered at random, some lying on their sides, others against the trees. The party-like chatter was coming from the cycle's owners, who were leaning against a post-and-rail fence that ran alongside the lane.

Mena slowed and stepped from her bicycle, walking with it until she drew level with the rest. She stopped. She couldn't quite believe her eyes but what had she expected? That she was the only girl within cycling distance of Camp Stoughton with cause to go there? A line of girls, wearing what Mena imagined were their brightest outfits, stood by the fence, chatting away and giggling with a line of men that was three deep in places on the other side. Their American accents told her she'd found the right place and as she dropped her bicycle and went to the fence herself, she saw that some of them wore the same smart uniform she'd seen on Danny yesterday, while others looked casual in loose-fitting jackets and trousers that were covered with baggy pockets.

Her heart began to race. She felt uncomfortable at first, but as she leant on the rail she was put at ease by a sudden eruption of laughter as one of the GIs - a small, dark-haired man - climbed onto the shoulders of the biggest man there and began to juggle what looked like three galvanised metal cups. She became so caught up in the scene, smiling and laughing with everyone else as the larger man wobbled and side-stepped beneath the juggler, that she was startled when another uniform rose up against the fence in front of her.

"Hey, doll-face! You wanna help win the war?"

Mena stepped back and the smiling soldier removed his forage cap. He clutched it to his chest and began to flash his eyebrows at her. "Tell me I never made it through Italy," he said, pronouncing the country as, *Idaly*. "Tell my mother I'm in heaven and I ain't ever comin' home!"

Another man quickly joined him, shoving him aside. He was smiling, too. Everyone was smiling. "Don't mind him, ma'am," he said. "Spiller's the regimental idiot! It's a mystery to us all how come he *did* make it through Italy." The GI reached a hand over the fence. "Names Montalvo," he added. "That's Vic to you. What's yours?"

Mena was hesitant. A girl standing beside her in a royal-blue dress turned and nudged her. She was no 'girl' at all, Mena thought. She had to be in her forties.

"Come on, honey. I don't bite," Montalvo said. "Not dames, anyways."

Mena shook Montalvo's hand and quickly withdrew again. "Mena," she offered.

Montalvo whistled, slow and long. "I like that. Say, that's almost as cute as you."

He sounded the same as Danny and the rest of the GIs, Mena thought, but there was something different about him: his skin was tanned, like the rest, but it had a waxy appearance like an olive, which by contrast made his teeth look whiter. His nose was small and his eyes were wide-set, and his hair showed oily black beneath his cap, which rested at an impossible slant on his head.

"So what brings you to Camp Stoughton?" he said.

"I'm looking for someone."

"Hey, ain't we all, sweetheart!" It was Spiller again.

Montalvo, the bigger of the two, reached an arm around Spiller's neck and pulled him into his chest. "He sure is a joker!" he said as he began to rap his knuckles on the man's head. When Spiller protested, Montalvo shoved him away again, watching after him as he moved down the line to annoy someone else.

"What's the lucky fella's name?" Montalvo said. "Maybe I can find him."

"Danny," Mena said. "Danny Danielson."

Montalvo looked like he was thinking about it. "Rings a bell," he said. "I couldn't say for sure."

"He's tall," Mena said. "About your height. He's got blonde hair and -" She was about to tell him about Danny's blue eyes, but she thought better of it.

"Blonde?" Montalvo said.

"Almost white."

Montalvo nodded. He smiled. "Yeah, sure. I think I know who you mean. There's a Blondie in H-company."

Mena reached into her raincoat pocket and produced a note in a sealed envelope. She read Danny's name on the front and smiled, chewing her lower lip, wondering if Danny would think it too forward of her until she began to feel light-headed. The envelope quivered as she handed it over. "Give him this will you?"

Montalvo took the note and turned it in his hands. "What if it ain't the right guy?"

Mena was thinking about it when she became aware that the woman next to her was leaning over the fence, kissing one of the GIs. It looked like the kind of kiss Mena had seen at the pictures, only these two really meant it. She thought it was enough to put Mary and Edward to shame. When the woman withdrew, her lipstick was smeared on both their faces and the GI was beaming as he handed something across the fence. It was a tan-coloured ball that unravelled as the woman took it and Mena saw that it was a pair of stockings. The woman kissed him again and the GI backed away.

"Hey, Victor!" several voices called out at once in slow, patronising tones. "Lover boy!"

Montalvo looked around. Spiller was there with several other men, presumably from his unit. They waved and pulled cutesy faces, and Mena saw that all the GIs were moving away from the fence now and she noticed that the smiles on the girls' faces were fading.

"Gotta go," Montalvo said. "Tell you what. Meet me back here, same time tomorrow." He backed away, still smiling. "I'll let you know if I found your man."

My Man, Mena thought. *My Blondie.* She liked the sound of that.

The next evening, Mena was out fire-watching with Joan Cartwright. It wasn't something they did in any official capacity; they received no pay and their services were additional to Oadby's regular fire-watch rota. Several of the local girls had volunteered their services a few years ago, when the air raids had been at their peak. Margaret Lasseter had been against any kind of duty that kept her daughter out after dark. But Mena had worked on Pop, who in turn had worked on her mother until it was agreed that until she was old enough to join the Land Army, she could fire-watch two nights a week as long as she had a friend with her and was home by midnight.

There was a building on the Leicester Road, next to the painters-and-decorators, which had a flat roof. The owner always left a ladder out so they could climb up and sit against one of the chimneystacks, looking out over the shops and houses for evidence of incendiary bombs. The regular fire-watchers who patrolled the streets in shifts throughout the night would always check on them as they passed, and whenever there was an air-raid they had to come straight down and get to one of the shelters, which wasn't so often lately.

It was a cool night. The clouds had moved out of Oadby by mid-afternoon and the stars and half-moon above the blacked-out streets were typically bright in the sky. Both girls wore coats and scarves with their inseparable gas masks in a box that hung around their shoulders. Their torches had cardboard over the lens with a hole cut in it to reduce the beam whenever they needed to use them and they each had a flask of hot soup to keep them going. For the most part they just sat in the moonlight, listening to the world below them: the muted revelry from a nearby pub and the clack of heels on the streets. That's when they could hear anything at all over the sound of their own gossip.

"Mary knows," Mena said, once she'd told Joan all about her visit to Shady Lane.

"You're kidding me," Joan said. "How?"

"I went back there today. I wanted to make sure Danny got my note. One of Mary's friends must have recognised me and told."

"Thank God she didn't tell your mother!"

"I know."

Joan had been Mena's best friend since either could remember. She had shimmering chestnut hair that fell past her shoulders in long waves, big brown eyes that were wide-set, and she always wore make-up these days, even at home. She produced a crumpled packet of

American Chesterfield cigarettes, lit one up and drew on it, leaving her lipstick on the paper as she handed it to Mena between long scissor-like fingers.

"And?" she said, her eyes growing with expectation as she spoke. "Did he get the note?"

Mena coughed and nodded. "He wants to meet me," she said. "Next time he can get out of camp." She coughed again and handed back the cigarette.

"And when's that?" Joan said, smiling and fidgeting.

"Next Friday night. At St Peter's!"

Both girls began to giggle.

"Great choice," Joan said. "Your mother won't go anywhere near that place."

"I know," Mena said. "She'd sooner cross the street than risk bumping into an Anglican."

Joan took a thoughtful pull on the cigarette. "What about your sister? How much does she know? D'you reckon she'll tell?"

"I told her everything," Mena said. "She wasn't happy about it, but I'm sure she won't say a word. She knows I'll be in for it if she does." She shrugged like she didn't care. "Mary worries too much," she added. "I'm nearly seventeen, aren't I? Feels more like I'm still ten." She took the cigarette from Joan and puffed heavily on it as if to prove the point. Then she rolled her head back with Joan's and blew smoke at the moon.

"You'll have to pretend you're fire-watching," Joan said a moment later. "It's the only way you'll be allowed out."

"It's not my night for it," Mena said. "Can't you call for me with some story? Like we're expecting a raid and they need all the volunteers they can get."

Joan gave a derisive laugh. "You wouldn't be allowed out at all if your mother thought there would actually be an air-raid." She sighed. "I can't anyway. I'm supposed to be looking after my pain-in-the-backside brother. Mummy and Daddy are going to a dance - some posh fundraiser in town I'd rather be going to myself."

Mena unscrewed the cap on her soup flask. "Never mind, I'll come up with something," she said. "Mary will be away again by then. I'll have to lie to Mother, of course."

Joan snorted, puffing smoke through her nose. "That's nothing fresh!"

Chapter Eight

By the time Mena's Friday night date with Danny Danielson came around, she had her mother believing that she'd swapped a fire-watch shift with one of her friends because her 'friend' had no one else to sit with her. She'd even stayed home when she was supposed to meet Joan on their usual night to make the story seem genuine, and it had worked a treat. She had until midnight.

It had been raining most of the day, but it was thankfully dry now. It was after nine p.m. and almost dark when Mena set out on her bicycle for the church. Double summertime hours, which had been in place between April and September since the war began, meant that it stayed light an hour longer than usual. Dusk was the time to go fire-watching and although she would have liked to go sooner, it had apparently suited Danny and she didn't want to do anything to arouse her mother's suspicion. To further maintain the lie, she had her gas mask, torch and flask with her in her bicycle basket, and as the evenings were still chilly, she wore her coat and scarf, which was just as well given what she was wearing beneath it.

Mena allowed her excitement to permeate only when her back was to the house. She kicked hard at the pedals and began to grin, in part because she knew how well she'd fooled her mother, but mostly because she was about to embark on her first proper date. Her skin began to prickle. She felt so alive and as bold as she'd felt when she wrote her note to Danny, asking to see him again. She pictured his face: his angular features and those piercing blue eyes that had tried to avoid hers out of shyness, she thought, on that day she first saw him. Surely he would forgive her forwardness. There *was* a war on.

Mena slowed as she came to the edge of the village. She felt her skin flush beneath her coat and she knew it wouldn't do to arrive at St Peter's glowing like a scullery maid; not this time. The streets were busier than she would have liked. At first she felt the need to look away from every face that glanced towards her, but her lie had been so perfect. It didn't matter if anyone saw her because she had her mother's permission to be there. After a while she found herself smiling and nodding at people she knew, although there were a good many nowadays that she did not. Every other person she saw wore a military uniform of one kind or another and it was apparent to her that Danny's pass was no special case tonight.

She was almost there. She could see the church spire above the rooftops ahead, stabbing into the clouds that were only just visible now in the rapidly darkening sky. She stopped short of the road that led to the church and pulled her bicycle into a side street where there was a terrace of houses with blacked-out windows. She propped her bicycle against a drainpipe and removed her coat and scarf. Beneath it she wore her favourite dress: the same blue polka-dot dress she had worn on Christmas day.

Mena checked her reflection in one of the windows. She straightened her hair and realised she'd have to be quick or she'd lose the light. She unscrewed her soup flask, which contained no soup tonight. She tipped it up and her lipstick fell into her hand, followed by an eyeliner pencil that she quickly began to use. When she'd finished, she stood back and pouted at her reflection, thinking her effort not bad at all under the circumstances. Not quite Veronica Lake, but it would do.

She draped her coat over one arm and continued the rest of the way on foot, wondering as she walked where Danny would take her on their first date. *Does he know anywhere?* she thought. It would never do to turn up at the same dance in Leicester that Joan's parents were going to. Wherever they went they would have to take the bus out of Oadby; it was one thing to be seen in her coat and scarf pretending to be out fire-watching, but it was another matter altogether to be seen out socialising after dark with a Yank.

The church was in front of her suddenly, like she'd lost track of time and had no recollection of how she'd arrived there since leaving her bicycle behind. She stood at the roadside opposite and stared past the high wall and the headstones, past the neatly trimmed evergreens and the trees beyond, towards the imposing body of the church then up and along the length of its spire. The *tring* of a bell forced her eyes away and she saw two GIs wobble down the street on a single bicycle that looked ready to collapse beneath them. Turning back to the church she began to wonder if Danny had been delayed. Or worse still, whether he was coming at all.

She crossed the road, sure that she had not arrived early. If anything she thought herself a few minutes late. When she reached the steps that led up to the church path, she looked back. The streets were quieter now that night had all but fallen on Oadby. The gas lamps would soon be lit, she thought, although since their windows had been painted blue, their effectiveness was limited. She ran up the steps to get a better look, but of the few people she could see, no one seemed to be heading for the church.

Disappointment began to smother her. She drew a slow breath and started walking aimlessly back down the steps, thinking she could wait a while, but knowing in her heart that Danny was not coming. In the stillness that accompanied the night she began to hear other people enjoying their lives: their distant laughter and the plink of a merry piano. Then she heard something else that caused her to spin around.

"Hello," she called.

Her heart began to race. She stared through the half-light towards the church and saw a faint red glow, hovering in the shadow of the church doorway. A moment later she saw a puff of white smoke rise out of the arch and dissipate on the breeze. She supposed the sound she'd heard was the snap of a cigarette lighter as it closed.

"Danny?" she called, smiling again. "Is that you?" She returned to the top of the steps and heard him call her name. She was beginning to like that American accent. "I thought you weren't coming," she said. She took a few quick steps along the path towards him. "But I'm glad you did," she added as the glowing tip of his cigarette came out from the doorway to meet her. She could just about make out his uniform now in the low light. She thought she caught the hint of a smile from that perfect mouth.

"We can go out this way," he said, taking the path that led around the side of the church.

Mena lost him then to the deeper shadows that were cast across the churchyard by the trees. She saw another puff of smoke and followed it, curious at his behaviour, concluding that he must be every bit as shy as she thought.

"We can go into Wigston if you like," she said. "I don't know if you've been there yet but -"

She paused, aware that she was probably being too forward. She'd asked him out after all. That was forward enough. Perhaps she should leave the details to him. She caught up and she could discern the outline of his broad back now. His pace slowed, inviting her alongside. She wanted to hold his hand as they walked but there was plenty of time for that.

"I really don't mind where we go," she said, laughing nervously. She thought she heard Danny laugh with her then and as she looked up to catch his eyes he stopped. His hands were suddenly on her shoulders, pulling her towards him.

"Surprise!"

The outburst startled Mena. She instinctively tried to pull away, catching only the flash of his impossibly white teeth. She began to struggle.

"Hold on there, beautiful!"

Mena's eyes were slowly adjusting to the darkness and although they sounded alike to her, she could see now that this was not Danny - not her Blondie. There was no bright fringe around the edge of this man's cap. His hair was black as the night.

"It's me!" the man said. "It's your old pal, Vic Montalvo!"

Mena kept struggling. Montalvo's grip grew stronger. He began to laugh in a condescending way that reminded her of how Mary would laugh at her when she wanted to let her know what a silly girl she was being.

"Easy there!" Montalvo insisted.

Mena began to shake her head as if trying to tell herself that this was not real. Words formed and caught in her dry throat.

"Danielson's no good for you," Montalvo said. "The bum stood you up last minute for some other broad."

Mena didn't believe a word of it.

Montalvo laughed again. "I felt kinda responsible on account of it was me who gave him your note. I came along in his place so's you weren't disappointed."

Mena didn't believe he'd even given her note to Danny. She thought now that he probably never intended to. She pulled away again and Montalvo's upbeat tone changed.

"Hey, what's with all the fuss? We got on just swell across the camp fence, didn't we?"

She felt his fingers press into her skin as he pulled and jerked her closer. His arms were suddenly around her like a clamp, holding her to him so tightly that she couldn't move.

"I thought you'd like to see old Vic again," he said. "I even brought you something. Look." He fumbled in his pocket and produced a small paper parcel, tied with string. He held it in front of Mena's face. "There's nylons in there, lipstick and candy, too."

The sour reek of whisky was strong on his breath. Mena struggled again and the package fell to the ground, but Montalvo regained his hold.

"What's the difference anyways?" he said. "We're all airborne, right? All American! All the way! That's why you went to the camp ain't it? That's why all you broads go there."

Mena couldn't breathe; the combined effect of Montalvo's arms squeezing her tighter and tighter and the anxiety that seemed to paralyze her.

"Come on, honey. Whaddaya say?"

Mena felt his mouth on her face, fighting to find her lips. She thrashed her head from side to side and in her mind she began to scream but no sound came out.

Why is it so dark? she thought. *Where's Pop? Where's Mary?*

She felt a hand fumble through her hair. Then her head snatched back and his lips were suddenly hard on hers, his tongue stabbing and writhing. A hand was suddenly firm around her throat, his coarse thumb scratching up and down, up and down.

"Take it easy," Montalvo whispered.

Mena felt another hand cup around her breast and when he squeezed it she began to shake like a deathly fever had taken her. When his hand moved lower over her dress and his mouth returned to hers, she gave no fight. All she could think about was last Christmas morning and how good it felt when Mary was drawing that comb slowly through her hair. How soothing it was.

"Now that's more like it," Montalvo said, and he was kissing, kissing, kissing - drawing circles down her neck with his tongue.

Her submission must have relaxed him.

Mena felt the restraint from his arms and hands gradually lessen as they continued to discover her body. Paralyzing fear turned to rage and she seized her chance. With as much strength as she could muster, she brought her right knee up until it connected with Montalvo. She heard a groan and in that instant she twisted herself free and she ran.

Chapter Nine

The taxi Tayte had picked up when he got off the train at Leicester station had brought him out of the city to the east, through suburban villages and beyond to a stretch of open countryside, wide and lifeless in the winter grey. It had stopped at the end of a gravel drive by a low, open gate, and Tayte could clearly see the Lasseter house through the bare trees that would otherwise have screened it.

It was a crooked old house of red herringbone brick, framed in squares of exposed beams like something from Shakespeare's time: Anne Hathaway's cottage on a bigger scale. It had a red, peg-tiled roof that sank in places between a number of small dormer windows with leaded lights and garages had been added in more recent years to accommodate the changing times.

Tayte paid the driver, wondering whether he should ask him to stick around in case no one was home, but he figured he was expected so he took the chance and the cab left him there, suitcase in one hand, his briefcase in the other. He paused and watched the cab go back along the narrow road it had arrived by, noticing that it was a very quiet area with no other visible houses nearby. He headed down the drive, crunching the gravel that slipped beneath his loafers as he walked. There was a little icy rain in the air and he was glad of his coat. It was nothing like as cold as back home, but it seemed to get to him more, maybe on account of the wind that came at him in daggers across the fields, rattling his cases and ruffling his lapels.

When he reached the front door, he didn't have to knock. It opened as he reached out to try and a tall, slim man who looked in his late fifties or early sixties appeared in the frame with a smile, which accentuated his chiselled features. He had tidy salt-and-pepper hair and wore chinos and a blue Oxford weave shirt, open at the neck.

"Mr Tayte?" the man said.

"Yes," Tayte replied, smiling back.

"I thought it must be you. We don't get many visitors out here. I'm Jonathan." He shook Tayte's hand. "Come on in."

Jonathan Lasseter took Tayte's coat and suitcase from him and led him into the sitting room. There was already a fire lit beneath the beam, which gave the otherwise modern, uncluttered and neutral decor a homely feel.

"My wife isn't back from town yet," Jonathan said, "but she shouldn't be long. She's dying to meet you so don't feel there's any rush. Can I offer you some tea or coffee?"

He was a well-spoken man who sounded very British, Tayte thought. "Coffee would be great," he said. "Might help to keep me going after the flight."

"Milk and sugar?"

"No thanks," Tayte said, thinking that every little helped and that he had some making up to do after going through that bag of Hershey's.

He sat on a brown leather armchair by the fire, briefcase at his feet, and warmed himself as Jonathan made the drinks. A few minutes later Jonathan came back and set a steaming mug in front of Tayte and sat on the sofa opposite him.

"It's instant, I'm afraid," Jonathan said. "We're a household of tea drinkers really. I only keep a jar in for guests."

"Just as long as it contains caffeine," Tayte said, "I really don't mind what kind it is." He took a sip. "Do you have other family living with you? Children?"

"No," Jonathan said. "The kids moved away years ago now. Jennifer, our eldest, took a job in Bristol where she now has a family of her own and Caroline went east to Norwich University. She married an accountant and settled in the area." He sat back with his tea. "But what about you and your client? And this little suitcase that's turned up out of the blue. You've no idea who sent it?"

Tayte took another sip of coffee and shook his head. "Without the packaging, we've no way of knowing where it came from."

"No, I suppose not. Still it's a shame."

Tayte agreed, but there was nothing to be done about it. "Maybe someone else can shed some light on that," he said. "I'm keen to talk to the family and anyone else who knew Philomena. I want to gather any information I can that might help me find her."

"I'll do all I can," Jonathan said. "And it's Mena. Dad always called her Mena. I never met her, of course, but he used to talk about her whenever anyone set him off down Memory Lane. It was always the same old story really, about how he went off to war and when he came home again, Mena, was gone."

"Was there any explanation?"

"Vague," Jonathan said. "Dad always maintained it was because she fell in love with one of those GIs so many girls were falling for at the time. He would have been with the 82nd Airborne, no question about it. The 504th Parachute Infantry Regiment was camped up at Evington for a time in 1944. There's plenty of local history about them if you know where to look."

Tayte took his notebook out from inside his jacket and scribbled the information down. It would help to identify the right man when he had the chance to look.

"Dad always said how sorry he was that he hadn't seen Mena again," Jonathan continued. "He said he'd even thought about looking for her once or twice, but I think life overtook him, as life has a way of doing if you let it. He married just after the war. I was born soon after that and my sister followed. I suppose Mena eventually became little more than a memory to him - a face in a photograph of someone he used to know."

"You said on the phone that you'd found a few photographs of Mena," Tayte said.

Jonathan sat forward. "Yes, of course. You must be itching to see them. I've got them in a box down here."

He reached beneath the coffee table and slid out a small mahogany chest that had brass corner caps. He set it on the table, opened it and pulled out a collection of photographs, sliding them across the table like he was fanning out a pack of playing cards.

Tayte leant in on his elbows to get a better look.

"This is a good one," Jonathan said, singling out the largest photograph. It was mounted in a sleeve like it had been taken professionally. "This was just before the war." He pointed to the figures in the middle. Everyone looked like they were dressed in their Sunday best. "That's Granddad Pop and my grandmother, Margaret," he said. "Dad and Aunt Mary are this side. Uncle Michael and Uncle James are on the other." He pointed to a small girl, sitting with her legs crossed in the centre of the photograph. "That's Mena," he said. "She would only have been ten or eleven then."

The girl's hair was in ringlets tied with a pale blue bow and from her get-me-out-of-here expression, Tayte thought she looked far cuter than she wanted to with her big eyes, dimpled cheeks and a flouncy gown that made her look even younger than she was.

"Here's one from the war years," Jonathan said as he slid another photograph across. "There aren't many from that time, I'm afraid. Most of these were taken afterwards so you won't find any more of Mena."

Tayte recognised her straight away. She was giggling as she saluted the camera, wearing a military cap and a short army jacket over her dress. "Who's that with her?" he asked, indicating the dark haired girl giggling along with her as two young men in army uniforms sat and watched in the background.

Jonathan took the photograph back and studied it. "Her name's Joan," he said. "That's Michael and James laughing in the background. I suppose Dad must have taken the picture."

"Joan?" Tayte said. "Another family member?

"No, Joan was Mena's friend. Her best friend, so Dad told me.

"Mind if I hang on to it while I'm here?"

"Not at all," Jonathan said. He continued to shuffle through the photographs. "Here's a better one of Aunt Mary," he added, handing it to Tayte. "That's clearly from the war years."

Tayte took it. It showed a man and a woman in military uniform, her arm linked through his. A happy couple.

"Aunt Mary moved away to South Africa soon after the war," Jonathan said. "She became a missionary. I've heard that Margaret was very religious so I suppose that's who Mary got her calling from. She married an Afrikaner called Ingram and took her middle name, Grace, although I always thought of her as Aunt Mary. She was in the ATS during the war."

Tayte tapped the photograph. "Who's the man here with her?"

"That's Edward Buckley in his paratroopers uniform - one of the Red Berets. Apparently Aunt Mary used to talk about him all the time. They were supposed to marry after the war, but it never happened. They were besotted with each other by all accounts and Dad always said that he sensed such longing and regret from her whenever she spoke about him."

"Do you know why they never married?"

"I really couldn't say, but it must have been something pretty serious to break that pair up."

"Is your Aunt Mary still alive?" Tayte asked, thinking it would be great to be able to talk to someone from the time when Mena was still around.

"Sadly, no." Jonathan said. "Although you've not missed her by much. She died last month. Lung cancer."

"That's too bad," Tayte said, wondering whether Mary Lasseter's death could be the catalyst he was looking for: a recent family event linked in some way to Mena's suitcase and why it had been sent to his client.

The sound of a car on the gravel outside drew their attention.

"Good," Jonathan said, getting up. "That will be Geraldine. Don't call her Geri, or we'll both be in trouble." He winked at Tayte as he went to open the door. "Of course, she'll insist you stay for dinner, unless you have other plans?"

"None," Tayte said. "But I wouldn't want to -"

"Good. Dinner it is then."

Six thousand miles away, a priest was alone in his chambers. He was sitting at his desk, preparing for the Saturday Vigil, just as the man who entered the room and silently closed the door behind him knew he would be. He adjusted the round, frameless glasses that were pinched to the bridge of his nose and stepped closer as the priest's eyes turned to meet him.

"I must confess my sins, Father," the man said through thin lips that barely moved as he spoke.

The priest stood up. He looked confused. "You shouldn't be here," he said. "This area is private."

"But I am here, Father," the man said.

The priest, a much older man, checked his watch and shook his head. "Maybe you could come back later?" he said. "I am about to -"

"It can't wait, Father," the man cut in. "You see - I keep secrets."

"Secrets?"

"Yes, Father. I'm keeping one now."

The priest smiled at him. "Keeping secrets is not such a sin," he said.

The man nodded slowly, audibly drawing air through his nose as he filled his lungs. "The way I keep them is, Father."

He reached beneath his jacket, never taking his eyes off the priest, who backed instinctively away. When his hand came into view again it was holding a Glock 19 semi-compact handgun with a silencer already attached. The priest cowered and without hesitating the gunman put two bullets into his chest. The priest fell into the desk and then to the floor, and the man stood calmly over him, expressionless and remorseless.

"Forgive me, Father, for I have sinned," he said.

Then he shot him once more in the head, turned and slowly walked out again, closing the door behind him.

Jefferson Tayte took an immediate liking to Jonathan's wife, Geraldine, who hadn't stopped smiling and talking all through dinner. Small talk had never been something that Tayte was any good at or even comfortable with, and like Jonathan, she'd made him feel right at home. He thought she was an attractive woman. She'd had her hair done in town, cut in a short, steely-blonde bob, and in black trousers and a loose-fitting lilac jumper, she'd returned home all set for the evening, as Tayte supposed she had intended.

They were still at the table in the dining room towards the back of a house that Tayte felt he could easily get lost in. Slow piano jazz continued to play in the background and Jonathan had managed to tease a glass of brandy into Tayte's palm against his better judgement; it wasn't yet nine p.m. but jet lag was knocking on his eyelids and he knew the alcohol wouldn't help.

"So are you both retired?" he asked.

Geraldine laughed at the idea. "Jonathan got out the year before last when he turned sixty," she said. "Personally, I wouldn't know what to do with myself."

"Journalist," Jonathan offered as if that explained everything. "Always on the go."

"I work for the Leicester Mercury nowadays," Geraldine said. "Not as active as I used to be, but I'm not ready to pack it in yet."

"And what line were you in?" Tayte asked Jonathan, figuring he never would be any good at casual conversation if he didn't at least try.

"I was a GP like my grandfather. Dad was going the same way before the war broke out. I don't think he had the stomach for it afterwards. He went into engineering."

"Tell us about yourself?" Geraldine said. "What do you get up to when you're not being a genealogist?"

Tayte couldn't think what to say to that. He stared at them blankly for a few seconds while he tried to think of something. Then he shook his head and said, "Nothing. I'm always being a genealogist, I guess."

He could see that Geraldine was studying his hands and knew where that was leading.

"No wedding ring," she said a moment later. "You're not married, then?"

"No," Tayte said, almost laughing at the thought.

"But you must have a girlfriend. Surely you can't get away with working all the time."

Tayte thought about the woman he'd met on the plane the last time he came to England. His relationship with Julia Kapowski, if he could even call it that, hadn't lasted and he figured it only began in the first place because she'd been so determined. In part, he blamed the distance: she was in Boston and he was in DC. But in the end he thought he'd probably just been taken in by the idea of having someone in his life over the reality it offered. She didn't feel right for him - not that he really knew what 'right' was because he'd had so little experience. Ultimately, she'd wanted too much of his time and he couldn't deal with that. At least that's how he saw it, but a part of him knew he was just running scared again like he always did.

"There's no girlfriend either," he said. "I think maybe my work gets in the way."

Jonathan cut into the conversation. "You're making our guest uncomfortable, Geraldine."

"No, it's okay." Tayte said. "It's been me, myself and my work for so long now, I've kind of accepted it."

"Well, there's nothing wrong with being dedicated to your work," Jonathan said and Tayte just smiled.

He put his nose to the rim of his glass and drew the brandy vapours in. He took a sip and the amber liquid stung his throat. Changing the subject he said, "You told me earlier, Jonathan, that Mena had a friend called Joan."

"Yes, Joan Cartwright," Jonathan said. "The family lost touch with her years ago, but she came to Aunt Mary's funeral. I don't know how she heard about it." He turned to Geraldine. "We exchanged Christmas cards, didn't we?"

"Yes, she gave us her address at the funeral," Geraldine said. "I had a good chat with her. She wanted to keep in touch."

"That's right," Jonathan said. "Fancy that after all these years. I heard she married well and moved away to Hertfordshire back in the fifties. Nicely set up."

"Twice divorced," Geraldine said. "She told me she gave up on men after that and went back to using her maiden name."

"Can I get her address from you before I leave?" Tayte asked, considering that Mena's best friend from the war years could be a vital source of information. "Do you have her phone number?"

"She didn't give her number," Geraldine said. "Just the address. I should think she's ex-directory."

"I guess I'll have to take my chances then," Tayte said. He

wondered who else he could go and see. Mary had died recently, but Jonathan had said that she'd married an Afrikaner. "Is Mary's husband still alive?"

Jonathan shook his head. "Long gone."

"Any children?"

"Yes, a son and a daughter. Her daughter didn't get on in South Africa. Or rather, she fell out with her mother over something, I don't know what. She came to England as soon as she was old enough and the family helped her out until she was settled. She lived on the other side of Leicester towards Birmingham."

"Lived?" Tayte said, wondering what mother and daughter had fallen out over.

"Yes, she died about six years ago now - her husband went a couple of years before that. Her son still lives in the area though and we keep in touch on and off. I can take you to see him if you think it might be useful. I know where to find him on a Sunday morning."

"Thanks," Tayte said. "That would be great. My hire car's being delivered to the hotel sometime tomorrow morning, but if you want to get an early start, I'd be happy to go along with you."

"Where are you staying?" Geraldine asked.

"I booked into the Marriott."

"That's in Enderby, isn't it?" Jonathan said.

Tayte nodded. "It's close by a main highway - a motorway, that is. I figured an out-of-town hotel would make it easier to get around."

"Sensible choice," Geraldine said. "The traffic around here can be a nightmare."

Tayte was still thinking about Mary and he didn't want to lose that thread just yet. "You said Mary had a son," he said to Jonathan. "Is he still alive?"

"Oh, yes. His name's Christopher Ingram. He's about my age. Doing very well for himself. We only really see them at weddings and funerals - mostly the latter these days. Mary and her husband set up a charitable trust that Christopher ran for several years. I believe he's taken a back seat on the board of trustees now. It was founded in South Africa, but they branched out into the UK a few years ago. I'm sure I could set something up for you there, too."

Tayte sipped his brandy and smiled, thinking that Jonathan was proving to be a great player to have on the team. There were already plenty of people who might be able to tell him more about Mena and it looked like getting to see most of them would pose no problem, but he hoped to learn more from Jonathan yet.

"Do you think there could be anything of Mena's still at the house?" he asked. "Any more photos? Any letters from that time?" It was a rambling old farmhouse. He thought it worth asking.

Geraldine answered.

"I don't doubt it," she said. "The attic's never been properly cleared out. It's a challenge just to get up there these days."

"That's true," Jonathan said. "There's sure to be something, but don't hold your breath."

"You never know," Geraldine said. "You might find something valuable up there."

Jonathan raised his eyebrows. "I very much doubt that. I'll take a look tomorrow afternoon, after our visit with Aunt Mary's grandson."

"Don't forget we're out for Sunday lunch tomorrow," Geraldine said.

Jonathan threw Tayte a wink. "After that then."

"Thanks," Tayte said. "And I'd be happy to lend a hand if you -"

"That's quite alright," Jonathan cut in. "I'm not sure it would be safe for two people to be up there at the same time. And the hatch is on the small side."

Tayte got the picture. It was no place for a man his size to go fumbling around.

Jonathan's cheeks flushed. "I didn't mean to say that -"

"It's okay," Tayte said. "I wouldn't want me in the roof space of an old house like this either." He laughed to make fun of it. "Actually, I have something of Mena's I'd like to show you," he added, changing the subject. "At least, it was in Mena's care. It's from her suitcase."

He took the library copy of *Madame Bovary* out from his briefcase, which he'd habitually brought into the dining room with him. He set it down on the table. "There's a military nametape inside," he said. "You mentioned earlier that your father believed Mena fell in love with a GI." He opened the book and slid the nametape out so Jonathan and Geraldine could see it. "Does the name, Danielson, mean anything?"

Jonathan sat up. "Danielson," he repeated. "That was it. I've been trying to think of his name all through dinner. I was sure Dad must have mentioned it. His first name was Danny. It's clear as crystal now."

Jonathan reached across the table and scooped the book up. He studied the nametape and the inside front cover where Mena's library card was, clearly reading the name and address that was written in Mena's own hand so long ago. He lingered over it as though cherishing something lost that had now been returned.

Tayte smiled to himself. "Danny," he said under his breath. He reached into his pocket for his notepad. "I'll see if I can find anything out about him when I get to the hotel."

It seemed highly likely to Tayte now that Mena and the GI had fallen in love during the summer of 1944, making Danielson a strong candidate for Eliza Gray's father. But the arrival of Mena's suitcase and the note that had accompanied it made him think that there had to be more to it.

Chapter Ten

July 1944.

June came and went for Mena Lasseter like so many lines of chalk scratched on a prison-cell wall, counting down the days until she could join the Land Army and get as far away from Oadby as possible. In that month she had become her mother's model daughter: she dressed conservatively, was never late for meals, and spoke only when spoken to. She rarely left the house all month other than to wheel her books in silence around the hospitals or to run errands, after which she always came straight home again. Her parents' roles as far as Mena was concerned had reversed that June. Her mother smiled whenever she saw her and her father often frowned, asking, "Whatever's wrong with my lovely Mena?"

By the end of the first week in June, Mena had learnt of the great allied invasion of Europe, codenamed Operation Overlord. She'd run into the yard with Pop and watched the skies with him as wave after wave of allied aircraft passed over Leicestershire. She never would forget that sound - that throbbing sky. Nor would she forget the sense of hope those iron angels carried with them.

Pop had later told her how upset Edward was that the 1st Airborne had been held back, serving only as a training unit in the build up to the campaign to help prepare those who were going. She also heard that most of the American soldiers camped at Shady Lane had been precluded from the fight and she wished they had all gone. All except Danny, whom she could not quite force herself to forget. By the end of the second week Pop was talking about V-bombs and the terrifyingly indiscriminate long-range attacks that the Germans had begun on London.

She observed less military matters largely through the eyes and gossip of Joan Cartwright, who - since Mena had also given up fire-watching - visited her often and had been tireless in her quest to understand Mena's changed behaviour and why she wouldn't let on about how her date with Danny Danielson had gone. Joan would chatter away about the Americans and Mena would listen without interest, bordering resentment as her friend told her about such trivial things as the van that drove regularly through the village, selling hotdogs and doughnuts, and how the children would chase after it shouting, "Yankee lorry! Yankee lorry!" Joan brought a packet of Wrigley's spearmint chewing gum with her on one visit, but this was nothing new to Mena as she'd already witnessed her mother's attempt to remove the sticky substance from the twins' hair, finally resorting to scissors and resulting in tears.

It was on such a visit, one mid-July afternoon, that Joan brought with her a gift that could not fail to cheer Mena up. It was a Sunday and such a hot day that all the windows in the Lasseter house were wide open, trying to tease in what little breeze there was. Mena was in her room, curled up in her day-dress on the chair by the window, her teddy bear in her lap for comfort. Through the pages of a book by Jonathan Swift, she had successfully managed to escape to Lilliput, but only until she heard Joan's voice, followed by Pop's as he called her down.

Mena found them in the conservatory.

"Joan has a present for you, Mena," Pop said, smiling as she entered the room and sat in a low bergère chair.

"Hello, Joan," Mena said. It's not my birthday for a whole month yet."

"I know that, silly," Joan said. "It's not a birthday present. Here." She produced an envelope that had been hiding in the folds of her elegant pleated grey dress and handed it to Mena with a grin. "Open it."

Mena turned to Pop with a look that was as much to ask if it was okay and Pop eagerly nodded back. She thought it odd that the envelope had already been opened. Inside was a card inviting Mr Childers and guest to a dance at De Montfort Hall in Leicester that coming Saturday. She looked up, confused to be given a dance invitation addressed to someone else.

"Turn it over," Joan said.

On the back Mena read that the dance featured the Glenn Miller Army Air Force Band and that it was supported by the 504th Parachute Swing Band. Her eyes lit up, but she was still confused.

"Who's Mr Childers?" she asked.

Joan sat forward. "He's a well-connected friend of my father's," she said. "He managed to get four tickets to the dance, and guess what?" She began to nod with enthusiasm. "He can't go and his wife won't be going either."

"So this is spare?" Mena said.

Joan continued to nod. “He’d invited mum and dad,” she said. “Then when he told dad he couldn’t make it, he said he could take whoever he liked in their place.” She stood with a little jump and crossed the room to Mena. “I asked if I could go and whether I could invite you along too.”

Mena looked at Pop and saw that he had that conspiratorial look about him; that amused smile that told Mena he’d already known what was inside the envelope. “What about Mother?” she said.

“I’ll tell her tonight,” Pop said. “It’ll do you good and I can’t see it being a problem as long as Joan’s parents will be there to chaperone the pair of you.”

“You’ll *tell* her?” Mena repeated. “Tell Mother?”

Pop’s face furrowed with determination. “That’s right,” he said. “I, your father and head of this household, will *tell* your mother that you are going to the ball.”

Mena knew Pop could never be so bold, but she didn’t mind how he went about it as long as she could go. She looked at both sides of the invitation again and then at last she returned Joan’s smile. “I can’t believe it,” she said.

The mood outside De Montfort Hall the following Saturday evening gave Mena goose bumps. There were more fancy cars circling the formal gardens to the front of the hall than she thought she could see in one lifetime, all gleaming in the late sunshine as ladies dressed to the nines made their way inside the hall on the arms of their uniformed partners. Older gentlemen such as Joan’s father wore sharp suits and black patent shoes, and the buzz in the air and the sense of high expectation that Mena continued to feel as she took it all in was enough to make anyone forget, for one night at least, that there was a war on.

“Stop gawping and come along,” Joan said.

The tug at Mena’s arm pulled her eyes away from the hall’s imposing facade with its numerous whitewashed Corinthian columns and the banner that reached the full width of the building’s front gable. The banner screamed Glenn Miller’s name and Mena couldn’t believe she was there, about to hear and see, live, the band that she had listened to so many times on the wireless at home.

She felt another buzz run through her as she turned her attention back to Joan, who continued to pull her through the crowd towards her parents and the entry tickets. The lace-trimmed skirt of Mena’s gown began to dance ahead of the music as she ran along with her friend, and Mena knew she would be eternally grateful for the loan of what was decidedly the most beautiful dress she had ever worn. It was emerald satin and one of Joan's favourites. It was a little tight in places but wasn't uncomfortable as long as she remained standing. The boned bodice fell to a wide black ribbon that accentuated her waist and went perfectly with her low-heeled court shoes.

Joan had even lent her a pair of long white gloves which, after helping with her make-up in the car, made her look every bit the Hollywood film-star. She wore real silk stockings, too, and although Joan wouldn't say where she got them, Mena could guess well enough. Joan's gown was eye-catching red and low-cut, revealing more cleavage than Mena's mother would have allowed her to admit to owning, and unlike Mena she wore her hair down in long sultry waves.

They looked a formidable pair.

The hall was decorated with flowers around its entire perimeter and hung with the red, white and blue of the British and American flags. Soon after they entered, Mr Cartwright became engaged in a conversation that neither Mena nor Joan had any interest in and Mrs Cartwright was soon chatting away with her counterpart, both ladies hovering thin white cigarettes between elegant fingers as they spoke. Mena felt another tug at her arm and the two girls split away.

"They won't even notice we're gone," Joan said, and the girls began to mill through the crowd.

They quickly lost themselves in the melee of gowns and uniforms and the smiling faces and polite conversations that all conspired to lift Mena's spirits and cause her to forget momentarily the events of May. She caught sight of the stage as they drew closer - a sea of gleaming brass and sharp-pressed American uniforms - and suddenly it seemed that what had happened at St Peter's was no more than a bad dream that belonged now to some other life-time.

A lone trumpet flared up. The first brassy note of the evening rasped out from centre stage, filling the hall, turning heads and ending conversations as a deafening applause quickly rose and slowly fell. Then it was Mena's turn to pull Joan's arm. She pulled her through the crowd to the edge of the dance floor in time to see the 504th Parachute Swing Band kick off their opening theme tune, *Sentimental Journey.* It sent a tingle down her spine. She was transfixed, like time had frozen around her.

"Doesn't look like there are many eligible bachelors in," Joan said, underlining her own priorities for the evening.

Mena didn't care. She began to sway in time with the music as the space before her started to fill with well-acquainted couples eager to start the dance. The stage ahead was elevated and tiered, with several steps connecting the two platforms so Mena had no trouble seeing the band members, who apart from the cellist were seated behind their boxy music stands. At the very back, a dark mahogany and brass-work organ practically filled the wall, its numerous vertical pipes reminiscent of the hall's grand pillared entrance.

"Let's get a drink," Joan said.

Mena couldn't take her eyes off all the entwined couples on the dance floor, gazing into each other's eyes like the music was taking them each on a sentimental journey of their own, perhaps stimulating fond memories of better times.

"Come on!" Joan had Mena's hand this time, leading her to the back of the hall. "I fancy a gin and lemon," she added, winking as she turned to Mena. "How about you?"

"Just the lemon," Mena said, recalling her mother's often voiced opinion about the sort of women who drink gin.

They reached the bar and Joan ordered two lemonades. She passed one to Mena then she was off again towards the sign for the toilets, stopping as soon as they found a quiet spot.

"Here, hold this," Joan said, passing her lemonade to Mena. She stood close to Mena for cover, lifted one side of her dress and pulled a hip flask from the garter belt at the top of her stocking.

"You're so bad, Joan Cartwright," Mena said as Joan poured a heavy splash of gin into one of the glasses.

Joan raised a questioning brow. "You sure you won't try some?"

Mena smiled and chewed at her lip. She looked over her shoulder like she half expected her mother to be there. "Just a drop then."

In the background the music really began to swing, taking on a quickstep tempo that set the girls' feet tapping.

"Still tastes like lemonade to me," Mena said, and before she could refuse, Joan had tipped in another splash - a big one this time.

"How about that?"

The next sip made Mena cough. The sip after that she rather liked.

"Come on, let's dance!" Joan said, her voice rising above the music as she took Mena's drink from her and set it down with her own. They were almost at a run to get to the dance floor, laughing by the time they reached it and in hold for the big-band rendition of George

Gershwin's, *But not for me* before the number had reached its first drum-roll.

"I'll miss you come September," Joan said. "It won't be the same around here and I know I'm going to hate the Civil Service. I sometimes wish I was going off to join the Land Army with you, but you know how my dad is."

"It's only for the duration," Mena said, already longing for her flat-soled, saddle shoes. "I'll be back before you know it. The war can't last forever." *Then I'll have to come home to mother again,* she thought, losing her smile and her step at the same time.

"I bet dad could get you a position as well if I asked him," Joan said. "You might have to wait a while for an opening. It's a reserved occupation so you'd really have to hope there's someone you can swap with who wants to join-up."

Mena stopped dancing. She held Joan's hands with rigid arms and stared her determinedly in the face. "I'm going," she said. Slowly, so it sank in.

Joan just smiled back. "Then we'd better make the next six weeks count," she said, leading Mena into a fast spin that got them both dancing again.

The band wound down their warm-up session with a cheeky take on Miller's own *Seven-O-Five,* by which time sandwiches had been laid out on trestle tables to the side of the dance floor. The girls re-joined Joan's parents for the interval and Mena slowly finished her 'lemonade'. Joan had downed three by the time their attention was drawn back to the stage. The bespectacled Glenn Miller appeared before his fifty-piece Army Air Force Band to rapturous applause, opening with their signature tune, *Moonlight Serenade,* as they did on their wireless programme.

There was something about that mellow melody, Mena thought, that stirred something in people; something even deeper than *Sentimental Journey* had. As she looked around at all the hitherto happy faces she saw a sudden change in every expression there. They were still smiling, but many had a tear on their cheek; such was the power of that tune. The band launched straight into *Little Brown Jug* after that. Then *In the Mood* instantly restored the evening's former gaiety.

While the dance floor filled, Mena just stood and watched the show, arms crossed in case Joan tried to pull her away again. And it was quite a show. A line of saxophone players were on one side, trumpets to the other. Each side stood up as they played, turning now and then in unison to a flash of polished brass. The trombone players behind them rose and fell in golden waves as they hit their notes, throwing their instruments into the air while Glenn Miller stood centre stage, playing trombone right along with them.

A few fast tunes came and went. Joan was dancing with just about anyone who cared to now, never leaving the dance floor. Mena was alone for the first time all evening, just listening and watching the band through her smile as she drifted without awareness closer and closer to the stage. The 504th band members distracted her momentarily as they came out for refreshments, smiling politely as they passed, and several tipped their caps. She barely looked at them, although she imagined Joan would make a beeline for them as soon as she spotted all those available uniforms. For herself, she just wasn't interested.

She turned back to the stage and quickly lost herself again as the tempo shed a hundred beats and *I know why* began to play. A moment later a woman in a long silver gown came onto the stage for the vocal and was met with warm applause. She had an unlit cigarette poised between her fingers. *So glamorous,* Mena thought, and as soon as the woman began to sing, Mena wanted to be her; wanted to look like her and to sing like her; wanted to travel the world with a big swing band and never look back. The woman seemed to look right at Mena. Perhaps it was that bold emerald dress that drew her eye, or because she was standing by herself. Either way, Mena felt as if she were singing just for her.

"Why do robins sing in December?" she began. "Long before the spring-time is due. And even though it's snowing, violets are growing. I know why and so do you..."

The woman turned away and Mena willed her to come back. But another voice suddenly demanded her attention, breaking the spell.

"Excuse me, ma'am."

Mena had half expected this moment would come when she saw the 504th band pouring into the hall, but she didn't want to dance. She turned, ready to give her apology, but her words lodged in her throat. Her lips parted but she was unable to speak.

It was Danny.

Chapter Eleven

Mena registered Danny's blue eyes and his white-blonde hair and she could hardly breathe.

"It is you," Danny said.

Mena just stared at him.

"I thought as much," Danny continued. "But…" He trailed off and shook his head. A big smile filled his face. "Wow!" he added. "You look so different in that dress. From when I last saw you, I mean. Say, how are your folks? And how's Eddie? I've not seen him in weeks."

Mena closed her mouth.

"You do remember me, don't you? Eddie brought me home for supper. You were late and missed all the eggs." He laughed.

As if I could forget you, Mena thought. She smiled, more to herself than to Danny. Then she let her smile flourish and said, "Of course, they're all fine. But what are you doing here? Are you with someone?"

"Sort of, I guess. I'm with the band. We're on a break until Miller's finished. Then I think we're set to join in. They sure are something, aren't they?"

Mena nodded. "I didn't know you played."

"Oh, I'm just a hack really. I'm standing in. Making up the numbers, you know. It's no secret around camp that I like to play. The band was a couple of boys down so they invited me along. I was tucked away at the back there, where I could do least damage."

"What do you play?"

"Trumpet, ma'am. Say, do you mind if I call you Mena?"

Mena took a deep breath at hearing Danny speak her name; at knowing he remembered it after hearing it only briefly almost two months ago. Suddenly aware that her lips were parted again and that no words were coming out, she just shook her head.

"Swell," Danny said. "And what about you? Are you with anyone?"

"My friend, Joan Cartwright," Mena said. "We came with her parents." She looked around for Joan and had to laugh when her eyes found her, still on the dance floor. She had a GI on each arm and a big grin on her face. "That's her there," she said. "In the red dress."

Danny laughed with her when he saw Joan. "Those boys'll be too tuckered out to play another note by the time she's finished with them," he said. "Do you like dancing?"

Mena nodded.

"Well, would you care to?"

I'd like that very much, Mena thought as she watched his hand extend towards hers. She took it and smiled, and a moment later they were dancing and she wanted Joan to come over and pinch her, to know that it was all real and not just some hallucination brought on by her first taste of gin. He spoke again from that perfect mouth and she knew that it was not.

"So Mena's gotta be short for something, right?"

"It's Philomena."

"Wow, that's a heck of a name."

"I know, but everyone calls me Mena - apart from my mother."

"I like Mena a whole lot better."

"Me too," Mena said. She closed her eyes and she was turning, turning with the music, wondering how fate could have singled them out so perfectly for this romance she knew was coming. She opened her eyes again, having recalled what Danny had said when he'd first introduced himself at the house. "You said people call you Danny because of your surname," she said. "Danny's not your real name then?"

Danny shook his head. "Uh-uh. Mine's a heck of a name, too."

There followed an expectant pause while Mena waited for Danny to tell her. When he didn't, she said, "So what is it?"

Danny laughed. "I don't think I know you well enough for that yet."

Mena stopped dancing. "Then I don't think I want to dance with you any more," she said, hoping that her wounded smile told him enough to know that she didn't mean it.

Danny looked like he wasn't taking any of it seriously. "If you don't dance with me you'll never know," he said.

"I'll ask one of your friends. You must have hundreds."

He laughed again. "Heck, they don't know!" He held her again and she fell into his eyes. "Dance with me until the band stops playing and we're the last couple out here and someday I'll tell you."

She took his hand again. "Someday then?"

"That's a promise."

Behind them, the band began to play *Stardust* and as she felt Danny's arms pull her closer to him it was like she was in one of her Hollywood movies, ready to steal her first screen kiss as the melody lifted and swept her off her feet.

Later that evening, when Mr Cartwright pulled up outside the Lasseter house and dropped Mena off, Joan walked with her to the door.

"So," Joan said, "are you going to tell me what you two were talking about all night?"

Mena's excitement, which had been subdued by her thoughts since leaving De Montfort Hall and Danny Danielson, suddenly rekindled, like she'd been holding everything in, waiting for Joan to ask her that very question.

"He asked if he could see me again," she said. "He wanted to call for me at the house. Well, you can imagine my reaction."

"What did you say? Did he kiss you?"

Mena nodded and felt a blush rise in her cheeks. "I told him I'd rather my mother didn't know about us just yet. Then he reminded me that it was my mother who'd invited him to call back the first time we met." She laughed into her hand. "I said I remembered, but that I was sure she didn't have this in mind."

"So where are you meeting him this time?" Joan said when they stopped laughing.

"He said he'd meet me at the bus-stop in the village so no one would know we were together - just two people waiting for a bus."

"Where will you go?"

"I told him I thought *Cover girl* was still showing and that we could take the bus up town. He said he hadn't been to the pictures in ages - he called it a *flick* - so that settled it."

Joan looked suddenly thoughtful and then a little puzzled. "You know, you two looked like you'd been waiting all your lives for each other in there tonight."

"It feels just like that," Mena said, curious at Joan's changed expression, yet unable to fathom it.

"I'll bet," Joan said. "It's easy to see why you're so excited about seeing him again, but I don't get it. Why didn't you go out on another date after you met him at St Peter's in May? Why wait to chance like this if you liked him so much."

Joan's earlier words replayed in Mena's head. *Where are you meeting him* this *time?* The significance suddenly struck home and her face dropped. As far as Joan was concerned tonight was, albeit unexpectedly, hers and Danny's second date, not the first date that it truly was. She felt Joan take hold of her hand and squeeze it tight.

"And why won't you tell me where he took you that night?" she added. "Why won't you talk about it?"

In that instant, Danny Danielson, the dance at De Montfort Hall and the Glenn Miller Army Air Force Band were far away. In their place all Mena could see was Victor Montalvo's slick black hair and those impossibly white teeth grinning back at her. She turned to go inside the house, but Joan held her.

"I thought we were best friends, Mena. You know you can tell me anything."

Mena wanted to tell, but she couldn't. She felt the blood drain from her cheeks so fast she felt giddy. She shook her head, fighting her emotions as her eyes began to fill with tears. She tried to pull away again, but Joan wouldn't let her. A horn tooted by the roadside. A light came on inside the house.

"Mena. What is it? Tell me."

The door opened and Pop was there, puzzlement and alarm cutting chasms across his face. "Mena?" he said. "Whatever's the matter?"

Joan backed away then and Mena ran upstairs to her room.

Chapter Twelve

Mena didn't see Joan again that month. She'd called at the house several times, but Mena couldn't face her. She knew that if she did they would get around to talking about Danny and Joan wouldn't be able to stop herself from asking about that night at St Peter's again. And Mena knew she would have to tell her; tell her what a silly little girl she'd been and where it had got her. They were best friends after all. If she couldn't tell Joan, whom could she tell?

But how could she?

Best friend or not, Mena knew Joan Cartwright well enough to know that she wouldn't be able to help herself. She was such a gossip that Mena thought she might as well put a poster up in Mr Hendy's shop window as to tell Joan such a thing. No, it would have to be her secret. Of course, she would tell her friend all about it someday - she knew that, too. Only not now. Not for a long time if she could help it.

None of that was on her mind today though as she lay on her bed late one afternoon towards the end of July. Today, she had something far worse to concern herself with. She tried to shut reality from her mind as she lay there. She thought about Danny as she often did, and they were good thoughts, which helped. She had been on two proper dates with him since the dance. They went to the pictures as planned and sat high up at the back in the 'kissing seats', and she knew as soon as the picture started that she would have to go. and see it again sometime to fill in everything she'd missed. They left the matinee in bright sunlight and they held hands and just walked until her feet were sore. They didn't need anything more to do with their time than that. Mena recalled that they hardly even spoke.

Danny couldn't get out of camp every day. Sometimes he couldn't get out all week, but they found ways to be together if only for half an hour at a time. Not all of the fence space around Camp Stoughton was in regular use by the soldiers and the local girls, so there were quiet spots to be found and Mena and Danny had theirs. When Mena wasn't wheeling her books around the hospital wards she'd be out on her bicycle, heading for Shady Lane where she would wait for Danny.

The other proper date was at the fish and chip shop in Wigston. You had to get in the queue early or the fish, which wasn't on the ration but was in short supply, would run out, and it was appreciated if you took your own newspaper or any kind of paper you had, although newspaper was best. It surprised Mena how romantic something like that could be.

"It's where you eat it," Danny had said, and he'd cycled back out of Wigston with Mena in his lap and the food in the basket until they came to a hay-meadow that was painted with wild flowers. He'd picked her a bunch and sat her down on his jacket. He had a candle for later and a couple of beers and they ate and just watched the sun go down.

That and the dance at De Montfort Hall was the part of July she really liked to think about when she was feeling sad. The part she was trying to deal with now she didn't like at all. She could still smell the wax polish that hung in the air as she sat in the dining room earlier. The polish tin had still been open at one end of the table and her mother was still wearing her cleaning apron. Mena could see Pop's hands shaking on the table in front of her; see the determination in his watery eyes as he tried to still the tremor of his lips. She could see her mother sitting beside him with one hand clasped to her mouth, the other clenching her wooden crucifix, and she could still feel the anxiety that caused her mother's head to shiver.

And, no matter how hard Mena tried not to, she could still see the telegrams that a kind-faced boy in a smart navy-blue postal-service uniform had just delivered. No one was actually crying. She felt bad about that now, but it had only been a matter of time. Perhaps it took a while to sink in. Perhaps she'd needed to read those telegrams for herself to make the words real. Or Perhaps James and Michael had just been gone so long now that they were already part forgotten and the family had become used to the idea that they would never be coming home again.

Mena didn't think any of that was true.

She could see her mother again, clearly now in her mind. She watched her rise from the table, scraping chair legs slowly back over the floorboards, and she never would forget that sound. She saw Pop stand with her, reaching out to comfort her. Then over and over again she saw her mother fall like an empty dress to the floor. Those things are not easy memories to misplace no matter how hard Mena tried.

Life will never be quite the same, she supposed as she lay on her bed, still staring at the cracks on the ceiling. It goes on, she thought, but it's a different life from the one you set out on. She imagined that hers and the rest of her family's, especially her mother's, would spend its remainder trying to get back to that time before. But of course, it never would.

Two things were certain now in Mena's mind. The first was that life is a fragile gift that could be taken back at any time and she promised herself never to let a single day slip through her fingers unaccounted for. The second was that her mother needed her and for now at least she wanted to stay. How could she go into the Land Army after this? And in little more than a month's time? The whole idea seemed too hard on her mother to contemplate.

And there was Danny.

The Land Army would have taken her away from home for a relatively short time, whereas Danny could take her away forever. And she would happily go - Mrs Mena Danielson. She liked the sound of that and besides, she had no idea how long Danny would remain in Oadby. His unit could be off into battle again at the drop of a hat and she wanted to be with him for as long as possible. She thought about those telegrams for the umpteenth time and the reservoir of tears she thought had long since run dry, flooded open again when she pictured herself reading such a telegram with Danny's name on it.

I must see Joan, she thought. She was keen to tell her that she wasn't going away now after all; desperate just to talk to her if she still wanted to after the way she'd treated her. Mary would come straight home as soon as the news reached her, of course she would, and Eddie was still in Leicestershire. She wished Peter could come home too and she thought perhaps he might be allowed to under the circumstances.

Pop had said that they often split family members up to reduce the odds of more than one being killed in action at the same time. James and Michael had been no exception to that rule, but there had been so much fighting in Europe recently and so many casualties pouring into the hospitals that it was perhaps not such great odds that they should both be killed within a few days of each other. At least, that was Pop's rationale. Not that it lessened the pain in their hearts.

Chapter Thirteen

Tayte had been staring out the car window since Jonathan had picked him up from his hotel, trying to get an idea where they were going. It was a quiet Sunday morning and having passed through a few sleepy villages, which afforded him no clue whatsoever, he was still none the wiser.

"I managed to do some research into Danny Danielson after I left you last night," he said.

"How did it go?"

Tayte scrunched his face. "Mixed at best. I checked with the US National Archives and Records Administration. I went into the US army enlistment records for World War II and I found several entries for people called Danny Danielson. I took some notes and started looking in the civilian records using the information I'd found." He shook his head.

"No good?" Jonathan said.

"No good at all," Tayte replied. "It's just too common a name. Until I can find out more about him I'd just be chasing my tail. I checked with the American Battle Monuments Commission in Washington, too. They keep records of American soldiers buried overseas and they were able to confirm that there's no Danny Danielson listed, and there's nothing on the Rosters of the Dead either, so there's every chance he survived the war at least. He might still be alive."

"That would be something," Jonathan said.

"Yes, it would," Tayte agreed.

The car was amidst the wintry countryside now - cold and naked farmland to either side of them. It made Tayte wonder all the more where they were going and he was about to ask when they turned into a muddy lane on their right where he saw two distinct 'H' shaped goal posts in the field ahead.

"He coaches junior rugby," Jonathan said. "Under sixteens. His boy plays."

"Great," Tayte said. "I'm a big American football fan myself. Washington Redskins."

"I wouldn't mention that," Jonathan said. "He doesn't get the whole padding and armour thing. He'll tell you that Rugby's a real man's game and we'll never hear the end of it."

They came to a busy car park and a low club building that carried the team's name, 'Leicester Cubs RFC'.

"He's been divorced a few years now," Jonathan said, continuing the character profile as they got out of the car. "Bit messy by all accounts, but he gets to spend plenty of time with his son, Josh, particularly during the season."

It was still raining, light but cold in the breeze; the sky like concrete. As they headed towards the activity and the confused shouts from the playing field grew, Tayte had to admire the young players' determination to get out there in the cold, wet mud on a Sunday morning. He pulled his collar up and wished he had a waterproof coat like Jonathan's and a hot cup of coffee in his hands.

They found the man they were looking for amidst an animated gathering of people standing at the edge of the pitch.

"That's him there," Jonathan said. "In the long black sports coat and bucket hat on the right. His name's Alan. Alan Driscoll."

He was a stocky man and well dressed for the occasion, Tayte thought. His own coat barely reached the hem of his suit jacket and his tan trousers and loafers were already spattered with mud.

"Alan!" Jonathan called and the man turned towards them, confusion meeting Jonathan's smile. "I thought I'd find you here," he added as they approached and Driscoll came to meet them.

"Morning Jonathan," Driscoll said, glancing at Tayte. "Something wrong?"

"No, no," Jonathan said. "I've brought someone to meet you, that's all." He turned to Tayte. "This is Jefferson Tayte. He's a family historian from America."

"JT," Tayte said, smiling as he offered out his hand. "If it's okay with you, I'd like to ask a few questions about the family."

Driscoll shook Tayte's hand and the furrows on his brow deepened. "I'm pretty busy," he said, indicating the playing field. "What is it you want?"

"I'm trying to find out about a relative of yours no one seems to have seen since the war years - Jonathan's aunt, Philomena. Jonathan tells me she went by the name of Mena. She was your maternal grandmother's sister."

"Mary-Grace," Jonathan interjected.

Driscoll was quick to reply, one eye on Tayte, the other on the game. “I’m sorry,” he said. “I’ve never heard of anyone called Mena. What’s your interest?”

“She had a daughter she gave up for adoption towards the end of the war. I’m trying to find out what I can about her for my client - locate her if I can.”

Unexpectedly, Driscoll wheeled towards the playing field, cupped his hands to his mouth and called out, “Tackle him, Jones! Don’t tickle him!” He turned back to Tayte. “Like I said. I’ve never heard of her. But then we’re not exactly what you’d call a close-knit family.” He glanced knowingly at Jonathan.

“That’s right,” Tayte said, keen to understand what Mary and her daughter had quarrelled about. “Jonathan told me your mother moved to England after she fell out with Mary over something. Did your mother ever say what it was about?”

“Not really,” Driscoll said. “Some silly argument. You know what mothers and daughters can be like.” He turned away again and shouted, “Pass the bloody thing, Reynolds! You’ve got twelve other players out there!” To Tayte and Jonathan, he added, “Christ! Everyone wants to be Jonny Wilkinson.”

“You said, not really?” Tayte said, hanging onto the hope that he might be able to offer a little information. “Was there something? Anything?”

Driscoll’s shoulders dropped. “Look, I don’t know. Mum never said why. All I do know is that they fell out and Mum came to England. Her brother got everything and we got nothing.”

“Mary disowned your mother because she left home?” Tayte said.

“I guess you could say that. My parents struggled all their lives and they died the same way. No one from that side of the family ever gave a toss. We never had any help from them.” He stepped closer to Tayte and Tayte could see that his face had reddened. “See that lad out there in the number nine shirt? The blue one?”

Tayte looked and nodded.

“That’s my boy, Josh. He means the world to me and he deserves better, but I can’t give it to him. I’ve been living in a one-bed flat since my divorce, struggling just like they did. Not much to show after forty-three years, is it?”

Tayte swallowed the lump that had risen and stuck in his throat while Driscoll was talking more at him than to him.

Driscoll wasn’t finished. He gave a small, sardonic laugh. “Talk about how the other half live,” he said. “I suppose you’re going to see them, too?"

Jonathan answered. "I'm trying to set something up." To Tayte, he added. "I called to speak to Christopher first thing this morning. Left a message with one of the staff."

Driscoll snorted. "Staff," he said. "See what I mean?" He spun away and shouted at one of the players. "Watch your flank! How many more times?"

Tayte had decided that he wasn't going to get anything useful from Alan Driscoll, who seemed to know little or nothing about Mena and was clearly preoccupied with the bad run of cards fate had dealt him. Tayte had encountered many such family divisions on other assignments and he wasn't surprised that Driscoll felt bitter.

"Well, thanks for your time, Mr Driscoll." Tayte said. He handed him a business card and added, "If anything comes to mind, please call me. I'll be at the Marriott hotel most of the week."

Driscoll took the card without looking at it or saying a word.

"We'll leave you to it then," Tayte said, glancing at Jonathan.

"Yes, thanks Alan," Jonathan said. "Drop in whenever you like."

Driscoll just nodded and went back to his spot on the sidelines.

"That was intense," Tayte said as they walked back to the car.

"Yes, and I'm sorry it wasn't more useful to you."

"It was worth a shot and I'm sure he knows something about why his mother fell out with the rest of the family. He changed the subject pretty quick, didn't he?"

"Yes, I suppose he did."

Tayte checked his watch. "Plenty of time before you have to be back for lunch," he said. "Let me get you a hot drink back at the hotel."

As he got into the car and the engine started up, he'd already begun to think ahead to Joan Cartwright. He hoped the afternoon would prove more fruitful.

Chapter Fourteen

Joan Cartwright's address in Hertfordshire was easy to find, courtesy of the satnav in the silver Vauxhall that had been waiting for Tayte in the hotel car park when he and Jonathan returned from the rugby club. Once they had parted company, Tayte took advantage of the all day dining in the hotel's Atrium Lounge and then he was on his way. It stopped raining soon after he set out and it wasn't a long journey, taking little more than an hour door to door in the easy Sunday lunchtime traffic - a sneeze compared to the long interstate drives he was used to back home.

It had been easier to persuade Joan to see him than he'd expected. Mena's library book and the story of how he came by it had played their part, but when he told Joan he had a photograph from the old days of the two of them together, Joan had wanted to see it. Tayte thought Jonathan's telephone number would seal it as he gave it to her over the intercom at the gates, but she hadn't used it. His story and the photograph had been enough.

They were sitting in easy chairs in the conservatory drinking pineapple juice, Joan in a red-and-gold embroidered housecoat and slippers, hair tied back. The chairs were set at angles to one another, looking out onto well kept gardens and what looked like a small woodland that Tayte imagined was part of the grounds. They appeared so extensive that he wouldn't have been surprised to see a line of deer stroll past the window.

It was a cool room, which was how Joan had said she liked it, despite the advice from her live-in help who were always telling her she should keep warm at her age. They were a married couple that had been with her for years, she'd said, adding that they always fussed too much. Tayte had his notepad out and his calling card was on the low glass table in front of them, briefcase open beside him. Joan had the copy of *Madame Bovary* in one hand and the photograph in the other. She seemed to lose herself in it.

"I know you," she said to the image as she adjusted her glasses.

Tayte couldn't be sure whether she was looking at Mena or the much younger version of herself as she spoke, but he figured the latter. He sipped his pineapple juice and set it back on the table. "There's plenty I want to ask you about Mena," he said, interrupting her memories.

She looked up and something playful seemed to spark in her eyes. "And there's plenty I can tell you," she said. "I'm eighty-four years old, but seeing this photograph again makes it all seem like yesterday." She smiled at Tayte. "Well, perhaps not quite yesterday."

Tayte returned her smile. "There's nothing better than a photo to stir old memories," he said.

Joan lifted the book and gave it a gentle shake, hands thin and contracted with arthritis. "I remember going to see the film with Mena," she said. "She took quite a shine to the eponymous Emma Bovary as I recall. I think something about that character caught her imagination." She paused and stared into the middle distance beyond the windows. "That was just after her birthday."

"1944?" Tayte said.

Joan nodded. "She'd just turned seventeen. I remember that because she wanted to join the Land Army and suddenly she was old enough to, but something stopped her. I don't recall what it was. I was glad she stayed in Oadby that summer, though."

"That was the last time you and Mena were together, wasn't it?" Tayte said.

"It was. Mena was so desperate to leave home and live her own life. It was inevitable that she would go sooner or later."

"Do you know why she left?"

"There was a lot of speculation," Joan said. "She wanted to get away from her mother, I know that much, but I don't think it was the main reason in the end."

"You weren't with her when she left?"

"No," Joan said. "We were best friends one minute and seemingly less than strangers the next."

Joan looked at the photograph of the two of them again and smiled sadly. She slipped it into the front cover of the book and saw the nametape that was marking Tayte's page halfway in. She opened it and turned her head sideways to read it, eyes widening as she did so.

"Danny," she said with a sigh.

"The GI Mena fell for. Jonathan told me."

"Oh, she fell for him alright."

"Can you tell me anything about him?"

Joan drew a long and thoughtful breath. When she let it go again she said, "I'm a little confused about Danny Danielson. I know Mena loved him, but -" She paused. "Do you mind if we don't talk about Danny just yet?"

"Not at all," Tayte said. He was intrigued by what he thought she might know about Danny, but it was clear that seeing his surname on the nametape made her uncomfortable and he didn't want to push his luck. "Maybe we could talk about Mena some more," he said. "Save Danny for later."

"Yes, I'd like that."

Tayte offered her a smile, knowing how difficult it must be to have a stranger turn up at your door trying to dig up a past you might sooner forget, but he sensed that some part of Joan Cartwright wanted to go back there. Why else would she have invited him in?

"You mentioned Mena's seventeenth birthday, he said. "Would you care to tell me about that? Did she have a party?"

Joan's face beamed as she seemed to recall it. She laughed. "Oh, yes," she said. "Mena Lasseter had a birthday party alright."

Chapter Fifteen

August 1944.

Mena's birthday was on a Saturday. The day before, on the 11th of August, General Eisenhower had paid a surprise visit to his 82nd boys at Shady Lane. There was an inspection at Stoughton Aerodrome and although Mena hadn't seen Danny yet to find out what it could mean, Pop had said that it had to be because something big was coming up.

That troubled Mena.

It had been a hot and sticky month so far, though it was thankfully cooler now. There had been a thunderstorm during the night and it had been raining hard all morning, which Pop had said was just God's way of clearing the air. It was drying now as Mena stood by the gate at the bottom of the garden, gazing out over the fields at the clouds that remained stacked on the horizon like a fleet of battleships at sea. She was thinking about Danny and the visit, wondering when their time together would be up and wishing that the summer of '44 would never end, despite everything. She drew another long breath, tasting the air that after rain had a sweet, mineral quality to it that she liked, like rusting iron. She had barely considered the more immediate problem of how she was going to tell her mother about Danny when she heard a call.

"Are you coming in?"

Mary was home and Mena was thankful for that. She'd arrived soon after the war-office telegrams and she'd been a great comfort to everyone. It seemed such a long time ago now, yet it was barely more than two weeks. No one really talked about it anymore, perhaps to avoid further upset or perhaps because the war effort kept everyone so distracted that they had little time to dwell on it. Mena knew there would be plenty of time for that later.

She turned away from the landscape and her floral-print dress became animated as a breeze pushed through the gate and played with the yellow ribbon that was tied in a bow around her waist. Mary was walking down to meet her. She was by the old well, waving at her with a cigarette between her fingers. Mena rarely saw her without one these days.

"Edward's just arrived," Mary called. "I think he has something for you."

She was smiling and Mena smiled back as she strolled towards her. Mary knew all about her and Danny. Not about Victor Montalvo being there in Danny's place that night in May. As far as Mary knew - and Joan for that matter - the two of them had met at St Peter's and had been going steady ever since. But Mena had told her about the dance at De Montfort Hall and every wonderful encounter since, saying nothing to suggest that she'd met him there for the first time, as she had with Joan.

Mary had told her she should just come out with it and tell Mother she was dating. And why shouldn't she? She'd always planned to wait until her birthday; like that extra year on her age would make all the difference. She considered that if she was old enough to leave home and join the Land Army then surely she was old enough to have a boyfriend, Yank or otherwise, and wear make-up too if she liked, although she hadn't found the courage today. The problem was that since turning seventeen she didn't feel any different. She'd thought about telling Pop, but that was no use. She knew Pop wouldn't mind just as long as she was happy.

"And?" Mary said as Mena arrived beside her. "Have you worked out what you're going to say when he arrives at the door with his flowers and that cheeky Yank smile? It won't be long now. We've finished the cake and tea's all set. I wonder if he'll have a present for you." She grinned like she knew she was teasing.

Mena sighed again and nodded. "I don't think I'll say anything."

"Just let it happen?"

"Something like that. I'll put my arm through his and everyone will get the picture. It's not like they haven't met him before and it was Mother who invited him back."

"I still think you should tell her," Mary said. "Get it out in the open before he gets here. Is he Catholic?"

Mena shrugged. "I never asked."

Mary stopped walking. She turned to Mena and the two locked eyes. "You love him, don't you?"

Mena didn't need to think about that. It felt like it was something she'd always known yet would never be able to explain to anyone. From her tone, Mary seemed to know, too, just from being around her this past week. Mena's eyes softened and she just smiled back.

"Then everything will be alright," Mary said, stubbing out the remains of her cigarette. "Isn't Joan coming? I thought she would have been here by now."

Mena wished she was. "She's away with her family," she said. "They won't be back until tomorrow."

They went into the house, through the kitchen and into the sitting room where Pop and Mother and Edward Buckley were sitting. The twins from London were sitting opposite one-another at a drop-leaf table in the front window, racing to see who could finish their jigsaw puzzle first, and Xavier and Manfred were asleep as usual on their settee at the back of the room. Edward, who had turned out in full dress-uniform, rose to attention, full of smiles as the girls entered.

Their arrival stopped Pop's conversation mid-sentence. "There you are, Mena," he said. He finished stuffing a pinch of tobacco into his pipe and Mary joined him with a cigarette and lit it for him. "I was just saying what a great disappointment it is to us all that last month's assassination attempt on Hitler failed." He glanced at Edward and under his breath he added, "Bloody war might have been over all the sooner if that bomb *had* got him."

"Pop!" Margaret said. "I'll have no swearing in this house. I don't care if there is a war on." She turned to Edward. "And you say it was one of their own, Edward?"

"A Colonel, Mrs Lasseter. Shenck, I believe he was called. They shot him the same day and I hear they hanged several of his co-conspirators from meat-hooks - with piano wire, would you believe?"

"Barbarians," Pop said.

Margaret winced and reached for the teapot that was set out with the rest of the crockery on a low table by the fireplace. Mena's birthday cake was there, too, and although not that big it was big enough and was as much as her mother could put together, even though she'd been saving the ingredients to make it for months.

"Happy Birthday, Mena," Edward said. "Look what I found." He reached down beside the settee and produced a parcel wrapped in brown paper and tied with string. He handed it to her with a kiss on the cheek. "Sorry the paper's so dull, but you know how it is."

The gift was heavy. Mena smiled then laughed as she wrestled it to the floor. She untied the bow and carefully unfolded the wrapping paper so it could be re-used. It looked like a battered old brown leather suitcase and she thought at first that Mary couldn't have told Edward that she was no longer going away to join the Land Army. But it was heavy. There had to be more to it.

"Open it then," Mary said.

It had clips on the sides and a button beneath the handle. Mena lifted the lid slowly, like she expected something to spring out and make her jump. It didn't, but what she saw still surprised her. Her jaw dropped.

"It's a phonograph," she said, scarcely able to believe it. The silver-coloured turntable had a green felt mat and the needle arm was of the same silver metal. "It's beautiful," she added.

"Look inside the lid," Edward said.

There was a divider to store records and Mena reached inside and felt the thin paper edges of more than one sleeve. She withdrew them and her birthday just got better. "Glenn Miller!" she said, her eyes scanning the blue-and-cream label. "Bluebird," she read aloud. "Electrically recorded phonograph recording."

"That's the label Miller and his band are signed with," Edward said.

Mena kept reading out the words. "In the mood - Fox Trot. By Glenn Miller and his orchestra." The other record was *Chattanooga Choo Choo* and it had a similar label.

"It's portable," Mary said.

"You wind it up," Edward added. "See the handle there?"

Mena picked it up by its brown Bakelite knob, looked it over and put it back in its place. She turned to her mother and was surprised to see her smiling back.

"You can listen to it in your room on Saturdays," Margaret said.

Mena got up and kissed everyone; even the twins, who proceeded to wipe their faces in disgust. Outside, Mena heard a car pull away. She looked out the window, which was still covered with condensation from the morning's rain and the twins' breath, but she was too late to see who it was. When the knock at the front door came she stared at Mary and froze for several seconds before she said, "I'll go." But her mother was already on her way.

A moment later she heard, "Philomena! There's someone to see you," and Margaret Lasseter came back into the room, her blank expression giving nothing away.

Mena let go of the breath she was holding when she saw Joan standing in the doorway. She was puzzled to see her, but pleased just the same. Her friend looked quite plain today, she thought. She wore a simple grey skirt and a lilac blouse. Her hair was tied back and she wasn't wearing make-up.

"Joan!" Mena said. "What a nice surprise."

"Hello Mena. Hello everyone."

Mena rushed over to greet her, eyeing the bright wrappings on the significant parcel she was carrying. "I thought you couldn't make it."

"I know, but I talked Dad into coming home early. Have I missed the cake?"

"Not a bit of it, and look what I got off Edward and Mary." She showed Joan the phonograph and the Glenn Miller records.

"That's a real humdinger," Joan said and Mena laughed at her.

"You've been around too many Yanks, Joan Cartwright."

Joan winked back as she handed her parcel to Mena. "Here, this is from me."

Margaret was on the edge of her seat. "What beautiful paper."

"I kept it from last Christmas, Mrs Lasseter."

The gift felt soft in Mena's hands, yet she unwrapped it like whatever was inside was made of crystallised sugar. She saw the colour first: green, like emeralds with the sheen of satin. She knew long before she took it out and held it up to her frame that it was the dress Joan had lent her for the dance at De Montfort Hall.

"I thought you might like to keep it," Joan said.

Mena's jaw dropped again. She just stared wide-eyed at Joan for several seconds while the lump in her throat stopped her from speaking. She was wondering how her birthday could get any better when she heard Pop say, "Excuse the pun, but look who's dropped in."

Mena spun around, still clutching the dress to her, and there beside Pop stood Danny, smiling at Mena like only Danny could. He looked smarter than ever, she thought, and he was clutching his flowers just as Mary said he would be. She hadn't even heard the knock at the door or noticed Pop leave the room to answer it.

"Mr Danielson!" Margaret began. His presence seemed to light a fuse in her. She was on her feet and fussing with the wrapping paper Mena had left all over the floor. "You took your time coming back to see us. You know Edward, don't you? Of course you do. It's our Mary you've not met and this is Mena's friend, Joan."

Danny nodded at Edward and offered Mary a polite smile. "I'm pleased to make your acquaintance, ma'am," he said. To Joan, he added, "How are you, Joan?"

When his eyes found Mena's, Mena found that she was lost for words. She tried to shake her head, like she didn't want to go through with this after all, but it barely moved.

"And you brought flowers," Margaret said. "How thoughtful of you." She reached for them and Danny stepped back.

"Well you see, ma'am, it's like this," he said. He looked at Mena again and Mena silently willed him not to say another word. Then he did. "The flowers are for Mena."

"For Mena?"

"That's right, ma'am."

Margaret's cheeks flushed. "Of course," she said. "How silly of me. Flowers for the birthday-girl." She looked puzzled. "But how did you know it was Mena's birthday?"

When it came down to it, Mena couldn't bear to stand there and watch Danny suffer any longer. "I've been meaning to tell you, Mother," she said. Her stomach was in knots. She couldn't look her mother in the eyes. Instead, she put an arm through Danny's, smiled and said, "We're dating." Just like she said she would.

Margaret's face dropped. Her thin eyebrows shot up towards her hairline, creasing her brow. "Oh," she said, and she sat down again.

"Well, that's splendid," Pop said. "And how long has this been going on?"

"Not long at all, really," Mena said before Danny could answer.

Margaret sat staring at Mena's birthday cake, absently toying with her crucifix. A moment later she picked up the cake-knife and indelicately chopped into it. An awkward smile twitched at the corner of her mouth. "Would you like a cup of tea, Mr Danielson?" she asked.

"That'd be swell," Danny said. He handed the flowers to Mena and kissed her cheek. "That's not all I brought," he said to Mena. He reached into a pocket and pulled out a fold of olive-green material. He held it in his palm and unwrapped it as Mena watched. "It's none too pretty for a girl like you," Danny added. "But it would do me a great honour if you'd wear it from time to time." He removed the material and Mena moved closer.

"See," he said. "No pretty thing at all, especially bashed up and all like it is. I made a hole in it and put it on a chain so's I could keep it around my neck as a reminder - not that I need one."

Mena studied it. It was a polished silver disc about an inch across. It had a deep depression close to its centre and there was a picture and several words engraved on it. She couldn't make out the detail.

"It's the coin that saved my life," Danny said. He indicated the depression in the centre. "See, that's where the round hit."

"Close call," Edward said.

"It sure was. I had a whole bunch of 'em in my pocket. Felt like someone just thumped me hard in the chest. Well it spun me round and down I went."

"Shouldn't you keep it?" Mena said. "I mean, if it was lucky for you."

Danny shook his head. "The way I see it, Mena, that silver dollar has served its purpose. They say lightning never strikes the same place twice so I don't suppose it'd be lucky for me again. Maybe it'll be lucky for you."

Mena lifted the coin from Danny's hand and slipped the chain over her head. It covered the small silver crucifix that was already there. "I'll cherish it, Danny. Thank you."

"It was made a few years after the last war," Danny added. "They called it the 'Peace Dollar' - ironic as that is. Like I said, it's not much to look at, but I wanted to give you something that was special to me and I can't say I have much else in this world that doesn't belong to Uncle Sam."

The room seemed to close in around Mena as everyone gathered for a better look; everyone except her mother, who remained seated. Mena held the coin out on its chain for all to see, knowing that it was a wonderful thing, simply because it had belonged to Danny. She also knew that it was something she never wanted to take off again.

Mena was naive enough to think that she got away with Danny Danielson that day, but she didn't. It was late now, barely an hour of her birthday remained and she was alone in her room, sitting up in bed, eager to try out her new phonograph. The afternoon had gone so fast since Danny arrived and she'd been so focused on him that she hadn't even heard it play yet. It was on the bed beside her where she'd been looking at it for half an hour or so. Her new dress was hanging on the back of the door where she could see it. All she needed now was Glenn Miller and she'd be back at De Montfort Hall in Danny's arms. Just a few seconds would be enough, she thought. No one would hear it and if they did, the music would have stopped again before they realised what it was.

Mena opened the lid and took out *In the Mood.* She removed the sleeve and set the hole in the middle of the record carefully onto the spindle. When she reached for the winding handle her breath caught in her chest.

It wasn't there.

She thought about her mother and how quiet she'd been all

afternoon. They had exchanged barely two words since she'd told everyone about her and Danny. She put her fingers into the recessed space where the winder should have been and felt around the lining. It was just like her mother. Sometimes harsh words and a slap were not enough. She thought about her *Merrythought* teddy bear. Pop had bought it for her when she lost her first tooth. That bear went everywhere with her.

Until she lost it.

Lost it, she thought. She recalled how she'd found it again several years later. It was in a box in the attic crawl space with her favourite hair-clip and a number of other items she'd expressed a particular fondness for at some time or another. A part of her now thought that she'd always known better - had always believed that it was her mother who had lost them for her. Now she had lost the winder to her new phonograph. She threw her head back into her pillow and a deep sigh trembled from her lips.

At least the records aren't broken, she thought, reading the labels again.

Chapter Sixteen

Mena spent little time at home that August. She sensed that her mother was waiting for her to mention the missing winder for her phonograph but she never gave her the satisfaction of believing that losing it hurt as much as it did. She knew her mother would only try to use it as leverage to stop her seeing Danny and her way of getting back at her mother was to see Danny as often as she could. Whenever she wasn't with him or waiting to be with him, she stayed at the hospital with her books, reading to the patients with such hunger for the words and the sense of escape they offered - which was as much now for her benefit as for theirs. Romance had become her new favourite genre.

It was the 25th of August when news reached Oadby that, after four years of German occupation, Paris had at last been liberated. It was a Friday and a dance was being held the following evening by the 504th Parachute Infantry Regiment in their mess-hall at St Peter's to celebrate the landmark allied victory. Spirits were high that weekend. The way most people were carrying on was enough to make anyone believe that the war was over. At least, that's what Mena saw in other people, but she couldn't share in their reverie. The thought of going anywhere near St Peter's again filled her with an inescapable sense of fear. She hadn't passed those steps that led up to the church, nor gazed along its path through the headstones where Victor Montalvo had led her, since that dreadful night in May. She did not want to go and yet she knew she had to. How else could she explain herself to Danny? She couldn't lie to him - not to Danny. And Joan was going, too. She knew Joan would see straight through any excuse she could think up.

She met Danny on the Stoughton Road at seven p.m. and they cycled into the village together. He had a friend with him this time, whom he introduced as Melvin Winkelman. He was hanging onto Danny's shoulders and riding the back wheel. He was a big man, too, Mena thought. No taller than Danny, but he was thicker set. He had close-shaved, dark hair that continued as stubble across his face and when he smiled Mena thought he didn't look so mean, but that wasn't very often. He didn't say much either; just enough for Mena to know that he liked to be called Mel.

It was a casual dance, nothing like De Montfort Hall. Wire-framed tables and chairs were arranged around the dance floor and there was no decoration to speak of: a few small flags, but that was all. The 504th held regular dances in the church hall and although the event was about as impromptu as things could get during war-time, as long as there was enough warm beer and a few bottles of gin to go around, and as long as the band kept playing, no one seemed to care what the place looked like.

It was packed out.

The girls, who were typically out-numbered, wore swing-skirts and saddle shoes, and within an hour of the band starting up, ties were off and collars were hot and ruffled. Cigarettes were plentiful and a thick, blue-grey haze clung to the ceiling like city smog on a hot summer's day. Seeing the church again and walking around the low wall beside the headstones had been difficult for Mena, but she'd been okay with Danny's arm to hold. They were sitting at a table at the back of the hall and the mood inside soon lifted her spirits. The band was kicking out a lively tune and Joan was dancing - always dancing. She'd brought a date along with her this time and Mena had lost count of how many Joan had had since the summer began; she never saw the same face twice. Mena was sitting this one out on Danny's lap and Mel was sitting opposite, sucking on a beer bottle, watching the dance with a distant stare.

"Jitterbug's a funny name for it," Mena said.

Danny smiled. "Come to think of it, I guess it is. What do you call it again?"

"It's a quick-step."

"Not as quick as a jitterbug, though. I've seen gals back home dance it like their feet were on fire."

"Do you have a girl waiting for you back home?" Mena said. She'd never thought to ask before.

"Well..." Danny began. He put a hand out in front of him and extended his fingers like he was counting all their curves and faces through his mind.

Mena caught him steal a glance at her out of the corner of his eye and he laughed at her as he made a slow zero between his thumb and forefinger. She slapped his hand away and laughed with him.

"You should've seen your face," he said. "I guess it's as well I *don't* have a sweetheart to go home to."

"Where exactly is home?" Mena said. Something else she'd never thought to ask. Perhaps it had seemed too trivial a question, or perhaps she was only just beginning to think that far ahead. "You never did tell me," she added.

Danny smirked. "We're trained not to. Just the name, rank and serial number, ma'am. Besides, you never asked."

"I'm asking now."

"It's a small town called Grantsville," Danny said. "In Calhoun County, West Virginia."

"What's it like?" Mena didn't really mind as long as Danny was there with her.

"Well, there's Main Street running down the middle and the whole place is cradled in the bow of the Little Kanawha River. There's water on every side save to the east. I guess you'd say it was kind of in a low valley. You can see the trees on the hills rising a little around you just about everywhere you go."

"It sounds lovely," Mena said.

Danny looked thoughtful. "Yeah, I think you'd like it," he said. "I'd sure like to take you there someday to meet my folks."

"Do you have a big family?"

Danny whistled and nodded. "Sure," he said. "Real tight-knit too, but don't let that scare you."

One of her mother's sour expressions popped into Mena's head and she knew that nothing about Danny's family could even come close. She looked over at Mel. There was something sad about him, she decided. Everyone there had a story. Some just hid theirs better than others.

"Where are you from, Mel?"

Winkelman's head snapped around. "Arkansas, ma'am."

Danny clipped the top off another beer bottle and slid it across the table. "That's about four states further west from me and little to the south. Hamilton, didn't you say?"

Winkelman nodded.

"The campaign in Italy had its way of making good pals of strangers," Danny said. He clanked his bottle against Winkelman's and thoughtfully added, "It's keeping 'em that's the hard part. When you look out at a bunch of fellas you've fought alongside and you see them enjoying themselves like they are right now, you're not really thinking about them."

"No?" Mena said.

Danny shook his head. "It's the faces you don't see anymore."

Winkelman nodded again, slowly this time, and they both drained their beers.

"Few more of these and we'll be *feeling no pain*," Danny said to Winkelman.

Mena gave Danny a curious smile. "No pain?"

"It's just an expression. You know, numb from the drink."

"Oh."

"Mel's from good old Arkansas farming stock," Danny said. "Built like an ox, too." He reached over and slapped his friend's shoulder. "Ain't that right?"

Mena caught that rare smile of Mel's then, this time tinged with embarrassment. It was worth the wait.

"And what did *you* do before the war started," Mena asked Danny.

"Same as my folks and my grand-folks. I worked the lumberyard. If not that - if this damn war hadn't started up when it did - I had an idea to go back to college."

Joan came back then. Her hair was up out of the way and her face was shiny. Her partner, a highly conditioned American soldier like the rest, had his hands on his knees, panting heavily.

"Phew!" Joan said. "I need a break." She pulled Mena up and whispered in her ear, "Look, do you mind if we slip out for an hour or so?" She gave Mena a telling wink and her cherry-red lips smiled with devilish intent.

"You're so bad, Joan Cartwright," Mena said.

"I know. See you later."

"Be careful," Mena added.

The GIs brought scabies with them from Italy and it was no surprise to Mena that Joan soon caught it. She'd never admit it, but Mena had seen her scratching a nail over her skin here and there. Goodness knows what else she might go home with if she wasn't careful. She watched Joan lead her man away and the music slowed to a waltz. She turned back to Danny and extended a hand to him.

"This is my kind of dance," she said. "Do you mind, Mel?"

Mel just shook his head and opened another beer.

When they were on the dance floor Mena felt Danny's hands slide around her waist and she caught her breath. She held his arms and didn't ever want to let go again.

"So what were you going to study?" she asked.

"That's just the thing. I never had a clue. It didn't seem to matter just so long as it was something that could take me someplace better than the lumber yard."

"It might not have brought you here."

Danny kissed her. "No," he said. "It might not."

She was lost in his eyes, but the dream ended abruptly when she saw a hand tapping on Danny's shoulder.

"Hey, d'you mind if I cut in?"

The couple parted and when Mena saw who it was her face drained of colour so fast she thought she would faint.

"Hi'ya, doll-face. Remember me?"

"Spiller," she said under her breath. She paid him no more attention. Her eyes were all over the room. Her chest felt tight suddenly; her breath short.

"Hey, sweetheart -"

That was all Spiller could say before Danny stepped between them. "Hey, joker. Can't you see you're upsetting the lady?" He walked calmly towards Spiller and Spiller moved back.

"All I want is a dance! No need for the greed, pal!"

"Trust me," Danny said. "She doesn't want to dance with you. Not now. Not ever."

Danny and Spiller were off the dance floor now, moving towards the door. The empty space they left soon filled and Mena could no longer see them. She was alone in a sea of happy faces, feeling anything but. Her eyes darted quickly from one face to the next until she felt dizzy. Her palms began to sweat. Her legs felt too heavy to move.

"Were you looking for me?"

She spun around and the nightmare she had tried so hard to forget suddenly caught up with her again.

He grabbed her and she began to tremble in his cold embrace. "I know you remember me."

He was grinning through those impossibly white teeth. She could smell his whisky breath again; feel his fingertips pressing into her. A scream was moments from her lips when she saw Mel Winkelman tower up behind him. Without speaking he pulled Montalvo's arms away and flung him back. The music stopped and the people cleared. Mena saw Danny again then. A moment later he had an arm around her.

"You okay?"

Mena nodded.

Montalvo was on his feet again. Spiller had worked his way around behind him and they had two other friends with them. Montalvo's smile looked mean and cocky, like his pride was hurt and he was trying to save face. He came closer. He was looking right at Danny.

"Hey, I saw her first, Blondie!"

"You're a disgrace to those stripes, Sergeant. Clear out."

Montalvo sneered. "Don't say she didn't tell you about us."

Mena saw nothing but confusion in Danny's eyes. She wanted to be sick.

Montalvo laughed. "You really don't know, do you, Blondie?" he persisted.

Danny took a step towards him and Mena reached out to stop him.

"I guess I'm not all that surprised," Montalvo continued. He leered at Mena. "I looked out for you by the fence as usual, sweetheart. I even hung around the churchyard in case you came looking for your old pal."

"That's enough!" Danny said.

Montalvo stepped up then and Winkelman stood between them. Montalvo pulled a knife. He began to wave it from side to side, tracing infinity through the air.

"Not such a hero now, are ya big guy?"

"Put it away, Vic," Spiller said. "She's not worth it."

"Yeah, c'mon Vic," another of his pals agreed. "Let's get outta here. It's a lousy joint anyways."

Mel Winkelman didn't seem to think about it. He just paced up to Montalvo. The knife lunged and he stopped it barely an inch from his stomach. He twisted Montalvo's wrist until the knife fell and Montalvo began to whimper. Then Winkelman hit him once in the face and he went down.

Mena turned away and stared into Danny's questioning eyes until the weight of those questions forced her to step back. He came closer and she began to shake her head as a lone tear broke and fell onto her cheek.

"Not now, Danny," she said. "Later, I promise."

She watched his chest rise and slowly fall.

"Let's get you home," he said.

Chapter Seventeen

It was the last day of August and it had been five days since Mena last saw Danny. He'd called at the house every day since the dance and she knew what an effort it must have been for him to get out of camp so frequently. She knew he must have skipped out on at least half the occasions - gone AWOL for her. She'd asked her mother to send him away again every time simply because she couldn't face him. Not yet. She'd given Danny a promise, but with all her heart she would not have him know anything of her acquaintance with Victor Montalvo or the truth of what happened that night in May. Yet not seeing him, even to hold his hand over the camp fence at Shady Lane, broke her heart.

Her mother had been all too happy to play her part. No doubt she thought some miracle of divine intervention had come between them, and although Mena had given her no clue as to why she wouldn't see him, it was apparent that her mother cared little for the reason. Danny, it seemed, was not for Mena after all. Her prayer had been answered and subsequently, on the evening of Danny's second visit, Mena found the winder to her phonograph again.

She avoided all the usual haunts where she thought Danny might find her and she cycled alternative routes to the hospitals she worked at. She even had her mother looking out for Danny before she left the house in case he was waiting for her. She needed time. The thought of losing him if he knew what had happened kept her distant for now, which is why she'd planned to stay in town after finishing work at the Royal Infirmary that Thursday night.

She met Joan at the clock tower: a nineteenth century Ketton limestone memorial with a clock face set into each of its four sides. She was outside Hilton's shoe shop, adjacent to the monument, looking up at an enormous *Bovril* sign that arched high up on the building next to Jay's. The memorial was set on an island at the junction of five roads and it was always a busy spot with people hurrying about on foot or bicycle, eager to get their shopping or to get home again afterwards. The trams were nearly always full at this time of day and there were always a few cars on the streets here despite the petrol rationing, although US military vehicles now considerably outnumbered them.

They were going to the pictures to see the 1933 adaptation of Gustave Flaubert's, *Madame Bovary,* which was showing that month at the Odeon on Rutland Street. The tickets were two shillings and threepence for the good seats and the decor was glamorous Art Deco, which Mena loved because to her it was the essence of Hollywood style. The film itself captivated her to such an extent that she wanted to stay in her seat at the end and watch it over again, but Joan was hungry, so they went for chips.

"What's wrong with the chips in town?" Joan protested as they collected their bicycles and made off towards Gallowtree Gate.

"I like the chips from Wigston best," Mena said. "Besides, it's nearer home and they're not mean with the scratchings."

They joined Granby Street and turned right onto Belvoir Street, heading for the Welford Road, which would take them all the way south to Wigston. As she pedalled after Joan, all Mena could think about was the film they had just seen and how much she identified with Emma Bovary.

"Of course, I'll have to read the book," she said to Joan when she caught up. "If I can find a copy."

"There's bound to be one at the library," Joan said.

Mena hadn't been to the general library in a while; there were plenty of books at home and at the hospitals to keep her going. "I'll take a look tomorrow," she said.

After joining the Welford Road they were soon cycling back past the hospital on their right, then past the cemetery a little further down and to their left. They kept a leisurely pace, nothing too strenuous. It was still warm enough out for light blouses, although they both had pullovers tied around their waists in case it turned chilly later.

"You know," Mena said. "I can understand why Emma Bovary wanted more out of life."

Joan scoffed. "And look where it got her," she said.

"I know, but she wasn't happy anyway, was she? What did she have to lose?"

"She would never have been happy, Mena," Joan said. If the wealthy Boulanger had married her, she would have tired of him soon enough, too. Then what?"

Mena shrugged. "I suppose so."

"The grass isn't always greener, you know," Joan said. "That's the message."

"I know," Mena said. "I just felt that we had a lot in common, that's all. I mean I can empathise with her even if I can't condone her behaviour - the lies and the cheating, and her poor husband, Charles. I could never be like that." She paused and then thoughtfully added, "My ideals are far simpler."

"Like getting away from your mother?" Joan said.

Mena didn't answer. She knew Joan was perceptive enough to need no confirmation but there was more to it now. Her own aspirations had deepened since meeting Danny and her thoughts had wandered to that river in West Virginia he'd spoken of; to the town he'd said he was from. Where was it? Grantsville. She supposed she couldn't get much further away from her mother than that.

"So how come you're not out with Danny tonight?" Joan said. "Not that I'm complaining. We just don't seem to see much of each other these days, do we? Not like we used to."

"I've not seen him since the dance," Mena said and she knew it was a mistake.

"Oh?"

Mena kept pedalling. She pretended not to have noticed Joan's inquisitive tone. She wasn't ready to explain why she hadn't seen Danny since the dance. Just thinking about it made her skin prickle.

"Where did you get to anyway?" Joan asked. "I couldn't find either of you when I got back to St Peter's."

Mena knew she had to change the subject. "I didn't think you were coming back," she said. "We left."

Joan gave her a wink. "Followed my lead, did you? Well, come on. Don't hold out on me. What did you get up to?"

She had that devilish gleam in her eye and Mena knew exactly what she was thinking. "It wasn't like that," she said. "I didn't feel well so Danny took me home." She hated lying to Joan and she hated Victor Montalvo all the more for giving her cause to.

She looked around for something, anything, just to turn the subject around, but her mind was back at the dance now and Montalvo was inside her head, blocking her thoughts. His words played over through her mind. *I saw her first*, he'd told Danny, like she was something you pick up in a January sale. And there was that sense that what had happened at St Peter's in May was somehow perfectly acceptable to him. Now he wanted more and he'd even been out looking for her. She felt ill just thinking about it, but she couldn't stop herself.

"So how come you haven't seen him?" Joan asked, adding further confusion to her thoughts. "You didn't fall out, did you?"

Mena was beginning to think that Joan's efforts in the Civil Service were a waste of her natural talents; that her friend could have provided a far greater service to her country interrogating spies. The thing she hadn't expected was that a part of her felt ready to break. Perhaps deep down she wanted to talk about it. Get it out in the open where it might catch in a breeze and blow away, all the sooner to be forgotten.

"Come on," Joan persisted. "Something must have upset the apple-cart. You've been in each other's pockets all summer."

Mena felt her breath quicken. Why couldn't she just leave it alone? She found herself nodding as she considered that something had indeed upset things. Now it was coming between her and the people she cared for - the people she loved. Her hands tightened around the handlebars and she kicked hard at the pedals, propelling herself ahead of Joan so Joan couldn't see the red-faced anger rising inside her. Her emotions were suddenly in turmoil. She felt like she was gasping for air and all she could see was Victor Montalvo, grinning down at her with those impossibly white teeth, letting her know that it didn't matter how fast or how far she went, she would never be able to get away from him. Never.

Joan caught up. "We said we wouldn't keep secrets from each other," she said. "Did you have a row? Is that it? I'm sure we can fix it."

She just wouldn't let up.

"It's not the first time either, is it?" she went on. "I bet something must have happened after your first date in May. That's why you couldn't talk about it when my dad dropped you home after De Montfort." She laughed like it was nothing. "It happens all the time," she added. "Tell me what it is. It's probably not as bad as you think."

Mena had switched off - tuned her friend out. All she could hear now was the whir of her spokes and the road beneath her tyres as it raced hypnotically beneath her. She was back at St Peter's church again. It was dark and Danny was there, only it wasn't Danny, it was Montalvo and he was pressing himself against her, feeling her and kissing her. Kissing, kissing, kissing until she broke free and she was running wild between the headstones - running and grazing her legs and tripping. And then feeling his hand, tight around her ankle, pulling her back through the grass.

"Mena? Are you okay?"

She could feel her whole body shaking. Tears soaked her face now as they had then. She was lying on her back in that black graveyard and all she could see was his grinning face as he forced himself onto her - Victor Montalvo. She recalled the fear and the pain and she knew that, to the contrary, it was every bit as bad as she thought.

Mena screamed. "He raped me, okay! Are you happy now?"

She felt dirty.

She could hear herself sobbing through the words as she spoke them and at the same time she stood on her pedals, channelling all that hatred fuelled adrenaline through them as she raced ahead, turning off the Welford Road onto any road she came to just to lose herself. She was scared. Telling Joan had brought her no solace. She felt more afraid now than ever; afraid because she knew she had to tell her mother and she would have to tell Danny too, of course she had to tell Danny. She would have to tell them all that she had been raped, and worse still, she would have to tell her mother that she was pregnant.

Chapter Eighteen

Tayte spoke very little while Joan talked about Mena, having learnt over the years when it was best just to listen. They had taken a stroll in the grounds as Joan had said she liked to do most days in the early afternoon, weather permitting. She only ever went to the stream and back nowadays - half a kilometre at most and at no great pace. "Use it or lose it," she'd said as she put on her coat and changed her slippers for daisy print wellington boots.

They were on their way back now, walking a bark-covered path that wound its way through formal displays of floppy winter pansies and bright cyclamen standing to attention. Joan had told him that she hadn't seen Mena again that year; that when the summer of 1944 ended it took their friendship with it because of what happened. Learning that Mena had been raped both shocked and angered Tayte.

"But I thought you were of the opinion that Mena was in love with Danny," he said. "Jonathan told me the same thing based on what his father had said."

"I think I've gone on too long about Mena," Joan replied, a slight tremor in her voice at thinking of those days again, despite the time that had passed since.

Tayte thought her pace quickened slightly. "But these are things I need to know about," he said. "For my client." He was beginning to feel so caught up in Mena's story himself that for a brief moment his client's needs seemed to come as an afterthought to his own.

"I'm telling you exactly what Mena told me," Joan said. "Do you think I could forget something like that?"

Tayte didn't, but he couldn't understand why she sounded so edgy all of a sudden. "And she was definitely talking about Danny?" he asked, needing further confirmation.

Joan stopped walking but she didn't look at Tayte. Not directly. "I've already told you that Mena met Danny at St Peter's church earlier in the year," she said. "I knew Mena was going there to meet him and she never gave me any reason to think otherwise. Then after we'd been to see *Madame Bovary* we were talking about Danny and she got upset and said, "He raped me." It just came out. And by the end of the year I heard that she was telling everyone she was carrying his baby. Danny's baby."

Tayte thought Joan sounded a little as if she was explaining things to herself rather than to him - like she was going over the details to confirm what she knew, or thought she knew. "So if Danny raped her, why did you tell me she loved him? It kind of contradicts, doesn't it?"

Joan turned away and started walking again. "Yes it does, but there it is. I don't know what else to make of it."

They continued in silence for a few long minutes and Tayte spent that time considering the uncertainty he felt had crept into Joan's voice. Could there be another explanation? Right now it seemed that Danny Danielson had raped Mena and was every bit his client's father. He figured Joan had no reason to lie about what she'd heard, but he sensed some doubt there. As they came back to the house and the conservatory they had previously left by, he thought that Joan's sudden, contemplative silence was telling enough and he wondered what else she knew that she wasn't saying. His instinct told him to drop it for now, but he thought he was close to something so against his better judgement, he persisted.

"Is there anything else you want to tell me?" he said.

Joan didn't stop or turn to look at him.

"Something about Danny perhaps?" He was fishing and he knew it, but he was sure she was holding something back and he wanted to know what that was. "What about Mena?" he added. "Was there something else about Mena?"

Joan stopped walking then and when she turned around she had tears in her eyes. "I think it's time you left, Mr Tayte," she said. "I'd like to be alone if you don't mind."

She tried to smile, Tayte thought, but he could see it was difficult and he immediately regretted trying to push her like that. It wasn't like him. He watched her step through into the conservatory and a moment later she handed him his briefcase.

"You can go around the house to your car," she said. "The gates will be open."

With that she closed the doors and disappeared into the house, still in her boots and coat, leaving Tayte confused if not surprised that his visit was over.

Chapter Nineteen

Tayte was less than a mile into his journey back to the hotel when his phone rang. He was still in the Hertfordshire countryside, driving down a leafless lane that looked much like every other. He pulled over to answer it and put his hazard lights on. He didn't have time to check who was calling.

"Jefferson Tayte."

"JT. It's Jonathan."

"Hi Jonathan. How's it going?"

"Good. I've managed to set things up with Mary's son, Christopher. Just got off the phone with him, actually."

"That's great," Tayte said. "When can he see me?"

"Right away."

"He's keen. I like that."

"Yes, perhaps. Although I think the main reason he suggested seeing you now was because he's flying to New York tonight and won't be back until Wednesday."

"I see," Tayte said. "Well, I'm glad he could fit me in. Where do I need to go?"

"He's at a gala lunch and conference in London," Jonathan said. "It's for the charitable trust I told you about. He said you were welcome to go along. You'll have missed the main course by the time you get there, but if you're quick you might catch dessert."

Tayte licked his lips. "Where's it being held?"

"It's at the QE2 Conference Centre in Westminster."

Tayte got out his pad, pinning his phone to his ear with his shoulder while he wrote the details down.

"I thought you wouldn't want to miss him, so I told Christopher you'd be there. He said he'd have your name added to the guest list. Just ask for him when you arrive."

"How long a drive do you think it is from Joan's house? I've only just left."

"I wouldn't drive," Jonathan said. "The traffic might not be too bad on a Sunday afternoon, but you'll still have a tough time parking anywhere close. I'd drive to the train station in Hertford if I were you. You can leave your car there and pick it up again later. The conference goes on into the early evening so you've plenty of time."

"I'll do that," Tayte said. "Thanks."

He was about to say goodbye when he thought to ask Jonathan if he'd managed to get into the attic.

Jonathan hesitated before he gave his reply. "I did," he said.

"No good?"

"No. There are just so many nooks and crannies that are hard to get at."

"That's no problem," Tayte said. "Thanks for trying."

With that he said goodbye and set the car's satnav for Hertford.

The Queen Elizabeth II Conference Centre wasn't difficult to find once Tayte arrived in London. He got off the Tube at Westminster by the bridge, and standing in what would have been the shadow of Big Ben if the skies weren't so leaden, he was given directions to Broad Sanctuary, which was just off Parliament Square. It was spitting with rain again, but it only took a few minutes to walk the rest of the way.

Inside the building, Tayte cleared security and reported to one of the reception desks. From there he was directed to the second floor. As the lift doors opened and he stepped out, a display screen bearing the word 'GIFT' greeted him. The 'I' was pictured as a gift-wrapped parcel in the style and colours of the South African flag and beneath it were the words, 'Welcome to the Grace Ingram Foundation Trust annual charity conference'.

Further in he gave his name to a young black girl wearing a floor-length dress that looked like the 'I' from the GIFT poster. She was standing beside a lectern next to a set of double doors and she had a big smile on her face that seemed to contradict the fading burn scars that reached up from her neck and fanned out across her cheek. Watching over her was a heavyset man in a tuxedo. The girl checked Tayte off the screen in front of her and she smiled again as the man opened the doors into a large conference room that was lit with subtle blue lighting around the perimeter and over the tables, which were laid out cabaret style in the middle of the room, seats facing the stage.

Another young girl, also gift-wrapped in the flag of her nation, ushered Tayte towards the front of the room, keeping to the edge so as not to block anyone's view of the stage. Looking around, it was apparent to Tayte that GIFT was a big-money business. He thought there had to be at least three hundred smartly dressed business men and women sitting at the tables, which were all crowded with wine glasses and bottles of water. He quickly noticed that the cutlery was gone, telling him that he'd missed both lunch and dessert. Ahead, the raised stage was lit up like a theatre set, minus the curtains, and the trust's logo, GIFT, appeared over the central podium. The woman speaker standing behind it was in mid flow.

"When my grandmother, Grace Ingram, began this trust almost fifty years ago," she said with a distinct South African accent. "She could have had no concept of just how much happiness her commitment would bring to so many lives."

To either side of the room, Tayte saw screens showing images of the work the charity was involved in. Some had pictures of smiling children, others of happy parents and of schools and hospitals. Several conveyed information about the corporations already involved with GIFT and every one showed an image depicting the results of GIFT's work in South Africa, rather than showing the often desperate images that necessitated its creation. He supposed the young girl at the door was reminder enough of that. He saw a number of men in tuxedos, standing in the shadows between the lighting, their hands clasped in front of them as they stood and watched the room like FBI agents at a presidential visit.

Tayte turned his attention back to the speaker as she continued her presentation.

"But just as the monkey-bread seed grows into the ancient and mighty baobab tree we call the tree of life - as it provides shelter, food and water in the dry savannah regions to both animal and human-kind alike, without intolerance or prejudice - so has the Grace Ingram Foundation Trust grown to replicate that design. For so many South Africans - like the baobab tree - GIFT has come to symbolise life."

Applause erupted from the room, which seemed to embarrass the speaker. She appeared humble before her audience as she put her hands together and pressed them to her lips as if in prayer, closing her eyes and bowing her head. Tayte arrived at a table at the front of the room and was invited to sit down. There were only two people sitting at this table and he supposed it was Christopher Ingram and his wife. He nodded and smiled and the bald-headed man beside him, dressed in a silver-grey suit, smiled back.

"That's my daughter," he said, indicating the stage, also exhibiting a strong South African accent as he spoke. "Her presentation is almost finished. We can talk after."

"Sure," Tayte said.

The applause began to fade.

"Thank you," the speaker said. "But that applause belongs to each and every one of you." She clapped back at them, turning in a slow semi-circle as she did so. "GIFT is a name that successful companies such as those represented here today want all the more to be associated with, and I thank you all for helping to make that happen. Now before the coffee is served, please take a moment to consider where your donations are going. Think to the future and about the many people your generosity is saving. Because the gift you give, truly is the gift of life."

The room fell silent. Heads began to bow. Then a moment later two sets of doors to the side of the room opened and a host of serving staff came pouring through with coffee jugs, stirring the room back to life as conversation erupted and the air began to buzz.

"I'm Christopher Ingram," the man beside Tayte said, and at that point the woman sitting next to him turned towards Tayte for the first time. "This is my wife, Sarah."

They all shook hands.

"I'm pleased to meet you both," Tayte said.

Ingram shifted in his seat until he was almost facing Tayte. "I wish my son was more like my daughter," he said, "but he has no interest in the trust. He prefers to climb mountains. Now, Jonathan tells me you're looking for my mother's sister, Mena Lasseter?"

"That's right," Tayte said. He was about to explain why when Ingram cut him short.

"There's no need to go into the details," he said. "Jonathan filled me in. I don't know how much I can tell you about her, but I'll do my best."

That he knew anything at all was a good start, Tayte thought. Before he could ask his first question, Ingram and his wife both stood up, their faces suddenly full of smiles. Tayte followed suit and as he turned around he saw the woman from the stage approaching.

"This is my daughter, Retha," Ingram said.

She offered her hand to Tayte and he shook it, thinking that she had a surprisingly strong grip for someone who on first impression looked so fragile.

"Unusual name," he said for want of something better to say.

He put her in her mid-thirties and up close he thought she was a striking woman. She had a pale complexion, straight blonde hair that was cut in a short bob and deep red lips, which gave colour and vibrancy to her otherwise monochrome appearance. Her petite frame was dressed in a burgundy trouser suit, no shirt or blouse visible.

"It's short for Margaretha," she said. "It's the equivalent of my English great-grandmother's name, Margaret."

"It's an old Afrikaans tradition," her mother offered. "It's an old Afrikaans tradition," her mother offered.

Retha came closer to Tayte until he could smell her perfume. "But you're American, heh? That's very topical," she said.

"It is?"

Retha nodded. "You've come at an exciting time. We're about to sign our first big deal with a major US corporation."

"Expansion," Ingram said. "We hope it will open the gateway for many more such partnerships. If we can make an impact in America..."

He left the notion hanging as the coffee arrived.

"Stay and join us," Ingram said to his daughter.

"I can't, really." Retha said. "I have to prepare for the next presentation."

"Of course, darling," Ingram said. He turned to Tayte. "She's such a hard worker. The trust really couldn't be in better hands."

Sarah Ingram moved around the table. "I'll give you a hand," she said to Retha. Then turning to Tayte, she added, "If you'll excuse me, Mr Tayte. I'll leave you both to chat."

"It was nice meeting you," Tayte said and he watched them leave.

"So tell me, Mr Tayte," Ingram said as they sat down again. "What is it that I can tell you?"

Tayte eyed the coffee as it was being poured. He drew a deep breath and wondered where to start. Then considering that Mena was reportedly out of the family's life before Mary went to South Africa and became Grace Ingram, he said, "How did you come to know about Mena?"

"Photographs," Ingram said. "Mamma kept a few around from her old life here in England and I came across them one day. I suppose I was in my late teens then. There was a photo of the two of them together and I asked who the other girl was. When she told me she had a sister called, Mena, naturally, I asked where she was because I'd never seen nor heard of her before then. She just said that she didn't know. That she ran away and was never seen again."

"Did your mother say whether she ever tried to find her?"

"I asked her that very question," Ingram said. He shook his head.

"No," he added. "She never tried. But you have to understand that her life changed quite dramatically when she became a missionary and founding the trust kept her busy, I can tell you."

All the same, Tayte thought she might at least have tried - unless perhaps she already knew or just didn't care. It was a cynical view, but he couldn't help seeing it that way.

"I don't suppose she talked about why Mena left?"

"No," Ingram said. "I don't recall ever asking her and she never offered up any stories from her old life."

"That's too bad," Tayte said. He could see this visit going about as well as his visit with Alan Driscoll at the rugby club. "Your sister moved to England some years ago," he added. "Did you keep in touch?"

"For a few years," Ingram said. "But families drift apart and ours was no exception."

"I've heard that she fell out with your mother over something. Do you know why? That is, if you don't mind me asking."

"You seem to know quite a lot about my family already, Mr Tayte."

"Jonathan gave me the background and I spoke to Alan Driscoll this morning."

Ingram nodded. "I see. Well that would explain it. What did Alan tell you?"

"Not much."

"And I don't believe I can tell you much either," Ingram said. "My sister and Mamma always had their differences. I wasn't surprised when I heard that she'd left."

"You weren't home at the time?"

"No, I was away at University."

"And your mother never explained the reason to you?"

"Like I said, Mr Tayte, they had their differences. It was always on the cards so to speak. Mamma didn't need to explain anything to me. She said she didn't want to talk about it and that was good enough."

Tayte got the feeling that no one liked to talk about it. He decided to move on.

"Did your mother ever mention someone called Edward Buckley?"

"I know the name," Ingram said, "but she never mentioned him as such. I saw his photo, too. It was an army portrait of a well-turned-out captain. A champagne cork was taped to the back. When I asked Mamma who he was, she told me his name, but that's all she would say about him. It upset her as I recall."

“They were engaged to be married during the war,” Tayte said.

Ingram raised his eyebrows. “Really?” he said. “I didn’t know that.”

“They also fell out over something,” Tayte said, “but no one seems to know why that was either. Do you know why your mother wouldn’t talk about him?”

“Who knows?” Ingram said. “Painful memories perhaps. I had no real interest in him. Just a young boy’s curiosity.”

Despite something having come between them to prevent their marriage, it was clear to Tayte from what Ingram had said that his mother had still cared for Edward. It led him to think that it was perhaps Edward who had called the wedding off. But why? And what, if anything, did it have to do with Mena? He felt himself going around in circles and coming back to the same empty answers: no one knew anything, or if they did, they didn’t want to talk about it. That was the message he was getting and the lack of any useful information had clearly contributed to the reason why Mena’s life had become a family mystery - and as far as Mary-Grace was concerned, it appeared that she had taken the answer to at least some part of that mystery to her grave.

Tayte had let his coffee go cold. He drank it down as the stage lighting changed, signalling that the next phase of the event was about to begin.

“Well, thanks for your time,” he said as he got up and shook Ingram’s hand. He passed him one of his business cards. “In case you think of anything else,” he added. “And good luck with your expansion plans in America. I’ll look out for you.”

“Thank you,” Ingram said. “I’m sorry I couldn’t be of more help.”

Chapter Twenty

Tayte's standard king room at the Leicester Marriott hotel looked like a hundred others he'd stayed at, although this one was brighter than some, clean and new and perfect for his needs. It had custard-cream walls and brown carpet, with two tangerine upholstered chairs and a table by the window. The usual desk with the in-house services guide and complimentary notepad ran alongside the wall at the end of the bed. He dropped his briefcase under the desk and threw his jacket onto the bed as he went to the window to look outside. It was a new development - not much to see beyond the car park below and the fringe of trees that were barely more than saplings.

It was just after six p.m. and he'd ordered a room-service meal at reception on his way in, as he'd grown accustomed to doing over the years because he was usually hungry whenever he got back to whichever hotel he was staying at, irrespective of the time. It saved having to call down later. He didn't like eating in hotel restaurants by himself. He'd tried it a few times, but he always felt uncomfortable and self-conscious sitting there by himself. Taking a book for company and pretending to read it never really helped either.

He hadn't stopped thinking about Mena and how bad his day had gone all the way back from London. Mary-Grace's descendants had offered him little beyond a better picture of how their respective lives had turned out and although Joan Cartwright had given him plenty to consider, he couldn't see how anything he'd heard was going to help him to find Mena.

He sat on the bed and kicked off his shoes, thinking that he might have a look around the local churchyards at some point, although he didn't really expect to find anything worthwhile. He hoped a visit to the local record office would turn something up though and he might have gone sooner if he hadn't landed at the weekend.

Moving to the desk, he consolidated his notes while he waited for his meal, which arrived with a knock at the door barely ten minutes later. Half way through eating, his jacket buzzed and the theme from one of his favourite Broadway shows, *Anything Goes,* started to play. He took out his phone and checked the display. It wasn't a number he recognised. He swallowed the mouthful of food he was chewing and answered.

"Jefferson Tayte."

"Mr Tayte, it's Joan. Joan Cartwright."

Tayte's eyes widened. He pushed his meal away. "Ms. Cartwright. I hadn't expected to hear from you again after -"

"Yes, and I'm sorry," Joan cut in. "The memories upset me, that's all. I was rude to you and I apologise."

"There's really no need to," Tayte said. "I fully understand."

"No, you don't," Joan said.

The phone went quiet. Tayte expected her to say more, but if she'd called to tell him something else, she was having trouble saying it.

"Is everything okay?" Tayte asked.

"No. Not really. I'd like to come and see you if it's not putting you out. There's something I need to show you."

"Of course," Tayte said, thinking that his luck might have changed. He wondered how she was going to get there. "Would you rather I came to you?"

"No, I have someone who can drive me," Joan said. "And you've been to see me once already today. I should have shown you then. I can be at your hotel around eight o'clock."

"Okay," Tayte said. "It's the Leicester Marriot. I'll be waiting for you in the lobby."

"Until eight then, Mr Tayte."

As soon as the call ended, Tayte gulped the rest of his meal down and hit the shower, buzzing with anticipation. *She has something she needs to show me*, he thought, wondering what it was.

Chapter Twenty-One

The hotel lobby was a modern, airy reception lounge with a high glass wall at the entrance and a vaulted ceiling. Tayte was sitting on a lime-green sofa surrounded by yellow armchairs and dark wood, all set on a psychedelic green rug that had waves running across it in colours that picked out the furnishings. He had one eye on the entrance and the other on his watch. It was a little after eight p.m. now and he figured Joan wouldn't be long. Maybe the traffic was heavy.

It was another five or six minutes before he saw Joan standing at the entrance, talking to the man he assumed had driven her to see him. He stood up so she knew he was there and he watched the driver go back out into the night, presumably to wait for her in the car. If Tayte hadn't been expecting her he didn't think he would have recognised her; she looked so different. She wore a turquoise trouser suit with a silk scarf in the neck and her hair was loose on her shoulders. She was wearing makeup, too, he noticed. It was light but the overall effect as she walked towards him seemed to have taken ten years off her. She had a smile for him as she approached and it put him at ease.

Tayte shook her hand. "Hello again," he said and they sat down.

He'd been looking to see what she'd brought to show him since he saw her at the entrance and he figured that whatever it was it had to be small because all she had was a black clutch bag.

"I'll try not to take up too much of your evening," she said. "I'm sure you have plans."

A part of Tayte wished that was true, but he had no plans at all beyond a little reading and an early night.

"Quite the opposite," he said. "Take all the time you need."

"First things first then," Joan said as a grave expression washed over her. "I had a phone call not long after you left this afternoon. I didn't mention it when I called earlier because I thought it could wait until I saw you, but the more I think about it now the more it unnerves me.

"What was it about?" Tayte asked, concern in his voice.

"It was about Mena."

Tayte sat up.

"I've no idea who the man was and at first I thought perhaps he was working with you, but then I realised you didn't have my number and there was something about his tone that didn't feel right."

"What did he say?"

"He wanted to know where Mena was, just as you do. He became quite insistent that I should talk to him. Then when I asked him how he got my number he wouldn't say, so I hung up the phone."

"Did he say why he was looking for her?"

Joan shook her head. "It was a very one-sided conversation, but whatever his reason, I believe it's important that you find her first." She opened her clutch bag and reached inside. "I don't know if it will help at all, but I've brought some letters to show you."

Tayte's eyes were on them the instant Joan withdrew her hand.

"They're Mena's letters from Danny," she continued. "Perhaps before you look at them I should explain how I came by them."

"Please do," Tayte said, unable to decide which he'd rather have first, the letters or the explanation. Both excited him equally.

"I saw Mena again," Joan said. "Not recently, but after she left home. It was early in 1945, Late January perhaps. I was still living in Oadby with my parents then and she was waiting for me when I came home one afternoon. I was quite speechless as I recall and she didn't say much either. I could see she'd been crying. She just thrust the letters into my hand and asked me to look after them until she came for them."

Tayte eyed the letters again. That Joan still had them was telling enough. "And she never came back?"

"No. I never saw her again after that."

"Did she say anything else?"

"She just said that she had to go, and with some urgency as I remember. She was heavily pregnant and I wanted her to come inside but she wouldn't. It can't have been long before the baby was due."

Before my client was born, Tayte thought. Then he wondered about the suitcase again and whether Mena still had possession of it at that time.

Joan passed the letters to Tayte and he unfolded them. The first thing he noticed was the stamp that all but one of them carried, centred at the bottom of the page. He pointed it out.

"V-mail," he said. "It stands for Victory Mail." He told Joan what he knew about it. "The US military borrowed the idea from the British Airgraph Service," he said. "It was designed to cut down on freight space so there was more room available for war materials. They photographed every V-mail letter sent to and from servicemen and women during World War II and they put them all onto microfilm, which was then sent to the States for censorship and forward processing. It meant that around forty sacks of mail could be condensed into one." He looked up from the letters. "Sorry," he said. I can get a little carried away at times."

"No, it's very interesting," Joan said. "I never knew. The microfilm must be a valuable resource to you nowadays."

"I wish that were true," Tayte said. "But it was all destroyed after the war."

He noted the boxes in the top right-hand corners of the V-mail letters and smiled to himself. Danielson's name and contact information at the time of writing were there. And so was his army serial number.

Touchdown!

He took out his notepad and wrote the details down, knowing that he would have no problem finding the right Danielson now. He ordered the letters by date, eyeing the larger boxes in the middle where the main body of the letter was written.

"They were strictly single page," he said. "This box is here to ensure that the sender couldn't take up any more space than the next guy." He smiled to himself. "I've seen some written with tiny writing so as to fit more in."

With that, he turned to the first letter and began to read.

Chapter Twenty-Two

September 1944.

Mena had never felt so alone. She hadn't seen Danny in almost three weeks and his attempts to call on her were becoming less frequent; he'd only tried twice in the last week. She was losing him. She knew that, but she couldn't bear to look him in the eyes and tell him what had happened and the longer she left it the worse it became. She was letting him go simply because she didn't know what else to do and it felt like the only good thing in her life was slowly dying while she just stood back and watched.

She couldn't see Joan again either. Sheer embarrassment and the disgusting shame of it all had come between them. What must she think of her? She'd written Joan a letter the night she came home from the pictures. She'd been in such a panic. She'd told Joan not to come to the house - not ever again. She was so scared that Joan would tell her mother or Pop. And she'd written some hurtful things in that letter - things that could not now be undone. She'd told Joan to keep her big mouth shut; told her what a busybody she was. She'd even threatened to write to her parents to tell them what the real Joan Cartwright was like. All those secrets. How that would shatter the illusion they must have of her. Joan was no little Miss Perfect either.

Mena regretted writing every word.

The result of her uncharacteristic behaviour that night, however, seemed to have had the desired effect and that was what mattered most to Mena. Joan hadn't once tried to see her and so far her parents appeared oblivious.

So far.

Mena put her book down and went to the full-length mirror next to her dressing table. It was late morning on a Tuesday. She was still in her nightdress and she hadn't done a thing with her hair. She stood sideways to the mirror and ran her hands down the front of her nightdress, smoothing the material over her skin. There was definitely a bump there, she thought. Was it bigger than yesterday? She thought it was. It was definitely bigger than it looked a week ago. She monitored her condition like this every morning and the truth of it was that to anyone else, if she was showing at all, it was negligible. She was thankful that the sickness seemed to have passed, which was something that until recently had also been part of her morning ritual.

She forced a breath out like she was practicing her contractions. Then she gripped her hair with both hands, scrunched her fingers into tight fists and began to pace the room in a silent rage. When her eyes fell on her book again, face down on the floor by the window, she sat and calmly continued to read.

She'd found a copy of *Madame Bovary* at the general library in town. That was the last time she'd been out of the house, when she delivered Joan's letter to the Civil Service offices. Since then she'd spent most of her days like this, analysing the life of Emma Bovary or listening to Glenn Miller on her phonograph, and in between, panicking and fruitlessly trying to think of a way out of her predicament before her condition became too obvious and people started talking. That was the reason she'd stopped wheeling her books around the hospital wards, too - why she'd stopped reading to the patients even though the beds had never been in such demand and their occupants never more in need of such comforts.

Mena went on like this for a few more days and then suddenly everything changed. On the Friday of that week Pop came to see her in her room with lunch and a glass of milk. He often did and with it he would bring news of the war and the outside world in general. He had a spam sandwich with him today, which he set down with the milk on the bedside table.

"There's been an uprising in Poland, Mena," he said. "The Russians are closing in on the capital and the Polish Home Army and the citizens of Warsaw are making a brave fight of it."

Mena feigned polite interest then asked, "Has Danny called?" It was always her first question and one that preoccupied her mind.

Pop sat on the bed. "Not today, Mena, no."

Mena's shoulders sank and she stared out the window. The low clouds seemed to suffocate the horizon, reflecting her mood. Her mother hadn't reported Danny calling at all that week.

"Mind you, I'm not surprised," Pop continued. "Word is that it's all gone very quiet down at Shady Lane. That can only mean one thing to my mind."

Mena spun back into the room. She thought about Eisenhower's visit at the end of last month and had a good idea what Pop was going to say next.

"They're packing up," he said. "I'm sure of it. And Edward's unit have been confined to barracks. Mary's trying to get to him now. I don't know how she does it, mind." He laughed to himself. "That girl could manipulate the stars."

"Will she be allowed to see him?" Mena asked.

"Hard to say," Pop said. "But she's going to try. She's convinced they're off somewhere." He shook his head. "She must be sick to her stomach, poor thing."

Mena shot out of her chair. "Thanks, Pop," she said. "If you don't mind, I need to get dressed."

All Mena could think about as she cycled to Shady Lane that afternoon, pedalling fast, fuelled by her emotions, was that she had left it too late. She'd been such a fool all year for one reason or another and she began to despise herself for letting it come to this. How could she stand back and let him go? She had to be more like Emma Bovary; she knew that now. She had to take control of her life, find Danny and tell him everything - to hell with the consequences. She had to tell him that she loved him, too. She couldn't recall ever saying it, not even during those tender moments when they had come so close to making love, and each time she had refused him because all she could see when he touched her in that way was Victor Montalvo.

She wished now that it had been otherwise.

It was spitting with rain by the time Mena reached the camp. It was cool out but she wore no coat, just a skirt and pullover that were soon damp, but she didn't care. She went to the main entrance this time and was directed to the regimental personnel section. It was an olive-green, cotton-canvas tent like all the rest and the man she'd been directed to see was busy with a clipboard, scribbling away at a folding table. He had a fat cigar in his mouth that he was chewing more than smoking. He waved her in and pointed at the chair opposite.

"I need to see Staff Sergeant Danielson," Mena said as she sat down. She thought that sounded more official, but it didn't seem to matter to the man sitting opposite.

He put his pencil down and rolled his cigar back and forth between his teeth. He looked her over briefly then shook his head, grinned and said, "I suppose you've come for your pound a week like all the rest?"

"Excuse me?"

The man seemed low on patience. He huffed as he leant in on his elbows and said, "For the baby. That's why you're here, ain't it? A pound a week for sixteen years. Believe me lady, you sure ain't the first."

Mena drew a sharp breath and held it. She just stared at him, dumbstruck. Finally, she managed to say, "A pound a week?"

The man nodded. "Or do you expect the joker to marry you?" He rocked back on his chair. "Look, lady. You seem real nice and I'm sure you deserve something for your trouble, but it takes two. Know what I mean? You've got just about as much chance of making the fella pay up or marry you as I have of making General."

Mena screwed her eyes at him. The conversation seemed too bizarre to contemplate, although she had to concede that he wasn't far off the mark. She shook her head and decided to start over. "I just need to see Staff Sergeant Danielson," she repeated.

Another huff. "What company's he with?"

Mena had no idea. Danny might have mentioned it, but she couldn't recall.

He shook his head and reached for a thick folder that was on the table beside him. "Danielson, you say?"

Mena nodded and the man began to rifle through what she supposed was some kind of personnel register. "He's got blonde hair," she said, trying to be helpful. "Almost white."

The man stopped what he was doing and looked up at her. "It ain't got no photographs in here, lady. Just names and numbers."

He continued and a moment later he tapped the register and said, "Danielson, E. There's only one listing here so I guess that's the little joker's daddy."

"I guess," Mena said.

They all seemed to refer to each other as jokers for some reason. Mena never asked Danny why. She noted the clue to his real name and wondered again what it was and whether she would ever now find out. It made her feel warm inside knowing that the man opposite her thought Danny was the father of her child. She liked the idea of that and wished with all her heart that it was true.

"He's in A-Company," the man said, interrupting her fantasy. "A for Able."

"So, can I see him?" Mena asked.

The man removed his cigar, looked into his lap and sighed. When he looked up again, he said, "No. I'm real sorry, lady. You just can't."

Mena's pulse began to race. "Why not?"

"As far as you're concerned, Able Company ain't here no more."

He stood up. "Now if you'll excuse me."

Mena got up with him and she felt so light-headed she nearly fell down again. She held on to the table to steady herself. Her mouth was suddenly dry - her hands clammy.

"You okay, lady?"

Mena took a few slow breaths and nodded. "Can you tell me where they are?"

The man didn't answer straight away. He just looked at her like he was weighing up whether or not to say anything further. Then he simply said, "No, I'm sorry," and headed for the exit.

Mena ran after him and caught his arm. "I have to see him," she said. "Please."

The man shook his head at her, but this time there was something that resembled a smile on his face. "Look," he said. "Best I can do is get a note to him. But don't take too long about it. There's paper and pencils on the desk there if you need 'em."

"But I may never see him again," Mena said. It was more a thought that just came out rather than something she meant to say, but the man heard her.

"Everyone had a chance to say their farewells yesterday," he said. "If Danielson chose not to spend his time with you, then - well, you can make up your own mind as to what that means."

Mena wanted to scream and cry and die right there and then. She wanted to hit that man, too. Hit him hard, like any of this was his fault. She knew Danny must have called at the house last night and that her mother had chosen not to tell her. She'd always told her before, like she was proud of herself. But not this time. Danny must have told her he was leaving and if Mena had known that yesterday, of course she would have seen him. She would have held him tight and never let him go.

But it was all too late for that now. She didn't cry or scream or hit out at anyone. She calmly went back to the table, sat down and began to write.

Chapter Twenty-Three

At breakfast the following Monday there was a letter waiting for Mena. Pop had taken the post in that morning and he'd arranged the envelope prominently on her placemat. Mena's eyes fell upon it as soon as she entered the room; she rarely received mail unless it was her birthday or Christmas and she could guess whom it was from. The envelope, bearing Danny's name and number along with a US Army return address left her in no doubt. She had butterflies in her stomach as she picked it up. She felt something else inside the envelope and she wanted to tear it open straight away, but she didn't. She glanced at Pop and coyly returned his smile.

Her mother, who was sitting opposite her, must have caught the exchange. Her stern face turned first to Pop and then to Mena as she said, "Are you going to open it then, dear?"

Mena shook her head. She hated it when her mother called her dear. She knew it was never well meant. "I think I'll open it later," she said, somewhat nonchalantly as she put the envelope to one side. She watched her mother's eyes drift after it and felt a degree of control she hadn't known before. She rather liked it.

After breakfast Mena set out on her bicycle for Wigston and the wild-flower meadow where she and Danny often went. Along with her letter, which she hadn't let out of her sight, she took her fountain pen and some blank airmail paper that Pop had given her, all pressed between the pages of *Madame Bovary,* which she thought would give her something firm to write on.

It was a fresh autumn morning. The early fog had given way to clear skies and it was cool out, but by the time she arrived she was glowing from the ride and the medley of feelings caught up inside her. The meadow had changed with the season and there was no scent of malt vinegar on the air this time, but as she sat down by the hedgerow and looked to the horizon, it wasn't difficult to find the memory of that special place.

She couldn't hold her smile back as she opened the envelope and saw what else was inside. It was a strip of olive-drab cloth bearing Danny's surname and she imagined he must have embroidered it himself, which made it even more special. She put it inside her book where she thought she would keep it as a bookmark. Then she turned to the letter, which was dated Saturday, September 17th; the day after she'd gone to look for Danny at the camp. She thought he must have read her letter and that this was his reply. She studied his handwriting first. Then she traced a finger over the ink, as if touching the words he'd written somehow brought them closer together as she read them.

Dear Mena,

I figured if you wouldn't see me then maybe you would at least read a letter. We're jumping into action tomorrow and I couldn't go without giving it one last try. If nothing else I had to say goodbye. They won't tell us what we're in for until the C-47s are in the air, but we've been issued with maps and currency so at least we've got some idea of where we're headed. It's ten p.m. now and it's raining real heavy as I write. It's like being inside of a tin drum, but the noise is kind of comforting in its way - it sure would be quiet in here otherwise. Most of the fellas are writing home or to their sweethearts. Some are just laid back on their cots staring up at the hangar roof and I can guess what they're thinking. Sleep won't come easy for anyone tonight, but when it comes for me I know it will be all the better for having written you.

Not seeing you for so long has sure made me realise how much I care for you, Mena. I don't know what happened that night at the dance, or what the deal was with that loudmouth drunk, but I want you to know that whatever it was, it doesn't matter an owl's hoot to me. It seems plain enough now that that joker was the reason you felt you couldn't see me again. I sure wish I could change that, but here we are. Today is all we have and tomorrow is for dreamers.

Mena, we've had such good times together, I can't begin to say how much I already miss you. Sitting here in this cold hangar waiting for the go makes it seem like I've already left England. I miss all that, too. It's a wonderful country, the likes of which I don't suppose I'll see again anytime soon. I guess I feel that way because of you, Mena. You remind me of all the beautiful things I'm fighting for.

Mena, there's a question just burning a hole in my chest. I would have asked it if I could have seen you last Thursday - everyone had a pass that night. It just doesn't seem right or fair to ask it now, not in a letter the night before I go back and face those Krautheads. Heck, what I need to say, Mena, is that I love you. The rest will have to wait until I see you again if you'll let me. For now, I just know this war would be an easier thing to get through if I thought you felt the same way. It'd be just swell to get a letter from you either way.

Danny.

Mena read the letter again. Was Danny going to ask her to marry him? She would need confirmation before breathing a word of it to anyone, but she could think of no other question in that context that was so important that he had to ask it in person. Neither did she want to. Her mouth remained open while she tried to take in its significance. Everything they had ever done together and all of the things they had yet to do rushed her at once until she was left an old woman sitting on a porch by a river somewhere in West Virginia. Although, it didn't take long for Mena's thoughts to come around to asking whether Danny was still alive. If the jump went ahead, he'd have been in action for over twenty-four hours by now and she thought that was a long time under the circumstances.

She didn't like to think about that.

Instead, she thought about the letter she'd written to Danny at the camp and she realised he couldn't have received it before he'd written this letter to her. She could only hope that he'd received it before he left and that at reading it he would know how sorry she was and how completely she returned his love. She hadn't written anything about the bad things that had happened that summer. Not yet. As much as she wanted to tell him, it hadn't seemed right to let him go with news like that.

After reading the letter for the third time, Mena took up her pen and began her reply, toying constantly with the coin on the chain around her neck as she wrote. She had a good idea how long it would take to find him from all the letters that had been sent back and forth between her brothers over the years. She knew she had to write straight away to confirm Danny's intentions so there was no misunderstanding. And she would say yes, of course she would marry him if that was what he wanted to ask. She didn't mind a jot if he wanted to propose in a letter and she would tell him so. She thought she'd tell him about Montalvo too, but she talked herself out of it. She didn't want to blacken things. She could write and tell him afterwards.

Chapter Twenty-Four

October 1944.

After that first letter in September, Mena wrote many more letters to Danny while she waited to hear from him again. She would lie awake most nights wondering how he was and what he was doing, and she was always up early to look out for the postman. She knew by now that Danny was in Holland because she'd received two more V-mail letters from him.

The first told her how happy he was at getting the letter she'd written when she went to the camp that day, and how sorry he was that she hadn't been allowed to see him. It reached him on the morning of the jump, he'd said, and he read it on the plane. He'd told her everyone was grey-faced and quiet as usual as the C-47s took off and crossed the English Channel, but not him. He'd said he was grateful to her for getting him through that and knowing she still cared for him like she did would get him through a great deal more in the weeks to come.

The second V-mail came a week after the first and in it Danny had explained that he hadn't had much chance to write. He'd been in the thick of it, he'd said, and she was left to imagine the rest because any mail was heavily censored and he couldn't go into details. Early in the month though, Pop had been able to fill Mena in a little on what Danny was doing.

They received regular letters from Mary, who received regular letters from Edward. It seemed that by the time Mena received Danny's second letter, the fighting in Holland - code-named, Market Garden - had moved on. Danny, with the 82nd Airborne had landed near Grave to take certain strategic bridges across the Maas River and the Maas-Waal canal, working their way to Nijmegen to take the main bridge there. Edward Buckley with the British 1st Airborne were to take the bridge across the Rhine at Arnhem and hold the town until relieved. Along with the US 101st Airborne the paratroopers were to pave the way for the British Guards Armoured Division who were heading the XXX Corps' advance: a combined force of several allied divisions with whom the various airborne units were to link up. Allied casualties were high and Pop had said that both Danny and Edward were fortunate not to have been killed or captured.

Mena wrote to Danny every day. She wrote silly things most of the time, she knew that. She wrote them in her room late in the afternoon, listening to the same two tunes on her phonograph until *In the Mood* was as familiar to her as a childhood nursery rhyme and her mother had to ask her to stop continually humming it. Mostly, she wrote about her day, which she soon realised was incredibly dull, so she took to updating Danny on what was happening in whatever book she was reading. She thought he wouldn't mind what she said in her letters as long as she kept writing them and as long as she told him how much she loved him at the end of every one.

She was waiting for the reply to the letter she'd written in the meadow at Wigston before telling him about the baby. She had to know that he was serious about marrying her first. Then she would just have to hope that he felt the same way afterwards. Danny would understand wouldn't he? It was just a baby after all - no fault of its own. She wished it was their baby as the man in the personnel tent at Shady Lane had assumed.

She often fantasised to herself that Danny was the father. Some days she would look at herself in the mirror for a whole hour or more, just staring at the bump like she could see the baby inside, and through her fantasy she'd learnt to smile at it. It was definitely showing now through all but the loosest of dresses and the close-fitting utility clothing everyone was wearing to save on material wasn't helping to hide it. She'd even felt it kick once or twice, or thought she had.

The letter she'd been waiting for came on a Wednesday. It was the middle of the month and Pop had just lit the fire in the sitting room and updated Mena on how the war was going, telling her on this occasion that after sixty-three days of fighting, Warsaw had fallen.

"The Russians weren't much help to them in the end," Pop said. "More politics, I suppose." He began to prepare his pipe. "It was a slaughter, I heard. Those who survived were evacuated and the city razed to the ground."

Mena was sitting with Pop by the fire in her dressing gown. She liked it when Pop was home, although she never knew any more than he did when he might have to go out on a house call. If he hadn't been out during the night, he was always first down and first to collect the post from the mat with his paper, and whenever there was anything for Mena, he would bring it straight to her with a secret smile that suggested he was as excited for her as she was for herself.

As soon as he gave it to her she knew this was the letter she had been waiting for. It wasn't a V-mail like the rest, presumably because this time Danny had more to say than could be written in the space that V-mail letters allowed. She didn't know how he managed to get it out to her but she didn't much care just as long as he had. Mena thought it had taken so long because it had travelled by regular mail. She found herself holding her breath as she tore the envelope open. Would Danny really ask her to marry him? She supposed he would.

It began with promise.

Dearest Mena,

I can't begin to say how happy I was at receiving your letter. Wigston will always hold a special place in my heart and boy, what I wouldn't give for a pile of chips and scratchings wrapped in old newspaper and covered with that malt vinegar you put on them. Those days seem like heaven to me now. Many's the time I've been reminded of England since I left. My ears seem tuned to that accent of yours - a 'blimey' here or a 'thanks awfully, old chap' there from your artillery boys. And it doesn't seem to matter how bad a situation is, they always find time for a 'spot of tea' - even with shells falling like raindrops around them. I guess that's where the British 'stiff upper lip' expression comes from.

I wish I could tell you that things over here haven't been so bad, but that would be a lie. It's been awful hard and, well, I've said it before - knowing you're there for me keeps me going. I took a piece of shell in the leg a few days back, but don't worry, it's healing well. Just a flesh wound, they said. It'll give me something to show the grandchildren some day and I guess it could have been a whole lot worse.

By the way, Winkelman told me a story the other day that you might be interested to hear. You remember Mel, don't you? Who could forget big Mel? Anyway, he told me there was a fight involving one of our boys and a Dutch fella one night. The joker had been drinking and it seems he took more than a fleeting fancy to one of the local girls. Well, the Dutchman was her father and he rightly kicked up a fuss. Our guy pulled a knife on the old man, but before he could use it the girl skewered him with a pitchfork! What do make of that? Well, I couldn't help but wonder if he was the same knife-happy joker at the dance that night. I know it's wrong of me, but I like to think so. You could say he had it coming to him, but I guess we'll never know.

There was this time... Oh hang it, Mena, I know I'm skirting the issue here with all this nonsense, aren't I? So here's the thing. Will you marry me, Mena? There I've gone and said it. I've asked the question I'd have liked to ask you in person, but I guess it's only right you should know what's in my heart. Say, how does that cabin by the Kanawha River sound. I just know you'd love West Virginia if you'd give it a chance. I'd pick you wild flowers every day and we'd get a boat and go fishing. That sounds real swell, doesn't it?

Well, I have to finish up now. I love you, Mena. Write me again as soon as you can.

Danny.

Mena's cheeks flushed. "Oh, Pop!" she said. She just stared at him for several seconds. Then she re-read the part of the letter where Danny popped the question. "He wants to marry me!"

Pop's moustache began to twitch until his whole face lit up with laughter. He reached across the settee, hugged her and said, "Then I'm as happy as any father could be. And don't fret yourself," he added. "That boy's a survivor. I knew it the first day I saw him."

As happy as Mena was, the moment did not last long. It seemed that their merriment had travelled and her mother now appeared in the doorway smiling along with them even though she could have no idea why.

"What's all this then?" Margaret asked. She came into the room and sat in the single chair by the fire, crossed her legs and clasped her hands together as if in prayer.

Mena couldn't speak. She looked at Pop and Pop looked at her. He smiled tentatively at Margaret and said, "Mena's had another letter."

"How nice," her mother said. "From the American boy?"

Mena nodded.

"Well, let's see it, dear."

Mena's eyes fixed on her mother's outstretched fingers until they began to flick with impatience. She hadn't asked to see any of her previous letters and Mena had done well to hide them from her. She could only suppose that her mother knew this was no ordinary letter and Mena had no intention of letting her read it. She wondered what Emma Bovary would have done. She thought she would have concocted some plausible story and dismissed the letter as something quite trivial and unworthy of her mother's attention, but Mena couldn't think of Danny's letter like that.

In the end she considered that Madame Bovary, once discovered, would have reacted more directly, so she faked a smile, stood up and said, "Mother, we're getting married."

There was no disguising the derision in her mother's laugh. "You're doing no such thing!" she said. "Now let me see it."

Mena held the letter behind her back. She could feel her jaw tightening, her teeth clenching. Her mother's nostrils flared back at her beneath eyes full of scorn, but Mena stood her ground even as her mother stepped closer. Mena would not be told whom she could love and she knew the words that would turn her mother to stone before she could take one more step.

"And that's not all," Mena said.

Her mother's advance faltered and Mena moved within slapping distance, smiling back to spite her hateful glare. "I'm having his baby!" she said, defiant in her moment as she watched her mother reel back onto the chair, face clasped between her hands as she crumpled into a pathetic, speechless heap.

Mena turned to Pop, whose expression still held concern for her, but it was now intermingled with the shock of her revelation. Her tone softened dramatically. "We're going to live in America after the war," she said. It saddened her to say that to Pop, knowing she would have to leave him behind with her mother and that she would perhaps never see him again after she'd gone. "West Virginia," she added, going to him and just holding him so tightly.

Chapter Twenty-Five

November 1944.

Mena Lasseter was having Danny's baby. That was the lie she would have everyone believe, and why not? Apart from Joan, no one else need know what had happened that night at St Peter's, although she supposed Danny would also know by now; she'd written straight back to him telling him all about Victor Montalvo: how she'd met him at Shady Lane that May when all along it was Danny she'd gone to see. And she told him how Montalvo had deceived her for his own unthinkable ends and of the fear and misery it had brought her.

She cried every word onto the page and wished her tears would wash each one away again as soon as she wrote it. But it was the truth, come what may. She had been raped and she was pregnant, and the man who wanted to marry her had to know everything about her if they were to live their happy lives together by the river Danny had spoken of.

And it could not come soon enough for Mena.

Her mother barely spoke to her any more, which was fine in itself as far as Mena was concerned, but it created such a disagreeable atmosphere in the Lasseter house that the place quickly lost everything that had once been good about it; even Pop's dependable smile, which seemed to take the very heart of the house with it. The twins from London had gone, too. Their mother had sent for them at the end of October and Mena missed the energy they brought to the house in the absence of her brothers, which could never now be replaced. Even Xavier and Manfred seemed different, as if sensing the changes in that perceptive way animals often do. They became aloof, like they no longer wanted to be there either, sleeping under beds and showing an uncharacteristic lack of interest at meal times. Mena thought the shine had gone from their marble eyes.

It all served to get Mena out of the house again. At the beginning of November she went back to her voluntary work at the local hospital libraries and she told everyone she knew, and even some she didn't, about Danny and the baby and about her plans for the wedding, which would take place at St Mary's just as soon as Danny could get back to her. She told her comforting lie so often that the truth behind it soon diminished in favour of this new ideal until, to Mena, it was no lie at all. It was no longer *her* baby it was *their* baby. Not that it would look much like Danny, she supposed, but they would be in America by the time any obvious inheritable differences began to show. Provided he took her news well and that it didn't come between them. And why would it? She hadn't cheated on him after all. She was the victim in all this.

So why hadn't he written back?

Love will guide him, Mena thought as she arrived home on her bicycle from the Leicester Royal Infirmary one afternoon late in the month. It was a cold and windy day with a heavy sky full of racing clouds that seemed so busy they had forgotten to rain. Mena thought they would soon remember though as she discarded her bicycle in the usual place beside the coal shed and came in through the back door. She went straight into the sitting room where she hoped to find Pop so she could ask him if there had been any post for her today. She still had her coat and scarf on and Pop was there, along with her mother and Mary, which was a pleasant surprise. They all stood up as she entered. They looked pensive, Mena decided as she stopped and stared back at them, her smile eventually fading.

"No letter?" she said to Pop.

Pop shook his head. He was frowning.

"What's wrong?"

"Sit down, Mena," her mother said.

She sat in one of the armchairs and everyone followed her lead, only they perched rather than sat.

Mena smiled at them and gave a nervous laugh. "Whatever is it?"

Her mother fidgeted. Her hands made knots with her fingers. "You've not heard from your American boy in a while now, have you?"

"He's called Danny," Mena said. "Can't you even say his name?"

"Not now, Mena," Pop said.

Mena sighed and turned back to her mother. "It's been three weeks," she said. "That's all. It's nothing."

"Three weeks," her mother repeated. "And you were receiving letters from -" She paused. "Danny - regularly before that, weren't you? "At least one or two letters a week. Isn't that right, Pop?"

Pop frowned again and slowly nodded.

Mena didn't like the line this conversation was taking. "It doesn't mean anything."

"You knew there would be risks," her mother said. "It's the same for Mary and - thank the Lord - she's still hearing from Edward almost every other day."

"It's true, sis," Mary said. "Three weeks is a long time."

Mena couldn't bear to listen to them, perhaps because they were voicing her own thoughts and in doing so it made it all the harder for her to ignore them. "There could be a hundred reasons," she said, though right there and then she could only think of one: that Danny had read her letter and wanted nothing more to do with her. She was dirty. She was spoiled goods and what man would want her now?

Pop came to her defence. "We'll give it more time," he said. "A letter could arrive any day now."

Mena caught the sharp-lipped glare her mother gave him for saying that.

"He's given her up," Margaret said. "It's quite obvious. Now he knows about the baby, he doesn't want the responsibility. He's been gone two months and that's long enough to forget our Mena. The longer we leave it, the worse it will be. People will talk." She clasped her hands to her mouth. "The shame of it!" she added. "The church will ostracize us."

Mena stood up. "The longer we leave what?"

Her mother looked up at her and sighed while Pop buried his eyes in the fire and began to fiddle with his pipe. She caught the odour of stale cigarette smoke and felt an arm around her. It was Mary, rubbing her shoulder, soothing her.

"What?" she said. "What is it? Tell me."

"Very well," her mother said. She was looking at Pop now. "We'll give it another fortnight, but no longer."

"Then what?" Mena said. She shook Mary's arm away. "Somebody tell me!"

Her mother stood up and her face conveyed no emotion as she said, "You're to be sent to a home for unmarried mothers."

Mena felt the blood drain from her cheeks. She staggered back on weakening legs and caught Pop's eyes at last as he slowly shook his head at her as if to say there was nothing he could do about it; that it was all for the best.

"You can start over," Mary said. "Put all this behind you, eh?"

"What about our baby?" Mena said.

"Trinity House is a good Catholic home," her mother said. "The Sisters of Enlightened Providence will look after you and the baby."

"They'll find a good home for it," Mary said. "Then you can come back and get on with your life like it never happened."

Like it never happened?

Mena couldn't believe those words came from Mary's lips. How could she of all people be so cold-hearted? Her head began to shake as she turned to Pop. She had tears in her eyes. "Pop?" she said, as if pleading with him to say something that would end this madness.

Pop bowed his head.

"Mary?" she said, her eyes wide as if to suggest that surely Mary would not allow this to happen.

"It's for the best, sis," Mary said.

Mena looked at her mother and her breath quickened in her chest. Her whole body began to shake until she felt too weak to stand. Margaret Lasseter made no attempt to disguise the satisfaction Mena knew she felt. Her thin lips twisted and one of her eyebrows slowly arched in triumph.

"No!" Mena screamed. "Pop, you can't let her!"

Chapter Twenty-Six

The Tanners Bar at the hotel Tayte was staying at was typically quiet for an out-of-town hotel bar on a Sunday evening. The decor echoed the lobby area, featuring more dark wood and bright furnishings, such as a line of acid-yellow stools at the bar that stood out all the more because they were vacant. Tayte had suggested to Joan that they go through for a drink after he'd read the letters she'd brought to show him and they had made themselves comfortable at one of the tables; Joan with a whisky and water, Tayte with a Jack Daniels over ice.

He'd made good use of his notepad, adding Mel Winkelman to the information he had on Danielson, and he'd tried to give the letters back to Joan, but she'd told him to keep them, saying that she'd held onto them too long already and that she thought he would be able to make better use of them now.

"So Danny proposed to Mena," he said, sipping his drink as he mulled the information over. He was thinking hard about what Joan had told him about Danny at her home earlier and how much the letters seemed to conflict with the idea that he'd raped Mena. Every instinct he had now told him that something wasn't right with that picture.

'I know what you told me about Danny earlier," he said, "but I can't believe that the man who wrote these letters to Mena could have begun such a relationship by raping her."

Joan took a deep breath. "That's why I wanted you to see them," she said. "I've doubted my own ears ever since Mena brought them to me. I've been confused about it for a very long time."

"And have you drawn any conclusions over the years?"

"No, not really. It's just a feeling, much like the one you now have after reading them." She paused, hovering her whisky glass before she took a sip. "You know, I often imagined that Mena had run away from home and had a good life, but when she never came back for her letters, as the years passed, I began to wonder if that could be true.

"Right now, I'm wondering why she felt the need to give them to you at all," Tayte said. "Why she felt that she couldn't keep hold of them herself. My only conclusion is that for some reason she was afraid of losing them and who better to give them to for safe-keeping than her best friend?"

"I've thought the same thing," Joan said. She gave a little smile and added, "I like to think that Danny came for her after the war and took her back to America with him. If he had it would explain why she never came back for her letters - because she was with Danny and had no further need of them. But I don't know."

"It's a possibility," Tayte said. He snorted. "Maybe I'm looking in the wrong country. I could have stayed home."

Joan wasn't smiling. She raised her glass to her mouth and drained her drink back. "Promise me you'll find out what became of her."

Tayte gave a slow and serious nod. "I promise I'll do my best," he said, wondering again who else was looking for her and why, and what it might mean if they found her first.

Joan reached into her clutch bag. "If you do find her - if she's still alive - will you give her this?"

She handed Tayte a pendant on a silver chain and he recognised it as a US dollar coin. It had a dent in the centre.

"Mena brought it to me with the letters," Joan said. "Something else she never came back for." She drew a deep breath. "I'll leave you to it then," she added. "I believe I've told you everything I know. I hope it will help."

She started to get up, but Tayte stopped her. "Before you head back," he said. "Do you have any idea who might have sent Mena's suitcase to my client?"

Joan settled on the edge of her seat. She seemed to think about it. Then she said, "There was a friend of the family called Edward Buckley. He was like another brother to Mena and I heard that he was somehow caught up with her leaving. Just gossip around the village, but there might be something to it. He would be my best guess."

"Jonathan mentioned him," Tayte said. "He told me that Mary and Edward were going to be married, only it never happened."

"That's right," Joan said. "They fell out over something towards the end of the war, before Mena left. I never saw him in Oadby again after that - or anywhere else for that matter."

"Do you have any idea where I might find him? If he's still alive, of course."

"I'm afraid I have no idea," Joan said. "All I can tell you is that his family lived in Hampshire at the time. They were titled, I believe."

"Hampshire," Tayte repeated, writing it in his notebook.

He stood up, keen to get started on the new information he had. With Danielson's service number he knew he could open up a wealth of information that might be useful to him, and if Edward Buckley was from a titled family they would almost certainly be listed in Burke's Peerage. Had he really helped Mena to run away? Tayte wondered why he would do that and whether the reason had anything to do with why he and Mary never married.

"Thank you, Joan," he said, offering his arm to help her up. "I'll walk with you back to your car."

Chapter Twenty-Seven

December 1944.

Two weeks had passed since Mena first heard about Trinity House and of her mother's plans to send her there and she had received no more letters from Danny. She was at a loss to understand how she could have misread him so completely that at hearing her news he hadn't even been kind enough to reply, if only to express his change of heart. It wasn't like him. Danny was never that cold.

She thought her mother might have taken to intercepting his letters but she'd seen the postman herself on every one of those fourteen days. She'd even searched her mother's room when she was out shopping, but she'd found nothing. Of course, with the war on there was another explanation as to why he'd not written, but Mena didn't like to think about it. She'd given his details to Mary who had offered to look into whether he might have been killed in action or was perhaps missing, in which case there might still be hope, however slim.

Now that her fortnight was up, Mena had been locked in her room, apparently to save her from herself, but it was clear to her that her incarceration was for no other reason than to protect the family's good name from the shame of her dissolute behaviour. Being isolated for long periods was nothing Mena wasn't used to, but it was different now. Now she was her mother's prisoner and the sentence she waited to serve felt like a death sentence to her. In less than a month her life had gone from salvation to ruin and as she waited for Pop to come for her she imagined that it was soon to become considerably worse.

She had been told to put on her yellow Sunday-dress. It had a high-buttoned collar and a white lace fringe and Mena hated it. It was old-fashioned and frumpy, which was why her mother liked her to wear it to church - and heaven help her if she left any of the buttons undone. There would be no church today, though.

When she heard the key in the lock and her bedroom door opened at last, her father stood in silence and waited. He had her coat and scarf with him, and as she passed him in the hallway, Mena thought how much older he looked today. He followed her without speaking and Mena wished he would say something - anything just to relieve the tension. Anyone would have thought they were going to a funeral were it not for that vile yellow dress. But she imagined he was hurting inside just as much as she was and although at times she would have wished him to be stronger, on reflection she would not have changed him.

It was the first Saturday of the month and it was a brighter day than Mena thought it had any right to be. Pop always said that skies like that were really the great shepherd's flock roaming amongst the cornflowers. She knew better now, of course, but she still liked to think of such skies in that way. Those days, forever gone, seemed so innocent and so distant to her now.

They approached the Morris on the driveway and her heart began to drum in her chest when she saw that her mother was already sitting in the back waiting for her; and it was made worse by the fact that she didn't even look at her as Pop opened the door and she climbed in. She sat as far from her mother as the limited space would allow and she kept her eyes fixed on Pop as he sat in front of her and started the engine. She watched him slam the door shut and it made her jump just the same.

It was some time before anyone spoke. They all knew where they were going and why and the occasion was hardly one to promote cordiality. Margaret Lasseter had a hat to match her pale-blue dress. She slid it from her lap towards Mena, filling the space between them and her eyes followed after it.

"Trinity House is the best home of its kind in the area," she said. "The Sisters of Enlightened Providence won't take just anyone so you'd better be on your best behaviour. If they like the look of you, I've arranged it so you can go at the beginning of next year."

Mena just kept breathing, staring through the windscreen at the road ahead. It felt like it took no time at all to get there. She saw the sign at the end of the driveway first. It was off a quiet country lane in the middle of nowhere for all Mena knew or cared. They turned in and drove a hundred yards or so through tidy winter gardens of trimmed shrubs, bordered with colourful pansies that always reminded Mena of the kaleidoscope she once had.

Trinity House was an imposing building of red brickwork and dark slate. It had a five by three matrix of Georgian sash windows and Mena could just see another row of tiny windows set into the roof-space, giving the building four stories in all. Pop parked the car and Mena and her mother got out. Her father, it seemed, was not going in with them. As Mena stood gazing up at the gargoyles squatting malevolently above the high dormer windows and over the main gables, she thought how much more she would fear the place if the sun was not on her face; how terrified she would be when night-time fell.

She wandered towards the main entrance with her mother as if in a daze, taking steady measure of the place, which did not take long. She heard someone speak her mother's name and two nuns in full grey-and-white habit, who did not return her mother's smile, greeted them and invited them inside. The interior reminded Mena of the Dickensian schoolhouses she'd read about in her books, but stamped with the obvious piety of the Catholic Church. There was a strong smell of floor polish, of brass metalwork and waxed wood - and of books. That was the only thing Mena liked about the place.

Their escort took them to a dark oak door. One of the nuns knocked once with firm authority, opened it and retreated silently into the shadows beyond the main staircase.

"Mother Superior," Margaret Lasseter began as soon as they entered. "So good of you to see us."

She was a short, thin woman who looked older than her mother, Mena thought. She had a gaunt face and a mole on her chin that had long grey hairs protruding from it. Mena supposed her lack of vanity prevented her from cutting them or plucking them out. She did not invite them to sit down. Instead she rose from her desk and came around it towards them.

"Let me have a good look at you," she said to Mena as she slowly and thoughtfully began to circle her, studying her in silence until Mena felt uncomfortable. She returned to her seat and waved them into theirs at last. "I'm sorry to say we only have one bed available," she said. "In such wicked times you were fortunate to contact us when you did. Now, when is the baby due?"

Mena was about to answer when she realised that the mother superior had directed the question to her mother.

"February," Margaret said. "So far as I can gather."

The mother superior nodded. "We charge no fee," she said. "Though donations are appreciated. Our girls are expected to work for their keep while they are here and they must follow the house rules at all times. We are strict but fair." She looked at Mena and added, "Discipline is the path to salvation."

Mena didn't like the way the mother superior's eyes seemed to look right through her as she said that, like she was reading her soul and knew whether or not discipline was something she was capable of. She gave a quick nod and the mother superior reached across the desk and spun a form around, sliding it towards her mother. She offered a pen and her mother took it.

"We must insist on the unequivocal right to govern our girls both morally and physically throughout their stay with us," the mother superior said.

Margaret Lasseter seemed to give the form no more than a cursory glance before signing it. It appeared to Mena that she couldn't give her consent quick enough.

"How long must I stay here?" Mena asked.

The mother superior seemed taken aback by the question. She stared at Mena like she'd only just noticed she was there, giving her a look that was as much to say, "How dare you?"

"Our girls do not speak unless they are spoken to," she said. To her mother she added, "I am surprised, Mrs Lasseter, that your daughter does not know better."

Her mother glared at Mena, embarrassment flushing her cheeks. "I can assure you she does, Mother Superior. But perhaps her time at Trinity House will remind her."

"I am sure it will," the mother superior said. She looked stern-faced at Mena for a long time before she turned back to her mother and handed her the pink carbon copy of the form she had just signed. "During her stay she will look after her baby and continue to earn her keep along with the other girls. Between prayers and on a roster basis she will clean the house and tend the gardens, help in the kitchen and wash the laundry. Our Lord does not suffer idle hands, Mrs Lasseter, and neither do I. Between her regular duties she will assist the war effort with a needle and thread. You will see that the question concerning the duration of her stay is made clear on the form," she added. "Simply put, your daughter must remain with us until the baby is born and a suitable home can be found for it.

Mena wanted to ask how long that would take but she was too afraid to say anything else. Then the mother superior seemed to read her mind, which made her feel all the more uncomfortable.

"Exactly how long your daughter will be with us very much depends," the mother superior continued. "Some of our girls leave us after six months or so, others stay a few years. We have one girl whose family disowned her and she had no-where else to go. She's been with us almost six years now."

Mena tried to swallow but her throat was suddenly dry. What if no one wanted her baby? She'd be trapped there forever unless she ran away. But where would she go? She wouldn't be able to return home or she'd be sent straight back again. And she thought as they only had one spare bed that it would naturally be in the attic space. And it was a bed, not a room. She imagined that several girls in her situation would all be sharing the same cramped and poorly lit space. And what about her books? She felt sure that her fondest pastime would be deemed idle in the eyes of the Sisters of Enlightened Providence, unless the subject matter was perhaps one of approved religious content.

This was not her life.

She would have run screaming from the room had her legs not felt paralyzed just long enough for her mother to conclude her business with the mother superior, who left Mena with the parting words, "Until the new year. When you shall be purged of your sins such that you may be born again."

Mena wished Joan was there. She would have known what to do and she certainly wouldn't have stood for any of this nonsense. She thought about Joan all the way back to the car. She knew how unkind she'd been to her and she wished she could see her again to tell her how sorry she was. But she didn't think she would see Joan again for some time now.

Chapter Twenty-Eight

Mena continued to wipe the condensation from her bedroom window as she looked out at the frost in the trees and at the freezing fog that hung low over Oadby's fields. It held a pale pink glow in the early sunlight and Mena wished it was last December again so she could start the year over. If only she hadn't gone to Shady Lane looking for Danny that day in May. If only she hadn't been so forward and had waited for their encounter at De Montfort Hall. But she could not live the year over. Danny had been right: today was all she had and tomorrow really was for dreamers. The winter landscape reminded her of how she'd been looking forward to Christmas last year and how she couldn't wait to join the Land Army. This Christmas would be quite different.

It was a little over a week since her mother had taken her to Trinity House and it seemed that everything was set. In two weeks she would be in the care of the Sisters of Enlightened Providence and their mother superior, who since having met her was the only person Mena feared more than her own mother. But Mena was resolved not to go without a fight, even though she had no idea how to turn her situation around.

Pop had been in to see her. He'd said he'd received a letter from Mary, saying that she'd found nothing to suggest that Danny was missing or had been killed in action. He frowned the whole time he was there and he said he was sorry at least three times before he left, presumably because it confirmed that Danny had no reason not to write to her other than through his own choice.

Danny was already beginning to feel like a sweet memory to her now: a beautiful dream that she had at last awoken from, and no matter how hard she rubbed at the coin around her neck before going to sleep, she could not find her way back into the dream. She had lost him, she knew that now and the realisation was bad enough in itself, but she could not bear the thought of losing their baby, too. The only obvious solution that presented itself to her was that somehow she had to escape - like Edmond Dantés in her favourite of all the classics, *The Count of Monte Cristo*. Although she had no clue as to where she would go or how she would survive the full term of her pregnancy alone.

But chance was a curious thing, Mena reflected later that day as she sat downstairs in her green day-dress and a long cream cardigan, having dinner in the dining room for a change. Edward Buckley had arrived unexpectedly and Mena had been told she could join them as long as she wore something loose-fitting and never brought the subject of her condition up.

She was reflecting on the nature of chance because the first thing Edward had said to her when he saw her was, "Don't worry. Eddie's got a plan." He whispered the words in her ear as he greeted her and kissed her cheek and she knew that Mary must have told him everything. Although, she thought it odd that Edward wanted to help her when Mary, who had sided so firmly with her mother, clearly did not.

It made for an intriguing dinner.

"We're glad to have you back, Edward," Pop said as they began the main course of mutton stew, which primarily consisted of root vegetables.

Margaret finished serving and sat back in her chair. "And we hope to have Peter back with us by spring."

Edward smiled. "Well that's splendid news," he said. "And I'm certainly glad to be back myself. Holland was no trip to the seaside, I can tell you."

"Pop tells us you were lucky to make it," Margaret said.

"It *was* luck," Edward said, thoughtfully. "Nothing more than that. Ten thousand of us went out there and eight days later few more than two thousand came back. We retreated across the Rhine to the south bank." He stared down into his stew. "We had to leave our wounded behind."

"All brave men," Pop said. "The finest."

Edward nodded. "And none more so than Colonel Frost and his battalion," he said. "Barely seven hundred and fifty men held our objective for four nights, which was as long as anyone thought all ten thousand of us could manage against such overwhelming numbers."

"What happened to them?" Pop said.

"About a hundred men finally surrendered. Two hundred or so wounded had already been evacuated by then."

Pop opened his mouth to say something else when Margaret cut in. "I think Edward's had quite enough for now."

Edward gave her a half-smile. "Thank you, Mrs Lasseter."

"Of course," Pop said. "Excuse an old fool, Edward. I don't know when to keep my mouth shut."

"That's quite all right, sir," Edward said.

Mena changed the subject. "Have you seen Mary lately?" she asked.

"No," Edward said. "But I expect I soon shall. With so few of us *Red Devils* left, word is that we'll not see any more direct action for a while. Has she been home lately?"

Margaret eyed him curiously. "Not since November," she said. "But didn't she tell you?"

Edward looked suddenly flushed. "Yes, I'm sure she did," he said. "I'm so forgetful these days."

Mena thought he dug himself out of that one rather well. This was intriguing indeed. "I'm sure she'll be home for Christmas," she said. "Mary loves Christmas almost as much as I do. And how about you, Edward? Are you coming again this year?"

"No, I'm sure I can't," Edward said, taking no time to think about it as he began to play with his food.

Margaret looked upset at the thought. "Really, Edward? What a pity. I was already used to the idea, wasn't I, Pop?"

"Yes, of course, Mother," Pop said. "It won't be the same without you, lad."

Edward smiled like he was embarrassed about something and Mena wondered if he might have fallen out with Mary, although she couldn't imagine anything bad enough to come between them. But why else wouldn't he do all he could to be with her over Christmas, or at least say he'd try? Especially as he'd already said that he was unlikely to see further active duty for a while. She was dying to ask, but how could she? It wasn't her place to and this was certainly not the time.

Mena also thought it curious that Edward did not stay long after dinner. He politely refused Pop's company by the fire, along with the cigar he'd offered him.

"I really have to get back," Edward said as they all stood in the hallway. "Thank you for dinner, Mrs Lasseter. It was very kind of you."

"Not at all, Edward," Margaret said, her tone conveying curiosity now, too. "You know you're always welcome."

It seemed to Mena that she had been the sole reason for Edward's visit. She walked with him to the front door, toying with the parlour palm on the jardinière as she passed it. She could feel her mother's eyes following her every move, as they had since she'd been allowed out of her room.

"Well, goodbye Eddie," Mena said, a little too loudly. "It was lovely to see you again."

Edward looked over her shoulder. He smiled at her and gave her a kiss on the cheek. "If you agree," he whispered, "be ready."

She felt something press into her hand and watched as he left along the path towards the gate. She stole a glance to see what it was. It looked like a piece of pale-blue airmail paper, folded to the size of a matchbook. She slipped it into her cardigan pocket. Her intrigue had deepened.

"Come away from the door, Mena," her mother called.

"Coming Mother."

As soon as the dishes were washed and dried, her mother escorted Mena back to her room, which was fine with Mena as she was dying to read Edward's note. Before her bedroom door had fully closed she threw herself onto the bed and began to unfold the message. She had barely glimpsed the words when the door shot open again and her heart raced as she quickly shoved the note under her pillow.

Her mother stood in the doorframe. "I'll send Pop in later with a glass of milk," she said. She paused like she wanted to say something else, or had perhaps intended to say something else all along but when faced with it she couldn't bring herself to.

Mena gave a half-smile and nodded, wondering perhaps whether her mother had wanted to thank her for behaving herself in company, or for not saying anything about her condition or causing a scene. Did she detect a shred of regret standing there; regret for keeping her locked in her room like a criminal? As Mena watched her mother go, and as she heard the key turn slowly in the lock, she supposed not.

Edward's note was short.

Dear Mena,

If you want to keep your baby, meet me in the lane an hour before daybreak on New Year's Day. Pack a small suitcase. Take only what you need. I'll be waiting for you.

Ed.

Mena's intrigue deepened. She had such a fierce sense of excitement and hope now that it made her skin tingle. She wondered again why Edward - kind-hearted as he was - would offer to help her like this and go against Mary. She wondered where he would take her and what kind of life awaited her if she chose to go. She thought about the Sisters of Enlightened Providence again and knew that none of the answers really mattered. She was going. There was no question in her mind about that.

Chapter Twenty-Nine

New Year's Eve, 1944.

It was almost seven p.m. and Mena could barely contain herself as she sat at her dressing table, struggling over the last few words of the letter she was writing to Pop. She had her little red suitcase packed and ready and a simple dress and cardigan to travel in were hiding beneath her bedcovers, waiting to make their appearance along with the New Year, if it would ever arrive. She'd spent all morning deciding what to take with her and what to leave behind, and she'd spent all afternoon getting herself ready for the evening *party* as her mother was calling it, although with only her parents and Mary there this year, Mena knew it would be nothing of the sort.

She wore the Emerald gown Joan had given her for her birthday, having let it out to accommodate her new shape with material from an old dress she no longer needed. It would never be quite the same again, she knew that, but she also knew that she wouldn't be able to take it with her and she was desperate to wear it one last time. She wore tan stockings, which Danny had given her, and grey leather court shoes with a peep toe. She particularly liked them for their *Movie-Mode* label and its obvious Hollywood connotations. She wore her hair up and she'd spent far too long fussing with it only to concede that nothing looked right without her makeup, which was already packed in her suitcase - not that she dare wear it. She did none of this directly for the sake of her mother's party. Mena's considerable effort was merely to go along with the illusion that this year was just like any other. She would do nothing to put her mother on her guard, taking the same care with her preparations as she always did so as not to give the slightest hint that tonight, once the New Year was in, she was leaving.

Xavier and Manfred were under the bed. Mena could see their snouts in the mirror, resting side by side on the floor by one of the bed legs. They came in at sunset when her mother unlocked her door for the evening and Mena supposed her mother had waited until then because she believed her little girl couldn't possibly run away in the dark, which made Mena smile. She would have liked to see her mother's face when she came to her room in the morning to find she'd done just that.

"The Hartwell's won't be coming this year," Mena said to her companions. "There won't be so many scraps for you, I'm afraid, but I'll see what I can do. We're having cold-cuts and potatoes and Mary's made her jelly-cream again. Poor Mrs Hartwell," Mena added. "I'm sure she must feel very offended, but Mother can hardly tell them why they can't come this year can she?"

She rested her pen and studied herself in the mirror again. The gown and her condition were decidedly at odds with one another, but what could she do? She turned back to her letter and the last task she had to perform before she could go downstairs and join the rest of the family. She owed Pop an explanation but why was it so hard? She'd been poring over it for almost two hours now and she was glad she wasn't wearing makeup because she knew it would have run several times over with her tears by now, and never more so than when she had written that after tonight she might never see him again.

It was nearly seven-thirty when Mena added the last kiss to her letter, sealed it in an envelope and left her room. She knew everyone was downstairs, but she still looked carefully around as she stepped into the hallway, watching the doors as she clutched her letter tightly. She could hear the wireless in the sitting room and the occasional line of indistinct conversation, and wary of just how well sound travelled through the floorboards, she trod them carefully in case her mother heard her and came up to see what she was doing.

There was a carved ebony cupboard above an old laundry trunk in one corner of the hallway where Pop kept his tobacco. He called it his *oh-be-joyful*, which was really just a synonym for *wotnot* or *thingumy*, because no one seemed to know exactly what it was or where it came from. Mena went to it, opened the door and slid her letter in beside one of the tobacco pouches. Pop would find it there soon enough, she thought. Tomorrow evening, perhaps. Then the mystery surrounding her disappearance would be a mystery no more.

Were it not for the shared sense of excitement and fear Mena had felt since leaving her bedroom, the closing hours of 1944 would have been without question the most boring hours of her life. Pop remained in the sitting room with his pipe most of the evening and hardly said a word, which was why the evening had been so dull. Although her mother seemed bent on making sure everyone enjoyed the party, continually forcing what food there was in front of them and insisting they play games like charades. This had the opposite effect on all but Mary, who appeared to be doing her best to go along with things for 'Mother's sake'.

To Mena the whole evening was a charade, made all the more ludicrous by her modified gown and the fact that everyone else had dressed relatively plainly: her mother in a floral frock, Pop in his usual jacket with the sagging pockets and Mary in a navy-blue belted skirt-suit. Mena was in the kitchen with Mary now, watching her fix herself another snowball. She'd lost count of how many that was, but the bottle of advocaat she'd bought only yesterday was almost empty. She watched her take a sip and light a cigarette.

"How come you're allowed to smoke in the kitchen?" Mena asked.

"Party rules, sis," Mary said. "One night only." She staggered a little as she sat against the kitchen table and drew deep on her cigarette. She let the smoke go and then drew it back in through her nose. "Want to try one?"

Mena blew a tune across the top of the cola bottle she'd been holding for the last hour or so. She shook her head, not letting on that she'd already tried one of Joan's and didn't much care for it.

"How's Edward?" she said. She was still curious as to why he was coming so gallantly to her rescue and why he hadn't been to see Mary at all over Christmas.

"Ed?" Mary looked surprised by the question. She knocked back half her snowball in one go. "He's fine. Why do you ask?"

"Oh, it's just that he usually comes to see you over the holidays, doesn't he? I wondered if everything was alright."

Mary pursed her lips and blew a sharp line of smoke at Mena. "Of course it is," she said. "Why wouldn't it be? There's still a bloody war on you know. Or had you forgotten?"

Mena shook her head.

"Well then," Mary said. "He couldn't get away this time, that's all it is."

Mena half-smiled and wondered whom her sister was trying to convince. She knew she was on to something so she persisted. "It's just that he dropped by and had lunch with us a couple of weeks ago and -"

"Yes, that's right," Mary cut in. "Mother said he'd popped in. That's not so unusual, is it?"

"No, not at all," Mena said. But what she did think unusual was that Mary had to find that out from their mother. Why hadn't Edward told her himself? He must have known Mary would find out. He would have mentioned it in a letter, surely. *Unless he's stopped writing to her*, she thought. She watched Mary stub out her cigarette with such purpose that she decided to let the matter rest.

"Let's go and listen to the wireless," she said.

Mena thought Pop looked dreadfully forlorn when she entered the sitting room and saw him fixed as usual by the fireplace like he was carved from the mantle itself. His head was bowed with his pipe, one ear trained on the wireless and George Formby's ukulele. She gave him a smile as she crossed the room and topped up her mother's sherry glass.

"Thank you, dear," her mother said.

Mena forced a smile. 1945 was less than an hour away now and in that time she had but one objective if her escape plan was going to work: she had to convince her mother that there was no need to lock her door tonight.

Mary came in and slumped down on the settee. "Careful Mother," she said. "You might get a taste for it."

Margaret's laugh mocked her. "There's the pot calling the kettle," she said, indicating the fresh snowball in Mary's hand.

"This is nothing," Mary said. Then as Mena sat beside her she quietly added, "I've a bottle of gin, too, and I might bloody well drink it before the night's out."

Mena kept her eyes on her mother's sherry glass, keen to see her drink as much as possible before midnight, thinking that it would serve her purpose better if she would just pass out. A series of cheerful tunes came and went on the wireless. Mary made several trips to the kitchen and gradually seemed to retreat into herself. Mena topped up her mother's sherry again and sat on the floor beside her chair. She sighed, purposefully.

"You know, mother," she said. "I've been thinking that Trinity House might not be such a bad idea."

Her mother sat up. "Really, Mena," she said, and her smile was the most genuine Mena had seen in a long time. "I thought we weren't going to talk about it at the party, but since you've brought the subject up." She leant in and cupped Mena's cheek in her hand. "What's brought you to your senses?" she asked.

Mena held her mother's hand to her face until her mother slowly withdrew it. She wanted to tell her that she wished to join a holy order and live a life of celibacy, married to God, but she thought that would be overdoing it.

"It's not the life I want for myself," she said. "I want a career and I want to travel. I can't very well do that if I'm left to bring up a baby by myself, can I?"

"A career?" her mother said. "You'd do better to meet a nice English boy and settle down in Leicestershire. A doctor, perhaps. Someone like your father. You must meet plenty of doctors at the infirmary."

"Yes, of course, Mother," Mena said. "I suppose what I'm trying to say is that I want options and I won't have many unless I go to Trinity House, will I? I mean, what doctor would want to marry me if I didn't?"

"Quite, Mena. You can see now that we're only acting in your best interests, can't you?"

"Yes, Mother," Mena said. "In fact, the next couple of days can't go quickly enough. The Sisters of Enlightened Providence will teach me how to sew properly, won't they?"

Her mother almost laughed. "Yes, and a good deal more besides. You'll leave Trinity House a fitting spouse for any Englishman, doctor or otherwise."

"I will," Mena said. "Would you like some more sherry?"

"Yes, dear. I think I would."

Pop tapped his pipe purposefully beside the clock on the mantle.

"Heavens, it's nearly time!" Margaret said. "Fifteen minutes to go!" she added. "Come along, Pop, have another stout." She got up and opened a bottle for him and topped up her own sherry.

Mena watched Pop take the bottle from her mother like it was too heavy to hold. She wished there was something she could say to him to make him feel better. None of this was his doing; she knew that. For a moment she wondered whether she could go through with it. It didn't seem right to leave him behind to deal with Mother all by himself, but she would be forced to leave him just the same if she stayed and for all she knew she might be trapped at Trinity House for years.

As the hands on the clock crept slowly around to midnight, she knew that her time at the Lasseter house had run its course. When the hour came she gave pop such a hug, and she thought she heard him choke back a tear, but when they parted again his eyes were smiling at her, giving her strength. She hugged Mary and her mother, knowing it was for the last time, and they all linked hands and sang *Auld Lang Syne*, just like they always did. When the moment had passed and the forced revelry had faded, Mena helped clear up. Then feigning tiredness she kissed Pop again, said goodnight to everyone and went to bed.

Chapter Thirty

Mena had been standing in the darkness behind her bedroom door for half an hour, counting her heartbeats as she waited and listened. It was after one a.m. and she had changed into her travel clothes; her suitcase was ready at her feet. She knew Pop was already in bed because she'd heard him snoring. She was listening for her mother now and after that she would listen for the quiet sounds that accompany the still of night: the faint tick of the clock on the mantle downstairs and the drip in the cistern that you could only hear when the Lasseter house had finally settled. When she heard that, she knew it would be safe.

Pins-and-needles set into her toes after a while so she sat on her bed and hoped that Edward would be outside in the lane as his note had said, but she had hours to wait yet. She began to feel herself drifting with her thoughts and she wanted to lie down but she knew if she did she would fall asleep and in all probability she'd be discovered fully dressed on her bed with her suitcase in the morning. She took a deep breath and was about to go back to the door when she heard a floorboard creak. She froze, wondering whether she should jump into bed in case whoever it was had come to look in on her. A moment later the decision was made for her.

She heard a key in the lock. It turned slowly and grated with such clarity that it set her nerves on edge. She shot up and was at the door in an instant. She wanted to turn the handle, open the door and run before it was too late, but when she heard the metallic thump of the bar going across, she knew that it already was. Her mother had locked her in. She felt sure she would have overlooked it tonight. She'd been good, hadn't she? She'd played along, giving her mother every notion that she wanted to go to Trinity House after all.

So why had she locked her in?

Mena paced the room, her face contorted by a jumble of thoughts. Instinct took her to the window and she threw aside the blackout curtains and opened it, allowing the cold night air to rush in. As she leaned out into the moonless night she saw that it had started to snow. The tiles below her dormer window would be slippery, but she thought the guttering would break her slide. From there it was only an eight or nine feet drop into the yard. But what if the guttering failed to break her slide? She shook her head, like she refused to believe this was happening. Then she sat in her chair, not stirring for several minutes, pondering the window and wishing there was some other way out of this nightmare.

When nothing presented itself she leant out of the window again to get a better idea of the distance. She sat in the frame this time and swung her legs out, testing what now appeared to be her only means of escape. The ground suddenly looked too far below her now and she caught her breath, legs dangling as she tried to reach the roof tiles. Then she stopped. What was she thinking? If she did slip - even if she survived the fall - what about her baby?

Mena came back into the room and sat down again, shaking with fear and anger; mostly anger. She was so close. How could her mother snatch her hopes away like that? How dare she? She stared at the door like she was willing it to open until her breathing at last slowed and her head began to rock and bow, and some time later she finally slumped in her chair and began to dream.

It was the sound of the key turning in the lock again that woke her. She came back to herself with a start, having no idea how long she'd been asleep. Her bedside clock told her that some hours had passed and there was a faint glow at the window. It was almost daybreak and she was suddenly in a panic. Her first thought was that she had to go to Edward, hoping he would still be waiting for her. Her second thought returned to the sound that had awoken her. Had she really heard a key turning? She thought it must have been a dream but she had to find out. She went to the door and slowly turned the handle, holding her breath like she was cracking a safe. When the handle stopped turning she pulled and to her surprise the door opened.

She thought it must be a trap; that her mother was playing one of her cruel games. Was she testing her? The hallway was dark and still. Perhaps it had been Mary? She hadn't heard her come up to bed last night and she thought she must have fallen asleep on the settee. She wondered whether Mary and Edward were in on this together. Perhaps Mary had been putting on a show for her mother? She smiled to herself, thinking that if she had been she'd made a good job of it.

Mena picked up her suitcase and crept towards the top of the stairs like a seasoned jewel thief. Her heart was beating so fast she felt that she could barely breathe. She descended, keeping to the edges so the steps wouldn't creak. When she arrived at the bottom she made straight for the coat stand.

A muffled cough stopped her.

She caught her breath and turned towards the sound. It came from the sitting room. The door was open. As she peered inside she saw that there was still a glow in the fireplace and before it she could see a thin line of blue-white smoke.

"And where are you stealing off to?" Mary said. She sounded half asleep and very drunk. "How did you get out of your room?"

"Someone unlocked the door," Mena said, certain now that it had not been Mary. She turned away, collected her coat and scarf and began to put them on, thinking only that she had to leave right away.

"He said he needed to think things over," Mary said.

Mena spun around to see Mary standing in the doorframe, leaning heavily against it for support. It took her a moment to realise she was talking about Edward and now she could see her sister better, it looked like she'd been crying. Her makeup was smudged. She looked like a rag doll.

"Quite the little detective, aren't you?" Mary continued. "Or should that be, little Miss Busy-body?"

"I don't know what you mean?"

Mary scoffed. "All those bloody questions last night. You knew how it was with Eddie and me, but you just couldn't let me get on with it, could you? Couldn't let me forget it just for one bloody night."

"I had no idea," Mena said. "I was concerned, that's all."

Mary staggered towards her. "So where are you going, Miss Busy-body?" She had a sarcastic smile on her face and her breath reeked of gin.

"Away," Mena said. She reached for the door, turned the key and opened it only for Mary to slam it shut again. The sound jarred Mena's nerves. She lashed out at Mary, hitting her with her suitcase. "I'm going!" she said. "You can't stop me!"

Mary laughed back at her like they were playing some childhood game. She continued to lean against the door, blocking Mena's exit.

"I'll hit you again," Mena said, "and you'll feel it this time. Now get out of my way!"

Mary laughed through her nose. "Go ahead," she said. "I'm sure I deserve it. Give it your best shot."

Mena swung her case back, ready to give it her all and send Mary flying into the Jardinière for all she cared. But when the case caught on something and she turned to see what it was, she felt her mother's hand slap hard across her face. It stung her cheek and knocked her sideways. At the same time, she felt the case go, tearing through her fingertips. As she recovered she saw her mother standing before her in her dressing gown, enraged eyes glaring like Mena had never seen before.

"You deceitful little harlot!" she said. "I've a good mind to let the Sisters of Enlightened Providence keep you!"

Mena watched in disbelief as her mother came at her again, this time with the suitcase raised above her, ready to bring it crashing down. She cowered from the blow, thinking only that she had to protect her baby, but the blow never came.

When she looked up again she saw Pop in his striped pyjamas. He was standing behind her mother and he had the suitcase in his hands. She watched him wrench it away from her mother with a determination Mena thought had long since abandoned him. She caught his eyes, alert and purposeful, his jaw firm with authority.

"Get up, Mena," he said. "Mary, come away from the door."

"You stay where you are, Mary!" her mother said.

Pop raised the back of his hand and Mena's mother cowered towards the stairs. Mena had never seen him do that before. He didn't hit her. He didn't have to.

"Mary, do as you're told," he said. "I won't tell you again."

Mena watched her sister drag herself away from the door.

"I'm sorry, Mena," Mary said. Her sullen tone sounded sincere, but through her drunken slur as she disappeared back into the sitting room it was hard to tell.

Margaret Lasseter looked livid. Mena could see the anger physically racking her body like she might explode again at any minute, but Pop's sudden change in character seemed to keep her in check. She was frozen to the spot, mumbling silent incantations to herself as she squeezed and rubbed her crucifix like a woman possessed.

Pop came to Mena and put the suitcase in her hand. He gave her a firm smile and produced her letter from the breast pocket of his pyjama jacket. "I must have gone through too much tobacco last night," he said, and his words immediately calmed her.

Just knowing that Pop had read her letter made her eyes well with tears; she could feel them straining behind her cheek bones. It was Pop who had unlocked her door. Pop who knew her plans long before they sang *Auld Lang Syne* together and yet did nothing to stand in her way. Quite the opposite.

"I only ever wanted what was best for all of you," Pop said.

Mena smiled kindly at him. "You'll say goodbye to Peter for me when he comes home? Explain things?"

"Of course."

"And if you see Joan, tell her I'm sorry. She'll know why."

Pop nodded. "I'll make a point of it."

Mena looked at her mother again and her mother turned away and sank her head, shaking it as if to say what a disappointment her youngest daughter was. Mena couldn't hate her. She felt sorry for her as she opened the door and drew in the cold early morning air. It tasted sweeter than anything she had known in a long time.

"Promise me one thing," Pop said.

Mena turned back to him and she could see that he had tears in his eyes, too. "Anything."

"Get as far away from here as you can and never look back," Pop said, his voice wavering. "You deserve better."

Mena could hardly speak. She sniffed and swallowed back the lump in her throat. Then she ran to him and embraced him. "I will," she said, and she cried so hard she thought she would never stop.

Chapter Thirty-One

Back in his hotel room, Jefferson Tayte was trying to sleep. He'd turned in at nine p.m. which was early for him, but he was tired from the day's travelling, or thought he was because it was now nearly ten p.m. and he was still wide awake. He supposed the jet lag was upsetting his biorhythms - his body still running on DC time. Or maybe it was the girl. He couldn't shake her from his head as he lay there and he realised after the first thirty minutes had passed that he didn't want to. She felt like something misplaced that had to be found and he knew he wouldn't get a good night's sleep again until he had.

He gave up trying and swung his legs out of bed. Then in stars-and-stripes boxers he strode across the room and put on his dressing gown. From his briefcase he took out the papers he'd gathered and he saw the photograph of Mena again. He sighed at it without really knowing why. Perhaps it was because it caused him to reflect on how young she was then and how she'd had her whole life ahead of her - and how that life must have been turned on its head by the events of 1944.

His thoughts spurred him on as he sat at the desk and took his laptop out. While it was booting up, he fetched his notebook from his jacket and found the information he had on Danny Danielson and Edward Buckley, deciding to look into Buckley first. He would be easier to get started on, he thought, and he was keen to go and see him if he could find him - assuming that he was still alive.

He logged into Burke's Peerage and Gentry where he had a paid subscription. Then he brought up the A-Z listing so he could see all the 'Buckley' entries at a glance. He scrolled down through the alphabetical list and found six in all, but there was only one Edward. He clicked the name and was presented with an address for somewhere called Bramshott House. He checked the county.

"Hampshire," he said to himself.

It tallied with the information Joan had given him earlier when she'd told him where the Buckleys were from. He thought an address was a good start, but he didn't have time to write to Edward Buckley to ask if he'd agree to see him. What he really needed was a phone number and he knew that wasn't going to be so easy.

Or an e-mail address, he thought as he brought up another browser.

He Googled Buckley's name and scrolled through several screens of search engine results, reaching several dead ends before he found something that looked relevant. It was a website for the British 1st Airborne and he knew from what Jonathan had told him that Edward had been a paratrooper with the Red Berets during World War II. It had a forum and a list of members among other things. When Tayte clicked on the list he was presented with the members' names beneath each person's online avatar.

He could see from the images that most of the members were too young to have fought in World War II and he figured they were the soldiers' dependents, carrying the flag for their fathers. But as he looked further down the list he saw a few older faces and then he saw the name he was looking for. The avatar was small. It was of a man wearing a red beret and a navy blazer with a bright red poppy pinned to the lapel. Tayte had little doubt that this was the right Edward Buckley. He clicked the image and was taken to a member profile page that gave some background information and a larger version of the image. Most importantly it had an e-mail address.

Tayte smiled to himself and marvelled as he often did at the power of the Internet. He clicked the contact button and began typing his introduction, briefly explaining his reason for writing and asking Edward Buckley if he would see him. Once he'd sent it he sat back and stretched and as he did so he eyed the sachet of hot chocolate that was on the tray by the kettle. He thought it might help him sleep. Reaching for it, he told himself that it was okay to have just the one as long as it was for medicinal purposes.

At a London railway station, standing beside a locker that was one of a hundred or more in the rack before him, a man in a long raincoat was about to put his key in the lock when his mobile phone buzzed. He adjusted his glasses and read the display. He wasn't expecting the caller to contact him again so soon, but in his line of work the parameters were prone to change.

"Hello."

He listened to the caller. Then he nodded and said, "The priest is dead."

He was silent again. Listening. A loud tannoy announcement caused him to cup his hand over the phone.

"The train about to depart from platform six is the ten-fourteen service to...”

He tuned the sound out, still listening. “Why the change of plan?” he asked. “Why the sudden urgency?” He nodded and continued to listen for several seconds. “Jefferson Tayte,” he repeated. “American.” He drew a deep breath. “I’ll take care of it,” he added, ending the call.

Inside the locker was another small case: this one moulded from black, ABS plastic. The man shuffled the travel case at his feet closer to the locker and unzipped it. Then he opened the ABS case and inspected the Walther P99 semi-automatic handgun that was nestled inside. Everything was just as he expected it to be, but he liked to be sure. He preferred the Walther, although international travel meant that he couldn’t be choosy and the Glock he’d used for the priest had served its purpose.

He closed the gun-case again and took a quick look around. There were plenty of people about - London never slept - but no one seemed interested in him. He lifted his travel case up onto his knee and slipped the gun inside, zipped it up again and made for his train.

Tayte dunked one of the hotel’s complimentary biscuits into his hot chocolate and opened his notebook to the page where he’d written Danny Danielson’s information. As he ate the biscuit he woke up his laptop and awkwardly tapped in the details for the US army enlistment records website. They were available to search in a number of places, but he typically used NARA - the US National Archives and Records Administration.

He went into the AAD - Access to Archival Databases - and was presented with two files: one for reserve corps records, the other for enlistment records. He clicked on the latter, which covered the period between 1938 and 1946. The first entry field was for the army serial number. Into it he typed Danny’s number and then he sat back with his hot chocolate while he waited for the results to come back.

There were almost nine million records in the file, but it only took a couple of seconds to pull out the one Tayte was interested in. On a single line he was presented with all the information that was pertinent to a US soldier’s enlistment into he army during World War II: name, residence state and county, place and year of enlistment and the year of his birth.

He noted everything down in his notepad and paused over the name. It was shown as Danielson, E. Not D for Danny. He supposed

'Danny' must have been a nickname or simply the name he commonly used, thinking that he really had no chance of finding the right man when he'd looked for him before.

His residence state was West Virginia and that put Tayte in mind of the name he'd seen on his client's original birth certificate. He thought it made sense that Mena would have chosen the name Virginia for her baby given everything he'd learnt so far. He underlined the words, wondering whether it was possible that Danny could have come back for Mena and taken her home to West Virginia with him. The thought made him smile, but it was just a thought.

He went back to the entry on the screen. The leftmost column had the option to view the record, which he did. It added the subject's specific date of enlistment, the term of enlistment, their race and education level, along with several other fields of information that were of less value to Tayte just now. What he really wanted to know was whether or not Danny had survived the war and what became of him if he did.

He sat back and pinched his eyes. Maybe it was the screen-work or the hot chocolate or both, but he was beginning to think that the pillow on the bed behind him was about ready to swallow him up as soon as he put his head on it.

"Just a little more," he said to himself as he brought up another browser screen, thinking to rule out the obvious possibilities before moving on to the more complicated process of getting to see Danielson's full army record.

He logged into the ancestry website he used for a large part of his everyday research and brought up the page with the heading, 'U.S. WWII Military Personnel missing-in-action or Lost at Sea, 1941-1946'. He already knew the statistics, reminding himself that of the sixteen million Americans who served during World War II, around four hundred thousand had died. Of those, seventy-nine thousand were unaccounted for and that number had only reduced by six thousand today.

As he typed the details into the search fields, he hoped that Danny wasn't one of them, but when the results came back he slumped in his chair and sighed. There he was: Danielson, E. He read the rank: Staff Sergeant. Then he confirmed the service number to be sure. There was no question about it. According to the information, the 'Date of Loss' told him that Danny had been missing-in-action since November 1944.

Unless he went AWOL for Mena.

He figured it had to be a possibility and missing-in-action didn't necessarily mean dead. Maybe Danny had engineered his way out of the war to be with Mena. As tiredness crept up on him, Tayte thought back to his earlier notion that Danny had taken Mena back to West Virginia. He thought about her little red suitcase again, considering that if Danny had managed to get back to her before the end of the war, their departure from England might have called for some urgency and that could account for why she had to leave it behind.

He liked that idea, but as he began to drift he knew it couldn't be that simple. If it was, why had his client been given up for adoption? He made himself get up and get back into bed, thinking that he needed to conduct further research into Danny Danielson and as much as he wanted to go on with it now, he knew he couldn't stay awake any longer. It would have to wait until morning.

Chapter Thirty-Two

By eleven a.m. the following day, Jefferson Tayte was driving through the English countryside, marvelling at how similar Hampshire looked to Hertfordshire, although it occurred to him that perhaps it wasn't so odd given their proximity to one another. It was all on a different scale from back home where driving from the middle of one state to another could take a day or more. According to the satnav, he was less than ten minutes from his destination: Bramshott House: residence of Edward Buckley.

He'd been awoken by the arrival of his room service breakfast that morning and it was unlike him to sleep so late, but he figured he must have needed it after last night's research. When he'd tapped his laptop back to life, ready to continue looking into Danny Danielson, he'd had an e-mail pop up on his screen from Buckley. It had simply stated that he was free to see Tayte any time in the morning before noon. No telephone number was given.

The arrival of Buckley's reply put everything Tayte had planned to do on hold - his Internet research and his breakfast - because an interview with Edward Buckley was something he could not afford to miss. He hoped Buckley might be able to tell him why he and Mary never married, and he could confirm whether he helped Mena to leave home. He also thought he might know something about what became of her afterwards and maybe even where she was now.

"At the next junction, turn right," satnav lady said and Tayte obeyed, turning off the main road.

It was a pleasant morning he thought as he continued to drive deeper into the countryside. Gone were the clouds that seemed to have followed him since he arrived in England. Now the sky was suddenly blue, the air crisp and cool and the ground drying after yesterday's rain. He looked up through the windscreen and smiled at it, thinking that the new week had begun on a promising note.

"You have reached your destination," satnav lady said and instinctively, Tayte stopped.

When he couldn't see anything obvious through the bare hedgerows to either side of him, he drove on again. The trees soon thickened around him, blocking his view, but after a few hundred metres, he came to a high, red-brick wall and then to a set of open gates that had the name 'Bramshott House' spelled out in wrought iron above them. He turned in and followed the pale gravel drive for a few hundred metres more, between towering, leafless oak trees and evergreen yews, until he came in sight of the house. He'd thought Joan Cartwright's home was impressive, but he had to whistle at this when he saw it.

Bramshott House was a 17th century stone manor house, built on three floors with a clay-tiled roof, mullioned bay windows and numerous high chimney stacks rising from every gable. The grounds appeared neat if not fancy and Tayte thought they had probably seen better days, or perhaps it was just the time of year. There was no obvious parking allocation, so he drove up to what looked like a disused island fountain with pieces of statuary set in various poses around a larger centrepiece.

Tayte turned around it and stopped by the steps that led up to the main entrance porch. He got out of the car and climbed them, briefcase in hand, thinking how quiet it was. Beyond the birds in the distant trees the air was still until he raised the heavy iron knocker and let it fall. It sent a booming echo through the building as it crashed down onto the oak door and Tayte stepped away and looked around, hands behind his back like he'd just broken something.

He waited several seconds but there was no answer. At first he thought he'd arrived too late; he couldn't see any other cars. Maybe Buckley had gone out earlier than he'd said. But the gates were open. Tayte figured if Buckley had gone out then the gates would probably have been closed. He checked his watch and the glowing red digits told him it was still forty-five minutes before noon. He knocked again and thought the sound was loud enough to get anyone's attention no matter how big the house was or even whether the occupants were all asleep. He imagined that even if Buckley lived by himself, he would have staff to keep the house going.

So why aren't they answering?

He tried again and he really threw the hammer down this time; so much so that he heard woodpigeons flapping in the distance. When no answer came again he shook his head and decided to take a look around, thinking that maybe he could get someone's attention through one of the windows. He also considered that Buckley was an elderly man now. Maybe he was deaf and the staff were on their morning off.

Tayte followed the gravel around to the right of the building and came to a block of stable-like garages. There were no doors. He could clearly see the cars inside and all the bays were full. Turning back to the house he began to peer in through the windows. The rooms were vacant and full of antique furniture and old paintings hanging from the picture rails. A cold breeze hit him as he arrived at the back of the house where he saw an expanse of winter countryside and there was evidence of what must once have been a fine parterre garden. Now, the low box hedging that framed and segmented it stood alone and unkempt.

He went up to the next window and then the next, and just as he stepped away this time, movement caught his eye. He went back to it, dropped his briefcase and cupped his hands over his face to block out the reflection. It looked like a study. There was a desk with a computer screen in the middle and the walls were decorated with bookshelves. He caught the movement he'd seen again and it drew his eye. Someone was kneeling on the floor by the desk, holding out a clenched fist. As Tayte's eyes adjusted to the light inside the room he saw that it was an elderly man and he supposed it was Edward Buckley. He looked in pain, like he was having a heart attack.

Without thinking, Tayte repeatedly shoved his elbow into the window until the leaded glass shattered and began to break away. When the jagged hole he'd made was big enough for him to reach through, he unlatched and opened the window then pulled himself up into the frame.

"Mr Buckley!" he called, "It's Jefferson Tayte. Hang in there!"

As he fell through the window and picked himself up again he heard Buckley groan. The man gave a sudden jerk and staggered back into the desk. He fell as Tayte ran to him, but Tayte was too late to help him. He knew Buckley was dead the moment he saw his ashen face and the blood that was seeping out across his shirt. This was no heart attack. He'd been shot.

Tayte was aware of a door behind him, directly facing Buckley and the desk. He spun around and saw a woman's body lying in the half-light beyond. As he went to it he heard a door slam, followed by the now familiar sound of the heavy iron knocker as it rebounded against the front door. He leapt over the body at his feet and ran towards the sound, but as he came out into the entrance hallway he stopped. Another body, a man this time, was lying just inside the front door and Tayte supposed that his killer had shot him dead as soon as he'd answered it.

Tayte went to the door, eyes on the dead body the whole time. He eased it open and peered outside but there was no one to be seen. Looking down at the dead man again - at the blood-filled hole in his forehead - he took out his phone and called the police.

Chapter Thirty-Three

It was gone four p.m. by the time Tayte had finished helping the Hampshire Constabulary with their enquiries. Three hours after that, he was back at his hotel in the Tanners Bar, getting better acquainted with Jack Daniels. His story about who he was and what he was doing at Bramshott House that morning had checked out easily enough. Jonathan had been quick to vouch for him when the police had called and Tayte had been able to show Detective Inspector Lundy, who was leading the enquiry, the e-mail exchange he'd had with Edward Buckley, validating his visit. He wasn't able to give him any idea as to why Edward Buckley had been murdered, but his questions had given Tayte cause to wonder at the killer's motive himself.

There had been no robbery. Buckley's murder appeared to be premeditated and the staff had clearly been in the way of the killer's objective. To Tayte, and he imagined to the police, it had looked like a cold-blooded assassination that he just happened to walk in on - albeit too late to prevent it. But then Tayte knew that he would also be dead now if he'd arrived at Bramshott House any sooner.

He picked his drink up off the bar and the pain in his left elbow reminded him that he'd not long since used it to smash through a window. It was just a bruise, he'd been told, but it hurt just the same every time he tried to use it. He swivelled around on the stool and switched hands. Then he took a big slug from the tumbler, rattling the ice, thinking of all the answers that must have died along with Edward Buckley.

He couldn't help but question the odds of Buckley being murdered on the same morning that he was due to meet him and he wondered if what he was doing in England had somehow helped to bring Buckley's murder about, in which case he figured they weren't such great odds at all. He'd been to see several people over the weekend and he'd asked some potentially sensitive questions - stirred up the past. Or maybe he'd simply arrived in the middle of something that was going to happen anyway and that his arrival had just sped things up. He ordered another drink, thinking that it wouldn't be the first time that had happened.

As his drink arrived he heard the theme tune to *Anything Goes* coming from his pocket - and so it seemed did everyone else in the bar. He took his drink out into the lobby and answered the call, seeing on the display that it was Jonathan. He sounded upbeat about something.

"How are you?" Jonathan said.

If Tayte was honest with himself, he didn't feel all that great. He'd pinned a lot on being able to talk to Edward Buckley and everything that had happened at the house and afterwards with the police had left him feeling in need of the second drink he was holding.

"I'm fine, I guess," he said, not wanting to dampen Jonathan's mood.

"You don't sound it. How's the elbow?"

"It'll mend."

"Good," Jonathan said. "Anyway, I've found something that should cheer you up. I went into the attic again this afternoon - into crawl-spaces I never knew were there - and I've found something I'm sure you'll be interested in."

"Go on," Tayte said. "What is it?"

"A tin box. It was locked and I had to break it open."

"What was inside?"

"Papers."

Tayte was smiling now. "What kind of papers?"

Jonathan didn't answer straight away. When he did he said, "I think it would be better to show you. Can you come over in the morning?"

Tayte checked his watch. It was still early: not yet seven-thirty. "Is it too late to come over now?" He really wanted to see those papers.

"It's not the hour so much," Jonathan said. "But we're just on our way out. Geraldine's got this thing about Pilates and I said I'd give it a try. She's been on at me for weeks."

Tayte didn't want to wait until morning, but it seemed he had no choice. "Okay," he said. "I'll come by in the morning."

"I expect you could use an early night," Jonathan said.

Tayte didn't feel much like sleeping. He still needed to calm down first. "I was going to look into Danny Danielson some more first."

"What have you discovered?"

Tayte told Jonathan what he knew.

"Missing-in-action?" Jonathan said. "Poor chap."

"Maybe," Tayte said, wondering again whether Danny could have gone AWOL for Mena. "He was listed in November, 1944," he added, and for the first time he considered how close that was to the time Mena left home. "I should be able to tell you more in the morning."

"Tomorrow then," Jonathan said. "Come as early as you like."

When the call ended, Tayte sat back and continued to sip his drink, thinking that he would be at the Lasseter house bright and early to see what was on those papers Jonathan had found.

"Family history starts at home," he told himself.

It was a reminder to him that it was essential to talk to the family first, and it wasn't just the information and the memories they could share, but the photographs and the documents that were so often hidden away, waiting to be found. He knew it could save time later on and he hoped it would now.

He considered everything he'd learnt about Mena so far. According to Joan, Mena had said that she'd been raped and Joan was of the impression - garnered from Mena herself - that it was Danny who had raped her. Then Mena had fallen pregnant and as if to confirm things, she was telling everyone that she was carrying Danny's baby.

But what about the letters?

They clearly conflicted with the idea that Danny could have raped Mena, not least because it was also clear from everything he'd heard and read that Danny and Mena had fallen in love during the summer of 1944. Tayte thought that Mena might not have become pregnant when she was raped, but had later become romantically involved with Danny and had conceived her baby as a result of that relationship. But it was all speculation and it didn't account for why Joan - until she had read Danny's letters - believed from Mena herself that it was Danny who had raped her. It all came back to that.

Joan had also suggested, from the gossip that had been circulating in Oadby at the start of 1945, that Edward Buckley had helped Mena to run away and he wondered again why Edward might have done that. He thought it could have something to do with the reason he and Mary never married, but it was just more speculation for now. He thought about Mary then, or Grace, as she had become, who in many ways had run away herself soon after the war. And there was her grandson, Alan Driscoll, who was clearly bitter towards the much wealthier side of the family - towards the Ingrams - because of an earlier family rift.

Tayte sighed as he got up and headed over to the reception desk to order his room service meal, thinking that it was all good background information to have, but he couldn't see how it was going to help him find Mena. He needed facts and as soon as he'd been to see Jonathan in the morning he was going to explore the archives at the local record office - although as Mena had run away from home he knew she could have gone just about anywhere. The local record office might not hold any information on her post 1944.

As he arrived at the reception desk he turned his thoughts back to Danny and the further research he wanted to conduct. He didn't expect to discover much, but he wanted to confirm his earlier findings and he thought that if there was more to Danny's story then it could take him closer to Mena, too.

Chapter Thirty-Four

Tayte couldn't stop smiling all the way to the Lasseter house the following morning and it wasn't because of the sun on his face or the promise of learning more about the documents Jonathan had found. It was because he'd made a discovery of his own and for Tayte there was no better tonic. He arrived around eight-thirty just as Geraldine was leaving for work. Ten minutes later he was in the sitting room with Jonathan, shoes off by the fire with a mug of coffee in his hand. Before he got stuck into Jonathan's find, he wanted to talk about last night's research while the details and his excitement about what he'd found were still fresh.

"I wanted to see if I could find out anything more about Danny Danielson before I went to bed last night," he said. "I've had a feeling that there was more to his missing-in-action status in light of everything I've heard and it turns out I'm not the only one."

"Interesting," Jonathan said, raising an eyebrow.

Tayte sipped his coffee, which was too hot to drink so he set it back down on the table. "I've had the notion that Danny might have found his way back to Mena," he said. "And I figured if he had then he must have generated a few records by now. Anyway, I wanted to see if I could turn anything up."

"And judging from your much improved tone this morning, I'd say you have," Jonathan said.

Tayte nodded. "I thought I'd Google Danny first. I got almost seventeen thousand results for his name, but things narrowed down when I added '82nd Airborne' to the search. There were only seven results then and one was for a website about a member of the 504th Parachute Infantry Regiment."

"Danny's regiment," Jonathan said.

Tayte gave another nod. "When I read the name of the person who'd set the website up, I had no doubt that I was looking in the right place. It was created by a man called Mel Winkelman. He was mentioned in a letter Joan showed me a couple of days ago. By all accounts, he and Danny were best buddies during the war. Mel died several years ago, but his grandson keeps the site running."

"And Mel didn't think Danny went missing-in-action?"

"No," Tayte said. "And he had a very good argument. You see, in November 1944, when Danny was listed missing, Paris was in allied hands - had been since the liberation in late August. Mel was with Danny and a few others from their company while they were there on leave. Apparently, it was the party capital of Europe at the time - a safe haven for battle-weary troops to get some well earned R&R."

"So the 'action' part of missing-in-action is somewhat at odds?" Jonathan said.

"Entirely. Mel says their unit went wild on the streets of Paris and generally made a bad account of themselves as far as the locals were concerned. After going through plenty of booze and French girls, the latter of which Mel was quick to report that Danny did not indulge in on account of his sweetheart, they split up for one reason or another. That was the last time Mel saw him, during or after the war."

"So why is Danny listed as MIA?"

Tayte tried his coffee again and this time he held on to it. "Mel goes some way to explaining that," he said. "Apparently, Danny was down as AWOL for a time, but Mel thought there must have been some mix up, or that someone was covering for him. He was concerned that Danny never said anything to him about going AWOL, and knowing him the way he did, he was certain that his friend wasn't the kind of soldier to walk out on a fight and leave his unit behind."

"Did he ever challenge Danny's status?" Jonathan asked.

"He did, but he goes on to say that no one in authority was ever keen to open an enquiry."

Tayte reached into his briefcase and pulled out several photographic printouts that he'd made at the hotel before he left. He passed them across the table to Jonathan.

"Mel spent years after the war gathering all kinds of information himself - conducting his own enquiry. He even went back to Paris on a number of occasions, talking to people, trying to retrace his and Danny's footsteps."

Jonathan was studying one of the monochrome printouts. "Gay Paree, indeed."

Tayte went over and sat beside him so he could see the images. "That's Danny there," he said, indicating a blonde-haired GI sitting at a table outside a café with several other soldiers. Everyone was laughing and drinking with a girl between each of them. "Someone in Danny's unit took that photo," Tayte added. "The rest of the pictures were taken by other soldiers in the area at the time. Mel said he'd found out who got passes to Paris that same week. Of those who survived the war, he's contacted most over the years and that's how he managed to gather all these pictures together. "There's a full-face portrait of Danny in there somewhere."

Jonathan flicked through them and found it. "Good looking boy," he said. "I'm not surprised Mena fell for him."

"That sharp dress-uniform must have helped, too," Tayte said.

Jonathan went through the rest of the images while Tayte looked on. They were happy scenes of people caught in the moment as if they hadn't a care in the world: a bottle of champagne being shaken over a crowd in celebration of just being alive - the cost of that bottle meaning so little at a time when the man holding it couldn't know whether he would live long enough to spend his pay. There was another soldier engaged in a kiss like he knew it might be his last, held for all eternity by the click of a camera shutter.

Tayte stood up and went back to his briefcase. "There's another image I want to show you," he said, and he was smiling to himself as he brought it out. It was attached by a paper clip to the morning newspaper he'd picked up in the hotel lobby on his way out. It was the main reason for his excitement. He handed the image to Jonathan, keeping the newspaper back for now. It showed a smaller group in the corner of a smoke-filled bar: two soldiers having a drink together, one with white-blonde hair who was clearly Danny. The other could have been just about anyone. Only Tayte knew now that it wasn't just anyone.

He let Jonathan study the image for a while to see if he could recognise the other man. When he didn't, he held the newspaper up in front of him and let it fall open on the front page. "He's with Edward Buckley," he said.

Jonathan looked at the newspaper and back at the image. "My goodness, I think you're right."

Tayte had no doubt. The photograph of Edward and Mary, which Jonathan had previously shown him, was small and less memorable, but the newspaper headline of 'Slain war hero!' and the full-page image of Captain Edward Buckley of the British 1st Airborne Division, made the comparison clear.

"So..." Jonathan said. "Edward Buckley was in Paris at the same time as Danny."

Tayte nodded. "And it could be more than just a coincidence. Mel had singled this photo out. It was the last picture he'd found of Danny before he went missing."

"Do you think Edward has something to do with Danny's disappearance?"

Tayte sat down again. "I don't know,' he said. "I really don't. Maybe he helped him go AWOL - helped him get back to Mena. Joan Cartwright told me there was a rumour going around that Edward had helped Mena leave home. Maybe he hooked the pair of them up."

"Maybe it has something to do with why Edward Buckley was murdered yesterday," Jonathan said, glancing at the newspaper again.

"Yes, maybe it has," Tayte said.

He'd been thinking about the connection since putting Edward and Danny together in that scene, but he hadn't really drawn any conclusions. Being with Danny at or around the time he went missing from his unit offered him no reason as to why anyone would want to kill Buckley. And why now, over seventy years later? Tayte didn't know. He thought there might be something to it, but he knew he didn't have enough information to take it anywhere, so he planned to focus on finding Mena now. As he figured he'd seen everyone he was going to see, he hoped Jonathan had something good for him.

Jonathan stood up. "Now, what about this tin I've found," he said as if reading Tayte's mind. "It's in my study if you'd like to follow me."

Parked in the lane outside the Lasseter house, screened by a tangle of brambles and low hawthorn branches, a dark green Land Rover Defender shook into life. It had been there since sunrise and the driver had been forced to start the engine from time to time to keep out the cold. He left it running and got out of the vehicle, dry leaves crackling beneath his shoes as he picked his way deeper into the verge, pushing the prickly foliage aside to get a clear view of the house.

When he found one, he removed the glasses that were pinched to the bridge of his nose and lifted a high-magnification riflescope to one eye. He used the limb of a branch to steady it, breath lingering like freezing fog around him as he scoped the house and the cars on the drive. There were two cars, but he was only interested in the silver Vauxhall that hadn't been there when he'd first arrived. He made a mental note of the registration and continued to study the house and the windows, looking for activity until the cold began to make the lens shake in his hands.

He went back to the car where he would wait. With Buckley taken care of he'd planned on paying Joan Cartwright a visit today, but he deemed that no longer necessary - just as it was now no longer necessary to visit with Jonathan and his wife. Anything they knew about Mena Lasseter was surely now known to the American.

Two birds with one bullet.

He knew Tayte would show up at the Lasseter house eventually, but that he had come to him so soon had been an unexpected bonus. It would save time and that was all-important to him. But he didn't want to be hasty. The American was going to find Mena for him. All he had to do now was to watch and be patient.

The tin box Jonathan had found in the attic was sitting on an old pine desk by a window that looked out onto bare fields, stripped and cold in the pale winter sunlight. Jonathan went straight to it and Tayte followed him, eyeing all the old medical books that were lined up on shelves around the room.

"Most of them belonged to my grandfather," Jonathan said, noting Tayte's interest. He picked the tin box up and handed it to Tayte. "And I suspect that this belonged to my grandmother, Margaret."

Tayte studied it, turning it in his hands. It was an old cash tin. He'd seen plenty just like it before. It was black and gold with a red line around the lid and there was a gold-coloured handle on top. He could see where Jonathan had attacked it, scarring the paint and twisting the metal. The hinges squealed as he opened it and inside he found a small stack of papers. Old family papers always put a smile on Tayte's face and this was no exception.

"I've been through them," Jonathan said. "I think you'll be particularly interested in the top two."

Tayte lifted them out and put the tin back onto the desk. The papers were pink and thin and as he unfolded the first he saw that the writing had faded to the point of being barely legible in places. The printed detail on what was clearly a carbon copy was much clearer.

"Trinity House," Tayte read aloud. "The Sisters of Enlightened Providence. Catholic home for unmarried mothers." He looked at Jonathan. "It's a consent form to a mother-and-baby home." He scanned the faded handwritten detail and could just make out the name, 'Philomena Lasseter'. It was dated December 1944, confirming his earlier idea that Mena had run away from home at the end of that year in an attempt to keep her baby. But Tayte knew she hadn't kept it and he thought maybe the contents of this tin box would confirm why.

"Look at the other form," Jonathan said, pre-empting his next move.

Tayte unfolded it, expecting to find it identical in every respect apart from the date. They were both consent forms to the same mother-and-baby home and both were signed by Margaret Lasseter, this one dated early February 1945. But there was one other significant difference.

"Mena Fitch," Tayte said under his breath, recalling the name on his client's original birth certificate.

The form had answered the question of why Mena was recorded under her mother's maiden name and he supposed that Margaret Lasseter had registered her under this alias to disassociate her daughter from the family and the shame she felt her condition had caused.

"So Mena came home again," Jonathan said. "How come Dad never knew about it? He was back from the war a few months later. Even if he hadn't heard directly, surely Granddad Pop would have told him where she was."

Tayte thought about that. It seemed probable that whatever plans Mena had when she left home didn't turn out how she'd hoped they would. Or maybe she had been found and brought back against her will. He thought about Mena's visit with Joan, when she'd taken her letters and her pendant to her for safekeeping, perhaps knowing that they would be confiscated either by her mother or the Sisters of Enlightened Providence. It was in late January, Joan had said. Mena clearly meant to return for them, but she had not - or she had been unable to. He began to wonder how long Mena might have been detained at Trinity House. He picked up the tin again and began to scratch through the contents looking for similar forms.

"Was there anything else from this place?" he asked.

"Not that I could see," Jonathan said.

Tayte kept looking. "Many of these mother-and-baby homes were little more than sweatshops," he said. "A throwback from the Victorian era." He found a receipt for something and quickly dismissed it. "In many cases you could only get out again if a member of your family came to claim you." He looked up from the tin and eyed Jonathan seriously. "Right now," he added, "I'm guessing that as your father didn't know what became of Mena, and as your grandfather doesn't appear to have mentioned anything to him either, I suspect that your grandmother, Margaret, was the only person in the family who knew Mena was there."

Tayte reached the bottom of the tin and a chilling thought gripped him. He hadn't looked into Mena's wider family. This assignment had so far been all about finding Mena - making the connection. Charting the family tree was something for later if his client wished it.

"When did Margaret die?" he said.

Jonathan scratched his chin. "Now let me think," he said. "I remember Dad telling me she died before I was born - that was in 1950. I only knew Granddad Pop and I was about five or six when he died." He scratched at his chin some more. "Now wait a minute. I know this one," he added, like he was in the middle of a quiz game. Several seconds later, he said, "George Orwell!"

"What, 1984?" Tayte said, confused.

"No, when the book was published. That was in 1948. Dad was a big Orwell fan. He was always filling my head with things like that."

"Are you sure?" Tayte said. "Or should I get my laptop out?'

"No, I'm positive. Margaret died in 1948. Just don't ask me what she died of."

"Three years after Mena went into the home," Tayte mused. "It's not long after, is it?"

"What are you thinking?"

"Right now I'm thinking the worst," Tayte said. "But I hope I'm wrong. If Mena was still with the Sisters of Enlightened Providence when her mother died, who else was there to go and claim her if no one else knew she was there? Under a partly false name she would have become lost in the system."

"I see," Jonathan said. "So she could have been there for a very long time?"

Tayte gave him a slow nod. "There, or she could have been transferred someplace else. There were numerous institutions like this around at the time - many of which still operated to the Victorian moral standards in which they were established."

"Well let's hope Margaret collected her before she died," Jonathan said. "Although, wouldn't Mena have come home if she had?"

Tayte had been thinking the same thing but he'd concluded that they couldn't know what Mena might do or where she would go. He thought that after being forced to give up her baby, maybe she didn't want to go home.

"I was planning on visiting the local record office today," he said. "I might get some more answers there and these consent forms should give me a head-start. Maybe you'd like to come along?"

"I'd love to," Jonathan said. "I've nothing planned for today. That's if you're sure I won't be in the way."

Tayte smiled. "Believe me," he said. "I need all the help I can get and I might have some more questions for you yet." He flicked a hand at the consent forms he was still holding. "I'd like to go and check out Trinity House first, though," he added. "It's probably the quickest way to find out if it's still there and I like to visit locations to get a sense of place whenever I can."

Jonathan leaned in and read the address. "It's just north of the city," he said. "Shouldn't take more than twenty minutes."

"Great," Tayte said. "See, you're helping already."

Chapter Thirty-Five

It took little time to discover that Trinity House was no longer at the address printed on the old consent forms. It was evident as soon as Tayte turned the car onto the road it once stood on that the whole area had been redeveloped into what was now a sprawling housing estate to accommodate city expansion and the inevitable growth of Leicester's population. The home for unmarried mothers that had once stood in the middle of it all was now a shopping arcade, which according to the plaque set above the main entrance, had originally been built in 1959 and it had since been expanded and modernised. That information set Tayte wondering what had happened to all the girls who were interned at Trinity House when it closed. As he turned the car around and headed back towards Leicester, he hoped he would soon find out.

The record office for Leicestershire, Leicester and Rutland, was located in the town of Wigston, which neighboured Oadby to the southeast, and although Jonathan hadn't been to the record office before, he knew the area well enough to tell Tayte where Long Street was. They took the ring road around the city and it didn't take long to get there in the late morning traffic.

Tayte parked in the visitor car park, collected his briefcase from the back seat and he and Jonathan strolled the short distance to the record office entrance. He thought it looked like a converted schoolhouse that had been extended over the years into the complex it now was. It had sections of tall, white-painted windows set into the red brick walls, behind which he could easily imagine school assembly and gym classes taking place.

As they drew closer, Tayte felt his pulse rise. He knew that adoption agencies and homes like Trinity House were originally only required to keep records for twenty-five years - a requirement that was extended to between seventy-five and a hundred years from the 1970s - but on so many occasions he'd found exceptions to the rules. That was what he liked about local record offices: you never really knew what you might find until you started looking.

Inside, Tayte handed over his briefcase in exchange for a numbered locker key and they had to register before they were allowed access to the archives. They were directed to a high-ceilinged room that had document boxes stacked on shelves around the perimeter, and in the middle of the room they passed a line of chairs at a long table loaded with microform readers. At the end of the table they came to an annexed reading room where a few visitors were sitting hunched over documents. To their left, a middle-aged woman sitting behind an L-shaped desk smiled and greeted them as they approached."

"Hello. How can I help?"

Tayte returned the woman's smile. "I'm looking for information about a local mother-and-baby home that operated in the 1940s. I know it's a long shot but do you keep anything here from that time?"

The woman's head started to shake even before Tayte had finished his enquiry. "I'm sorry," she said, "So few records of privately run homes for unmarried mothers survive today. We don't have anything here at all."

Tayte's shoulders slumped. He thought there might have been something.

"The main items we have that might be of interest to you," the woman continued, "are for the Diocese of Leicester Board of Social Work - formerly the Leicester Diocesan Moral Welfare Association. It was established for young people in moral danger, such as unmarried mothers, and it became an adoption society in 1943, although that function ceased in 1980."

"Of what religious denomination is the Diocese of Leicester?" Tayte asked, thinking there might still be some hope if the Diocese was Catholic.

"Anglican," the woman said, killing that hope dead.

Tayte sighed. "I see. Well, thanks for your time." He turned away and headed out.

"So that's it?" Jonathan said as he caught up with him.

"I need a coffee," Tayte said. "I saw a machine on the way through. I need to think."

The coffee machine was in a small rest area close to the main reception desk. They stood with their drinks as they talked.

"If Mena went to Trinity House in 1945," Tayte said. "Then as I see it there are only three ways that she left. Reason one - someone claimed her. Two - she died while she was there. Three - she was transferred, either in 1959 when the home closed or sometime before."

"I think we've already ruled out option one," Jonathan said. "If Margaret - perhaps being the only person who knew she was there - had claimed her, she would have brought Mena home again and I know that didn't happen or Dad would have said."

Tayte agreed. "And I'm pretty sure that we can rule out option two. If she'd died while at the home, I would have found a record in the local indexes. I've already checked them for Mena Lasseter and Fitch."

"So you think she was transferred?"

"It seems the most likely scenario of the three and that raises two new questions. Where and when?"

"But isn't there a fourth scenario?" Jonathan said. "She could have escaped."

Tayte had considered that but he'd ruled it out for the simple reason that if Mena had escaped, she would have gone to Joan for her letters and pendant.

"No," he said. "She didn't escape." He gazed thoughtfully out the window and watched the lunchtime traffic go by. "To find out where Mena was transferred," he added, "I need to find records for a Catholic home whose records no longer exist."

"Quite a conundrum," Jonathan said.

Tayte drained his coffee back and tossed the paper cup into the waste bin. "I'd better drop you home," he said. "I need to think my way around this and it's not going to be much fun. Sometimes you just have to grind things out and I think this is one of those times." He fished in his pocket for his locker key so he could reclaim his briefcase. As they headed for reception, he added, "I'll call you as soon as I get a breakthrough."

Tayte stepped outside with Jonathan and noticed that it was getting much colder, which he put down to the clear skies. The air numbed his nose and dried his throat and every breath seemed to freeze in front of him as he let it go. As they joined the pavement, slotting in with a few other people going about their business, Jonathan turned to him with a puzzled expression.

"I've been thinking about that photo you showed me earlier," he said.

"Mel's photo? Danny and Edward in Paris?"

"Yes, there's something familiar about it that's been bugging me all morning and I can't seem to put my finger on it. Can I have another look?"

"Sure."

Tayte slowed the pace and popped the clasp on his briefcase. With his free hand he rifled through the contents and pulled the image out.

"Here you go," he said, handing it to Jonathan.

They were ambling now, Tayte with his briefcase tucked under his arm as Jonathan studied the image again, screwing up his face as he did so. Tayte watched him with eager eyes hoping for some new revelation, but none came. When they reached the car park entrance, Jonathan shook his head and handed the image back.

"I'm sorry," he said. "It's not helping."

"Maybe it'll come to you if you stop thinking about it," he offered. "It works for me."

He balanced his briefcase on his knee and tried to slot the sheet of paper back inside, which quickly resulted in him hopping and stumbling and dropping the case. The contents spilled out across the pavement and Tayte cursed under his breath. Jonathan came to help him, but another man beat him to it. Tayte looked up as someone in a navy pinstripe suit squatted beside him.

"Madame Bovary," the man said. He picked up the book and adjusted the glasses that were pinched to the bridge of his nose as he opened it. "It's a little overdue," he added.

"It's not mine," Tayte said.

"So I see," the man mused, studying the inside cover. He opened the book at the page Tayte had marked with the nametape. "I'm partial to the classics myself. Poor old Charles, eh?"

"I haven't finished it yet," Tayte said, still putting all the papers back into his briefcase.

"Well you must finish it soon," the man said. He closed the book and passed it to Tayte, holding on to it as he looked him in the eyes and added, "I have a fear of dying partway through a book - of never knowing the ending. It's silly, I know, but it makes me a quick reader."

"I'll bet," Tayte said. He offered him an awkward smile and the man released the book. "Well, thanks for your help," he added. Then he turned, exchanged bemused glances with Jonathan and the pair of them headed into the car park.

Chapter Thirty-Six

By nine p.m. that evening, Tayte had a pile of room service trays filled with dirty crockery on the floor and not too many Hershey's miniatures left in the emergency bag he'd been saving for his return flight home. The crockery was piling up because he had a 'do not disturb' sign on the door as he didn't want anyone coming into the room to take the old trays away, distracting him any more than was necessary to bring them to him in the first place. The desk he'd been sitting at with his laptop all this time resembled a field of crop circles where his coffee cup had been filled and refilled and spilt so many times, but he paid no mind to any of it.

Grind it out. Grind it out.

He kept thinking that and saying it to himself whenever he lost the thread on his latest line of research, which was often. It was a familiar phrase that took him back to the long days and nights where he would shut himself away, trying in vain to research his own family history - the deep stuff. He wasn't drinking this time, though. He needed a clear head and knew from painful experience that Jack Daniels wouldn't help him to find what he was looking for.

So how do you find records for a home whose records no longer exist?

The obvious answer was that you couldn't, so Tayte knew he had to find a way around the problem. First, he wanted to be sure that Mena went to Trinity House; the consent forms showed her mother's intent to send her there, but it didn't prove that Mena actually went. After that he wanted to know when she left and he knew she had to have by 1959 because that was when the home closed down. Most importantly, if Mena was at Trinity House, he wanted to know where she went from there.

From those questions, Tayte figured that if he could answer the last one first, he would in effect answer all of them together. That was his way around the problem of there being no surviving records for Trinity house, but after several hours of trawling the Internet, following every Mena, Philomena, Lasseter and Fitch result he could find, he concluded that working his way around the problem had been the easy part. His hair was already sticking up and out every which way through continually shoving his frustrated fingers through it. He did it again and then popped another *Mr Goodbar* miniature into his mouth, having saved the best for last.

So where would everyone from a Catholic mother-and-baby home go when that home closed down?

Tayte must have asked himself that question ten times already. He was fixated with the idea that they would have been sent to another Catholic home. The Catholic Church was very tight knit, but in his experience it was also very guarded. He was beginning to suppose that might be the reason he couldn't find anything.

What if Mena was transferred before it closed down?

He thought it was time to move on to another line of investigation because the mini bar had started calling to him and he knew he wouldn't be able to ignore it if he didn't get a breakthrough soon.

Why would she have been transferred?

The reasons were limited as he saw it. Either she was too unruly for the home to manage - in which case she would have been sent somewhere with more discipline and control - or she was physically or mentally ill. If she was ill she would have been sent to a hospital, maybe with a view to being returned, or maybe not if the home had closed down in the meantime. Either route presented many possibilities and further problems, but Tayte figured he had all night and all day tomorrow if it came to it.

Or the day after that.

It was just after eleven p.m. when Tayte thought he'd exhausted the direct approach and it had yielded nothing. With the advent of the World Wide Web and its exponential growth in the last decade, Tayte was more and more of the opinion that any information you were looking for was out there somewhere in one form or another. What was becoming all the more important was that you had to know what you were looking for or the data would drown you.

Tayte felt like he was drowning now.

He got up and made a fresh jug of coffee and when he sat down again he finished the last of his Hershey's and turned his thoughts to the indirect approach. He couldn't find Mena, but perhaps he could find someone who knew her. He started with a search for the Sisters of Enlightened Providence, but with no matching results he quickly moved on.

Running a general search for Trinity House was something Tayte had hoped to avoid because it was such a common name, but he had no choice. He began with the address but that was too specific and also returned no matches. When he Googled 'Trinity House' he found that there were almost one million results worldwide. He thought to narrow it down to the UK, but how could he know that the link he hoped to find wasn't on a server in some other part of the world - a reference to the home, made by someone who now lived abroad?

"Gotta be thorough, JT," he told himself.

He added Leicester to the search thinking that any reference to the home had to include at least its broad location, but there were still some two hundred thousand results. He sat back with a sigh, drank his coffee and refilled it from the jug, knowing that it was going to be a very long night.

Two hours later, he concluded that he had to try another approach again because after all that time it was clear that he hadn't even scratched the surface. A few links had looked promising enough and had kept him going but they had subsequently led nowhere. There was just so much reading to do - scanning through the details.

The pain that was building in the centre of his eyes told him they were bloodshot. He rubbed them and yawned. Then he picked up the hotel phone and ordered a snack from the 24-hour room service menu to keep him going. Pushing on again, he added 'Catholic' to the search, having no idea whether one or more of the twenty thousand results would yield any reference to the Trinity House he was looking for. He scanned pages and pages of data. Then at around four a.m. he sat bolt upright up in his chair.

He was looking at a name that filled him with dread from all the stories he'd read about in recent years: *Magdalene*. He clicked the link and was presented with a website for survivors of the now infamous Magdalene asylums or laundries as they had later become known, which began in Dublin, Ireland, in 1765 and by the 20th century operated in countries throughout the world. He'd read that they were little more than labour camps and that many were operated like prisons to serve the local communities under the guise of rescuing fallen women, who could be sent there for little more reason than being thought too attractive to the opposite sex and therefore in 'moral danger'. Right there and then Tayte hoped with all his heart that Mena had not ended her days in such a place.

The last laundry had closed as recently as 1996 following public scandal over the discovery of the remains of one hundred and fifty-five bodies three years earlier, when the Catholic Sisters of Our Lady of

Charity sold one of their properties in north Dublin to developers in order to raise funds. Of all the exhumed remains only seventy-five deaths had been registered and of the eighty remaining, twenty-four could not even be sufficiently identified. It put Tayte in mind of the protestant-run, Bethany Home: another religious place of detention he'd heard of which had faced similar outrage in the 1970s, reminding him that such homes were not unique to the Catholic religion.

Tayte scrolled down, looking for the connection to Trinity House. He saw images of several women and began to read a little of each account - of the hidden attitudes and conditions that surely belonged to the Dark Ages and yet were as recent as the latter half of the twentieth century. When he saw the reference to Trinity House he leant in closer, hoping that it was the connection he was looking for, yet at the same time praying it was not.

"Audrey Marsh," Tayte said under his breath.

He was looking at the image of a grey-haired woman he thought was in her mid to late seventies, noting that her entry had been added to the website a little over a year ago. He began to read through her account, which told the harsh and often brutal story of her life at a Magdalene laundry. Then when he came to the reference to Trinity House he paused. There it was. He read 'Leicester' and the year '1959', which was the year Trinity House had closed down and Audrey Marsh - perhaps with all the other girls who were then in the care of the Sisters of Enlightened Providence - had been transferred to a Magdalene laundry. It made perfect sense. All Tayte wanted to know now was whether Mena had been transferred along with her.

He sat back and let out a long sigh. He'd been staring at his screen for so long now that the text had started to look fuzzy. Every now and then the words seemed to jiggle in front of him. There was a comments box at the bottom of the screen. He expanded it and saw several comments and responses, some as recent as a few months ago. They offered no further answers but every comment had been responded to, so he quickly registered with his email address and typed in a comment of his own, stating who he was and whom he was looking for, ending with the key question of whether Audrey knew Mena Fitch or had ever heard of her.

As he closed his eyes and laid his head on the desk - *just for a minute*, he thought - he hoped that Audrey Marsh was still monitoring the website and that she would get an email alert to notify her of his comments.

"Sometimes, you just have to grind it out," he mumbled to himself - right before exhaustion overcame him and he fell asleep.

Some hours later, Tayte awoke with a start. He sat up and looked around the room like he didn't know where he was for a second. Then as consciousness fully caught up with him and he saw his laptop on the desk in front of him, he noticed that he'd received a new email. It must have been the sound of its arrival that woke him. He sniffed and drew a deep breath, yawned and rubbed his neck and the side of his face that felt numb from being pressed against the desk for so long. He checked his watch as he opened the email. It was a little after eight a.m. Wednesday.

The email was a private message notification from the website he'd used to contact former Trinity House and Magdalene laundry intern, Audrey Marsh. He followed the link and read the message.

Hello, Mr Tayte,

Yes, there was someone called Fitch at Trinity House while I was there - although as I recall, she didn't like being called Fitch by the Sisters. I don't know why. I'd completely forgotten her first name until I read your comments. My mother took me to the home in 1955 when I was sixteen and Mena was already there when I arrived. She was much older than me, or so she seemed at the time, and I never really knew her - I don't think she had many friends. I remember her because she always used to talk when she wasn't supposed to, even though she knew she would be beaten for it. There were only around 30 girls at the home, so it was easy to stand out.

Please let me know if there's anything else I can help you with.

Audrey.

"Beaten," Tayte said under his breath. Audrey's email was the proof he was looking for, but reading it had angered him. He checked the timestamp against Audrey's message and noted that it was only five minutes old. He quickly hit the reply button and sent another message, asking whether Audrey knew what became of Mena. Had she been transferred with the rest of the girls when the home closed down? Was everyone transferred to Magdalene laundries? He sent it and sat tapping the desk while he waited for an answer. When none came he got up and set about making a fresh pot of coffee. He was in the bathroom washing his cup out when he heard the new message alert and raced back to his laptop.

Hello again, Mr Tayte,

Mena left the home a couple of years before the rest of us - sometime in 1957, I think. I believe she was sent to the 'Borough'. All the girls called it that but I never knew what it meant. I'm sorry I can't be more specific.

Audrey.

Tayte was glad to hear that Mena had at least avoided the Magdalene route that Audrey and so many other girls had suffered. But where had she gone?

"The Borough?" he mused.

He wondered what that was, concluding that he didn't have much to go on, although he'd already considered the kind of places Mena would have been transferred to. He thought it had to be another Catholic home or a hospital. He opened another Web browser and typed, 'the Borough'. Then he added, 'Leicestershire', thinking to start the search locally. There were half a million results. He added, 'home', which didn't help. Then he tried 'hospital' which was worse, increasing the results to over a million and none of those on the first few pages were of any relevance; most being references to the Leicester borough council.

He decided to put the search on hold while he had a line of communication open with Audrey. He had some more questions to ask and he didn't want to lose her, so he sent another message, asking if she recalled anything that Mena used to talk about when she wasn't supposed to talk. It had intrigued him that she would blatantly go against the rules, knowing that she would be punished. He wondered what was so important to her that she couldn't seem to help herself. The reply came back within a few minutes.

Mr Tayte,

Mena used to talk about the war as I recall. She would say that when it was over her husband was coming for her and that they were going to live somewhere far away from there. I don't recall where, but she used to talk about a river. It was a little fantasy she'd made up, I suppose, because of course if she had been married she wouldn't have been at Trinity House in the first place.

She was a quiet girl most of the time. Then suddenly she would start talking and talking and none of the sisters could stop her. I remember laughing at her the first few times and I came to be very sorry for doing so when I saw the trouble it got her into. It was 1955 and she seemed to think the war was still on. One of the older girls - we were all 'girls' to the sisters regardless of how old we were - used to try to tell her that the war had been over for years, but she wouldn't believe it. She would get angry in the long run and the orderlies soon came for her then. I suppose her rationale was that if the war was over, her man would have come for her. But because he hadn't - because she was still there - the war must therefore still be on.

That's about all I remember about her. It's funny how some things stay with you, isn't it? But then I can still recall so much about those years, even though I would sooner forget them.

Good luck with your search, Mr Tayte.

Audrey.

Tayte sent a final message to Audrey, thanking her, knowing that it must have been painful for to recall those times. He read through her last message again and it seemed clear to him that by 1955, when Audrey was sent to Trinity House, Mena was already suffering a mental breakdown. He wondered how bad she was and would later become; what drugs and treatments had been administered and whether any of it had helped her or made matters worse. He went back to his Google search and added the word, 'Asylum', which he knew was still a common term for psychiatric hospitals at the time, despite changing attitudes to such naming conventions. The first three results that came back were links to the UK National Archives.

He followed the first link and quickly learned that the Leicester Borough Lunatic Asylum had indeed changed its name at some point to the Leicester Towers Hospital. The catalogue referred largely to building works so he checked the second link and this proved more useful. It contained an administrative history that told him the asylum had opened in 1869, that it had changed from lunatic asylum to mental hospital in 1912, and that it had acquired its present name of the Towers Hospital in 1947, which had been its registered name when Mena was admitted in 1957.

She would have been in her late twenties - maybe thirty, Tayte thought, wondering how old she was when she left.

He scanned the catalogue entries, which were exactly what he was looking for: admission and patient registers, observations, treatments and discharge books. He saw that the records had been deposited at the record office in Wigston and he hurriedly wrote the catalogue reference number in his notepad. Then he held his breath as he read the words, 'Mental health has always been a sensitive social issue. Therefore, this collection is closed for one hundred years in order to protect patients both living and within living memory.'

Tayte just stared at the text. Of course they were closed. Such records invariably were, he knew that. He figured he was just so tired and so caught up in the chase that he hadn't given it a thought until it had hit him in the face.

"That's just great," he said to his laptop screen. "Now I need to see records that *do* exist, but which I'm not allowed access to."

Knowing that they were just a few miles from his hotel room didn't make him feel any better and he started to wonder how he could get to them, maybe under the pretence of seeing something he was allowed to see. Then, when no one was looking, he could... He curled his hands into fists and pressed them into his temples.

"Get a grip, JT," he told himself. "This is real life, not some damn movie." He stood up. "More coffee. More research. That's what you need."

He scanned the detritus around him - the battlefield that had become his hotel room - and thought that he needed to clean the place up - and himself while he was at it.

Soon, he thought. *Let's just find out some more about the Towers Hospital first.*

A few minutes later he was sipping hot coffee at his laptop again, promising his groaning stomach that he would feed it soon. On his screen was a website that told him the hospital had closed to patients in the summer of 2005. He saw images of an imposing three-storey Victorian gothic building with a black slate roof, stone mullioned windows and Dutch gables. He learnt that this was the original part of what had since become a sprawling fifty-eight acre complex. Other images showed parts of the complex, inside and out, that looked like they hadn't been touched in years, although there was no indication as to when the photographs had been taken.

He moved on, gathering information. On another website he read that the hospital had sold off parts of the complex to housing developers who planned to turn the original grade II listed building into apartments. That news made his heart sink until he read that the Leicestershire NHS Partnership Trust had its headquarters in part of the hospital complex and that it still employed hundreds of people.

Hundreds of people...

He started to wonder where all the patients went when the hospital closed in 2005 and he realised then that it had only closed to new patients. Since then the hospital had gradually been wound down. He didn't like to think that Mena could still be there after all this time, but he thought there was a chance that if not then maybe some of the patients were. Why else keep staff at the premises?

He drained his coffee back and stood up. If he wasn't allowed to see the hospital records, he was resolved to go there and see what else he could find. He thought he'd call Jonathan to see if he wanted to go along, but not until he'd shaved and showered and felt human again.

Chapter Thirty-Seven

Outside, it was another bright and crisp morning, the pale sun still low over Oadby's fields as Tayte pulled up outside the Lasseter house. He was about to get out of the car when he saw Jonathan come to meet him and he grinned to himself at seeing this man, who had so willingly become his assignment companion, skip across the gravel as he fought to put his coat on. He had something in his hands, which he began to wave at Tayte as he approached.

"I've realised what else was familiar about that photo from Paris," he said, his face alive with enthusiasm. "Can I see it again? Do you have it with you?"

Tayte wondered what he was holding. It looked like another photograph.

"It's in my briefcase," he said as he reached behind him and retrieved it from the back seat.

Jonathan got in. "It's Mary," he said. "I'm sure of it, but I'd like another look just to be certain."

"Mary?"

Tayte wondered what he'd missed. He quickly found the photograph and passed it to Jonathan, who placed his photograph alongside it. It was a family scene with George Lasseter - Pop - and his wife, Margaret in the foreground, and various other family members were in the background.

"See here," Jonathan said, tapping the image of one of the background figures, whom Tayte clearly recognised as Mary Lasseter in her ATS uniform. "Look at the pose," Jonathan added. "Note the cigarette."

Tayte nodded. "Got it."

"Now look at this." Jonathan slid his hand across to the Paris bar scene. There were people in the background there, too. "He tapped a finger on an indistinct shape, a silhouette almost, of someone standing further back and to the left of Edward Buckley. "I'm sure that's Mary," he said. "Look at the way she's holding her cigarette."

Tayte leant in and brought the images closer together until they overlapped. There was no way of knowing who the person Jonathan had highlighted in Mel's photograph was, but the size and shape of what was evidently a woman's figure was very similar. He studied the way Mary held her arm at her side, elbow bent in a V-shape so that the cigarette in her hand hovered close to ear. It was perhaps not a unique way to hold a cigarette, but it was identical in both images.

"It has to be her," Jonathan said. "It's been bothering me all night and this morning after you called I started going through all the old family photos again. I must have seen it when we looked through them before."

Tayte was still studying the images. "If it is her," he said. "It's some coincidence that they both happened to be there in what we know to have been allied occupied Paris around the time Danny was reported missing."

Tayte liked the coincidence less for knowing now that Danny had not gone AWOL for Mena. He had not come back for her as he'd hoped. At least, if he had then he had not found her - and how could he when she'd been secretly incarcerated at the Trinity House home for unmarried mothers and later transferred to the 'Borough' mental hospital?

So why did Danny Danielson go missing in allied territory in November 1944?

He turned to Jonathan, thinking the unthinkable and seeing those dark thoughts reflected in Jonathan's earnest stare.

Did Mary or Edward have anything to do with it? Could they both be implicated?

His thoughts strayed to Buckley's murder two days ago and then to the man who had telephoned Joan Cartwright, looking for Mena. *Was there a connection?* He supposed there was and he thought again that whatever was being played out now had been triggered by Mary's recent death - the catalyst that had caused the ghosts of the past to catch up with the present.

Tayte picked up the images. He knew he could speculate all he wanted to on why Edward and now Mary, it seemed, were there in Paris with Danny around the time he went missing, but what did he have? A photograph of three wartime friends in Paris. It didn't mean a thing and he knew that it proved even less.

He turned to Jonathan again. "Let's not get carried away," he said. "Do you mind if I keep both pictures together for now?"

Jonathan shook his head and Tayte slid them into his briefcase.

"I'd like to stick with trying to find Mena for now," he said. "Do you know where Humberstone is?"

"It's just a few miles north-east from here."

"Good. I have a feeling that if we can find Mena, we'll find the answers to a lot of things."

Chapter Thirty-Eight

When they arrived at what was formerly the Borough Lunatic Asylum, Tayte thought it looked every bit as gothic as it had in the images he'd seen online. What he hadn't been able to appreciate on his small laptop screen was the almost overwhelming size of the 19th century main building, with its watchful towers and myriad windows, behind which he imagined countless rooms linked by endless corridors. On the way there, Tayte had brought Jonathan up to date with his research and the reason he wanted to visit the site.

"But surely you don't think she's still here?" Jonathan said.

Tayte turned the car off Gipsy Lane, heading further into the complex. "No, I don't," he said. "I just wanted to see the place and ask a few questions if I can. You never know when another door's going to open and apart from getting an idea of how someone lived, visiting the places they inhabited can be a great stimulus."

Jonathan was still taking it all in, eyes fixed out of the front window as they drew closer. "It's hard to believe that Mena was so close to home all these years and no one knew," he said. He sighed. "And while I was growing up, enjoying a normal, happy childhood."

Tayte didn't know what to say about that so he said nothing. Out of the car windows to either side of him he saw line after line of galvanised wire fencing surrounding the buildings to keep people out. It was clear that the developers who had bought the property - whose banners he could see flapping in the light breeze - were well under way with their plans. Further on he saw a sign inviting him to view one of the recently converted show homes and he began to question what he expected to find here, more than a decade after the hospital had closed. He could hear the hum of builders' machinery somewhere nearby and he wondered where all the health service staff were. The only people he could see were two men in grey suits and white hard-hats. He pulled over just ahead of them and got out of the car.

"Excuse me!" he called, stepping around the car to meet them. "I was under the impression that the hospital kept a staff on after it closed." He looked around at the obvious lack of any activity other than building works. "Doesn't seem to be the case."

The shorter of the two men - surveyors, Tayte assumed - stepped closer. “You’ve come to the wrong block,” he said with a strong east-midlands accent. “The NHS reoccupied some of the newer buildings further down.” He pointed over Tayte’s shoulder. “If you go back out onto the main road and -”

“Reoccupied?” Tayte cut in. “So they can’t have kept any existing patients on,” he added, more to himself than to the surveyor.

“I shouldn’t think so,” the man said. “I believe it’s all admin now and they won’t be there much longer.”

Tayte paused, staring at the car while he tried to figure out his next move. It seemed clear to him that if the buildings had been empty and only later reoccupied, he wasn’t going to find anything out from the staff that were there now. In all likelihood they hadn’t been there more than a few years. He turned back to the surveyor.

“Thanks,” he said. “I’ll find it.”

With that he got back into the car and drove out the way he’d come.

“We’ll go and ask a few questions while we’re here,” he said to Jonathan, but I’m not confident that we’re going to get any answers about a girl who was admitted more than sixty years ago.”

Sitting in a dark green Land Rover Defender, set back in a siding off the main road opposite the former asylum complex, the man at the wheel sat up when he saw Jefferson Tayte’s hire car pull back out onto Gipsy Lane. He turned his key in the ignition and slowly left the cover of trees that lined the roadside, watching intently as the silver Vauxhall completed its right turn. Approximately one hundred metres further along the road, it indicated right again and turned out of sight.

The man in the Defender sped up, turning as the Vauxhall had turned, entering through galvanised steel gates by a blue and white sign that read, ‘Leicester Partnership NHS Trust - George Hine House.’ There was a small car park beyond the gatehouse buildings and the man held back when he saw his quarry stop and get out of the Vauxhall. He watched them march towards the buildings until they disappeared behind a fringe of trees and shrubbery, and when he could no longer see them he selected an appropriate parking space from which to monitor their return.

And there he waited.

Fifteen minutes later he heard a familiar American voice and saw Jefferson Tayte and his companion walking back across the car park, engaged in conversation that he couldn’t make out, but from the body language and the dour expression on the American’s face, he could see that their visit had not proven fruitful. He watched them go to their car and get in, and he was ready to start the Defender up again, but the Vauxhall did not move.

Tayte stared out of the windscreen with his hand paused on the ignition key. "I should have known that would be a waste of time," he said.

"It was worth a try," Jonathan offered.

"Yeah, I guess. It's just so frustrating being referred back to records you know you're not allowed to look at.

He started the engine. Then he stopped it again, wondering how long Mena had been at the hospital and what treatment she might have undergone. He imagined her condition had begun at Trinity House as a form of nervous or mental breakdown, brought on by everything that had happened in 1944 and soon after: being raped, falling in love and being denied that love, and the great injustice of being incarcerated on the brink of womanhood through no fault of her own. He thought it was more than enough to drive anyone to a place like the former Borough Lunatic asylum.

"Where might Mena have gone when she left here?" he said, thinking aloud.

"Are you sure she survived the place?"

Tayte gave a slow nod. "I've thought about that a lot and I'm certain of it. A hospital like this would have registered her death and no death has been registered for Mena Lasseter or Fitch in this county."

"So she could have left any time between 1957 and 2005?" Jonathan said. "That's forty-eight years. It doesn't help to narrow things down much, does it?"

"No, it doesn't," Tayte agreed.

"Do you think she could still have been here when the hospital closed?" Jonathan asked.

"If she was, and presuming that she still needed care, she would have been transferred to another hospital that could take care of her. But it's a long time. I can't see her being here for forty-eight years."

"No," Jonathan agreed. "Although we can't rule it out, can we?"

"No, we can't," Tayte conceded. He just didn't want it to be true; for Mena's sake and because if she had been transferred to another psychiatric hospital as recently as 2005 he knew that he would never find her. He unclipped his seat belt and slouched a little in his seat.

He wasn't going anywhere yet, not least because he didn't know where else to go. "Let's look at what I believe is the only other possible scenario," he said.

"Which is?"

"Which is that somewhere between 1957 and 2005 Mena had recovered sufficiently to be discharged into the community. In which case, where would she go? What would she do?"

"Well she didn't come home," Jonathan said. "That much is certain."

Tayte scoffed. "And who could blame her? I shouldn't think she'd want anything more to do with her old life after all she'd been put through. How could she go back to a family that had abandoned her like that?"

"Yes, I suppose she must have seen it that way."

They both fell quiet with their thoughts and Tayte went over all the checks he'd already made back home. All he'd found for Mena was a birth certificate. If she had been released into the community he thought there would be some other trace of her, but he recalled that when he'd checked online before leaving Washington there wasn't even an entry for her in the recent electoral roll registers - not one match. He thought she couldn't have vanished more thoroughly than if she'd entered into a Federal witness protection programme.

And changed her identity...

Tayte sat up and turned to Jonathan, wide-eyed. "What if she took another name? One she chose for herself this time. Maybe her mother gave her the idea when she sent her to Trinity House under the name of Fitch."

"But didn't you already check?"

"I did. But when you change your name by deed poll in the UK, it isn't automatically logged in any central register. I find that a little scary myself, but it's true. If the person changing their name elects to enrol the details then it gets recorded in the Enrolment Books of the Supreme Court of Judicature and subsequently gets printed in the London or Belfast Gazette where the details are easy to find. But most people who change their name do so with good reason - they don't want to go public."

"So just because you can't find a change of name, doesn't mean it didn't happen?"

"Exactly."

Tayte thought it would explain why he'd found so little information when he'd looked before, and what better way to put such a traumatic past behind you than to disown that past completely and become someone else? Given everything he'd heard since arriving in England, from talking to the family and friends and those who had come to know Mena at one time or another, he didn't have to think twice about the name she would have chosen. It seemed entirely obvious to him now.

"Danielson," he said. "She would have become Mena Danielson."

"Of course," Jonathan agreed.

Tayte twisted around and grabbed his briefcase from the back seat. "According to Audrey Marsh, who was at Trinity House while Mena was there, Mena was telling everyone she was married - that she was waiting for her husband to come and fetch her once the war was over - but it was sheer delusion."

"Perhaps that's how she managed to deal with her situation."

"I don't doubt it," Tayte said. "And she began to believe in the dream. And later on she took his name. It makes perfect sense."

He slid his laptop out from his briefcase and booted it up, wondering if it was possible, even now, that Danny had managed to find her and that she had taken his name without officially marrying him, which would have made them both easier to find if anyone came looking. *Were they together now?* Tayte hoped so and he thought he might soon find out.

"There's a way we should be able to prove this theory," he said, tapping keys. "If she did change her name to Mena Danielson it should appear on the electoral roll registers. Normally it's no good unless you have an address or at least a street name to search by because that's how the original documents are sorted. But the electoral rolls from 2002 are available online and you can search them by name."

There were several websites providing this service: some gave free teaser information, but all charged a fee for the full details. Tayte brought up his preferred website for electoral roll searches - one of many subscription websites he used - and entered the name, 'Mena Danielson' into the search field. His shoulders slumped when the search returned no matches and he crumpled over the keyboard like the wind had just been knocked out of him.

"Come on," he said to the screen. "She has to be there." He needed her to be there.

"Try Philomena Danielson," Jonathan said.

Tayte sat up again. He punched the name in and started the search again. When the result came back this time he just stared at the screen and shook his head. "Nothing?" He turned to Jonathan, his head still shaking. "This can't be right."

"Maybe she chose a different first name, too," Jonathan offered.

Tayte liked the idea. If Mena wanted to leave her past behind, she couldn't very well have kept such an unusual name as Mena or Philomena. He'd come across a few mentions of those names in his earlier searches, but they were few and those that he'd found, other than for her birth certificate, hadn't offered any connection to the Mena he was looking for. The big question now was what name she would have chosen.

"Any thoughts?" he asked. "Any names you've heard from the time she would have been at the house?"

"There were two Great Danes," Jonathan said, "But they were called Xavier and Manfred."

"There was a teddy bear in the suitcase that was sent to my client," Tayte said. "Any idea what she called it?"

Jonathan shook his head.

"I'll do a broad search for Danielson," Tayte said. "See if any of the names ring any bells."

He typed 'Danielson' into the surname field and this time he left the first name field blank. There were 184 matches: male names, female names and some entries with just an initial. He slid the laptop around so Jonathan could better see it and slowly began to scroll through the list.

"Shout out if anything jumps at you," he said. Then as he started to scan the list himself, something did.

"Emma!" he said. He turned to Jonathan with a wide smile on his face. "Emma as in Bovary - from the book. Maybe Mena escaped her past through the character in her book."

Tayte hoped he was right. The age guide seemed to fit well enough, indicating that the subject was between seventy-five and seventy-nine years old at the time the details were recorded. He clicked the name and was presented with another screen that gave details from the 2002 electoral roll, being the first year that it was possible to opt out of the public register. That there wasn't a more recent entry told him that this person had chosen to opt out of all subsequent registers. There was an address in Leicestershire, which was also encouraging.

"It's to the southeast," Jonathan said. "On the border with Northamptonshire."

It was the name of the residence Tayte was interested in. As he took his notebook out and wrote it down, his confidence that he had at last found Mena peaked. "It's a care home," he said.

Chapter Thirty-Nine

Logan House Care Home was on the outskirts of Market Harborough, a rural market town divided from the county of Northamptonshire by the river Welland. The near twenty-mile drive took Tayte no more than half an hour and it was almost midday when the voice from the satnav told him he'd reached his destination. The building was a modern structure, painted white with walls of glass and a slate roof that was fitted with solar panels. It was set in open countryside between weeping willows that had long since shed their leaves, their branches draping like veils over the brook that ran close to the property.

Tayte glanced at Jonathan, smiling pensively as he pulled onto the forecourt and parked the car, knowing there was every chance that he was about to meet the girl - the now elderly woman - whose suitcase had brought him all the way from America. And yet he was nervous about what he might find now that he was there.

They got out of the car together and Tayte collected his briefcase from the back seat. He paused as he looked more closely at the place - only the sound of birdsong in his ears.

Could she really be here?

He had to remind himself that although someone called Emma Danielson had without question been resident at this care home in 2002, he had yet to prove that she and Mena were one and the same person, despite growing odds in favour of that being true. He took a deep breath, knowing there was only one way to find out. They made their way inside.

"Seems nice," Jonathan said.

Tayte just nodded as he took the interior in. It was a bright reception area, made all the more cordial by the expansive windows and unhindered sunlight that washed through them. He expected to see old people and walking-frames being shuffled from one place to the next, but he saw nothing of the kind. Of the few residents he could see, both here and through an open door that looked in on what appeared to be a visitor and patient lounge area, he saw only women and they were of various ages: some old, others less so. One woman who was sitting by the window in the lounge looked closer to his own age.

As he approached the smiling face that greeted him from behind a curved birch-wood reception desk, he saw that Logan House was not a stereotypical, government run home for the elderly but a privately run facility catering for somewhat different needs. He smiled back at the young rosy-cheeked woman behind the desk, who was dressed in a smart, pale blue tunic, and wondered who was paying Emma Danielson's bills.

"Hi," he said. "I've come to enquire about a woman who was staying here in 2002 and I was wondering whether you could tell me if she's still here. Her name's Emma Danielson. She'd be around eighty four years old."

Tayte held on to his smile while he waited for a reply. Then an answer came that told him he was about to hit another barrier.

"Are you next of kin?" the woman asked.

Tayte grabbed Jonathan's arm and pulled him closer. "No, but this is her nephew, Jonathan Lasseter," he said, still smiling. "He's a doctor," he added, like he'd just produced a backstage pass.

"Retired," Jonathan corrected.

The receptionist began to suck air through her teeth. She shook her head. "I'm sorry," she said, "but we're only allowed to give information out to the immediate next of kin - parent, husband or child. Is there someone else you can come back with? We'd need to see two forms of identification as well."

By now, Tayte had already lost his smile. "Her parents are dead," he said. "To my knowledge she never married and her daughter - whom she was forced to give up for adoption a long time ago - lives in America. I think long-haul travel would be an issue for her."

"I see," the woman said. "Well, her daughter can apply for information by post." She swivelled around in her chair and reached beneath the desk. She brought up two forms and slid them towards Tayte. "She'll need to fill these in and send them back to us with her ID, and we'd also need to see her adoption records."

Tayte sighed as he took the forms, knowing the process could take weeks if not months to complete.

"Can't you at least check your records and tell us if she's still here?"

"No, I'm sorry. We have a duty of care to our residents. Their needs must always come first. I'm sure you understand."

Tayte did. Fully. He supposed that this care facility was full of women who had led difficult, probably traumatic lives. The rules were there to protect them.

"I'm sorry," he said. He gave a weak smile and picked up the forms. "Thanks for your time," he added as he turned away.

He had only taken two paces when he stopped himself and turned back to the desk.

"What am I thinking," he said. "My client's adoption records won't mention Emma Danielson. You see - that's not her real name. I mean it's not the name Emma Danielson was born with. She changed it." At least, Tayte hoped that was the case.

The woman smiled sympathetically. "Several of the women staying with us are understandably here under a different name," she said. "Most want to forget their past and we offer to help with that if a guest wishes it. We keep records of any changes of name that occur while a guest is in residence with us."

"That's great," Tayte said, expecting worse. At least there was a chance that Mena had changed her name after she came to Logan House, although he knew there was every possibility that she'd changed it beforehand, in which case the care home would have no record of Mena Fitch or Lasseter and they would not release any records they held for Emma Danielson.

"If your client returns the forms with her documentation," the woman reiterated, "we can go from there, but there's really nothing we can do until then."

"Of course. Thanks for your time," Tayte said. Then he turned away again and headed outside.

"What do we do now?" Jonathan asked as soon as they were out on the forecourt.

"I'm going to call my client and tell her I'm coming home with these damn forms," Tayte said.

"So that's it?"

"What else can I do? If Mena came here under her own name we'll find out more when the home writes back. If she's moved on, we should at least get a forwarding address. Then we can confirm for sure whether it's Mena and try to make contact."

They reached the car.

"So close," Jonathan said.

Tayte shrugged. "Sometimes that's just the way it is." He didn't like it, but there it was.

He opened the passenger door and put his briefcase on the seat while he put the forms away. He checked his watch and reached inside his jacket for his phone. It would be early morning in Washington DC, but he couldn't wait to call his client and he thought she would be keen to hear what he had to say. The call only rang twice before it was answered.

"Mrs Gray?" Tayte said. "Eliza, It's Jefferson Tayte. I hope I haven't disturbed you."

"JT," Eliza said. "No, of course you haven't. I've been up almost an hour. What have you found?"

Tayte gave his client a brief summary of the research that had led him to Logan House and how he believed that Mena had changed her name to Emma Danielson. He sensed her hopes lift each time he came to one breakthrough and another, and then he felt that hope deflate again when he told her he could go no further.

"They gave me some forms for you to fill out," he said. "I'm afraid it's going to take longer than I'd hoped."

"Oh, dear," Eliza said. "Could I talk to them on the phone, do you think?"

"I'm afraid not. They need to see some proof of ID and your adoption records."

The line went silent for several seconds.

"Eliza?"

"I'm coming over," Eliza said. "I'll bring all the paperwork with me."

Tayte knew how much this meant to his client and he understood that she wanted to speed things up. He did, too, but he knew that it would be an uncomfortable journey for her and he hadn't fully been able to confirm that Emma Danielson was Mena yet.

"I'd like to be certain that I've found the right person first," he said.

"Can you do that?"

Tayte bit his lip. "Through the forms, maybe."

"But not without them?"

"No, not really. I think I've exhausted just about every other avenue I can."

"And you say there was only one Emma Danielson listed on the UK electoral register?" Eliza said.

"That's right."

"And she's roughly the same age as Mena would have been at the time the register was taken?"

"To within a few years," Tayte said.

"And don't you think it's a big coincidence that the only Emma Danielson on the register was living in a women-only care home in 2002?"

Tayte sighed. "I guess, but there's another complication. You see, depending on when Mena changed her name, they might not have any knowledge of Mena at all, in which case they won't be able to give us any information for Emma Danielson."

"I don't see how that really changes anything," Eliza said. "The forms are the only way we're going to find out, aren't they?"

Tayte had to agree.

"Well then it's settled. I'll get myself organised and I'll be there the day after tomorrow. You can pick me up from the airport."

Tayte knew there was nothing he could say to dissuade Eliza and a part of him was glad she wanted to make the journey. As they said goodbye he just hoped that his research had led him to the right person, although despite his need to be thorough, he felt sure that it was. Eliza had been right there; it had to be Mena. He turned to Jonathan who had been listening to the conversation from the other side of the car.

"She's coming over," he said, in case Jonathan had missed anything. "She'll be here the day after tomorrow."

"I shall look forward to meeting her," Jonathan said.

"What am I going to do with myself until then?"

"I'm sure we can find something to keep you amused. Geraldine's swimming tonight - water aerobics. You wanna go along?"

Tayte snorted. "Definitely not." He got into the car. "I could use some lunch, though?"

"Good idea," Jonathan said. "I know a pub not far from here. It's on the way back."

As Tayte started the engine his phone rang. Glancing at the display, he saw that the caller's number was withheld.

"Hi," he said. "Jefferson Tayte."

"DI Lundy, Mr Tayte. We spoke on Monday following the murder of Edward Buckley at his home in Hampshire. Whereabouts are you?"

"Market Harborough," Tayte said, looking at Jonathan.

"Good," Lundy said. "I was on my way to Leicester to see you, but if you could make your way to the police station at Market Harborough, I'll make a detour and meet you there. I'm less than an hour away."

"What's it about?"

"Oh, it's nothing to worry about, Mr Tayte. You're not a suspect or anything. There's been a further development, that's all. I've got a few more questions I'd like to ask you and I've got something to show you. Just ask for me when you get to the station and someone will look after you until I get there."

"Sure," Tayte said. "No problem."

Tayte ended the call and arched a brow at Jonathan, wondering what DI Lundy had to show him.

"I suppose that pub-lunch is off then?" Jonathan said.

"I guess so. I'm sorry." Tayte checked his watch: it was just after one p.m. "There isn't really time to drop you home," he added. "Will you be okay to wait?"

"Of course," Jonathan said. "I'll get a bite to eat and take a look around the shops."

"Any idea where the local police station is?"

"No, but I'm sure we can find someone to ask."

Chapter Forty

Detective Inspector Lundy was a stocky, dark-haired man in his early fifties who walked with a slightly hunched gait as he led Tayte and his briefcase into an interview room at Market Harborough police station. Tayte thought he looked like a man who had seen as little sleep as he had over the past couple of days. His eyes were red and puffy and it seemed to take all his energy to drag his chair out from behind the desk.

"Sorry to have kept you waiting, Mr Tayte," Lundy said. "Please take a seat."

The ground floor room was plainly decorated with minimal furnishings and three small windows set high up in the far wall for privacy. Tayte sat down and Lundy sat opposite, placing a manila folder on the table between them.

"I'll try not to keep you too long," Lundy said as he opened the folder and sat back with it. "Firstly, I have some information that might be useful to you. You mentioned a suitcase that was sent to your client in America. Something that once belonged to a girl called Philomena Lasseter."

"That's right."

Lundy slipped a piece of paper across the table. "Is this your client's address?"

Tayte sat forward to read it as the phone in his jacket pocket began to play its show tune. He reached in and silenced it without looking to see who it was, thinking that it must be Jonathan. "Sorry," he said, turning back to the piece of paper. "Yes, that's her address. Where did you find it?"

"Edward Buckley kept an address book, as most people do," Lundy said. "I think it's safe to say that your suspicions as to who sent the suitcase were right."

Tayte thought that was good to know, but he was still trying to figure out why Buckley had sent it after all these years and whether it had anything to do with Grace Ingram's recent death. The next piece of information Lundy imparted came as something of a surprise.

"Edward Buckley was arrested in January, 1945," he said. "It was for the abduction of Philomena from her home in Oadby,

Leicestershire."

"Abduction?" That information didn't tally with the story Tayte had heard.

"Apparently so," Lundy said. "Philomena's mother -" He paused to check his notes. "Margaret Lasseter - she raised the charge against Mr Buckley and her daughter was later found at his home in Hampshire, which is what led to his arrest."

"Was he charged?"

Lundy shook his head. "No, the case against him was dropped as soon as Philomena was returned to her mother's care, but I can see how it could have been very damaging to the Buckley family's reputation if she had chosen to proceed. Local scandal was already brewing at the mere mention of Buckley's arrest by all accounts."

Tayte had been wondering why Edward Buckley would choose to help Mena leave home as he had, seeming only to forget about her afterwards. But then how could Buckley risk stirring Margaret Lasseter's wrath for a second time, knowing that she would re-open the case against him and that his name would be dragged through the courts and all the major newspapers, accused of the abduction of a seventeen year old girl?

"How do you know all this?" Tayte asked. "If Buckley wasn't charged, I mean."

"There's the original arrest sheet," Lundy said. "And there are other resources I'm sure you're familiar with."

"Newspaper archives?"

Lundy nodded. Then he began to scratch at his eyes, making them water. "Excuse me," he said. "I'm trying to switch to contact lenses and the bloody things are irritating the life out of me." He took a tissue from his pocket and wiped his eyes. "I'm beginning to wonder if they're worth the bother," he added as he put the tissue away again and turned his attention back to the manila folder.

"We found something else at Edward Buckley's home that I'm hoping you can help me with," he said, sliding another piece of paper from the folder, this one large and folded. "This newspaper page was on his desk. It's been torn out of *The Times*."

Tayte pulled it closer and unfolded it. It was from the foreign affairs column; dated three days ago on the Monday he had gone to see Edward Buckley. A quick glance revealed several articles from the previous week up to and including the weekend.

"Look here," Lundy said. He reached across the table and indicated one of the articles.

"Priest murdered in Cape Town," Tayte read aloud. The article was brief, presumably only having made the paper because of its widespread shock appeal; it wasn't every day that a priest was gunned down assassination-style in his own chambers in the middle of the afternoon. Tayte read how the murder had taken place at St Mary's cathedral in the middle of Cape Town last Saturday: the day he'd arrived in England.

"See the pen marks beside it?" Lundy said.

Tayte had. There were several ink dots like someone - presumably Edward Buckley - had been tapping the paper as they read it, indicating their interest.

"I was hoping it might mean something to you," Lundy said. "The MO in both cases is identical and the killer had enough time to get from South Africa to England to Kill Edward Buckley afterwards, although the ballistics don't match. A different firearm was used."

Tayte was nodding his head. "It does mean something," he said. "And I think it could come to mean a great deal." He reached into his briefcase and brought the copy of Mel Winkelman's photograph out. "I came across this during my research," he added. He showed it to Lundy. "It was taken in Paris in 1944. The man in the middle here is called Danny Danielson. That's Edward Buckley drinking alongside him." He put his finger on the silhouette of the woman in the background. "I believe this is Mary Lasseter. She was engaged to Edward Buckley at the time, but soon after the photo was taken the marriage was called off. Then Mary moved to South Africa, married someone else and became Grace Ingram."

Tayte went on to tell Lundy about the Grace Ingram Foundation Trust, GIFT, and how he'd been to see its founder's son, Christopher Ingram, recently. Then he told him what he knew about Danny and how the GI had been listed as missing-in-action in November 1944, around the time the photograph was taken.

Despite his niggling suspicion that there was something sinister lurking behind the scene, he had to remind himself that it was still just a photograph of two or maybe three friends at a bar in wartime Paris. Although with Buckley's murder and now the murder of a priest in Cape Town just the day before, it stacked up in Tayte's mind as something too suspicious to ignore. He could see from the look on DI Lundy's face that he thought the same.

"I'd suggest you confirm where Grace Ingram attended Mass,"

Tayte said. "And I'd have a word with her son. If someone's trying to make sure that the past stays where it is, in light of what we have here I'd say that Christopher Ingram would be the best person to help with your investigation."

"What about motive? Any thoughts?"

Tayte thought the motive was obvious after everything he'd said, but maybe he'd missed some salient point.

"To protect the good name of the trust," Tayte said. "If its founder was implicated in the disappearance of an American GI during the Second World War, the reputation of the Grace Ingram Foundation Trust would be damaged beyond repair."

Lundy began to nod.

"Hang on a minute," Tayte said as something else occurred to him. "When I went to see Christopher Ingram, I heard that the trust was about to expand into America. If Grace Ingram did have something to do with Danny's disappearance, given that he was an American GI, what American business - or any other business for that matter - would want to associate themselves with GIFT then?"

Tayte hoped he was wrong about these things that now seemed so clear to him. He hoped the answer was simply that Danny had come looking for Mena and maybe he never went back to his unit because he never stopped looking for her. Perhaps it took him the rest of the year to get back to England travelling through unofficial channels and by the time he reached Oadby, Mena had gone. But something told Tayte that a different answer was waiting to be found and it made him even more determined to find out what it was.

"I'd like to make a copy of this before you go," Lundy said, indicating the photograph and stirring Tayte from his thoughts.

"Keep it," Tayte said. "It's on my laptop."

Lundy's eyes lit up. "In that case, I'd like a copy of the file if you don't mind. Save me a trip to the scanner."

Chapter Forty-One

It was just after six p.m. when Tayte arrived back at his hotel. He'd dropped Jonathan home in twilight and left again in darkness, having taken him up on his offer of coffee and biscuits, which was all he'd eaten since breakfast that morning. As he walked the quiet corridor to his room, he could hear his stomach groan beneath his jacket and he supposed it was fitting punishment for having eaten all those Hershey's miniatures last night.

He turned a corner and saw his room ahead, prompting him to reach into his pocket for the key card. He was thinking about his client, wondering whether she would get an overnight flight tomorrow or would wait until the next morning. It didn't really matter. All he had to do now was wait for her call. They would take the next steps towards finding Mena together and the rest was in the hands of the police. He just had to switch off, have dinner, finish his book and get an early night.

Thinking about phone calls reminded him that he'd missed one while he was with DI Lundy. He paused a few steps from his room and checked to see who had called, thinking it can't have been Jonathan or he would have said. He checked the details. It was a local landline number he didn't recognise, but he called back anyway as he continued towards his room. It rang several times and then went to a voice messaging service that told him he'd reached the voice mailbox of Alan Driscoll. Tayte ended the call, thinking he'd try again later.

Alan Driscoll... What did he have to say?

As he put his phone away he knew he hadn't called to chat about rugby and that whatever it was he would find out soon enough. He was about to put his key card in the slot when he noticed the 'do not disturb' sign on the handle. He couldn't remember leaving it there, but he'd been in such a hurry to get out that morning, head spinning with thoughts of finding Mena, that it didn't surprise him.

He entered his room, dropped his briefcase and hung his jacket in the wardrobe, half expecting to find his breakfast tray still on the desk where he'd left it; his bed covers still draped on the floor. But when he flicked the main lights on he saw that his room had been serviced and the reason for the sign on the door became clear.

He was not alone.

Sitting at the table by the window was a man in a navy pinstripe suit whom Tayte vaguely recognised. Maybe it was the frameless glasses he was wearing, or perhaps it was that suit. It didn't matter. All Tayte could think about now was the gun in his hand as he raised it towards him.

"Sit down, Mr Tayte."

The man flicked the muzzle of his gun at the vacant chair opposite him, but as Tayte tried to comply he wasn't sure that he could. His legs suddenly felt so heavy he didn't think he could move at all.

"I said, sit down."

With the gun now levelled at Tayte's head, he managed to do as he was told. *Who is this man? Why is he in my room? Whose are those legs on the floor beside my bed?*

"You two have met, I believe."

Tayte sat down and stared at the body. "Driscoll?" he said, coughing the word out, his throat suddenly parched.

"Don't feel too bad about him," the man said. "He was already on my list, although it might not have come to this. You've stirred things up here, Mr Tayte."

"Am I supposed to feel guilty about his and Edward Buckley's death? The priest, too?"

The man shifted on his chair. "No, not the priest," he said. "Perhaps not Buckley, either, although I'd say you took a few days off his life."

Tayte didn't know whether to look at the body or the gun, but the gun with that stubby silencer attached to it had an immediacy about it that was hard to ignore. "Driscoll had a son."

"Someone's father dies every second of every day," the man said. "You can't afford to be sentimental in my line of work."

Tayte doubted the man had a sentimental bone in his body. "Why did you kill him?"

"Isn't it obvious? You don't think I brought him here, do you?"

Tayte didn't answer.

"Clearly he came to tell you something and in doing so he made it clear to me that he had something of interest to tell."

Tayte thought it had to be about why his mother fell out with her mother, Grace Ingram, and why she broke away from the family. "And I guess I'm next?" he said.

The thin line that passed for the man's lips twitched slightly.

"There's no rush," he said. "Tell me, did you finish Madame Bovary?"

"No, I didn't."

"That's too bad. But I gave you fair warning."

Tayte began to feel light-headed - a little nauseous.

"You see? Everyone assumes they will reach the end of their book when they start it, but you never know do you? How many unfinished books are out there, I wonder? How many people have died without knowing how the story ended?"

Tayte had no idea and he really didn't care. "Now I suppose you want me to tell you where Mena is before you kill me?" he said. He figured that was all there was between here and the grave, but he wasn't going to give up the information easily.

"No," the man said, very calmly, chilling Tayte to his core. "I've been following you all day. I know about your visit to Logan House."

Tayte smiled to spite the man. "You won't find Mena there."

"Mena? No. But Emma Danielson - I'll find her. That's the name you gave your client, isn't it? That American voice of yours carries."

Tayte tried to think of something else he could say to stay his execution, but he couldn't. When he stopped thinking he felt himself relax for the first time since he'd walked into the room, like everything that had ever concerned him no longer seemed to matter. "You don't need anything from me, do you?" he said.

The man shook his head.

"So what are you waiting for? Why don't you just do it?"

"Okay." The man was quick to reassert his grip on the gun, aiming it more precisely at Tayte's chest. He paused. "Call it a professional courtesy," he added, "but which would you prefer? Head or heart?"

"What?"

Tayte had heard the question but he had to ask to make sure he'd heard it right. The man didn't say it again. He just moved the muzzle of his gun slowly from Tayte's chest to his head and back again.

"I guess I can't talk you out of this, can I?"

"No," the man said.

"And if I go for the door, you'll shoot me in the back, right?"

"No."

"No?"

The man shook his head only slightly. "You wouldn't make it out of your seat."

Tayte tried to swallow, but he couldn't. He knew he was going to die. A part of him had known it the minute he'd walked into the room and saw this man sitting there. They were both very calm about it and somehow Tayte wasn't surprised by how he felt. He knew it was going to happen. They were resolved between them to kill and be killed. *Head or heart?* What kind of a choice was that?

"Does it matter?"

"Not to me," the man said. "But if you choose heart, there's a small chance the first bullet will miss. Your head on the other hand..."

Tayte tried to imagine what a head shot would be like. Quicker perhaps. But what if the bullet went in through his eye? He winced. It didn't bear thinking about. He really did not want to be having these thoughts.

"Will it hurt?"

"I'm not going to tell you that you won't feel a thing, Mr Tayte. But this is not personal. I'm not here to hurt you. Either way, the pain won't last long."

Tayte turned away and looked down through the window, thinking that this man was as cool as the January night that had settled an early frost on the cars below. He breathed deeply and wondered where the time had gone. His time. He thought how ironic it was that he should die a lonely man in some nondescript hotel room trying to connect another client with her birth parents while he still had no idea about his own. How could he die without knowing who he was? He scoffed, thinking that death would certainly spare him that pain.

How had it come to this?

"Head or heart?" the man opposite him repeated, and now that the moment had arrived, Tayte knew he would have endured any amount of pain to find his own answers. But he supposed it was too late for that now.

"Before you pull that trigger," he said, "will you tell me why you're looking for Mena? I should at least like to know how her story ends, even if I can't finish reading her library book."

The gunman's expression did not waver. There was no emotion behind his eyes as he replied. "No," he said.

"You know you're leaving quite a trail behind you. The police have already tied Buckley to the priest. That was Grace Ingram's priest you killed wasn't it?"

"Who's Grace Ingram?" the man said.

"Alan Driscoll was her grandson. Don't you think they'll make that connection?"

"I'm paid to keep secrets, Mr Tayte. That's all I do. I don't ask why. Now I'll ask you one more time and then I'll choose for you. Head or heart?"

The next few seconds passed in a blur. One moment Tayte had his eyes closed, ready to let the killer decide, the next he heard a tap at the door and someone on the other side called, "Room service!" Tayte opened his eyes and saw that his executioner's attention had been diverted. In that instant, Tayte jumped to his feet, lifting the table with him.

"Come in!" he shouted.

He ran for the door and the table crashed down behind him. When the door opened he saw a smiling waiter holding his meal on a tray. Then Tayte watched his smile turn to fear as he bowled into him, knocking him back, sending the tray and his dinner flying.

"Sorry!" Tayte yelled. "Get out of here. He's got a gun!"

Tayte thundered down the corridor. He followed the signs for the fire exit, turning around one corner and then another, hoping to reach it before the gunman had another chance to fix him in his sights. He didn't look back until he saw his way out. He took one glance over his shoulder, noted that he was in the clear and then he slammed into the fire exit door and burst out onto the iron stairway, catching his breath as the cold night air filled his lungs.

Chapter Forty-Two

Tayte reached the hotel car park out of breath, his heart racing so fast it was almost painful. As he continued to run, all he could think about was the tray of food he'd sent flying and the room-service routine that had just saved his life. He saw his hire car ahead and thought about his keys, glad that he hadn't had time to take them out of his trouser pocket before the gunman had ordered him to sit down. Right now all he wanted to do was drive as far away from there as possible. His phone was back in the room hanging up inside his jacket. That wasn't so good because the other thing he wanted to do was call the police.

As he reached the car he thought his exit from the building would have set off an alarm somewhere and that hotel security would investigate it, but he didn't plan to stick around long enough to find out. He took a quick glance around before he got in, noting that there were plenty of people around and there were other cars coming and going. All good signs, he thought as he hit the accelerator and pulled away hard, setting his wheels spinning on the frosty Tarmac.

He saw the gunman again then.

In his rear-view mirror he caught him running across the car park and the sight of that gun bunched in his hand made Tayte feel the cold through his thin shirt for the first time since he'd taken flight. He changed gear and accelerated harder. The man was gaining and Tayte realised the car wasn't going anywhere. His wheels were spinning, losing too much traction.

The wheels suddenly bit and the car lurched forward. Tayte looked back again and he could see the man more clearly now. He watched him bring his gun up ready to take a shot despite the attention it would draw. Then as another car passed him, heading towards the gunman, his pursuer dropped his gun arm to his side and stopped.

Tayte kept on the accelerator. He screeched out of the car park onto the hotel access road, thinking that he should drive straight to the nearest police station. He wished he knew where that was. Then he realised he had to go to the Lasseter house. He had to warn Jonathan. They had been together all day. Jonathan knew everything he knew and that put him in the same mortal danger. He could call the police later.

As he joined the traffic on the main road, heading towards Oadby, he heard another car screech in the near distance behind him and he knew he had to hurry. He swerved out into the oncoming traffic and overtook the car in front of him. He tried to repeat the manoeuvre but quickly realised he didn't have time. The oncoming van flashed him and a horn blared past as he ducked back in. A few seconds later he tried again, thinking only that he had to get to the Lasseter House first and with enough time to get Jonathan out.

The early evening traffic soon became heavy and he knew he had to get off the main road so he activated the satnav and brought up Jonathan's address, which he'd set up when he first arrived. It gave him the obvious route first - the route he was now on - so he asked for another and another until he found one that avoided all the main roads, which he knew would be clogged with people travelling home from work. When he found one that didn't seem to take him too far out of his way, he selected it. Then he heard a car horn behind him and checked his mirror. He saw headlights in the other lane briefly before they ducked back into file.

"In two hundred meters, turn left."

It was satnav lady and if she had a face Tayte would have kissed it.

"Thank you - thank you," he said, looking for his exit. There was no time to risk overtaking again and the oncoming chain of headlights told him it would be suicide to try. He just hoped his pursuer thought the same.

When the junction came, Tayte swung the wheel hard and lost the back end of the car for a split second, but it was nothing he hadn't done a hundred times or more in his Thunderbird. He counter-steered and regained control, all the while checking his mirror, hoping that the man who was trying to kill him hadn't seen him turn off or thought to do the same.

After several seconds passed he began to breathe a little easier. He was on his own - just him and the voice coming periodically from the satnav, guiding him to the Lasseter house as fast as the car and his nerves could manage.

There were no other cars outside the Lasseter house when Tayte arrived. The silver Vauxhall slid several feet through the gravel as he stepped on the break pedal, locking the wheels. He ran to the front door and banged on it with his fist.

"Jonathan!"

He flicked at the letterbox several times and thumped on the door again.

"It's JT!" he called. "Open the door! We have to go!"

He was about to thump the door again when it opened and a startled looking Jonathan Lasseter stood in the frame.

"Where's Geraldine?" Tayte asked.

"Swimming," Jonathan said. "You remember, I -"

"Good," Tayte cut in. He grabbed Jonathan's arm. "Let's go. We don't have much time."

"Time for what?"

"I'll explain later. Just get in the car."

"Can I put my shoes on first? What about my coat?"

Tayte glanced down at the paisley slippers Jonathan was wearing. "There's no time," he said. Then as he pulled Jonathan out onto the drive with him he heard a sound that froze him to the spot. It was another car and the wailing engine note told him that whoever was driving it was in a hurry.

"He's here," Tayte said, thinking fast.

"Who's here? What's going on?"

Tayte ran towards the Vauxhall taking Jonathan with him but before they reached it a green Land Rover Defender turned onto the drive at speed, spraying gravel in its wake, full beam floodlighting the house.

"Shit!" Tayte said, turning back to the house. He let go of Jonathan's arm. "Get back inside!"

They ran back to the house together, their backs to the Defender as it drew rapidly closer. Tayte turned as he reached the door to see the man in the pinstripe suit lean out of the window and take aim. A shot was fired. It clipped the door and went clean through. Then as Tayte slammed the door shut and shot the bolt across, another bullet tugged at his shirtsleeve.

"Did he get you?" Jonathan asked.

"I don't think so. Move away from the door."

"Who is he? Why is he doing this?"

"I don't know who he is," Tayte said. "He was waiting for me in my hotel room. He was going to kill me and he'll kill you, too."

"Why?"

"Because we're looking for Mena. He's used us to find her and now he has to stop us. To keep a secret."

There was a telephone on a half-table against the wall further into the hallway and Tayte quickly found it. He ran to it but stopped himself halfway. This was no place to be caught when the gunman came through that front door and he knew that would be soon. A second later the expected thud came and it jarred his nerves.

"Where's your cellphone?" he asked.

"In the kitchen."

The door thudded again as the gunman tried to force it. Tayte went to the stairs.

"Is there another phone up here?"

"In the bedroom."

The stairs creaked as they ran up into the darkness and seconds later a volley of shots was fired at the door.

"Maybe he'll think we ran out the back," Tayte said as they reached the top and turned around the bannister. "It might buy us enough time to get a call out."

"Then what?" Jonathan said.

Tayte didn't answer. He knew they didn't have much time and he thought if they could just call the emergency services, help would come. All they had to do was hide until then. It was a big house and it would take time to search it. Maybe they could go up into the attic and block the hatch.

Another thud sounded below. This time it was followed by splintering wood and Tayte knew the gunman was inside. He stopped moving partway across the landing and caught Jonathan's arm. He locked eyes with him and put a finger to his lips, warning him not to make any sound that might give them away. Right now he figured the slightest creak from a floorboard would kill them and every step he'd taken since they climbed the stairs had caused the old house to groan in protest. He listened in the darkness. The house was deathly still.

Seconds later he heard a door click somewhere downstairs like a handle had just been turned. The sound told him it was time to move again, but he thought it was best to stay put and let Jonathan make the call. He urged him on towards the master bedroom and in the half-light now that his eyes had adjusted, he watched him walk slowly towards it as if stepping through a house of cards. Another sound came from below, this time more distant. The bedroom door was open and Tayte could just see the silhouette of the phone on the bedside table inside. Jonathan reached it and carefully lifted the receiver.

The next sound Tayte heard startled him. It was a single creak at the bottom of the stairs. He held his breath and turned back to Jonathan who was already staring back at him. He had a finger paused over the phone's keypad, ready to make the call, but the sound had stopped him. The next creak was lighter and it was followed by faint footsteps in the hallway below, like the gunman had started to climb the stairs and changed his mind for some reason.

Tayte gave Jonathan a nod and Jonathan tapped out three nines for the emergency services. Even if he just left the call hanging without saying a word, Tayte thought it might be enough to bring someone out to the house to check. But as Jonathan hit the last digit there was a clatter in the hall below and when Tayte turned back to Jonathan he was holding out the handset, shaking his head, letting Tayte know that the line was dead. The clatter he'd just heard was clearly that of the master telephone socket being kicked off the wall, cutting them off from the outside world and ending any hope they had of calling for help.

The noise in the entrance hallway continued for several seconds and as soon as Tayte realised what was happening he used that sound to mask his own movement. He ran to Jonathan who stepped back as Tayte reached the bedroom and left the door ajar behind him.

"We have to get out," Tayte whispered.

"What about my mobile? Maybe we could double back to the kitchen when he comes upstairs."

Tayte shook his head. Even if they made it down the stairs, he figured the noise would draw the gunman straight to them.

"Is there a window we can climb out of?" he said. "Somewhere with a ledge?"

"There's an extension at the back of the bathroom," Jonathan said. "It wouldn't be hard to climb down from there. The windows are small, though," he added. "And the bathroom's at the top of the stairs. It would be too risky."

A succession of creaking floorboards told them that the gunman was now on the stairs. Tayte went to the bedroom window.

"It's a sheer drop from there," Jonathan said, stopping Tayte in his tracks.

Tayte spun around and voiced his earlier thoughts. "Can we get up into the attic? Maybe we could shut ourselves in and wait it out."

"We can't wait," Jonathan said. "Geraldine's due home soon. She'll walk right into all this if we don't do something." He went to another door - a smaller door at the back of the room. He opened it.

"Quickly. Through here," he added. "It links to one of the old bedrooms. We use it as a dressing room now. We can try the window in there."

"Is there another way in?" Tayte asked, assuming there must have been at some point.

"From the landing," Jonathan said. "But it's got no handle and there's a wardrobe behind it."

As they went through Tayte heard a voice on the landing that was so close and unwelcome it sent a shiver through him.

"You're beginning to make this personal, Mr Tayte."

It was already personal as far as Tayte was concerned. He pulled the door shut behind him. Then he followed Jonathan towards the moonlight at the end of the narrow corridor. He thought it must be coming from the window they were heading for, the curtains undrawn.

"Come out now or I'll make this very painful for both of you," the gunman called.

Tayte crept through after Jonathan into a room predominantly filled with pine wardrobes. There was an old dressing table inside the door and Tayte wondered if this might once have been Mena's room and whether she had sat and gazed at her reflection in that same mirror. It was a fleeting thought that he didn't have time to dwell on.

Jonathan went straight to the window and opened it while Tayte looked around for something to block the small doorway with - anything to buy them time if it came to it. He could see the main door that led onto the landing, which was half blocked by one of the wardrobes as Jonathan had said. The dressing table was the only thing in the room he thought small enough to be able to move quietly but which was large enough to offer some resistance.

"Jonathan," he whispered, calling him back from the window to help lift it into place. Tayte didn't think it would hold for long and he supposed the gunman would find his way to it soon enough. All they had to do now was get out of there before he did.

The moonlit view from the window wasn't encouraging. Below the dormer, Tayte saw frost covered roof tiles that sloped several feet down to the guttering and there was a drop of eight or nine feet below that. The slide wouldn't be too difficult, he thought, having no doubt in his mind that he would slide. Catching the guttering to stop himself would be the hard part.

"Will the gutter hold?" Tayte asked, thinking aloud.

"I should think so," Jonathan said. "It's tough old ironwork."

"Okay. You'd better go first."

Tayte figured that if push literally came to shove then being the heavier man he was best placed to keep that dressing table against the door. He didn't want to think about the bullets that would come through it if the gunman knew he was there.

Jonathan climbed into the frame and swung his legs out. He turned to face Tayte and lowered himself down onto the tiles. Then he slipped as he tried to get his footing. He grabbed the windowsill for support, rattling the catch. They froze, making no sound beyond their own heavy breathing. A second later Tayte felt a rush of adrenaline as he heard the gunman on the other side of the main landing door. He began to slap at the wood.

"I know you're in there," the man called, chanting the words like they were playing a game of hide and seek.

"Go!" Tayte said, and Jonathan let go of the windowsill. He began to slide on his hands and knees, scrabbling for purchase that didn't come until his feet caught the guttering.

The door behind Tayte began to bang and shake in its frame and Tayte hoped the wardrobe would hold. He turned back to Jonathan in time to see him lower himself to the guttering where he grabbed it and twisted around. Then Jonathan lowered himself further until all Tayte could see was the whites of his knuckles. A moment later Tayte heard him drop into the garden below.

He turned back into the room. The banging at the door had stopped, which unnerved him. The gunman was either looking for another way in - the way they had used - or he was heading outside.

"Come on," Jonathan called. "I'm okay."

Tayte copied Jonathan. He climbed into the window-frame and swung his legs out. Then he heard a sound that made him jolt so hard he almost fell out. The gunman was at the small door, thumping and shoving. Tayte saw the dressing table begin to slide. He twisted around and lowered himself out onto the roof tiles as the door opened a little more, enough to see the gunman's face. They locked eyes briefly. Tayte saw him raise his gun and shots were fired. Glass shattered around him and suddenly Tayte was sliding and rolling. He tried frantically to grab hold of something but he was disoriented and confused. A second later, the ground knocked the wind out of him and he found himself staring up at Jonathan.

"Are you hurt?"

Tayte wasn't sure. He quickly checked himself for blood. Nothing.

Then he grabbed Jonathan's arm and got to his feet, knowing only that he didn't have time to worry about it. They ran around the house, heading for the car, and Tayte knew then that something was wrong with his left ankle. A sharp pain caused him to wince every time he put his weight on it and he had to limp most of the way, going as fast as he could but quickly falling behind.

His lack of speed made no difference.

As they came to the front of the house and Tayte's eyes fixed with hope on his hire car, he saw that another car had pulled onto the drive. At first he thought it must be Jonathan's wife, Geraldine, returned from her swimming classes, but Jonathan had stopped running and Tayte questioned why until he saw the driver get out. It was Retha Ingram. She had a black attaché case in one gloved hand and a gun in the other. Her unmistakable, pale complexion appeared ghostly drawn in the cold winter moonlight.

Chapter Forty-Three

Retha shook her gun towards the house. "Inside," she ordered. "Both of you!"

Jonathan looked confused. "Retha?"

Her appearance at the Lasseter house, and the gun in her hand, surprised Tayte less. Retha Ingram was the ambitious head of a well respected and soon to be expanding charitable trust that had been founded on Grace Ingram's good name. It was that name, and no doubt the financial benefit the business afforded her, that Tayte knew she was there to protect tonight.

"I'm sorry Jonathan," Retha said, her South African accent conveying no warmth. "I was hoping it wouldn't come to this. Where is your wife?"

Jonathan continued to stare at the gun she was holding. It was a small gun as handguns go, but no less deadly at such close range.

"She's out," he said. "Swimming."

"That's lucky for her," Retha said.

"Why are you doing this?"

Tayte wanted to hear the answer to that question, although her presence there only helped to confirm what he'd told the police earlier: that Mary Lasseter, latterly Grace Ingram, was implicated in Danny Danielson's disappearance in 1944. Perhaps even his murder in light of the measures Retha was clearly prepared to take to keep her family's secret. It strengthened his need to know what had happened that night in Paris, but as Retha's hired killer joined them he knew that now was not the time to ask.

Retha flicked her gun again and the man in the pinstripe suit stepped aside as they filed back into the house. Tayte limped past and the man spoke quietly in his ear.

"Don't worry," he said. "That ankle won't bother you much longer."

Tayte tried to ignore the jibe, but the man slammed the butt of his gun into the side of his head, reminding him who was in control. It didn't knock Tayte down, but it came close. He wavered as he took another step, seeing double.

"Enough!" Retha barked. Her eyes glared at the man for whom

Tayte supposed she afforded little regard - just business between them.

"I owed him that," the man said and he shoved Tayte towards the living room with the muzzle of his gun as if to defy her. "Do you have the rest of my money in that case?"

"It's not your money yet," Retha replied.

The Lasseter house sitting room seemed to Tayte like a different place tonight, devoid of the warmth and homeliness he'd felt on previous visits. It was like he'd just stepped into an alternative dimension that was bereft of anything good or wholesome. The curtains were drawn and the lights were on but the glow that filled the room felt cold and unwelcoming to him now.

"Sit down," Retha said. "On the floor."

Tayte and Jonathan locked eyes with one another as they sat on the rug in front of a heatless fireplace that was full of grey ash, each silently asking the same questions: *what are we going to do now? Is this the end?* Now that there were two guns to contend with Tayte felt more helpless than he had when he'd been alone with the gunman in his hotel room. On top of that he now had an ankle he couldn't run on. He looked up at Retha, trying to make eye contact. Failing.

"So how come you're doing your own dirty work tonight?" he asked her. "Or maybe you just wanted to watch. Is that it?"

Retha seemed to ignore him and it occurred to Tayte that that was not it. She was taking a big risk by coming to the Lasseter house. It told him she must have felt she had no choice. He was supposed to be dead by now and yet his escape from his hotel room cannot have been the complication that had brought her there. To get there so soon after the killer she must have already been on her way. Tayte didn't think Retha had come to kill Jonathan in person either. His murder would surely be difficult for her and she had no need to do it herself if that was all that remained to be done tonight.

So why is she here?

The hired gun stepped closer to Tayte. "Let's get this over with," he said. "It's taken too long already."

He raised his gun level with Tayte's head and as futile as Tayte knew any effort to overcome the two of them would be he decided he wasn't going down without a fight. He was about to jump up and throw himself at the man when Retha spoke, although her words were not encouraging.

"Wait!" she said. She put the attaché case down on the sofa and stepped closer until she was standing beside the gunman. "We'll do it together. I'm sorry Jonathan," she added.

Then with speed and precision she brought the gun up beneath the gunman's chin and pulled the trigger, sending his head jolting back. He fell crashing onto the coffee table behind them and Tayte didn't have any more time to react to what had just happened than the man in the navy pinstripe suit had had to prevent it. The next thing he saw was Jonathan getting to his feet, an elated smile slowly emerging as he rose, as though Retha had come there to save him. But Tayte knew better. He was beginning to understand the need for Retha's visit and the small gun that had now turned back to Jonathan confirmed it.

"Sit down, Jonathan!" Retha ordered. She picked up the dead man's gun and aimed it at Tayte.

Tayte watched Jonathan's smile turn to confusion again. "She's not here to help us," he said, eyes on Retha. "She came here as soon as she heard that Alan Driscoll was dead. Isn't that right?"

Retha said nothing.

"Driscoll's murder was too close to home," Tayte continued. "And it wasn't part of the plan." He faced Jonathan. "I'm sorry," he said. "I'm sure you weren't part of the plan either until I showed up. Now Retha here thinks that if she gives the police the killer, the case will be closed. They'll ask a few awkward questions, sure, but ultimately they'll have their man."

"Is this true, Retha?" Jonathan asked.

Retha ignored him. "I like intelligent men, Mr Tayte. Perhaps you can tell me how the rest of the plan goes?"

"Well, let me see. You'd have to shoot both of us with this man's gun." Tayte indicated the body. "Then you'd have to make it look like one of us had your gun to shoot him with. But how's that going to work? Why would either of us have a gun. And a small gun like that? I'd struggle to even get my finger through the trigger guard, and how would I have brought it into the country?"

Retha smiled. "It's his gun, too," she said. "At least that's how it's going to look."

She went to the attaché case and opened it, keeping the small gun on them as she set the other down. There was no money inside. A moment later she pulled out a holster that had short fastening straps.

"It goes around the ankle," Retha said. "A professional killer might have such a gun, hey? The police are going to find it strapped to him and the wear marks will show that this gun fits it perfectly."

"So how does the gun-play work?" Tayte asked.

Retha pointed the dead man's gun at Jonathan. "Mr Killer here shoots Jonathan first. When he does, you rush him. There's a struggle between the two of you and the ankle-gun is brought out. You grab it or he grabs it. It doesn't matter. He shoots you and you shoot him. The only difference is that you kill him outright and the stomach wound he inflicts on you means that you bleed to death some time afterwards. I've heard that stomach wounds can be very painful."

Tayte swallowed the lump that had risen in his throat. Then he asked the same question he'd already asked the dead man. "Why are you trying to find Mena? Why is she so important to you?"

Retha gave a wry smile. "Let's just say that she has something I need."

Tayte thought he had a good idea what that was. "Your grandmother's confession?" he said. He supposed there were few other reasons to kill a priest. Sacramental seal or not, Retha clearly wasn't taking any chances.

Retha didn't reply.

"What happened to Danny Danielson?" Tayte asked. "Why didn't he come back for Mena?" He answered the question for her. "He couldn't, could he? So was it Mary or Edward? Did they kill him? Is that it? And you're trying to keep a lid on it. And what do you have planned for Mena when you catch up with her?"

"Enough questions," Retha said. "I think you should be more concerned with yourself now, hey Mr Tayte?"

"You don't have to do this," Jonathan said.

Retha reasserted her aim at Jonathan's chest. "It's all too late for that now," she said.

"Just wait a minute," Tayte said. "You're making a mistake. There's something you don't know."

"Really? That's quite pathetic. I've covered every conceivable angle."

Her gun arm flexed, like she was about to pull the trigger.

"You don't know about the photo," Tayte said, his tone urgent. "The photo that was taken in Paris in 1944 just before Danny went missing. It shows that Edward Buckley and your grandmother were there with him." Tayte knew the image of the woman in the background was too vague to pass in court, but he figured Retha didn't have to know that. "The police have a copy of the photo," he added, 'and I've told them everything I know. They know about the priest, too, and they already suspect that his and Buckley's murders are connected. As soon as they confirm it was your grandmother's priest, they'll be all over you."

Retha's gun arm relaxed and Tayte could see that she was thinking through the implications of what he'd said.

"You think that what you're doing here tonight will sever any connection between you and the murders," Tayte added. "But you're wrong."

Retha took a step closer to Jonathan. "Then I'll have to take my chances, won't I?"

Her gun arm was rigid now. It began to shake and Tayte knew she was about to pull the trigger. Then bright headlights illuminated the curtains at the window.

"Geraldine!" Jonathan said. "Please, Retha. Don't hurt her."

Retha backed away. Outside, a car door slammed and seconds later footsteps sounded in the hall. Retha took aim at the door. Then as it started to open, Jonathan sprang to his feet.

"Geraldine! Go back, she's got a gun!"

Retha fired twice through the door panel and Jonathan stopped in his tracks, his face suddenly ashen. They heard a groan from the other side of the door and it opened further as someone fell into the room. It wasn't Geraldine. It was Retha's father, Christopher Ingram.

Tayte saw the flash of confusion in Retha's eyes - saw the gun drop to her side as her arm went limp. By the time the reality of what had happened sank in, Tayte was already on his feet. As Retha went to her father, he grabbed her wrist and wrenched the gun from her hand. She offered no resistance. Her entire focus was now on the man lying at their feet.

"I came to warn you," Ingram said.

Then his whole body seemed to sigh and Tayte knew he was dead.

Chapter Forty-Four

Two days later.

Jefferson Tayte was driving east with his client towards Sutton Bassett: a small village amidst patchwork fields roughly four miles from Market Harborough in the county of Northamptonshire. Eliza Gray had arrived at Heathrow airport early that morning and on the drive out of London Tayte told her everything that had happened that week, sparing no detail when it came to Joan Cartwright's account of how Mena had said she'd been raped. The news angered Eliza, as Tayte knew it would, but he thought it best to prepare her in case it was later proven. She was also upset when he told her about the attempts on his life that had twice come so close to fruition. She had even apologised to him, like any of it was her fault.

Following the shootings at the Lasseter house, Tayte spent much of the night at the hospital and later with the police. From the hospital he was glad to learn that he hadn't broken anything, although the sprain in his ankle still made him wince whenever he put too much weight on it. From the police, who had been keen to speak to him following the discovery of Alan Driscoll's body in his hotel room, he'd gained no further confirmation of the Ingrams' motives. Retha Ingram had not spoken again that evening, having withdrawn into herself by the time she was taken into custody, and according to DI Lundy she had maintained her silence throughout questioning.

Tayte supposed that Christopher Ingram had panicked when Lundy paid him a visit with the copy of Mel Winkelman's photograph. Ingram had clearly gone to the Lasseter house to warn Retha about the connections the police had made, perhaps to stop her from carrying out the plan Tayte had no doubt he was in collusion with. But it had backfired.

That father and daughter were complicit in hiring a killer to keep their family's secret surprised Tayte, but he supposed they thought they had good reason to if Tayte's belief around what had happened to Danny Danielson was correct: that instead of Danny finding his way back to Mena, he had been murdered that night in Paris in 1944. Tayte didn't expect to discover any answer other than that now, but he did hope to find out what had happened.

He pulled the sun visor down as the road turned and the low, early afternoon sun shone into his eyes. Eliza was sitting in the front passenger seat in a burgundy trouser suit with a black and gold silk scarf tied at her neck.

"We're nearly there," Tayte said as Sutton Road became Main Street.

He glanced across at Eliza and thought she looked nervous, which was understandable given who he hoped they were soon to meet. From Logan House they had learnt that Mena had been staying there until 2003, having changed her name to Emma Danielson soon after her arrival. The records they were permitted to see showed that Mena entered the home directly from the Towers Hospital in 1975. She had been there for eighteen years and at Logan House for twenty-eight, and as much as Tayte would have liked confirmation that it was Edward Buckley who had found her again and arranged for her transfer to the care home, her benefactor was not named.

The most important thing they had learned from the home's records was Mena's forwarding address, which was where they were going now. Tayte had tried to get a phone number so he could call ahead, but no number was available and Eliza had said she was glad about that in case Mena refused to see them. Turning up unannounced was far from subtle, but Tayte saw her point. She hadn't come all this way to get a telephone rejection.

Eliza had been accompanied on the flight by her eldest son who was now being looked after by Jonathan and his wife. They had agreed between them that it would be better to continue the journey towards finding Mena with as few people as was necessary so as not to overwhelm her if and when the time came. DI Lundy was also very interested in the answers Tayte hoped to find and Tayte had some difficulty persuading him to allow them to proceed without a police escort. But Tayte managed to convince Lundy that tact was required if they were to learn anything further and he gave his promise to hand over anything that might be useful to the investigation, which Lundy had eventually accepted.

Ahead, the countryside changed from open fields of churned winter earth to bare trees and what looked like a few farm buildings, which according to the road sign Tayte could see marked the start of the village they were heading for. At the sight of it Eliza began to fiddle with her thumbs, turning one around the other and back again.

"I thought it was always raining in England," she said. "Or if it wasn't, it was about to."

"It was raining when I arrived," Tayte said. "But it's been clear like this for a few days now. Maybe it's a record." He could see she was tense. He gave her a smile. "It's no good telling you not to worry, is it?"

"No," Eliza said. "No good at all."

They passed a public house called the Queen's Head Inn and the satnav informed them that they had reached their destination. Tayte scanned the houses and soon saw what he was looking for. His throat felt dry all of a sudden and he imagined Eliza's was too.

"Here we are," he said, pulling the car over.

The house they had been directed to was a modest-looking, semi-detached property with a slate tiled roof and a small courtyard garden at the front. Tayte left his briefcase on the back seat and helped Eliza out of the car, still limping as he made his way around to her door.

She shook her head at him. "We're quite a pair now, aren't we?" she said.

Tayte took her walking sticks and helped her out of the car. "Yes, we are," he said. "Are you sure you're ready?"

Eliza took a deep breath. "As I'll ever be."

"Good. Here, take my arm. We'll walk the path together."

They entered through a low iron gate and Tayte felt his pulse quicken as he stepped onto the path amidst clipped shrubs and violas that added a splash of seasonal colour here and there. When they reached the front door, Tayte stepped forward and rang the doorbell. A tune played inside the house and several seconds later a thin-framed man came to the door. Tayte put him in his late seventies. He wore grey trousers and a chequered sports jacket with a plain shirt and tie in the neck like he was going somewhere or had just come back.

Tayte flourished his best smile and hoped it didn't look too cheesy. "Hi," he said. "We're looking for someone called Emma Danielson. Can you tell me if she still lives here?"

The man eyed him quizzically. He looked like he was about to speak but he hesitated first. "Do you mind my asking who you are?"

"It's a little delicate," Tayte said. "My name's Jefferson Tayte. I'm a family historian and this is my client, Eliza Gray. We have good reason to believe that Emma Danielson is Eliza's mother and she's travelled all the way from America to see her."

The man seemed to study them. Then he asked, "How did you get this address?"

"We were given it by the care home," Tayte said. "Logan House. On the other side of Market Harborough."

The man gave a small nod. He smiled at Eliza and stepped back into the house. "I think you'd both better come in."

Chapter Forty-Five

Tayte and Eliza were shown into a sunlit dining room at the back of the house, where French doors looked out onto a tidy rear garden and views of open farmland. It was a large room that seemed full of family heirlooms and memories and a heady smell of polish hit Tayte as soon as he entered. His eyes were immediately drawn to the numerous silver photograph frames that were arranged on the sideboard at the far end of the room.

"Have a seat," the man said. "I'll make some tea."

He turned and left the room before Tayte could express his preference for coffee if there was any. Although the man's haste to put the kettle on made Tayte realise that the proffered tea was not an option. He turned to Eliza who had already sat down.

"When in Rome," he said.

Tayte was wondering now where Mena was and he supposed Eliza was, too. That they had been invited into this man's home was telling in light of their reason for being there, and that the man who had invited them in had not denied knowing the woman they had come to see or redirected them to another address compounded Tayte's belief that they had reached journey's end. But where was Mena? Tayte pondered the question as he gravitated towards the photographs on the sideboard.

There were around twenty pictures in all - of family scenes in frames of various shapes and sizes - and somehow Tayte knew he was looking at Mena when he saw her in one photograph and then in another. She was an old woman now, but her eyes seemed to transcend time, as if he were looking at the young girl he'd seen in the photographs Jonathan had shown him on his first visit to the Lasseter house.

He must have become lost in those images longer than he realised because it seemed like no time had passed before the dining room door opened again and the tray of tea arrived. The man carrying it set it down on the table on a large round mat and Tayte went back to his client and pulled out the chair beside her. The man began to pour and the heavy-looking teapot caused his hand to rock the spout from side to side as the steaming brown liquid filled the cups.

"You can't beat a good, strong cuppa," he said. Then he paused and looked up. "I'm forgetting my manners," he added "I'm Kenneth Wells. Please help yourselves to milk and sugar."

Eliza sat forward, reaching for the milk. "Thank you," she said and Tayte noticed that Wells was studying her. He was blatant about it and Eliza soon noticed. "Is something wrong?" she asked.

Wells' cheeks flushed. "I'm sorry," he said. "No, there's nothing wrong. It's just that you look so much like her. I mean how she was when we first met."

"Is my mother here?" Eliza asked.

Wells drew a deep breath. He pulled out a chair and sat opposite them, heavy limbed, like it took all his effort to do so. He shook his head. "I'm sorry," he said. "She passed away almost a year ago."

Tayte's eyes were drawn to the milk jug in Eliza's hand as her strength seemed to give out and the jug crashed down onto the table, spilling the milk.

She tutted and shook her head at herself. "Look what I've done."

"Think nothing of it," Wells said. "I'll fetch a cloth in a minute. It'll soon clean up."

Tayte turned to face Eliza. "I'm so sorry," he said, and he could see that Eliza wanted to smile back but she couldn't.

Wells put a teaspoon of sugar in his tea and stirred it in, tinkling the china. "I wish I could have broken the news to you more gently," he said. "But I'm not much good around these things."

"That's okay," Eliza said. "And thank you for the thought. Some things just have to be said, don't they?"

Wells nodded. "I had no idea Mena had any children. That's come as something of a surprise to me."

"It was to me," Eliza said. "I only wish I'd found out sooner."

"Quite," Wells said, gently nodding his head.

Tayte picked up on the name Wells had used. "You called her Mena?"

"Yes, I knew her several years before she changed her name. She was always Mena to me."

"How did you meet her?" Eliza asked.

"It was at the Towers hospital in Leicester where I worked as a librarian. I suppose you could say that we had our love of books in common because she later told me she used to distribute books around the wards at the Leicester hospitals during the war." Wells raised a smile to the memory. "She was my best customer," he added.

"Looking back, I've no doubt that she preferred to live inside her books over the real world and I can't blame her. When I retired I used to take my own books to her and sometimes I'd read to her. She liked that. We'd become good friends by then and when I heard she was being transferred to the private care home in Market Harborough, I moved here to be closer. After a time I persuaded her to come and live with me."

"How did she cope with that?" Tayte asked. "I mean coming out into the world again after so long."

"It must have been difficult for her," Eliza added.

Wells smiled again, more fully this time. "It took years off her in a matter of days," he said. "We had ten good years together after she left Logan House and I'm thankful for every day. I'll never forget the first time we went to the British Library. Mena was like a child again. Overwhelmed, she was. I never managed to get her abroad, but she had a grand tour of Britain, I can tell you. My wife died when I was still a relatively young man and I found it very difficult to be with anyone else after that. I think we helped one another a great deal. At least, I like to think I helped her as much as I know she helped me."

"From what you've told us, I'm sure you did," Tayte said. "So you and Mena never married?"

"No. Neither of us wanted that. Our relationship was born out of good friendship and that's how it remained. We were two people sharing our lives with one-another. And with the ghosts of our pasts, you might say."

"Danny Danielson?" Tayte said, knowing that Wells couldn't have been referring to anyone else.

Wells nodded. "Danny, yes. Mena never really got over her Danny and I suppose I was the same about my wife, Fiona. We didn't want to get over them, you see?"

Wells settled back on his chair for the first time since he'd sat down. "Mena would talk about Danny all the time when I first met her - when she didn't have her head in a book. She'd tell me about the dances they would go to and the dreams they shared. And she would go quiet after a time, as if by talking about those days she somehow managed to find her way back there - to her Danny. She could be gone for hours then, just staring out the window or at the wall. She never stopped waiting for him, although she spoke of him less when she came here." He laughed to himself. "I suppose she was kept too busy with all the family around her then. I know she liked that."

"Can I ask how Mena died?" Eliza said.

Wells leant in on his elbows again. "She had a cranial aneurism," he said. "That's what the doctors told me. Neither of us knew anything about it until it was too late. It happened one night last March. I managed to get her to hospital, but it was too severe - inoperable they said. She passed away a few hours later and I was glad to have had the chance to say goodbye. The last thing she said to me was that she was going to West Virginia. She was smiling at me and talking about a river and a low valley, describing everything like she really could see it. It gives me a great deal of comfort knowing that she at least believed it was true."

Wells went on to recount Mena's life from the day she came to live at Sutton Bassett. They talked for an hour or more, eventually migrating to the garden where the pale sun had begun to slip towards the horizon. Wells largely revealed those years that Mena had been with him through the photographs he'd taken of her and of the family that had embraced her into their lives, and Eliza had remarked that Mena looked happy in every single image, which seemed to lift her spirits. Tayte was sorry to have missed Mena by so few months, but he was glad to learn that her life had found such kindness before its end.

When they came back into the house, Tayte felt his palms go clammy and it wasn't because of the sudden change in air temperature. It was because he had a question that he was compelled to ask and although his client appeared to be handling the emotional turmoil of both finding her birth mother and losing her again in such a short space of time, he knew it had to be difficult for her.

"I don't wish to appear insensitive," he said, addressing Wells, yet looking at Eliza initially. "But someone else has been trying to find Mena recently - I believe in connection with Danny Danielson. I was wondering if you have any idea why that might be."

Wells didn't take any time to reply. "Yes, I think I might," he said. "I was going to show you something before you left. I'll go and fetch it."

They waited in the dining room and now that they were alone Tayte asked Eliza how she was.

"Oh, so-so," Eliza said. "I don't really know how I feel to be honest. I have no memories to look back on. It's not like I knew Mena, is it? Only what you've told me. But it upsets me to think that I never will."

Tayte just nodded and wished he was better at this sort of thing.

"I should like to visit her grave before we go home," Eliza added.

"Yes, of course," Tayte said. "We'll go directly after we've finished here. There should be enough light."

Wells came back into the room. He was carrying a brown jiffy bag.

"This arrived in the post a few weeks ago," he said as he sat down. "It was originally sent to Mena at Logan House and they sent it on."

Edward Buckley, Tayte thought, supposing that he had to have been the one who sent it. Wells slipped the contents of the envelope out and Tayte took a closer look at the packaging. The postmark told him it was from Hampshire, confirming his thoughts.

"It's a bible," Wells said, holding up a black book that had a large golden cross in the centre. "There are some letters, too."

Chapter Forty-Six

Wells slipped two letters from the bible and laid them out on the table. "I've read everything," he said. "And there's a logical order to it. You should read this introductory letter first."

He slid a folded sheet of cream-coloured paper across the table.

"Shall I read it out?" Tayte asked Eliza.

"If you wouldn't mind."

Tayte unfolded the letter. The paper was crisp - recently used. "It's dated December 14th," he said. "It's signed by Edward Buckley."

Dear Mena,

How can I ever begin to explain the things that I have waited so long to say? And yet, now that Mary has at last found peace I feel that I can - that I must. You may ask why I've waited all these years and I would answer that I have waited for Mary. And yet, now that the time has arrived, my words and my actions feel entirely selfish, and while they will offer you no consolation I can only hope that if nothing else they will provide you with a degree of resolution. Some things should not be taken to the grave.

Enclosed you will find Mary's bible, sent to me shortly before she died, and an airmail letter. Together they will explain everything, although no forgiveness on my part is sought, for I surely deserve none.

Your servant,
Edward Buckley.

Tayte handed the letter back to Wells. "It arrived too late for Mena," he said, thinking that it was perhaps a good thing for her sake given what he expected to find in the bible and the remaining letter. He expected Wells to pass the other letter to him now, but he didn't.

"This comes next," Wells said, handing Tayte the bible."

It was heavier than it looked for its size: the pages thin and densely packed between the covers. Tayte supposed from its worn, almost threadbare appearance in places that it must have been Mary's for most of her life.

"If you look towards the back," Wells said, "You'll find two handwritten accounts. One from Mary - the other from Edward."

Tayte opened the bible and flicked to the further handwriting that was written at the back as though to attest to its whole truth and nothing but the truth: Mary's and Edward's sworn statements. Mary's came first and it was written in what appeared as a child-like scrawl, as though the writer was fighting to control the pen. Tayte thought he would struggle to read it, but it was nothing he wasn't used to from the countless old transcripts he was often faced with. He cleared his throat and began to read Mary Lasseter's words.

My dearest Mena,

What became of our youth? Where did those happy days go? I am trying to find my way back there now - to those innocent times before the war began, when we were sisters again, you and I. But I cannot. 1944 is like a fog in my mind, so dense that neither eyes nor memory can penetrate it. If I could find those days again, Mena, I would live so happily there with you forever. But I am sorry to say that they are long gone now for both of us, and with such pain in my heart I must tell you why.

Towards the end of 1944 I received word from Edward that he would be in Paris for a short time, so I applied for overseas service and within a week I was transferred to SHAEF - the Supreme Headquarters of the Allied Expeditionary Force, which was based in Paris at the time. I hadn't seen Edward since he'd left for Holland two months earlier and after the fighting at Arnhem I knew I had to see him if I could.

A week or so before my transfer, I received a letter from home. It was from Mother. She was upset, saying that you intended to marry Danny and that you were going to live in America after the war. Then I received another letter - this time from Joan Cartwright. It was brief and to the point. Joan wrote that Danny had raped you at St Peter's church on your first date together. She said that you had told her this yourself and it left me so confused. I could not understand why you still wanted to see this man, let alone marry him and go off to live in America with him. Joan said that she was writing to tell me this for your sake, Mena, adding that she thought someone in the family should know. Naturally, I thought you were making a terrible mistake.

I didn't tell Edward about the letters. We shared five happy days and nights together in Paris and in all truth the whole matter could not have been further from my mind. Then on our last evening together we were going out for a meal at La Closerie des Lilas in the Montparnasse district. I remember it vividly. But then how could I ever forget it?

November 1944. Montparnasse District, Paris.

It had been raining hard all afternoon and apart from the few busy tables that sheltered beneath the restaurant canopy, the chairs outside *La Closerie des Lilas* - the pleasure-garden of the lilacs - were tipped in to allow the rain to run off. It was early evening and the streets were as lively as ever since the liberation despite the inclement weather.

The damp had penetrated Mary Lasseter's coat. A shiver ran through her and she pulled harder at Edward's arm as they skipped between the trees on the boulevard outside the restaurant, giggling as lovers might in the rain. She wished she'd parked the staff-car closer, but she hadn't wanted to risk getting into trouble over the misuse of army property - not that it mattered now. They were almost there and the soft amber glow at the restaurant windows looked warm and inviting.

"Quickly!" Mary called.

She tugged Edward's arm again and they made it to the canopy, still laughing as they removed their hats and coats and straightened their hair. They were both in dress uniform and although Mary thought Edward looked as handsome as ever, she was sick of the olive drab and khaki she'd become too accustomed to wearing, even down to her underwear.

Edward held her back as she made to go inside. "Wait," he said. "I've a surprise for you."

Mary smiled. "What?" she said. "What is it?"

Edward grinned. "Come with me," he said, and he took her hand and pushed through the doors. He stayed ahead of her as they fought their way through the crowd.

"Un moment, Monsieur." It was the maître d' in a black suit and bow tie: a middle-aged man who, judging from his paunch, had eaten well during the occupation. "Avez-vous une réservation? Nous sommes très occupés ce soir."

"Naturellement," Buckley replied. He winked at Mary and said, "Apparently they're very busy this evening. Good job I booked." He turned back to the maître d'. "C'est Buckley. Une table pour trois."

The maître d' checked his reservation list, running a firm finger down the page. He smiled. "Oui, naturellement, Capitaine Buckley," he said. He collected two menus from a side table. "Veuillez me suivre."

"He wants us to follow him," Buckley said, and they moved through the restaurant, passing a barman in a white shirt and apron who was tending a crowded, well-stocked bar laden with bottles that were stacked three shelves high. "At least *Jerry* didn't leave the place dry," Buckley added.

The restaurant furnishings were rich mahogany and red leather and the tables were neat with starched white cloths. At a glance, Mary thought they all looked to be taken. She wondered where the maître d' would fit them in.

"Did you say table for three just now?" she asked.

Edward looked over his shoulder, still holding her hand as he followed the maître d'. "What was that?"

"I said," Mary began, raising her voice, but she trailed off. The place was too lively now they were amidst the hubbub, with conversation and laughter spilling from every closely bunched table. She couldn't even see where she was going beyond Edward and the maître d' as they moved in tight single-file between the tables. It wasn't quite what she had in mind for their last evening in Paris.

"Votre table, Monsieur," the maître d' said, handing Edward one of the menus. He smiled at Mary - still partially blocking her view of the corner table he'd brought them to. "Mademoiselle," he added as he offered her the other menu.

Mary wondered what Edward was so excited about. Then as he moved to one side and the maître d' moved to the other, she saw him. There was Danny Danielson, wearing his Class A uniform and a bright-toothed smile, full of eagerness and a sense of occasion. She watched him run a hand over his short blonde hair as he stood up.

"Mary!" he said, like they were good old friends; like he imagined she had no idea what he'd done to her sister.

"See," Buckley said. "What a surprise!"

Danny moved out from behind the table so Mary could squeeze in between them. "It's swell to see you again, Mary," he said. "How's Mena? Have you heard from her lately?"

Mary didn't return his smile. At least, the expression on her face didn't feel much like a smile, however it might have looked. She sat down, suddenly without appetite. "Mena's quite well," she said.

"Getting on with things. You know how it is." She opened her cotton-canvas shoulder bag and took out a packet of cigarettes.

Edward was there with a light from the complimentary matchbook on the table before the cigarette reached her lips. "I got in touch with Danny after Holland," he said. "I had some time on my hands and I found out he was taking it easy in Reims." He threw Danny a cheeky grin.

"Mighty caring of you, Ed," Danny said, grinning back.

"Nonsense. I was just checking up on you for Mena's sake. Well, I said I was coming to Paris for a spell before heading back to Blighty and Danny said he was waiting on a pass. Before we knew it we'd arranged to meet up."

"And I had to lie to my buddies about it," Danny said, "or they'd have insisted on coming along with me!"

Edward laughed. He reached across and held Mary's hand, pulling it up onto the table. "You didn't mind my little game did you, darling?"

She gave no answer. She wasn't smiling or laughing.

"Mary?"

She turned to Edward suddenly, like she'd just snapped out of a daydream. "No, of course not," she said, rushing the words. She blew a line of smoke out from the corner of her mouth. "How are you, Danny?" she added without so much as glancing at him.

"I'm missing Mena all the more for seeing you two love-birds," he said. "That's some knot you've tied there."

They let go of each other's hands immediately and Danny burst out laughing.

"I'm just messing," he said. "You go right ahead and canoodle all you want." He fidgeted in his seat. "Say, I guess you've heard the news, haven't you? I'd have liked to ask Mena in person, but I guess a yes is a yes whichever way it comes."

"Of course we've heard, haven't we, Mary?" Edward said. "Congratulations, old boy."

Mary just kept thinking that Mena was making a terrible mistake. She had no idea how Danny could appear so charming and caring on the outside, yet be capable of the dreadful things Joan Cartwright had written to her about. *Does war make such monsters of men?* she wondered. It had certainly done no such thing to Edward.

Danny was still smiling. "Mena's about all that's kept me going these past months, I reckon. Just thinking about getting back to her...

Well, I hate those Krautheads all the more for keeping us apart."

He looked right at Mary then and she couldn't avoid those intense blue eyes that seemed to make everything he said so deeply heartfelt.

"Picturing Mena and me back home in West Virginia someday," he added. "That's what keeps me sharp - and you have to be. You can't go soft out here. When you do that, you're finished."

Mary swallowed dryly and looked down into her lap where his eyes couldn't find her. *The hypocrite,* she thought. How could he claim to feel any such love for Mena after what he'd done?

The sommelier arrived and hovered expectantly as Edward, who had neglected to look at the wine list until now, quickly scanned it and said, "We'll have a bottle of the 1935, Gevrey-Chambertin, Clos St Jacques." Then in a lowered voice to Mary and Danny, he added, "Great year for Burgundy."

The sommelier replied in accented English. "An excellent choice, Monsieur. But I must inform you that I 'ave just one bottle remaining."

Edward smiled. "Oh, I'm sure we can find another little gem in there somewhere," he said. "Merci."

Mary couldn't wait for the bill to arrive. This was not how she'd imagined her last evening in Paris at all. All she could think about was her little sister and the hell Danny must have put her through. She wondered whether Danny had some hold over Mena - something strong enough to force her to marry him. Although Mary knew that Mena was desperate enough to take up with the first ticket out of Oadby just to get away from home and their mother. She recalled how jealous Mena had been over her own engagement to Edward. She thought about that time in the garden before Mena's birthday, when she'd asked her if she loved Danny. A humourless laugh rose in her throat. Mena had her as fooled as she had fooled herself.

It was an uncomfortable evening. The meal came and went with the wine and the chat that Mary barely listened to or contributed to. She hardly touched her food. Danny just kept looking at her and smiling and somehow that made everything worse - like he was gloating about it. She thought he was so full of himself, sitting there laughing and joking with Edward as if nothing so evil had happened that summer.

They were waiting for the dessert menus to arrive and the subject had turned to their own forthcoming marriage and the likelihood of children soon to follow. How Danny could talk so openly about it was beyond Mary's belief.

"And it seems we're going to have a baby of our own to bring up," Danny said, like he'd only recently discovered the consequence of his actions and was wholly proud of himself. He lost his smile suddenly. "You know all about that, I suppose."

Mary nodded back at him, a sense of loathing suddenly suffocating her. "I know," she said in a low monotone.

"I told Mena in my last letter that what happened before didn't matter a hoot to us now," Danny said.

Mary bit the soft flesh inside her lip so hard she could taste blood. How could he say such a thing? And Mena was a bigger fool than she took her for if she believed that what Danny had done didn't matter or that it wouldn't happen again, perhaps over and over again throughout her entire miserable life if she went ahead and married this monster. She thought the best thing Mena could do was give up the baby and have nothing more to do with Danny. But then Mena was too young and altogether too naive to know what was good for her.

Mary couldn't bear to listen to him any longer; could not suffer his company at such close quarter for one more second. "I'd like to leave," she said. "It's too loud in here."

"But we've not had pudding yet," Edward said.

Danny patted his stomach. "That's okay, Ed. I've been eating too well just lately and I'm not real big on dessert anyway."

"How about another drink then?" Edward said. "It's not late. I know a quiet little spot not far from the car. We can drop you back at your hotel afterwards."

"Thanks," Danny said. "I'll take a drink with you, but I can get the Metro back."

"Nonsense. Where are you staying?"

"It's over the river on Rue La Fayette," Danny said.

Mary stood up. "I need some air," she said. "Will you excuse me?"

Edward stood to let her pass. "I'll get the bill," he said, raising an arm towards one of the serving staff. "Excusez-moi. L'addition, s'il vous plait."

Chapter Forty-Seven

At the house in Sutton Bassett, Tayte was coming to the end of Mary's words.

"There's just one more paragraph," he said.

His eyes wandered ahead and he thought how much Mary's already poor handwriting had deteriorated during the course of his reading; how difficult her account of what had happened that night in Paris must have been to write.

"I'm sorry, Mena," Tayte read, "but I cannot go on. I had thought that after all this time I would have found the strength, but I have none left and must hope now that Edward will continue it for me."

Tayte stopped. "That's it," he said. "Mary's words end there."

Eliza looked at him questioningly. "So Danny did rape my mother?"

Tayte still found that hard to believe. "From what I've seen and heard this week, I really don't think so," he said. "To my mind there seems to have been some confusion between Mena and Joan over the matter, Maybe Edward's account will clear it up."

"I hope so," Eliza said. "I'd formed a better opinion of Danny myself from what you've told me."

"Well let's see what else this bible has to say," Tayte said as he turned the page. "Edward's account begins without further introduction." He scanned ahead. "It continues from where Mary left off," he added. Then he continued to read.

Mary was waiting for us beneath the canopy outside the restaurant when we came out. It was still raining, but on reflection I don't believe she cared too much about the weather by then. She chain-smoked her cigarettes all the way along Boulevard du Montparnasse.

'One for the road then, old boy,' I said to Danny when we reached the bar. I don't recall the name of the place now. It was just somewhere off the beaten track, away from the crowds. Mary said she didn't want to go in, that she'd prefer to wait in the car, but I wouldn't hear of it.

Of course, Mary hardly said a word while we were in there. She'd only had one glass of wine at the restaurant and she wouldn't have anything from the bar, but she had the car to think about. She just waited with her cigarettes while we sat and drank and talked about Holland most of the time. There were plenty of GIs in the bar and everyone wanted to buy Danny and me a drink, but Mary soon put her foot down. She told me I'd had enough - she wouldn't speak to Danny - and we left soon afterwards. It was ten o'clock. I've always remembered the time - but then some things have a way of sticking in your mind.

November 1944. Paris.

The tree-lined pavement along Boulevard du Montparnasse shone dark and wet from all the rain that had fallen that night as Edward Buckley followed Mary out of the bar. He raised a flat palm to the sky and noted that it had stopped raining, although as he looked above the street-lamps the sky remained overcast and inky-dark.

Plenty more where that came from, he thought.

He had a hand on Danny's shoulder, partly for support, but mostly for the camaraderie. He could feel the effects of all the brandy he'd just knocked back on top of the wine he'd had at the restaurant, although it seemed that Danny was a long way off 'feeling no pain' as he phrased it.

Mary was ahead of them - a long way ahead of them, Edward noticed as he watched her khaki-stockinged legs switch back and forth double-time. He wondered what had come over her since dinner. It wasn't like her at all, he considered, supposing that it was all his fault for not telling her about Danny joining them, or perhaps just for inviting him along to share their last evening together in Paris in the first place.

Danny slapped him hard on the back, jolting him forward. "She's a peach of a gal, Eddie."

"She is," Edward agreed, a little soberly despite the drink. "A bit off colour tonight though, don't you think?"

"Pshh! You know how gals are," Danny said. "I probably shouldn't have come. Three's a crowd, right?"

"Nonsense," Edward said. "You're almost family."

Danny flashed his eyes. "Maybe sooner than you think, ol' buddy."

They stopped walking and Edward saw that Danny had a mile-wide smile on his face. "How do you mean?"

"You promise you won't say anything?" Danny said. "I don't want to spoil the surprise."

Edward smiled along with him. He crossed his chest. "Upon my family's honour," he said and they started walking again.

"Okay then," Danny said. "As it is such an honourable family." He lowered his voice, although by now they had turned off the boulevard onto a dimly lit side street.

Tenement blocks, three storeys high, rose to either side of the narrow street. There were no lights on in any of the windows and many looked to be broken, the paintwork scarred and peeling.

"There's an airfield south-east of here," Danny said. "Orly airfield?"

"I know it," Edward said.

"Well they're making supply runs to England all week and I aim to board one of those birds."

Edward laughed at the idea. "How do you expect to pull it off? They'll have you up on a charge before you can say, 'Jack Robinson'."

Danny winked. "Let's just say I know a fella who knows a fella."

"You'll have to get back too," Edward said. "Three days, you say? Even if you do get to England, how do you plan on getting back again?"

"Hell, I'll figure that out when the time comes," Danny said. "Same ways I guess, but who cares? A couple of days with Mena's gotta be worth anything Uncle Sam can throw at me. I even packed a spare parachute so she can make herself a wedding dress for the big day."

"A *spare* parachute?" Edward said.

"Well it was just lying around," Danny said with a grin.

Edward laughed. "I've got to hand it to you Yanks," he said, then he saw the car headlights ahead and they stopped.

"Not a word to Mary," Danny said. He kicked his heel against the kerb as they waited. His face was still full of smiles. "Just in case."

"Mum's the word," Edward said, and the car crawled closer, its low engine note rasping off the buildings.

"And what about you?" Danny said. "Have you set a date yet?"

"We'll be announcing it this Christmas."

The car drew closer.

"That's swell," Danny said.

The bright lights dazzled Edward and he turned away. He heard the engine note change then, revving hard suddenly like the throttle was stuck open. He turned back in time to see the car mount the kerb, out of control, tyre rubber squealing as the engine raced.

Then it began to scream.
"Danny!"

Chapter Forty-Eight

Tayte looked up from Mary's bible, staring into space as he considered everything he'd just read. Was it a dying woman's confession? If so, then it was clearly the reason Retha Ingram and her father were so desperate to find Mena: to recover the bible Mary had sent to her via Buckley. And yet Mary had not confessed to killing Danny. That had been left to Edward.

Or had it?

Tayte thought there had to be more to it. He turned back to the bible and quickly found his place. Then he continued to read Edward's account.

The engine continued to wail long after the car stopped, and that sound has haunted my sleep to this day. Mary remained in the car. I could see her behind the steering wheel, clenching it like she couldn't let go if she wanted to. She looked deranged - I can find no more suitable word for her expression. She just stared at me, sitting by the roadside in the headlights with Danny in my arms.

Danny wasn't dead. Not then.

He was coughing blood and his head was badly injured and bleeding, but he was a strong man with an even stronger will to live because of Mena. I thought he must have hit his head on the curb after the car hit him and I thought he might make it if we could get him to a hospital. My own head was spinning. I thought about many things while I held on to Danny, but I knew what I had to do.

I had to protect Mary.

I had no idea at the time why she had done this and right there and then I didn't care. Mary was everything to me and whether Danny lived or died I knew how bad it would go for her. So I just continued to hold Danny, rocking him back and forth in the headlights, staring back at Mary. I had my arm around Danny's neck and I was holding him so tightly, slowly hugging the life out of him.

'It's okay, Danny," I kept telling him. 'Shh, Danny. It's okay.'

I cannot write of the things I had to do before that night was out, but by morning the rain had returned to cleanse the streets and it was as if we had never been there. And how much I have wished that were true. Of course, Mary told me why she had run Danny down that night. She told me all about Joan's letter, saying that Danny had raped you, Mena - had raped the little sister she would have done anything for. And she told me about the letter from Margaret Lasseter saying that you were going to live with Danny in America after the war. At the time, Mary truly believed that she was doing it for you - to save you. But I could never believe that Danny was capable of such things. I knew him better.

There was another letter, Mena.

It wasn't until sometime in December - a month later when we were both back in England - that we fully knew what we had done. Your mother had kept Danny's last letter to you. She showed it to Mary, saying that she had kept it from you because she didn't want you to go to America - didn't want the family split up like that. When I saw the letter, I took it from Mary and I kept it, and that was the last time we saw each other - neither one of us being able to look upon the other's face again without seeing Danny and being reminded of what we had done.

We denied our love as we had denied yours, Mena.

After that I vowed to do whatever I could to make up for the terrible wrong I had done, but your mother would not let you go and I lost you for many years. Then when at last I found you again, your life seemed too settled to warrant further upset from me, so I did what I could for you, knowing that it would never be enough. For all of this I am truly sorry.

When Tayte stopped reading the silence in the room seemed to reflect how everyone around the table felt. No one spoke for several seconds.

Today is all we have and tomorrow is for dreamers, Tayte thought, recalling the line from one of Danny's letters to Mena. He thought how prophetic it was in light of what had happened to him.

"That's all there is," he said. He placed the bible on the table and flattened the cover with his palm. "I've reached the end of the account."

Wells sat forward in his chair. "I believe this is the other letter Edward Buckley refers to," he said as he slid it towards Tayte.

It was written on blue airmail paper, the thin edges yellow with age. Tayte unfolded it. It was dated Saturday, November 18th, 1944 and it was written by Danny. Tayte gave it no more than a cursory glance before he read it out.

My darling Mena,

I was more upset than I can say at hearing what happened to you back in May. I wish with all my heart that you had told me sooner so I could have done something about that no good rat, Victor Montalvo. He should have been strung up for what he did to you and I can see how scared you must have been. Telling me about it was a brave thing to do, Mena, and I want you to know that it doesn't change a thing between us. I'll help raise the child as if it were my own. Heck, we'll have a whole bunch of kids if you like so don't you worry yourself. I'll take good care of the both of you. We'll get married just as soon as I can get back, which might be sooner than you think.

There's talk of extended leave for those of us who pulled through Holland. We're in France now and I can't tell you where but there's talk of passes to Paris. I don't want to raise your hopes, Mena, but I'm going to see if I can cut Paris short and catch a ride to England afterwards. So don't be surprised if you see me walking down the lane toward your house one fine day, whistling a tune with my hands in my pockets, looking like I was the happiest man alive.

By the way, Mena, I never did get the chance to tell you the name I was born with. I made that promise to you so I'll tell you now. What you have to understand is that my folks settled in America from Norway and they're a traditional bunch even to this day. My mom called me Ednar. I can see you smiling at that as everyone who hears it does, and I'm sure you can understand why I kept it to myself when I enlisted. No one outside my family ever pronounced the 'R' so it sounded more like Edna, which was hardly right for a fighting man in the tough 82nd Airborne.

I'm so keen to post this letter to you, Mena, that I'll end now. I miss you more each day and I just wish I could hold you in my arms until I knew you felt better about everything bad that's happened. I'll write again soon, but if I get that pass I could be with you before another letter has chance to reach you.

I love you, Mena.
Ednar 'Danny' Danielson.

Chapter Forty-Nine

Sutton Bassett was one of very few villages in England to have a church without a cemetery, having been built as an annexe to the church at nearby Weston by Welland. Tayte had driven there with Eliza under the direction of Kenneth Wells soon after reading Danny's last letter and Wells had told them that Mena had been laid to rest in the Wells family plot, having come to be considered over the years as family in all but name.

As they entered beneath the lych-gate in the shadow of the church's Norman tower, Tayte looked up into the late afternoon sky and thought about the irony of what had happened to the Lasseter family. If Margaret Lasseter hadn't kept Danny's letter, the misunderstanding between Joan and Mena would have been undone before any lasting damage could have been caused. *That was the real catalyst in all this,* he thought. The very action Mena's mother had taken, believing that it would keep the family together, tore it apart.

"The weather's going to turn," Wells said as they walked the path towards the church, pea-gravel crunching underfoot. He pointed out to a grey horizon beyond the pallid winter blue, to where a storm front was building.

"After the sun, the rain," Eliza added.

"Quite so, Mrs Gray, quite so. The world keeps turning and we must turn with it."

A moment later Wells said to Tayte, "I've been wondering what to do about that bible and the letters. It's a murder confession after all and I thought perhaps I should show it to the police. It just seems such a long time ago now. I shouldn't think they'd be all that interested."

"I'm sure they're going to be very interested," Tayte said, knowingly, thinking that it was so much more than a past murder confession. It was the motive for three recent murders, too.

When they came to the church they continued to follow the path around it, keeping it to their right as they walked at an amble towards the bell tower, and Tayte thought that Eliza commanded her walking sticks with great authority and determination as they went. A gust of wind arrived unannounced. It stirred what remained of the autumn leaves from hiding and his eyes followed their dance over the headstones in the graveyard until Wells brought them to a stop at the foot of the tower.

"I'll let you go on without me," he said. To Eliza he added, "I'm sure you'd like some time to yourselves."

"Thank you," Eliza said.

"It's easy to find," Wells added. He pointed across the graveyard. "See the circle of angels? That's where you'll find Mena."

Tayte took Eliza's arm as they stepped off the path and picked their way across the grass between the burial plots. It was the kind of graveyard that looked like it had always been there, Tayte thought. The numerous headstones were nearly all thin and grey, and time had taken their once erect posture and leant them over like old men, whose many words had faded to the point of obscurity beneath their beards of ancient lichens.

"Mena never knew Danny's real name," Eliza said.

"No. I guess she didn't."

"Do you know anything about this Victor Montalvo mentioned in Danny's letter?"

Tayte shook his head. "That was the first I'd heard of him."

"Good," Eliza said. "I don't want to know anything more about him. When I think of Mena, I'll picture Danny beside her. I'll imagine that I came out of their love for each other as Mena had wanted it to be."

Tayte thought that of all the things to have come out of what happened back then, Eliza was just about the only good thing. He reminded himself that she had three sons and a daughter, each with children of their own, and that none of them would otherwise have existed today. And who knew what might come from that branch of her family tree? GIFT was perhaps another good thing, he supposed, but now that he understood the motive behind its creation, any good that came out of the charity was diminished in his eyes. Mary had spent her life atoning for her sins and he saw the trust now as little more than her path to salvation.

They came to the statue Wells had directed them to - to the circle of angels that all seemed to be dancing in a ring and smiling at the heavens, as if rejoicing at the unity of one more soul that had found its way home. Tayte scanned the headstones before it and he was drawn to Mena's, being of new white marble and the most recent addition to the plot.

"Here she is," he said, and as he looked at Eliza he could see that her emotions had finally overcome her. She wiped her cheek with the back of her hand and stepped closer.

"In loving memory of Emma Danielson," she read, her voice low and tremulous. "My mother," she added, trying to smile yet succeeding only slightly.

Tayte read over the inscription and thought that no one else would ever know that, or be able to connect Emma Danielson to the Lasseter name. Any genealogist trying to build the Lasseter family tree after him would draw a blank when they came to hear of Mena, the seventeen year old girl who had run away from home with her little red suitcase at the end of 1944 never to be seen again. He thought it was perhaps for the better and he thought that was how Mena would have wanted it.

And who could blame her?

There was a trowel in the loose soil at the base of Mena's headstone, where purple and yellow pansies had been planted. Eliza surprised Tayte when she went to it. She dropped her walking sticks and awkwardly knelt on the grass. Then she picked the trowel up and began to turn the earth over. Tayte went to her and squatted beside her. He didn't know what to make of her actions at first.

"There's just one more thing to do," Eliza said. "Then we can go home."

She continued to dig at the ground and when she'd finished she set the trowel aside. She reached into her coat and brought out a thin blue airmail letter.

"I picked it up off the table before we left the house," she said. "It was Danny's letter and it was meant for Mena. Her mother had no right keeping it from her." She placed it gently into the ground and brushed the soil over it with her hands. "There," she added. "Mena has it now and she knows that her Danny was coming back for her." She looked up at Tayte, eyes glistening. "And now she knows his real name so she can find him and they can be together again."

Tayte put his arm around her. He leant in and brushed his hand over the soil and helped to pat it flat again. He hadn't felt this close to an assignment in a long time, perhaps because Mena's story hadn't happened so long ago or perhaps because of its tragic and unjust nature. Whichever it was, he had a tear in his eye for Mena, too.

He clenched his jaw and sniffed back the cold January air. He wasn't a great believer in heaven or hell, or anywhere in between that you couldn't reach by land, air or sea, but he liked Eliza's sentiment.

He liked to think that what she'd said over Mena's grave as she buried Danny's letter was true: that now Mena knew his real name and what was in his heart, she would find him again.

Epilogue

Jefferson Tayte was back home in Washington DC where he lived in a minimalist one bedroom apartment on tree-lined, North Carolina Avenue. It was an open-plan bachelor pad with hardwood floors and beige walls, a short walk from Lincoln Park, which was located between the United States Capitol Complex to the east and the Robert F Kennedy Memorial Stadium to the West. It was a rainy Thursday afternoon, almost a week after he'd returned from England. He was sitting on his couch drinking coffee and try as he had he still couldn't shake his last assignment from his head.

It hadn't helped that Mel Winkelman's grandson had contacted him that morning, although he'd been expecting him to get in touch. On his return from England, Tayte had left his contact details on the 82nd Airborne website where he'd previously come across Mel's photographs from 1944, and now he'd been able to tell his grandson what he'd found out about Danny. The information had come several years too late for Mel, but Tayte thought his family should know and his grandson had thanked him for the closure it gave them. That's what had started Tayte thinking about the assignment again and he was still thinking about it now.

He'd been glad to hear that Eliza Gray was going to keep in touch with Jonathan and his family, and with Jonathan's and Joan Cartwright's permission, he'd given Mena's peace-dollar pendant to Eliza along with the remainder of Danny's letters. He hoped they would give her some comfort whenever she thought about Mena and Danny and in many ways they belonged to Eliza now that Mena was gone.

Tayte recalled how upset Joan was when he'd told her what had become of Mena and that he'd found her grave, and she'd been inconsolable when he'd explained to her why Danny couldn't come back for her. Joan had immediately blamed herself for having told Mary what she'd heard. 'I was always such a gossip,' she'd said, adding that the significance of her writing to Mary hadn't occurred to her when she and Tayte had spoken, and why would it? Neither had known then what consequence it had contributed to.

It wasn't Joan's fault. Tayte had to tell her that several times before she would believe it. It was no more her fault than it was Mena's for propagating the lie that Danny was the father of her child, which had only served to compound the confusion between them over what had happened that night at St Peter's. Although, with the social stigma around unmarried mothers at the time, Tayte understood why Mena had wanted everyone to believe that Danny, who planned to marry her, was the father of her child.

Tayte sipped his coffee and turned his thoughts to Retha Ingram again. He supposed that her trial would continue for some time, although the conclusion seemed inevitable given the evidence against her. He felt no need to follow it further and he imagined that her unwitting act of patricide would only add to her punishment in the years to come.

Edward Buckley had been on his mind, too. His and Mary's story was another tragedy in itself and he believed that Edward had been a good man at heart, forced into what must have seemed like a surreal and hopeless situation. Whichever path he had chosen as he held Danny in his arms, he had ultimately lost the woman he loved.

Tayte was just wondering how Edward had known where to send Mena's suitcase - concluding at the same time that he'd had his whole life to find Eliza Gray - when the phone on the side-table at his elbow rang. He sat up and answered it.

"Jefferson Tayte," he announced, expecting it to be another client, but it wasn't.

"Jefferson! It's Marcus. I just got back from France. Emmy said you've been trying to contact me."

Tayte couldn't think of anyone he'd rather talk to right now, which only seemed to add to his melancholy when he thought that most men his age had a wife and family at the top of their list. But Marcus Brown was like family and Tayte was well aware that he was all he had.

"Marcus, hi. So what were you doing in France?"

"Oh, just a project I'm working on. Something for myself actually."

"Who's the family?"

"No one you'll have heard of. It's early days yet. I'll tell you all about it sometime. Did you need something?"

"No, I just called to catch up. I thought I might visit with you both while I was in England this time."

"I'm sorry I missed you," Marcus said. He paused. "Is everything okay? You sound a bit low."

"I'll buck up in a day or so," Tayte said. "I've just taken another assignment that should keep me busy. That last one got to me a little, that's all. It didn't turn out the way I'd hoped."

"Do they ever, Jefferson?"

"I know. I just think I got a little too close to the subject this time."

"Ah, the girl with the red suitcase."

"Mena," Tayte said, nodding to himself. "I guess I just didn't want to find another headstone this time."

"Family history isn't full of happy endings, Jefferson. You know that. And isn't that one of the allures of the job? It's the skeletons in the closet that get people like us out of bed in the morning, isn't it?"

Tayte had to agree. Tragedy, injustice and misfortune were commonplace in genealogical research and those elements of people's lives were a part of what made going back through time so compelling.

"I guess," Tayte said with a sigh.

"Oh dear," Marcus said. "You are in the dumps. But what about your client? The past is the past, Jefferson. You can't change it. It's what you do right here in the present that matters and you've changed your client's life for the better, haven't you?"

Tayte knew Marcus was trying to cheer him up and he supposed he was right as always. Another eventful assignment had reached its conclusion and although it had begun too late for any kind of reunion between Eliza and Mena, he had re-connected her with the family that until a few weeks ago she never knew she had. Perhaps more importantly, now that she did know, she wouldn't wake up each morning wondering who she was like he did.

"I know what you need," Marcus said, interrupting Tayte's thoughts. "You need a girlfriend, Jefferson, that's what you need."

"Please don't start that again."

"And someone in the here and now," Marcus added. "Not in the past where they can't hurt you."

Tayte knew exactly what Marcus meant by that. He meant that he'd come to prefer spending his time with the people whose lives he researched - the dead over the living - perhaps because their paths had already been determined. They could not refuse his company or turn their backs on him as his own mother had. Back there he was in control.

Tayte laughed it off and changed the subject like he always did. "So when's your retirement party? I'll bet you're looking forward to that."

"In the summer, Jefferson. And yes, I'm looking forward to spending more time with Emmy and working on my own projects."

Tayte laughed. "Don't tell her that last part," he said. "I'm sure she's looking forward to having you all to herself."

"Why don't you come along," Marcus said. "You'll be forty soon. We can have a double celebration."

Tayte didn't like to make a big thing of his birthday. It always seemed such a farce to him because he had no idea when his real birthday was. It was just some date that had been picked for him because no one else knew either. He certainly didn't want a party.

"I'll see what I can do," he said, thinking that it really would be good to see Marcus and Emmy again. Maybe he could take a vacation. He smiled to himself. He couldn't recall the last time he'd done that.

"Good," Marcus said. "Now get stuck into that new assignment you mentioned. The matrix of human life is full of broken links and it's -"

"I know," Tayte cut in. "And it's up to you and me and all the other genealogists out there to find them and put them back together."

"Precisely. And there's no better tonic for what's troubling you than a fresh assignment. What's it about?"

"It's just routine stuff," Tayte said. "An origins assignment. First generation ancestor settled in New York in the 1800s. Probably of Irish descent."

"Oh," Marcus said. "Still, you never know what you'll uncover until you start digging, do you?"

Tayte smiled to himself. "No, you really don't," he said knowingly, already thinking about Ellis Island and the immigration registers.

The world keeps turning, he thought. *And we must turn with it.*

Acknowledgements

My sincere thanks to the members of the Goodreads UK Amazon Kindle Forum and the Kindle Users Forum (KUF) for all their support and encouragement since launching my debut book, *In the Blood,* in June 2011, and to those readers who have written to me and/or written reviews for my work. Our lives are often busy and to have taken time out from yours in this way will always be very much appreciated.

Special thanks to Kath Middleton, Madeleine Paine, Patricia Elliott and Karen Watkins for their help with proofreading this book, and to my wife Karen, without whom Jefferson Tayte would not have been able to make the leap from my head to yours in the first place.

About the author

Steve Robinson was born in coastal Kent, UK, and now lives near London on the Essex/Hertfordshire border. His passion for writing began at the age of sixteen when he was first published in a computer adventure magazine and he has been writing by way of a creative hobby ever since. When a career in software and telecommunications ended in redundancy he began to write full time. His debut novel, *In the Blood*, was the result, with *To the Grave* following a year later.

I write for the crime, mystery and thriller genres with a family history angle, having become interested in genealogy as a means to tell the story of In the Blood and perhaps because I have no idea who my own maternal grandfather is, which is something that has always intrigued me. He was an American GI billeted in England during the second world war and to my knowledge a few years after the war ended he went back to America leaving a young family behind and no further contact was made. I traced him through his enlistment record to Arkansas and know very little else about him. Perhaps this is also why my lead character is an American genealogist.

If you would like to contact me, you can visit my website at www.steve-robinson.me or send an email to mailspr@yahoo.co.uk. I'd love to hear from you.

Lightning Source UK Ltd.
Milton Keynes UK
UKOW040054030113

204317UK00001B/132/P